Wilhelm Baur

Religious Life in Germany During the Wars of Independence

a series of historical and biographical sketches - Vol. 2

Wilhelm Baur

Religious Life in Germany During the Wars of Independence
a series of historical and biographical sketches · Vol. 2

ISBN/EAN: 9783337388904

Printed in Europe, USA, Canada, Australia, Japan

Cover: Foto ©Andreas Hilbeck / pixelio.de

More available books at **www.hansebooks.com**

RELIGIOUS LIFE IN GERMANY

IN TWO VOLS.

VOL. II.

RELIGIOUS LIFE IN GERMANY

During the Wars of Independence

IN A SERIES OF HISTORICAL AND BIOGRAPHICAL SKETCHES

By WILLIAM BAUR

MINISTER OF THE ANSCHAR CHAPEL, HAMBURG

TRANSLATED WITH THE SANCTION OF THE AUTHOR.

IN TWO VOLS.

VOL. II.

STRAHAN & CO., PUBLISHERS
56 LUDGATE HILL, LONDON
1870

PRINTED BY TAYLOR AND CO.,
LITTLE QUEEN STREET, LINCOLN'S INN FIELDS.

CONTENTS OF VOL. II.

CHAPTER VII.

CHAPTER VIII.

CHAPTER I.

THE SIN OF NAPOLEON.

THE religious aspect of the revolt against Napoleon which we have presented to our readers in the foregoing sketches will become more intelligible, when we consider the ground offered by the character of Napoleon for a religious movement, an appeal to heaven against him. He was an extraordinary element in the world's history,—one of those mighty spirits upon whom God has specially reckoned in carrying out His plans for the human race; but he was certainly not among the good spirits. He appeared to devout people as an embodiment of self-sufficiency, daring to set itself up against God; as a type of wickedness, a demon whom God permitted to plague the German nation, as Job was once for a time given over to the devil; and many who were looking for the fulfilment of the prophecies of the Revelation in the events of the time, saw in him the Apollyon of that sacred book. The people were surely justified in praying against him, and in asking for aid from the avenging arm of God, for the contest with him was a contest between truth and falsehood, between justice and injustice, and those who were engaged in it seemed to be taking the side of God against the devil.

To portray the mighty conqueror is a task for which we do not feel equal, nor is this the place for it. It is only our intention to delineate a few features of his character, in order to explain why the national mind recognized in him the Apollyon of the Apocalypse, and why the poet could exclaim with truth—

> "'Tis not a war in which crowns are at stake;
> It is a crusade, 'tis a holy war."

The certificate which he received on leaving the military school at Brienne at the age of fourteen in some respects indicates his subsequent career :—"Good constitution, excellent health ; submissive, honourable, and grateful character; distinguished by his taste for mathematics. He has a competent knowledge of history and geography, but does not excel in recreative exercises, nor in Latin, in which he has only reached the fourth class. He will be a distinguished sailor."

It is also said of him, in his school days, that he was obstinately punctual, eager in the acquisition of knowledge, reserved from pride, and yet there was a shyness in his demeanour which perhaps gave the idea that he was submissive. He was grateful for what pleased him, but without any of the affection which generally binds heart to heart at that period of life. So, also, when he was emperor, he loaded with honours those who were devoted to his personal interests, but no noble or disinterested affection for his fellow men was ever traceable in his character.

He was not insensible to the charms of poetry, and took poetical works with him on his voyage to Egypt.

He was attracted to Rousseau by the peculiar combination in his mind of solidity and imagination, of the poetical and philosophical elements. The French dramatists not only gave him the taste for a heroic career, but afforded him examples, of which he gladly availed himself, for theatrical conduct and pompous speeches in important periods of his life. He is said to have read Goethe's ' Werther ' seven times ; and his letters to Josephine show that he was not a stranger to the style of enthusiastic love. But, like his affection for Josephine, all poetical taste was made to give way to the great object of his life, to stamp the impress of himself upon the world. Among all his gifts and tastes, it was his genius for mathematics which most fully served the purposes of his life ; indeed, the essence of all that he was and did may perhaps be described as the result of a mathematical genius in the service of immeasurable egotism. His pride, his scorn, and ambition caused him to ignore all considerations of convenience, humanity, or historical associations.

Human beings, with their rich individual life, were but ciphers to him, and kingdoms were nought, —he set himself up above them as a mighty unit ; the riches of national life were but mathematical formulas for his Titanic projects ; countries were but *tabulæ rasæ* through which he drew straight lines according to his pleasure, in order to create new empires, without any regard for ancient boundaries or the sanctities of national life.

When egotism like this is coupled with genius

such as his, great things are sure to be accomplished; but the national mind revolted against him as against a calculating demon, against a mighty spirit who had no concord with God or with love; and by this national spirit all the calculations of the great mathematician were confounded in the end.

The revolution and Napoleon were each ready for the other. The first outbreak of the democratic spirit greeted the young lieutenant at twenty years of age. When the monarchy was overthrown, he was a Jacobin, and called himself Brutus Bonaparte. As early as 1793, when he joined the campaign against the royalists and Girondins, in a letter to two deputies of the Convention, he betrayed the cold mathematical spirit of which we have spoken :— " Citizen representatives, From the field of honour, marching through the blood of the traitors, I rejoice to send you the news that your commands have been carried out, and that France is avenged. Neither age nor sex has been spared. Those who were only wounded by republican cannon have perished by the sword of liberty and the bayonet of equality. —BRUTUS BUONAPARTE, Citizen Sans-culotte."*

No man was so worthy as he to be the heir of the revolution. He was the revolution personified. Thiers gives a striking description of his entrance into its paths :—" A miracle of genius and passion, suddenly appearing in the chaos of a revolution, he spread his branches in it, took root in it, he ruled it, substituted himself for it, adopted its energy, its rashness, its intemperance. The successor of people who set no bounds for themselves, either in virtue or in crime, in heroism or in cruelty, sur-

* Leo, ' Universal History.'

rounded by men who denied nothing to their passions, he denied nothing to his own. They wanted
to turn the world into a universal republic, he into
a universal monarchy; they made a chaos of it, he
an almost tyrannical unity; they threw everything
into disorder, he reduced it to order again; they
treated sovereigns with contempt, he dethroned
them; they put people to death upon the scaffold,
he upon the battle-field, but veiled the bloodshed
behind the fame. He sacrificed more lives than
did the Asiatic conquerors; and upon the narrow
space of Europe, peopled by resisting nations, he
traversed more space than did Tamerlane and
Gengis Khan over the uninhabited countries of
Asia."

Further on, he says, "Utter want of moderation
is therefore the distinguishing feature of his career.
It is on this ground that, if it were not for Alexander, we must call this profound general, this wise
lawgiver, this consummate administrator, the most
foolhardy statesman that ever lived. If statesman-
ship depended only on intellect, he certainly would
have outwitted the most crafty politicians; but it
depends more upon character than intellect, and it
was in this that Napoleon was wanting."* We are
quite content to adopt this verdict of the French
historian. Napoleon was a great genius, but his
failing was want of character. He was a fool, in the
Old Testament sense of the word, as one who sets
himself up against the living God, and who is therefore sure to be ruined in the end.

It is easy to imagine what must have been the
religion of the man who made self his god. Not

* Thiers, 'Histoire du Consulat et de l'Empire.'

but that hundreds of nominally Christian rulers may have had the same superficial and political ideas of religion that he had, but few have made so revolting a use of them. It must be granted that, in a certain sense, he restored the Church and advanced its interests, in opposition to the sacrilege of the Revolution; but it was a thoroughly heathenish spirit in which he handled the subject, and the more closely we examine it the more revolting it appears. We have before remarked that it was an element of heathenism to regard religion as an aspect of nationality, so that if a man belonged to a nation he acknowledged and practised its religion as a matter of course. Thus, because Napoleon was born a Roman Catholic, he took part in the worship of that Church, without adopting the positive doctrines of the system. In the beginning of his career he said to Monge, "My religion is very simple. I behold this great, this manifold, this glorious creation, and I say to myself that it cannot be the result of mere accident, but the work of an unknown almighty Being, as far above all human beings as creation is superior to our most perfect machines." He said further, "Let it be allowed, then, that religion tells man all that he wants to know, and let us honour what she tells us. It is true that what is taught by one religion is contradicted by another. But I form a different opinion from this, from that of Volney. Because there are various religions which contradict each other, he decides against them all; he pronounces them all bad. I am more inclined to think them all good, for the groundwork of all is the same. They are only in the wrong when they persecute one another, but this must be prevented by good laws. The Roman Catholic religion is the religion of our country, that in which we were born."*

In the same spirit he expressed himself at St. Helena. After acknowledging his faith in a God as merciful as He is powerful, whom, in spite of his errors, he approached with calmness, he continues, "But as soon as I enter the region of positive religions, I feel less secure. There at every step I meet the hand of man, and it often confuses me, and is repulsive to me. . . . . But one must not give way to this feeling, with which much human pride is mingled. When we set aside the national traditions which have been woven into religion, we find the acknowledgment of God and of good and evil clearly defined in all, and that is the essential thing. I have been in the mosques, and have seen people in them on their knees before the Eternal Almighty; and although it may have been repulsive to my national feeling, it never appeared to me in a ridiculous light. Calumny, which has burlesqued all my actions, has declared that at Cairo I acknowledged Islam, while at Paris I was devoted to the Pope of the Catholics. There is some truth in it, for I did see something venerable in the mosques; and although I could not be affected in them as in the Catholic Churches, to which I have been accustomed from childhood, still in them I beheld man confessing his weakness before the majesty of God. Every religion which is not barbarous has a claim to our respect; and we Christians have the advantage of having one which has its source in the springs of the purest morality. If we ought to esteem all, we have double cause to esteem our own; for the rest, every one ought to

* Thiers.

live and die in the religion by which his mother taught him to worship God. Religion is a part of our destiny. Together with the land in which we live, its laws and manners, she forms the sacred whole which we call our country, and which no man ought to forsake. At the time of the Concordat, some old revolutionists talked to me about making France Protestant. I was indignant. It was as if they had proposed to me to renounce my identity as a Frenchman, and to become an Englishman or a German."*

"Is Protestantism, then," he exclaimed at that time, "the ancient religion of France? Is it the religion which has come victorious out of long civil wars, out of a thousand struggles, as that best adapted to the manners and spirit of the nation? Putting oneself in the place of a nation, is it not plain that it would be a most arbitrary thing to attempt to force tastes, customs, and reminiscences upon it which are not natural to it? The chief charm of religion lies in the memory of the past."*

"Last Sunday," he relates, "I was walking in the gardens of Malmaison, amidst the universal stillness of nature. The sound of the church bell at Ruel fell suddenly upon my ear, and renewed all the impressions of my youth. I was quite affected by it, so strong is the power of early associations; and I said to myself, if this is the case with me, what an effect such memories must have upon simple devout people! Let your philosophers look to it. The people must have a religion." And this was his opinion to the end. For the people he considered a positive religion necessary; for himself the most scanty conception of it sufficed.

* Thiers.

Before his death he asked for a Roman Catholic priest at St. Helena. His uncle Fesch sent him two good but not superior men. "I should like to have had a learned priest," he complained, "with whom I could have discussed the dogmas of Christianity. He certainly would not have made me believe more firmly in God than I do already, but perhaps he would have confirmed me in some points of the Christian faith; but I cannot expect anything of that sort from my two priests. However, they can read mass to me; they will do for that at any rate."

The Roman Catholic Church has the satisfaction of knowing that the great man died in her faith; but we can scarcely imagine a more barren, superficial conception of religion than his. To him it was nothing of a light from God, adopted by faith, and penetrating the spirit of man; it was only an aspect of national and natural life which we possess just as we do our existence, without any conflict of the conscience, any feeling of victory through divine grace. No wonder that he accommodated himself to all religions according to convenience, and thereby incensed all against him. Had he been merely personally indifferent to religion, he would no more have incensed the national mind than the innumerable people who are so. But that he went so far as to deny Christianity when policy required it, the national Christian conscience could never forget. But what offended it most of all was the pretence of religion with which he invested his mission, his tyranny, his self-deification.

As Satan gladly transforms himself into an angel of light, so Napoleon represented himself as having a mission from God, and it was always welcome to him when flatterers greeted him as a political Messiah. But God was to him, merely necessity, power; he was much more sincere when he talked of destiny.

The star in which he believed for himself and his family was but a poetical name for inexorable fate, of which he considered himself the instrument.

A few days before he landed in Egypt, he issued the following proclamation to the army :—" We shall undergo some fatiguing marches, shall fight several battles, and be successful in all our undertakings, for destiny is in our favour."

In order to render his divine mission plainer to the Mussulmans, he did not hesitate to proclaim himself the completer of the work which Mahomet had begun, and to affect a belief in the Prophet. Leo truly calls it a heathenish proclamation which he issued to the troops in Egypt. "The people among whom we shall now live are Mahometans: the first article of their creed is, 'There is but one God, and Mahomet is his prophet.' Do not contradict it. Treat them as you have treated the Jews and Italians; have respect for their muftis and their imams, as you have had for the rabbis and the bishops. Have the same consideration for the ceremonies prescribed by the Koran that you have had for monasteries and synagogues, for the religion of Moses and Jesus Christ. The Roman legions protected all religions."

He went still further. On landing in Egypt, he put forth a proclamation in Arabic, which ran as follows :—" I honour God, his prophet Mahomet, and the Koran." And in Syria his proclamation began, " In the name of the Almighty eternal, everlasting and allwise God, who was never created and has no son ;" and in order to gain the favour of the Mahometans, he took credit to the French for having abolished the Pope. When he entered the tombs of the Pyramids, he exclaimed, "Glory be to Allah! There is but one God, and Mahomet is his prophet." The mufti who accompanied him said, "Thou hast spoken like the most learned prophet."—"I can mount a chariot of fire from heaven, and cause its course to be guided to earth," continued the young general. "Thou art the great captain," answered the mufti, "to whom Mahomet will give the power and the victory."

But when in spite of his playing this repulsive part, French blood had been shed in a tumult, Bonaparte revenged it by shedding the blood of the Mussulmans, and put forth his proclamation to the inhabitants of Cairo. " Sheriffs, ulemas, and preachers in the mosques, teach the people that those who are at enmity with me will find no refuge either in this world or the next. Is there any one so blind as not to see that all my undertakings are shaped by destiny ? Is there any one so unbelieving as to doubt that everything in this great world is under the dominion of destiny ? Teach the people that since the world began, it has been decreed that after the annihilation of the enemies of Islam, and the overthrow of the Cross, I should come from the West in order to carry out the mission assigned to me. Let those who are only hindered from cursing us by fear of our arms, change their minds, for in offering prayers to heaven against us, they pray for their own damnation. Let true believers offer up prayers for the success of our arms. I could call you all to account for what passes in the most secret recesses of your minds, for I know everything, even what you have not told to any one; but a day will come when it will be clearly seen that I am guided by a higher power, and that human efforts will avail nothing against me."

The young general may have felt himself specially at liberty to say what he pleased in Egypt, and much of this may have been mere bravado, but it certainly was his opinion that by his means destiny was marching with iron tread through the world, and this opinion remained just the same when he made use of the holy name of God.

In 1802 he wrote to the Dey of Algiers, " God has decreed that all those who act unjustly towards me shall be punished." And after he had elected himself emperor, he wrote to the Archbishop of Mayence, " As I perceive that I am called by Divine Providence to assume the Imperial dignity, I submit myself to the Almighty guidance of the Highest."

And he carried this illusion of his divine mission to an awful extent of self-glorification, for it is reported that on the 18th Brumaire, 1799, he said in council, " We will have a republic, based upon true liberty, on the freedom of citizens, on a national representation. We will maintain it. I swear it in my name." But his most extraordinary attempt to make himself imposing to the people consisted in the Imperial Catechism, put forth in 1806.

It was not merely obedience to the government in general that was enforced, but his name was specially introduced :—

" Christians owe to the princes, their rulers, and

we especially to Napoleon I., our Emperor, affection, reverence, obedience, faith, military service, and all the duties which are ordained for the defence of his empire and his throne; we also owe him earnest prayer for the prosperity of his empire, spiritual and temporal.

"*Ques.*—Why is it our duty to fulfil all these duties towards our Emperor?

"*Ans.*—Firstly, because God, who creates kingdoms, and distributes them as it seems good to Him, in that He has richly endowed our Emperor with His gifts, for times of peace as well as of war, has appointed him to be our ruler, and has made him the servant of His power and His representative upon earth. In honouring and serving the Emperor, therefore we honour and serve God Himself.

"Secondly. Because Jesus Christ, as well by His teaching as by His example, has instructed us in our duties towards our rulers. He was born subject to the Emperor Augustus; He paid the prescribed imposts; and while He commanded to render unto God the things that are God's, He also commanded to render to the Emperor the things that were his.

"*Ques.*—Are there not special reasons which should strengthen our devotion to our Emperor Napoleon I?

"*Ans.*—Yes. For he it is whom God the Lord has raised up, under most difficult circumstances, to be the restorer of the public practice of the holy religion of our forefathers, and the protector of the same. By his profound and energetic wisdom, he has restored and maintained peace and order; he is the defender of the State by the power of his mighty arm, and by means of the holy oil which he has received from the hands of the Pope, the head of the Church universal, he is become the Lord's anointed.

"*Ques.*—What is to be the thought of those who do not faithfully perform these duties towards their Emperor ?

"*Ans.*—According to the teaching of the Apostle Paul, they resist the ordinance of God, and are in danger of eternal damnation."

And this catechism was not intended for Catholics alone, it was taught to the German youth on the left shore of the Rhine.

What sort of impression could be made by his boasted profession of protection of all religions when he insulted the Christian faith by such repulsive self-deification.   He endeavoured to accommodate himself to all creeds, but he incensed the people against him by the contempt for all religious fervour which was in the background ; and one after another, Islamism in Egypt, Roman Catholicism in Spain and the Tyrol, the Greek Church in Russia, and Protestantism in North Germany, resisted him unto blood.

And when, dazzled with his fame, his flatterers handed him one intoxicating draught after another, when a French Major said, "God created Napoleon and then rested from His labours," when a preacher in the Confederation of the Rhine exclaimed from the pulpit, "Napoleon the next after God !" when he was even lauded as the Son of God, and, instead of rending his clothes like Paul, was pleased with the incense offered him, no wonder that religious people began to think, He is " that man of sin, the son of perdition, who opposeth and exalteth himself above all that is called God, or that is worshipped; so that he as God sitteth in the temple of God, showing himself that he is God ;"* he is the king " which is the angel of the bottomless pit, whose name in the Hebrew tongue is Abaddon, but in the Greek tongue hath his name Apollyon ?"†

Even if it is allowed that there was any right or necessity in his conquests, we must consider as disgraceful the licence which he permitted himself in breaking treaties, and the manner in which he treated his allies. When he was at war with Austria, in 1805, Prussia was neutral. But it was desirable for Napoleon's troops, under Bernadotte, to march through Anspach. He ordered this violation of the treaty to be carried out as politely as possible, but the instructions ran as follows :—" I must gain the victory; if I suffer it to be lost through false scruples, if I am beaten, Prussia will ally herself with the coalition, because I am unfortunate ; but if, on the contrary, I gain the victory, I shall be sufficiently justified for this breach of national rights."

Never was selfish ambition exhibited in so great a degree in a man endowed with great gifts, for even the most noble actions which were related of him, were performed towards those from whom he expected services ; he had nothing of the magnanimity towards an enemy which distinguishes the true hero. Even Thiers ascribes his fall to his immoderate am-

* 2 Thess. ii. 3, 4. † Rev. ix. 11.

bition. He points out six great errors in which his "*intempérance morale*" was inimical to his policy.

1. That in 1803 he forsook the strong and moderate policy of the Consulate, broke the peace of Amiens, and began to throw stones at England, which it was so difficult to reach.

2. That after the subjection of the Continent in three battles, Austerlitz, Jena, and Friedland, in 1807, he did not return to a moderate policy, and that instead of subjecting England, by means of uniting the Continent against the Island Empire, he took the opportunity of endeavouring to found a universal monarchy.

3. That at Tilsit he allowed this universal monarchy to depend upon the interested complicity of Russia, which could only last while it was paid for by giving up Constantinople.

4. That he buried himself in Spain, that bottomless abyss in which all our powers were in danger of being swallowed up.

5. That he did not persevere in trying to put an end to this war, but endeavoured to solve in Russia the difficulties he could not surmount in the Spanish Peninsula, and which led to the unheard of catastrophe at Moscow.

6th, and worst of all, that when, after he had again obtained victory for our arms at Lützen and Bautzen, he rejected the Peace of Prague, which would have left us a territory larger than policy could have hoped or wished for.

If a French historian, very sensitive for the fame of Napoleon, and that of France through his deeds, speaks like this, what shall the Germans say, at whose expense most of this fame was acquired, and who were the greatest sufferers from the Satanic arrogance of the conqueror?

Nevertheless, admirers of Napoleon were not wanting in Germany. Princes of the Confederation of the Rhine, after they had succumbed to force, endeavoured to gain as much honour and profit out of their subjection as they could. The people on the left shore of the Rhine, freed from the burden of feudal service, for a time hailed the conqueror with acclamation. And between the highest and lowest classes, there were learned men and authors, infected with the cosmopolitan spirit of the times, who expected to find the past glories of the German empire revived under the universal empire of Napoleon.

No one could be indifferent to him; he was either adored or hated. Johannes von Müller, who had resolved not long before to sacrifice everything in opposing the *parvenu*, after a conversation with him, found it desirable to change his mind; and another celebrated historian, Heeren, at Göttingen, offered his homage to the "Hero of the Age" as long as his power lasted.

The wife of Frederic Schlegel, a clever woman, was present in the summer of 1804 at Cologne, when Napoleon and Josephine made their entry there; and a letter that she wrote at the time is full of admiration of the Catholic *fêtes* and the imperial presence. After describing the entry, she says, "The emperor was much pleased. Cologne is enchanted with him; and the more he gave himself up to enjoyment, and the more confidential he was, the better the people liked him. And he was more

open and agreeable, even confiding, than he often
is.   One evening he conversed upon the most various subjects,—upon religion, the immortality of the
soul, his maxims of government,—and he said that
he considered the first virtue of a ruler to be moderation.   Then he spoke of the philosophy of Kant,
and of German literature in general.   Of the former
he said, that it was a useless and groundless chimera,
and that the latter had neither worth nor merit.
Afterwards he talked of business matters.   He
showed the most profound knowledge of trade, and
all subjects connected with it, to the great surprise
of all present.   His whole demeanour was amiable,
and gained all hearts.   He is now quite secure of
the affection, and of living in the memory of these
good people.   And he appeared to be touched by
the impression he had made on the hearts of the
citizens.   His last words here were, ' *Cologne, con-
tentement.*' "

We have here an instance of the ease with which
some people adopt new ideas, which is the reverse
side of our national many-sidedness.   Napoleon's
contempt for the philosophy of Kant and for German literature, which afterwards shot fatal arrows
against him, did not prevent this philosophical and
literary lady from joining in the admiration which
originated in the weakness and vanity of the human
heart.   It was against such phenomena that the
following burning words of Arndt were directed :—
" If Satan were to come forth out of hell, in order
to become king of the Germans, thousands and tens
of thousands of pens would immediately be in motion to prove, from all imaginable reasons and with
double-refined logic, that it is a great happiness for

the world, and especially for the German nation, that the Lord Satan is pleased to assume the government of them." And in the end Arndt's opinion gained the day. There was nothing in Napoleon's character which answered to the true German's ideal of what was noble in human nature.

We have good reason for attaching some importance to Arndt's opinion of Napoleon. It was formed before he had trodden on German soil; it remained the same during the years of humiliation, and of the revolt against him; and in spite of all the judgments formed of him, and of all the historical works relating to him with which Arndt, who so long survived Napoleon, became acquainted, his first opinion never changed. Arndt and Napoleon were born in the same year. As it was the impulse of the latter to subjugate nations, so it was the unceasing endeavour of the former to appreciate their various peculiarities, to assign to each member of the great human family its fitting place; and, above all, to secure to the German nation its essential qualities, its rights, and its historical vocation.

His unmitigated opposition to Napoleon arose from his profound conception of national life, from his conviction that no nation should oppress another, that the diversity among nations is intended to increase the rich variety of human life, that they should live near one another and for each other in a spirit of freedom, and that the German nation has a special calling to advance the best, the most moral, and intellectual interests of humanity.

In his work called 'Germania and Europe,' published in 1802, he says of Napoleon, "His love of pomp proves that he is vain. Vanity appears through

all his greatness, like crackers that insult instead of
illuminating the majesty of night.   And he is even
cowardly, as is shown by his anxiety about police
regulations.   How little, when a man, and even a
great man, makes his own little person the centre
round which heaven and earth revolve !   What
vanity to think that France hangs on his destiny !
What is this secret police ?   Woe to the ruler who
cannot defend himself by the affection of his people
from the cold steel of the murderer !"

In the second part of the ' Spirit of the Age,' of
which Stein justly remarked, that it was written
with fearful truth, Arndt's righteous indignation
against Napoleon knows no bounds.   The subjuga-
tion of Germany had been accomplished.   "Thou
art a brave and successful warrior, a cunning de-
ceiver, a great immortal monster, the terror of the
world.   Small and great give thee credit for all
this.   But what art thou more ?   A narrow, faithless, greedy, blood-thirsty soul, who wishes that the
whole world had but one neck, that thou mightest
subjugate it as easily as thy Frenchmen."   Then
Arndt says that he is not to be compared to any of
the heroes of antiquity.   He reminds him of his
want of generosity in his treatment of the subjugated
German nation, and especially of the unchivalrous
manner in which he had insulted the Queen Louisa.
" How foreign to the better spirit of these times, to
the spirit of Christianity and princely dignity, is the
spirit which thou hast shown ; thou who wouldst
fain be thought a chivalrous hero !   He who can so
misuse his good fortune, he who can mock at misfortune, he who can insult fallen majesty, may well
fear retribution."

Again, he says, "He is possessed by the most wicked and cunning devil who has ever played a part on earth in human form, and therefore he is a wonderful sign to this weak and spiritless generation. For the devil was an angel of light, created after the image of God, and endowed with glory and strength; but he fell, and through abuse of his divine nature he became the representative of evil, the prince of darkness, the enemy of the children of light. Every unprejudiced man is reminded of his course, when a mortal man misuses his great strength and rare talents, and the wonderful gift of success, and desolates and enslaves the earth which he might have set free and made happy.

"If you will bow the knee, my befooled compatriots, before such a divinity, we have nothing in common. Such a virtuoso of evil the previous ages of Europe have never brought forth."

Again, he says, "But thou and thy works will prove, at last, that no skill or cunning will suffice to hinder the almighty power which we can faintly discern through all these terrors, upsettings, and revolutions. Go on then in thy vain and perilous course. When the work is done, Providence will destroy the instrument." Arndt expressed himself more calmly in calmer times, but his views remained the same.

After Napoleon's death he found in Stein's library the 'Vite e Ritratti d'illustri Italiani,' and among them a portrait of Napoleon. "I have often lifted up my voice against him, and must do it once more at the sight of this portrait. Admire him as a great general, admire the concentrated condensed strength of the man as much as you will, but do not represent him to me as a creative genius, or as a civilizer, or as one who ever had a thought of doing anything noble, divine, or humane. In the broad and sublime brow of an Alexander, a Cæsar, and a Frederic II., one may imagine that there is an expression of nobility, of longing, of something unattainable even by the most victorious hero, but there is nothing of the kind in Napoleon's countenance.

"He had the narrow, low, hawk-like brow by which many rapid conquerors have been distinguished. The forehead and nose, and the upper part of the face altogether, are good and regular, though the small sharp eyes always looked like lamps gleaming out of a doleful prison, but the lower part of the face is commonplace and empty. Let history assign a place to him, as in part an enigmatical instrument in God's hands, but do not attempt to impose him upon me as a benefactor or friend of the human race, or as one whose dark soul was ever illumined by one thought of ennobling it or making it happy." Much more might be added. Philosophers and poets, students of prophecy, and newspaper-writers, beheld in Napoleon an incarnation of the enemy of God, of a principle that was ruinous to humanity, and therefore Germany confidently appealed to an avenging God for help. This indignation of the peaceful German people is remarkable. They have not the French reverence for a *fait accompli*, success does not yet justify an action to German eyes, the dazzling splendour of fame does not conceal the uncleanness within. The German loves to judge things from a religious and moral point of view, and to recur to first principles. But he is long-suffering under oppression; so that the fact that all the power of

German conscience and Christian faith rose up against Napoleon, is a proof that the tyrant was threatening the kingdom of God upon earth, and endangering their highest possessions.

And if at that time Christian conscience, less enlightened than now, recognized in him with a healthy instinct, not only the enemy of the nation, but also the enemy of Christendom, it is to be regretted that at the present time, of these two principles, which should ever be united, patriotism and Christian faith, the first only is armed against Napoleonic ideas?

It should never be forgotten that in Napoleon was opposed and conquered, revolution personified in a despot; the outrage of rights and treaties, the illusive idea of a universal empire, involving the extinction of genuine nationality, though often disguised under a flimsy pretext of protecting it; and, above all, the arrogance with which he set himself up for an instrument in God's hands. A mortal man presumed to proclaim himself as the centre of humanity, as the axis upon which the world's history was to turn; a dignity which belongs alone to Him who died that man might live. But when the tyrant, to whom neither human life nor human rights were sacred, tried to exalt himself to such a pitch of honour, all who had a spark of faith or conscience gazed at him in anxious suspense; they could not doubt that God must reject one who, without a divine mission, assumed to be God's ambassador. And this faith was crowned, and wonderfully confirmed by the fearful fall of the mighty conqueror.

CHAPTER II.

CLAUDIUS AND JUNG STILLING.

THESE names recall the memory of two venerable old men, with devout faith in their hearts, gentle wisdom on their lips, and countenances expressive of serene peace. It is not amidst strife and tumult that we find them; their voices are not heard on the battle-field. For many years they have lived far removed from outward conflict, and have only been accustomed to wage war with sin and unbelief. From the secure stand-point of vital Christianity, and with eyes enlightened by the Spirit, they surveyed passing events, and they summon us to withdraw from the tumult, and retire into the closet; their departure is at hand, and they would fain teach us the lessons which should be learnt from subjection and misery, war and victory.

We willingly listen to their words, and thank God for giving us men who, in the time of religious declension, regarded Christ as their guiding-star, and who heard the still small voice of God amidst the thunders around them, and spoke of it to the people.

Their talents and the sphere in which they worked were similar, yet not without that diversity which God observes in distributing His gifts; and during the course of a long life both exercised great influence by their writings. Both were born in 1740, the year in which Lavater and Oberlin also first saw the light,—four powerful witnesses in a Christ-forgetting age.

Claudius was a native of the most northerly district of Germany, where the country presents an aspect of quiet and uniform beauty. He sprang from a race distinguished by sober and solid worth, and the course of his life was an even and straightforward one. Stilling was born in a mountainous district of central Germany, amongst a population in which, ever since the beginning of the eighteenth century, a pietistic separatist movement had penetrated to the lowest classes of the people; and it gave rise to many a peculiar and fanatical phase of religious life.

Notwithstanding that he was a partaker of the peace of God, Stilling strikes us as a man with an impulse to perpetual motion; and this tendency occasioned frequent vicissitudes in his fortunes, in spite of his confidence in God's guidance. Both received deep religious impressions in their early homes. Claudius, brought up in the Lutheran faith, was more disposed to contemplation; Stilling belonged to the Reformed Church, and was more fitted for action in a larger sphere.

Claudius belonged to a family in which the pastoral office had been hereditary ever since the Reformation; Stilling's family belonged to the class of peasants, accustomed, for one generation after another, to walk in the ways of their fathers. Both had a strong family feeling, and took a pride in looking back to a long line of ancestors. It was the movement which was taking place in the literary world which incited Claudius to make his voice heard, while Stilling was rather induced to do so by the impressions he received among the "quiet in the land." Both ended their lives in truly patriarchal style, amidst the happiness of a German Christian family life.

It is seldom that the long life of a distinguished man has run so even a course as that of Matthias Claudius. He was born in August, 1740, at Reinfeld, in Holstein, two miles west of Lübeck. The place is picturesquely situated amidst fruitful hills; the parsonage is buried amongst fruit trees, close to the garden is a little lake, two others enliven the landscape, and woods of oak and beech offer pleasant resting-places for the eye in the extensive plain.

Claudius always clung with affection to his native place; and perhaps scenery of this quiet and peaceful sort exercises no less an influence upon character than the more changeful and striking aspects of a mountainous country.

His early training was in harmony with it. His father appears neither to have felt himself called to enmity with the world by any tendency towards pietism, nor did rationalism entangle him in its snares. The Bible was everything to him, and in important moments of his life he often expressed himself in Scriptural phrase.

When "things were not as they should be," the boy often devoutly sang with his mother,—

"Commit thy way unto the Lord."

When Matthias was nine years old he received a Canstein* Bible as a present, on the fly-leaf of which his mother had written the words, " My son, ' Remember now thy Creator in the days of thy youth, while the evil days come not,' and fear God, for that is the beginning of wisdom. And this wisdom maketh rich, and bringeth spiritual and temporal blessings with it. Above all things, thank God for everything that befalleth thee, and pray Him to direct thee to act according to His word in all thy undertakings. May the word of God be thy most precious treasure, for it can make thee wise unto salvation ; and whatever thou doest, think of thy end, and then thou wilt never do wrong. This is my maternal admonition ; if thou followest it thou wilt certainly attain the end of our faith, even the salvation of the soul. May the Lord in His mercy grant it ! Amen !"

After a childhood blessed with such pious influences he went, at fourteen, to the grammar school at Plön, then the royal residence and capital of Holstein. The town lies upon a narrow strip of land which stretches out into one of the largest of the Holstein lakes ; other lakes, reflecting the shadows of lofty beech woods, enliven the landscape ; and a park, with groups of fine old trees, slopes down from the palace to the lake.

His school life did not interfere with the gradual

---

* In 1712 the Baron von Canstein, regretting the scarcity and dearness of Bibles in Germany, obtained subscriptions, and devoted a large part of his own property to establish a press at Halle for printing Bibles and Testaments. They were eagerly purchased. Many thousands were issued and sold at a low price.—Tr.

development of his character. Latin was made the supreme object, but the pupil appears to have diligently studied, on his own account, Greek, modern languages, and mathematics.

A Christian tone was maintained in the school, for lessons were preceded by singing a hymn, and reading a chapter in the Bible. The rector Alberti was every inch a schoolmaster, and his motto was that " the schoolmaster should die in his desk."

Well informed, and accompanied by excellent advice from his father, but with no special development of his intellectual powers, Claudius went, in 1759, to the University of Jena.

He gave up studying theology, in consequence of delicacy of the chest, and attended lectures on jurisprudence and political economy, but he took no special interest in them, and regarded them merely as studies which would enable him to get a livelihood. The philosophy then reigning in Jena, which alike attempted to prove things which are obvious to every one, and those which are incapable of proof, was very repulsive to him, and he afterwards assailed it with his humour. His attention was principally occupied with ancient and modern languages, and music enlivened many a lonely hour, for he kept much aloof from the wild life of the other students.

He had a solemn admonition in the early days of his university life, for his brother Josiah, who was also a student at Jena, died of the smallpox.

Claudius was doubtless much affected by his loss, but the funeral discourse which he delivered before the rector and the mourners is an instance of the manner in which at that period the natural springs of feeling were suppressed by lifeless forms. The same amiable and affectionate being who afterwards gave vent to his feelings in the most simple and touching tones at the grave of his father, at twenty years of age had nothing to say over his brother's grave but words " unrefreshing as the misty wind, that whistles through the falling leaves in autumn," and discussed in the dryest style of scholastic philosophy the question, " Whether, and how far, God determines the death of men ?"

The poetic muse had not yet inspired him, though he was not without thoughts of becoming her disciple, but the muse that first attracted him, was not the lovely German maiden as beheld by Klopstock, but a muse in the form of Gottsched of Leipzig, as he is described in Goethe's 'Wahrheit und Dichtung,' the stiff professor who boxed your ears if you had not your wig on. Claudius became a member of the " German Society " established in accordance with Gottsched's ideas, and under its influence he produced his ' Trifles ' (*Tändeleien*), rhymes without any poetic value.

His student life at length came to an end; it had only been to him a sort of process that had to be passed through; it had not given him any definite aims, or introduced him into any sphere of action.

His renunciation of the study of theology, and absence from home, had somewhat estranged him from its spirit, and he now returned to it without having made choice of a profession. What was to be done next? He was never very anxious about the future, and was a stranger to the feeling with which Schiller's Carlos exclaims, " Three-and-twenty years, and nothing done for immortality." He stayed quietly at his father's house, and it was a fortunate thing for him that Gottlob Friedrich Ernst Schönborn was then living on an estate not far from Reinfeld. He was afterwards well known from his political missions abroad, and his association with Klopstock, Stolberg, and Goethe.

He was a poet of moderate pretensions, but satisfied only with poetry of the highest standard; he had an equal taste for philosophical research and political action, and was a man of a Faust-like nature, gifted with the Promethean tendencies of the " Sturm und Drang"* period, and open to all great influences.

It was a great advantage to Claudius that Schönborn directed his attention to the beauties of Homer and Shakspeare, and induced him to give up the rigid forms of Gottsched's style. Under Schönborn's auspices, Claudius went to Copenhagen in 1764 as secretary to a Count of Holstein. The state of things in the Danish capital a hundred years ago was very different from what it is at present. A genial German spirit prevailed there. The minister, Count Bernstorf, had summoned Klopstock thither; J. A. Cramer, the friend of Klopstock's youth, and an author of hymns, was court preacher; H. P. Sturz, a German author of merit, was a member of Bernstorf's ministry; the poet Gerstenberg, captain of horse in the Danish army, wrote poetry himself in an original and earnest style, and gave encouragement to poetic efforts by means of a periodical which he edited. Claudius seemed to breathe a different mental atmosphere. Christian and patriotic topics, as well as nature, presented themselves to him as proper themes for poetry. Klopstock, without doubt,

* An expression denoting a state of peculiar ferment and excitement either in the sphere of literature or politics.

exercised the greatest influence over him. But he did not long retain his appointment; for in 1765 we find him again in the parsonage at Reinfeld, and for three years he enjoyed its repose. We do not precisely know how he occupied his time, but it would seem as if the strong impressions he had received resulted in the development of his peculiar character amidst the rural repose and salutary influences of his home. For when in the autumn of 1768 we find him at Hamburg as editor of the 'Adress Comtoir Nachrichten,' to which he contributed short essays on life and literature, we already trace his characteristic humour. He records in the simplest tones the impressions produced by the charms of nature, the affections, the creations of genius, and the artificial relations of life, and aims to attach to them their true value.

He was in the midst of the exciting life and animating controversies of Hamburg. Lutheran orthodoxy found a mighty champion in the head pastor, Götze, who held his opinions with the pertinacity to which there is still a tendency at Hamburg, while modern intellectual ideas were represented by the pastor Alberti, the philosopher Reimarus, and the dramatist Lessing. But the glories of the city could not console Claudius for the loss of the peaceful quiet of the country; and when he addresses the Hamburgers in the character of editor, he speaks the language of a simple countryman. Thus the peculiar character of the 'Wandsbeck Messenger,' grew to maturity. Hamburg was to him no abiding city; he could only be happy beyond the gates. About the time that he gave up his connection with the 'Adress Comtoir Nachrichten,' and, on the invitation of the author and bookseller Bode, began to assist in the little weekly paper called the 'Wandsbeck Messenger,' he was brought into association with the third of the great renovators of German poetry. He had formed a warm attachment to Klopstock at Copenhagen, had been a sincere admirer of Lessing at Hamburg, and now Herder passed through the city. From the wonderful originality and versatility of his mind, he was peculiarly adapted to exercise a beneficial influence on the simple and impressible nature of Claudius. Herder describes Claudius as "an 'angelic soul,' a noble young man of eager glance, and with a gentle and simple heart, the purest of men;" and Claudius wrote to Herder, though he was not much given to enthusiasm, and always independent in the presence of the greatest, "Your love is to me like the love of women."

On the 1st of January, 1771, the 'Messenger' took its start from Wandsbeck. Its aim was honestly to seek for the good in everything, to penetrate to the kernel of the subjects it handled, to notice modern publications, and in short, striking articles, to keep before the attention of its readers all that is of true and lasting import, to present to them the charms of nature, and to remind them of Him of whom she speaks to us. It preserved the same humorous tone both in prose and rhyme; the poetry was often prosaic, and the reviews poetical; little importance was attached to the form, so that the subject was rendered intelligible. Claudius's choice of a wife was very characteristic. Rebecca Behn, his "peasant girl," was the daughter of a master carpenter; she was young, pious, simple, poor, but she had a fine figure and noble bearing, delicate features, brown eyes, and thick brown hair; a genuine German maiden, capable of the highest culture, though not possessing much; not too refined to bear the heavy burden of domestic cares, but sufficiently so to share the intellectual tastes which Claudius prized so highly. The eccentric manner in which the marriage was celebrated in May, 1772, was not much like a prelude to the future Christian family life. Claudius had invited a number of his most intimate friends, among them Klopstock and Schönborn, not forgetting the clergyman of Wandsbeck. During this social meeting he talked of being married; at first as if in joke, but, as it proved, in earnest, for he produced the royal licence, and requested the pastor to pronounce the blessing over himself and his Rebecca. The early days of their married life appear to have been passed in much simplicity; for a time they maintained a neighbourly intimacy with John Henry Voss, who once wrote to a friend: "We spend the whole day with brother Claudius, and mostly lie in the shade on the grass near an arbour, and listen to the cuckoo and the nightingale. His wife, with her little girl in her arms, lies beside us, with her hair all loose, and dressed like a shepherdess. Then we drink tea or coffee, smoke our pipes and chat, or compose something jointly for the ' Messenger.'"

The sphere of outward life was a restricted one, but that of mental interests was for ever enlarging. Acquaintances multiplied; among them were the brothers Frederic Leopold and Christian Stolberg, and their sisters Augusta and Catharine, and his writings brought him into correspondence with Ha-

mann and Lavater, which developed his religious
life. His views gradually ripened and acquired
precision, and he never gave expression to more
of religious truth than he had himself experienced.
If only time were granted him, it was impossible
but that the healthy germ of honesty and simplicity
in his character should ripen into Christian conviction and decision. The Cross contributed its share
to the process. Two daughters were already born
to the young couple, and their income was very
small. In 1775 he had retired from the ' Wandsbeck Messenger,' and had published on his own
account the first and second parts of his ' Asmus
omnia sua secum portans.' But it was very difficult to live by the pen, especially for a man like
Claudius, whose writings were mostly fragmentary,
outpourings of the heart, or brilliant mental flashes,
very pleasant to read, but not bringing in much
profit. It became a duty to look round for some
appointment. Herder who was then counsellor of
the consistory at Bückeburg, interested himself for
his friend, and through his connection with Darmstadt, the President of the Government there, Von
Moser, jun., offered him an appointment. Claudius
was greatly surprised, and explained clearly what
he could, and what he could not do, and what sort
of an office he wished for. He wrote to Herder :
" As far as my inclination is concerned, I would
rather have had a less brilliant and a quieter post,
such as superintendent of some hospital in the depths
of a forest, or some other benevolent institution,
steward of a hunting-seat, inspector of gardens, or
magistrate of a village, so that I should have had
time to follow my own devices." He, however, was

appointed to be Commissioner of the Oberland, with a salary of 800 florins.*   His duties were to work as member of a commission, the object of which was to develope the material resources of the country, as well as to improve the mental and moral condition of the people.   In March, 1776, Claudius and Rebecca, and two children, took their journey southward.   They spent a week with Herder at Bückeburg, and their warm friendship rendered it a time of high enjoyment.   Moser's reception of them was friendly rather than gracious.   Claudius was installed into his office, but things did not go altogether smoothly; for though the post suited him pretty well on the whole, difficulties connected with some of the details of business soon presented themselves.   Among all the duties which devolved upon him, the one that suited him best was the editorship of a paper published for the benefit of an asylum for invalids.   Darmstadt was not an unpleasant residence; there was still a circle of eminent men there, whose society frequently attracted the youthful Goethe; the country was varied and pleasant, and there were always dry walks under the evergreen shelter of the fir-trees in winter. Whether correct or not, tradition points out the place where he composed his ' Evening Hymn.' Be that as it may, the scenery exactly answers to the description.

> " The moon hath risen on high,
>   And in the clear dark sky
> The golden stars all brightly glow ;
>   And black and hushed the woods,
>   While o'er the fields and floods
> The white mists hover to and fro.

---

* About £66.

" How still the earth ! how calm !
      What dear and home-like charm,
From gentle twilight doth she borrow !
      Like to some quiet room,
      Where, wrapt in still soft gloom,
We sleep away the daylight's sorrow.

" Look up ; the moon to-night
      Shows us but half her light,
And yet we know her round and fair ;
      At other things how oft
      We in our blindness scoff'd,
Because we saw not what was there.

" We haughty sons of men
      Have but a narrow ken,
We are but sinners poor and weak ;
      Yet airy dreams we build,
      And deem us wise and skilled,
And come not nearer what we seek.

" Thy mercy let us see,
      Nor find in vanity
Our joy ; nor trust in what departs ;
      But true and simple grow,
      And live to Thee below,
With sunny, pure, and childlike hearts.

" Let death all gently come
      At last to take us home,
And let us meet him fearlessly ;
      And when these bonds are riven,
      Oh, take us to Thy heaven,
Our Lord and God, to dwell with Thee.

" Now in His name most blest,
      My brethren sink to rest ;
The wind is cold, chill falls the dew.
      Spare us, O God, and keep
      Us safe in quiet sleep,
And all the sick and suffering too."*

------

* Reprinted, by permission of Messrs. Longman and Co., from
' Lyra Germanica.'

But the spiritual atmosphere of the place did not suit him, and so the " fine Darmstadt air " did not suit him either.

Before a year had passed, Moser and Claudius came to an explanation, which resulted in his return to Wandsbeck. In his pecuniary embarrassment he applied, with his accustomed candour, to Jacobi at Düsseldorf, who had been represented to him as a wealthy and noble-minded man. He received a favourable answer, but it found him on a sick-bed. In the meantime, Herder, who was then superinten-dent-general* at Weimar, had obtained the money for the return journey of his stranded friend from the youthful Duchess of Weimar.

As soon as he was recovered, he cheerfully turned his steps northward again. To Herder's very natu-ral question, " What he was going to do at Wands-beck?" he returned answer, " Make translations, publish a continuation of Asmus, and—commit my way unto the Lord."

In May, to the surprise of friends and neighbours, they arrived at Wandsbeck. Claudius wrote to a friend, " The doctrine about the climate did not altogether satisfy them. " But God was with him. He did not again leave Wandsbeck of his own accord, though the troubles of war sent him forth as a wanderer in his latter days. He lived for nearly forty years in this quiet place, which became in consequence one of the best known spots in Ger-many. The children multiplied; he persevered in his plan of translating, publishing a continuation of ' Asmus,' and committing his way unto the Lord; and when his difficulties appeared insurmountable,

* A dignity in the Lutheran Church.

Frederic, Crown Prince of Denmark, gave Claudius out of gratitude, a pension of two hundred dollars, and, at his own request, he afterwards received the appointment of chief auditor of the Schleswig-Holstein bank at Altona. The office gave him little trouble, he could continue to live at Wandsbeck, and the salary was nearly a thousand dollars per annum.* Thus his outward life was provided for, and his inner life daily increased in depth and fervour. He remained, as he had before in jest described himself, a " man of letters."

Authorship was the talent with which God had intrusted him for the benefit of his countrymen. As we have seen, it was long before his vocation became clear to him ; in fact, it was not until German poetry had perceived its true mission. His early attempts at poetical composition shared the prevailing faults of the time,—poverty of matter, and rigidity of form. The odes of Klopstock, the creations of Goethe's poetic genius, the acuteness of Lessing, and the originality of Herder, all combined to elicit whatever was good and genuine in the mind of Claudius ; his simplicity, sincerity, and fidelity to nature. And when he tuned the lyre, he affected nothing artificial or assumed, but simply gave expression to his own mental mood. In a greater degree than any other poet, Claudius regarded nature and creation, not as a work distinct from the Author, but as an image of God, on which may still be traced the impress of the divine finger, which is still illumined by the reflection of the satisfaction with which God beheld His work, and over

* The Danish dollar is worth about 2s. 3d. sterling. The salary and pension would, therefore, amount to £135.

which, with vivifying power, the Spirit of God still moves.

"Poets," he said, in an imaginary audience of the Emperor of Japan, "are bright transparent flints, which give out sparks when struck by the beautiful heaven and the beautiful earth, and our holy religion."

He never stops short at the mere description of natural objects, he rises to the contemplation of the moral and spiritual, to the spirit of charity. His loving nature causes him to see the love of God in creation ; he extols the happiness of a pious peasant race, to show men how happy they may be in humble circumstances. Love made his own domestic life a scene of constant enjoyment, alternating in work and peaceful rest ; and a neighbour in distress was never forgotten.

Patriotism, too, was often the subject of his song. In poetry like that of Claudius, which always unconsciously breathes a spirit of piety, the transition was natural to special religious subjects. Besides poetry, his writings comprise fables, proverbs, and many prose pieces, some of them in aphoristic style, some in the form of treatises.

The peculiarity of his style consisted in a certain humour, which, however, was in nowise discordant with the Christian tone of his works, for none but the Christian who forms a just estimate of the essential nature of things can play as he did with their outward manifestations. The jocular tone of the 'Wandsbeck Messenger' was only the reverse side of the true earnestness with which, as a pilgrim here on earth, he sought an abiding city to come. His happiest hymns are in the style of those of Paul Gerhardt, and his descriptions of natural scenes, and the incidents of human life, may be compared to some of Goethe's, such as his ' Artist's Morning and Evening Hymns.'

Claudius was certainly "homme de lettres," but his authorship was never anything distinct from his life; it was the expression of his own experience. The mainspring of his life was therefore the main-spring of his writings, and that was Christ. He never belonged strictly to any party; his views were not orthodox in the ancient acceptation of the word, nor was he a pietist of Spener's school, nor yet a rationalist, but he was ever gradually attaining to more settled religious conviction. He may be described as a mystic in the best sense of the term. His views of life, of the will, of love, of communion with God by its means, of the reality of a future glory, of which we have here but the faintest shadow, were all based upon the word of God. He was strongly opposed to the deadness of the letter, to a mere belief of the understanding, to controversies about words, and to that short-sighted wisdom which thinks it has attained to all knowledge. The most correct description of him is, that he was a simple biblical Christian, and, as such, he bore his testimony in a period of religious declension. As a messenger from God he journeyed far and wide, offering the truths of salvation in various attractive forms. The firmer his faith became, and therefore more and more unintelligible to the wise of this world, the more he experienced the truth of the following lines :—

> " The Christian's inner life keeps fresh and green,
> Although without the burning sun oppress ;
> What God hath given His own no eye hath seen,
> They only know the treasure, who possess."

In the midst of a time which said it was "rich and increased with goods," he distinctly proclaimed that humanity stood in need of a Saviour. It was impossible for one to despise creation, regarding it, as he did, as pervaded by the blessing of the Creator, but he could not ignore its defilement by sin. He regarded man as the crowning work of creation, and said, "Every living thing that he sees around him dies, but he knows of immortality; everything that meets his view in external nature is temporal and local, but he knows that there are things eternal. Destined for the liberty of the children of God, he has fallen into the bondage of sin." He did not despise reason, nor deny that the heathen retained traces of the original revelation; and, although he considered it an exaggerated toleration which declared that the ancient philosophers were Christians, because they taught a lofty morality, still he said, "Water, no doubt, extinguished fire even in those days, and self-denial produced excellent results." But he had little taste for controversy of this sort; his creed was, "We poor sinners are conceited creatures, but it is very little that we know."

In times when the multitude does not believe, and an individual testifies of his faith, he naturally adopts a personal tone, but it comes from the heart, and reaches the hearts of others. Some of our readers may remember being touched by such words as these :—

"You would like to know more about our Lord Christ? Andreas, who would not like to know more of Him? But it is of no use to come to me. I am no friend to novel opinions, and keep close to the written word. And I hate puzzling over the mysteries of religion, for I consider that it is just because we are not to know them yet that they *are* mysteries. Since we cannot see Him ourselves, we must trust to those who did see Him. I cannot see that any other course is open to us. Everything that we find in the Bible about Him, all the glorious stories and sayings, are not Christ certainly; they are only testimonies concerning Him; only the fringes of His garment; still they are the best things that we have on earth, and they comfort us and rejoice our hearts by showing us that man may become something different from, and better than, what he is."

Then he describes our need of redemption and the Redeemer as the Gospels represent Him, and exclaims,—

"Andreas! have you ever heard anything like it? Do not your arms drop down by your sides in amazement? Certainly it is a mystery entirely above our comprehension, but it is a mystery from heaven and from God, for it bears the stamp of heaven, and overflows with the mercy of God. One would be willing to be branded or broken on the wheel for the bare idea of it; and he who can laugh and mock at it must surely be out of his mind. He whose heart is in the right place will put his mouth in the dust, and worship and adore."

Again he wrote:—"He who will not believe in Christ must see how he can get on without Him. Neither you nor I can. We want some one to support and sustain us while we live, and to put his hand under our heads when we die, and, according to what is written of Him, He is abundantly able to do it, and we know of no one by whom we should so much like to have it done."

In all the writings of Claudius there is a certain domestic tone. It is not only that the events of his life may be traced in them, he is fond of adopting the form of confidential conversation or correspondence. He was thoroughly a family man; "he himself believed and his whole house." From the tying of the marriage knot to the end of his life, when eleven children had been born to him, he lived entirely for his home, and for his country only so far as was compatible with that. It was an exemplary household, for, as the outward means were limited, the inner life was all the more sedulously cultivated. There was neither the affectation of genius scorning the labour of the hands, nor so much occupation of time with work that it was considered a sin to take up a book. All worked hard: the father in his study and with the children, the mother in her nursery, kitchen, and garden, and the children at their tasks. But there was time for morning and evening prayers; grace was said at table; there was music, singing, and reading; the best music was heard in the house, the best literature lay upon the table. Sometimes pupils, sometimes visitors were added to the family circle; the vibrations of the intellectual world were felt within the house; the most eminent men knocked at the Messenger's door, but the home preserved its simplicity.

His poems indicate his deep interest in family life; his Rebecca often appears in them. There were cradle songs, and others dictated by little daily family events; and he had a happy fertility and humour in inventing simple little domestic festivals. Then we find him in all seriousness writing for his children, 'A Father's Account of the Christian Religion,' composing a hymn on the death of his little girl, or closing a last will and testament for his son John, with the following lessons of Christian wisdom :—

"When I am dead close my eyes, and do not mourn for me. Be helpful to your mother; honour her as long as she lives, and bury her near me. Meditate daily upon death and upon life, so that you may find it. Be of a cheerful spirit, and do not go out of the world without having publicly testified of your love and reverence for the Founder of Christianity."

It may be remarked that nothing that we have related of Claudius has any particular connection with the renewal of religious life during the wars of independence; and the simple Wandsbeck Messenger certainly was much less mixed up in public events than any of the characters whom we have hitherto presented to our readers. Nevertheless he did contribute to that end. It was partly owing to his unobtrusive influence during previous years that some of the best men in the nation passed through those troublous times in the devout spirit that we have described. Gratitude demands that a place should be accorded to Claudius among our heroes as a forerunner of the renewal of faith. It was, as it were, raised upon his shoulders that the deeds of some of the younger generation were achieved. We can scarcely think of such men as Perthes, Stolberg, or Nicolovius, who either by deeds or words took so active a part in public events, apart from the influence of the Wandsbeck Messenger, whom they honoured as their spiritual father.

We close our sketch with a few words on the relation of Claudius to the conflicting opinions of the time. The Wandsbeck Messenger spoke decidedly from the first against the French Revolution, when the greater number of his countrymen were cheering on the French in their revolt against royalty, and Klopstock was so far carried away as to greet it with spirited odes. It was not that the heart of Claudius did not beat warmly for the happiness and freedom of the people; he hated all injustice and oppression, especially the conjunction so frequent in the eighteenth century of the servitude of the people, and luxury among the great; but he was himself too good, too submissive in a Christian sense, not only to the good and gentle but also to the froward, ever to advise an appeal to force.

Claudius loved a paternal government and a child-like submission to it, and it was only on a Christian foundation that this appeared possible to him. The horrors of the revolution, the rebellion against the throne and the Church, and all authority human and divine, excited his utmost abhorrence. He at once began his opposition to the 'Modern Policy,' and published his remarks upon the 'Modern System' and the 'Rights of Man.' No doubt he was often mistaken, and scarcely admitted the good which God permitted to arise out of the Revolution, but from his point of view he was certainly right in lifting up his voice against its godless excesses. His opinions were shared by many in Holstein; counts Reventlow and Stolberg from their noble birth and religious opinions entirely agreed with him. The German

fugitives from the South and West who turned their
steps towards the North when French disorder en-
croached on German soil, Jacobi and Schlosser could
find no words strong enough in which to express their
horror of the Revolution.　In association with such
men, Claudius was more and more confirmed in his
views, and he broke forth into the following lament :

> " They would not have a God, would cast away
>   His being from their thought,
>   And so He left them to their evil way,
>   He gave them what they sought.
>   That germ of heavenly light and love,
>   Which God implants in every breast,
>   And hath with His own seal impressed,
>   And which by every one possessed,
>   If duly nurtured, watered, dressed,
>   Shall grow till he is truly blessed
>   With choicest blessings from above—
>   That germ of heavenly light and love,
>   Was stifled in their hearts, and still,
>   They mocked at goodness, worshipped ill,
>   They prayed to folly, and the devil praised,
>   To horrid cruelty their altars raised,
>   Have pity on them, Lord !"

At the age of seventy-three, Claudius, who amongst
other ways had proved his patriotism by contributing
to the ' Patriotic Museum,' established by his son-
in-law Perthes, was placed in painful outward circumstances and much mental perplexity.　As an inhabi-
tant of Holstein his fate was bound up with that of
the King of Denmark, but after June 1813, Denmark, repulsed by England, had entered into alliance
with France.　Wandsbeck was therefore an enemy's
territory to the allied troops stationed on the banks
of the lower Elbe, and Claudius thought it best to
leave with his Rebecca before the conclusion of the

armistice. Assisted by a sum of money sent him from Elberfeld by some unknown hand, he wandered from place to place, sometimes finding refuge with a friend, sometimes with a brother. At the beginning of November he joined his daughter Caroline Perthes and her children at Kiel, but in January he thought it best to go to Lübeck. There his circumstances were most needy. He wrote to Caroline Perthes: "We are so far well, we have a little room in which there is a bed and a settee, but there is no room left to turn round. We cook our meal and potatoes for ourselves, but fuel is very dear; you will have learnt from the papers that Wandsbeck is in the hands of the allies. Fritz is there and keeps house, and has sold the cow, and in the larder it looks as the earth did before the creation, desolate* and void."

But his keenest sufferings were not occasioned by hunger, cold, and nakedness. He loved his King, who as Crown Prince had shown him much kindness; he regarded him with a sentiment of ancient German fealty, but he also loved his German fatherland, and hoped that it would be victorious; but the success of Germany involved the defeat of his sovereign. So that even at that time the union of Holstein with Denmark produced hopeless confusion.

But this perplexity did not deter him from addressing his countrymen on the signs of the times when the German arms had proved victorious. He published a 'Sermon for the new year 1814, by a lay brother' on the text, 'and Moses said unto God, who am I that I should go unto Pharaoh?'†

---

* Luther's translation is, "Wüste und leer."
† Exodus iii. 11.

This, if nothing else, would entitle him to a place among those who contributed to the renewal of religious life at this period. It began with Martin Luther's hymn,—

> " It was a strange and awful strife,
>   When life and death contested ;
> But death was triumphed o'er by life,
>   And life from death was wrested."

He then continues :—" Germany had forgotten its ancestral virtues.   The ancient spirit of uprightness, brotherly love, and manliness was extinguished, and irreligion, luxury, and effeminacy had taken its place ; thus it became possible for an enterprising neighbour to accomplish what would have been previously impossible.   He advanced boldly, sowed discord, prevailed against us, brought us into subjection, and divided the spoil, and our free brethren looked on, and allowed themselves to be played with as puppets and slaves. Germany had forgotten her ancestral virtues, and had fallen into a deep slumber. But when awakened by a mighty voice from the North, she began to look about her ; the ancient spirit revived ; great was the company of heroes, and their united power and wisdom put an end to the mischief. And having so long conferred everlasting obligations upon Germany, they will finish their work, convert us from the error of our ways, cause justice to be respected, and ensure peace and safety to us and our posterity. But we have paid, and must still pay dearly for this. Germany's hills and valleys are streaming with blood, her plains are strewn with corpses, her villages and towns are lying desolate and waste, the inhabitants have fled, and are roaming about wretched and forlorn.

It remains for the princes and fathers of the people to honour the memory of the heroes who have fallen in the service of freedom and their country, to provide for their widows and orphans, to gather the fugitives together, to build up the waste places, and, as far as possible, to counteract the evil that has been done. But that is but a part of the duty which God has laid upon them, and by far the smallest part. Here on earth we are clothed in flesh and blood, but we are not flesh and blood. Man is immortal! Man's true nature is imperishable, and destined to rule over perishable nature, and to be God's image and representative upon earth. This is what he was originally, and he may be restored to his pristine glory. But this cannot be effected by the powers of perishable nature; it must be effected by the first and most glorious of Beings, of whose nature we partake, the fountain of all goodness, the source of all power, and of all our faculties, and in whom they are all united. None but Him can help and succour us! With man it is impossible, but with God all things are possible."

Further on he says, " Perhaps there never was a time since the introduction of Christianity, when the ground was so well prepared for it as now; God has prepared it, for as gentle measures did not avail, He has inflicted severe and general chastisement. War, which has never before so raged through the length and breadth of Germany, and in nearly all the countries of Europe, has snatched from men the treasures wherein they sought their happiness, in order that they might turn to those which cannot be taken from them, or at least be convinced of their transitory nature, that thus their attachment

to them might be lessened. War has brought down
the conceit and self-reliance which caused men to
hold their heads so high; it has taught them to
submit to the mighty power of God, and injustice
and violence, losses and misery have broken and
contrited their hearts. In a word, it has made them
ready to receive help from the only true source of
help.

"And you mourners and sorrowing ones far and
near, who are weeping for the loss of your sons,
your friends and lovers, do not despair! If you
cannot take comfort in the thought that they suffered and fell in the cause of liberty and country,
there is a prospect for you beyond death and the
grave and all earthly things, which will dry your
tears."

It was with such words as these that Claudius
took leave of his countrymen. Once more, in the
fulness of his love, he called upon them not to neglect the time of their visitation, but both individu-
ally, and as a nation, to give heed to the things that
belonged to their peace. Then he peacefully went
his way to his everlasting rest.

On returning to Wandsbeck he found his house
in a desolate state, after its occupation by soldiers;
and after he was again settled in it, he did not regain his previous vigour either of body or mind.
He once more cheerfully celebrated his birthday on
the 15th of August, 1815, but his health soon afterwards declined, and at the beginning of December
he yielded to the wishes of his daughter Caroline
Perthes, and went to her house, in order that medical aid might be nearer at hand. There he passed
the last few weeks of his life in weakness, but with-

out pain, full of love and gratitude towards God and man, rejoicing in the blue sky or a fine sunrise, and regarding his wife, his children, and grandchildren with affectionate delight. The final conflict lasted for a week, and he was fully conscious of his approaching end. He had hoped before his release to have been favoured with one of those special illuminations which have been the lot of some, that he might have gazed into the land beyond the bridge of death. But it was not granted him, and he acknowledged it as a mercy that his mind was permitted to remain clear and his faith firm. He prayed fervently that suffering might not prove too strong a temptation for him. Thinking of the mystery of the separation of soul and body, he said, "I have been studying all my life to prepare myself for this hour, and now I do not know how it will end."

When he felt his departure to be very near, he said once more, "Lead me not into temptation, but deliver me from evil," and shortly afterwards, "Good night! good night!" Speech then failed him; once more he opened his eyes, and, turning them on his Rebecca with a look of blessing, he departed. It was on the 21st of January, 1815. His children laid him in the coffin; by his own wish, no stranger touched him. He was taken to Wandsbeck, and buried near his daughter; and a cross, inscribed with the text, "For God so loved the world," etc., marks his resting-place.

Great changes have since taken place in his dwelling-place; but on the hundredth anniversary of his birth a simple monument of granite was placed in the wood at Wandsbeck, as a memorial that the Wandsbeck Messenger once listened to the voice of God under the shade of the trees, that he might deliver to his countrymen at the right moment, and in well considered words, the message of salvation.*

Stilling's voice was more powerful than that of Claudius, and his character was by no means so unassuming. Whilst Claudius couched what he had to say to his countrymen in the modest form of a message, and simply styled himself a "lay brother," —when the great events near the close of his life caused him to address an admonition to them, Stilling assumed the prophet's mantle; and he, who once earned his bread by working as a tailor in his father's attic, beheld an emperor and princes reverently listening to his words. Both were students of the Bible, but the favourite portion of Claudius was the Gospel, of Stilling the Revelation of St. John.

Stilling has himself given us a picture of his life in a book which has been much read, and deserves to be read again and again. A rich vein of human, German, Christian interests runs through it. All conspires to produce a striking effect; beautiful and romantic scenery, and a thorough appreciation of it; the elements, legends, and presentiments are curiously blended with the actions and feelings of men. Mountains and forests, and the varying aspects of nature, seem to him to speak in parables of human experience. Strong passions were con-

* 'Matthias Claudius, der Wandsbecker Bote. Ein Lebensbild von Wilhelm Herbst.' Gotha : F. A. Perthes.

'Matthias Claudius' Werke.' 2 Bände. Siebente Auflage. Hamburg und Gotha : F. A. Perthes. 1844.

trolled by Christian training, and we are presented with an interesting picture of very various individual character, in a setting of religious, rural, domestic life.　How distinct are the characters of the patriarch Eberhardt and his son William, the old pastor Moritz, Margaret, and Dortchen !　The garden behind the house, as it sloped up the hill, seemed only like a natural extension of the dwelling ; and when quiet and seclusion were not to be had within, or when the space seemed too narrow to contain the overflowing feelings of the heart, or when these singular people were in mournful or meditative mood, they would wander alone, or in company with wife or child, over the wooded hills, and fancy they heard spirit voices in the sighing of the wind or the song of the nightingale.

Daily labour at the plough or at charcoal-burning did not preclude occupation with the problems of science.　The search for the philosopher's stone, of which we find traces in Stilling's youth, is a sort of poetico-religious embodiment, in a speculative age, of an endeavour to solve the mysteries of nature. The quadrature of the circle, with which Eberhardt occupied himself at his charcoal burning, incited his son John to cultivate a taste for mathematics, which resulted in his obtaining a useful and important situation.　Daily toil did not blunt the keen interest of these mountaineers in the investigation of the properties of natural objects ; and in religious matters they did not pin their faith upon the minister, but searched the Scriptures for themselves, and obtained other books, which they read in the same reverent spirit as the word of God.

They thus became possessed of an eccentric mental culture, but still the best thing about them was their warmth of heart.

We are fascinated with the creations of a great poet's genius—Shakspeare's, for example—when he weaves into a living picture of human life, history, legend, the phenomena of nature, and the knowledge of mankind; and in Stilling's life we have the same, with the additional charm of its being reality. The book contains many descriptions of the passions which agitate the breast of man, but controlled by the power of religion, which no poet could surpass. But we must resist the temptation of culling anecdotes from the story of Stilling's youth. It delighted the youthful Goethe so much at Strasburg, that he zealously forwarded the publication of it. Stolberg sang its praises, and in later times it has been extolled by poets differing so widely from each other as Schenkendorf and Freiligrath, and it has never been surpassed by any of our painters of popular life, not even by Immermann, Auerbach, Gotthelf, or Glaubrecht.

We must confine ourselves to seeking out the elements in Stilling's memoirs which combined to form his peculiar character.

The little village of Grund, in the parish of Hilchenbeck, in which, in September 1740, Heinrich Jung Stilling was born, belonged at that time to the Prince of Nassau-Siegen, now to the Prussian province of Westphalia. "In this country," he says of himself, "where the smelting of ore, iron foundries, mining and agriculture, were carried on, Stilling's youth was passed, among peasants, miners, and smiths." Stilling's family were mostly charcoal-burners, but his father was a tailor, and the boy was brought up to this trade, sometimes going into the fields with the women of the house; but it is probable that his grandfather's occupation of charcoal-burning, the life in the woods, the view of the mountains, the seclusion in the forest glades, which leads to an intimacy with birds and flowers, made a strong impression on him. At any rate, Stilling grew up with an unusually strong love of nature, and was a close observer of her.

The district was peopled by a sturdy race, professing the reformed faith. When Eberhardt Stilling looked forward to the glories of the future life, he hoped to find himself in the company of Luther and Calvin, Zwingli, Œcolampadius, and Bucerus. The pastor with whom Stilling came into contact in his youth had an overweening sense of the dignity of his office. But Eberhardt Stilling, the elder of the church, was by no means intimidated by it; his own faith was firm, he was fully conscious of his dignity as the head of a family; and, when occasion required, he was quite ready to stand up for his rights in opposition to the pastor. But there were other peculiar elements in the religious atmosphere by which Stilling was surrounded in his youth. The district was one of those in which the pietistic separatist movement was most strongly developed. All Protestant sects which were subject to persecution elsewhere, were welcomed in the neighbouring territories of Wittgenstein and Berleburg. The district had been visited by Zinzendorf, Rock, Hochmann, and Dippel; and the writings of Spener, Francke, Petersen, Anna Lead, and Mme. Guyon, were eagerly read. Many people thought themselves inspired by the Spirit of God, and that the fall of Babylon was near, and they were united in the bonds of close fellowship. Men who had once imbibed worldly wisdom at the universities, wandered about as pedlers from house to house, extolling, with their wares, the grace of God as the pearl of great price. Pious countesses gave their hands in marriage to pious peasants. There was much fanaticism, and sometimes much carnal-mindedness, but, nevertheless, Christ had many true disciples in the country.

There was no Separatist congregation formed in Stilling's native village ; but many were favourably disposed to this sect who did not leave the church, and sometimes attended the separatist meetings to supplement the spiritual edification to be obtained from their own pastor. To this class Stilling's family belonged. In his maternal grandfather Moritz, who had been dismissed from his office of pastor for practising alchemy, he saw an example of unrestrained fanaticism ; while his grandfather Stilling was a champion of ecclesiastical orthodoxy. After his mother's death, in the views which his father adopted, he made acquaintance with the hidden life of the " Quiet in the Land," a party who sought to withdraw entirely from the world ; and as soon as he left home, he was brought into contact with all sorts of religious opinions.

Stilling never attempted to conceal his connection with this classic ground of sectarianism, and his writings have a flavour of separatist opinions.

Although he considered himself a member of the reformed church, he was so indifferent to creeds, that towards the close of his life he resolutely refused to say to which he gave the preference.

But the effect of family influences was still stronger upon Stilling than that of scenery or associates; for the Stillings were distinguished by a remarkably strong feeling of family affection, which reminds us of the ancient patriarchs of the Bible. When taking a walk with his grandfather in the wood, Stilling once began asking him about their ancestors. Father Stilling smiled, and said, "It would be hard to make out that we are descended from any prince; but that is all one to me, and you must not covet it either. Your forefathers were all good and honourable people, and there are very few princes who can say that. You must consider it the greatest honour you can have that your grandfather and great-grandfather and their fathers were men who were beloved and honoured by everybody, although they had nothing to rule over but their own households. Not one of them ever married disgracefully, or acted dishonourably towards a woman. Not one of them ever coveted what did not belong to him; and they all died full of days and honour." Henry was pleased to hear this, and said, "I shall find my forefathers in heaven then."—"Yes," answered the grandfather, "that you will; our race will thrive there. Henry, I hope you will remember this evening as long as you live. In that world we shall take a high rank; mind you do not forfeit your privileges! Our blessing will rest upon you so long as you are good; but if you are godless, and despise your parents, we shall not recognize you in eternity."

Stilling's great-grandfather lived to be 104, his grandfather and father attained to a great age, and he reached that of 77 himself. He regarded his grandfather Eberhardt as a venerable patriarch, and always revered the memory of his grandmother, who took charge of him after his mother's death. Traits of the character of his mother, the gentle, susceptible Dortchen, were deeply engraven on his mind; and when at the height of his fame, he had the satisfaction of receiving his father—then a venerable and weary old man—into his house at Marburg, and of caring for him till his death. His strong regard for family ties was very early indicated. When his grandfather died, a son-in-law, of the name of Simon, became master of the house. Stilling says, " He was not a Stilling, and the oak table that had been witness of so many blessings and so much hospitality—the useful old table—was exchanged for a yellow maple one, full of locked-up drawers; the other was put up in the loft behind the chimney. Henry sometimes went up there, lay down upon the ground near it, and cried. Simon once found him there, and said, " Henry, what are you doing there ?"—" I am crying about the table." His uncle laughed, and said, " What, crying about an old oak table !"   Henry was provoked, and said, " My grandfather made that lap to it, and that leg, and that carving in the lap; nobody who loves him would like to see it destroyed."   Simon was angry, and retorted, "It was not large enough for me; and, besides, where was I to put my own ?"—" Uncle," said the boy, " you ought to have put that up here, till grandmother was dead, and all the rest of us were gone away."

The national and family influences amidst which a man grows up are doubtless very important in determining his future career, but they are not the most important element in so doing. It consists in the special divine idea of which his life is to be the exponent, the essence of his individuality, which though influenced by race and nation, like the plant by air and soil, is yet developed in accordance with its own peculiar characteristics.

Stilling early excited observation, both among his own family and others. His grandfather often said, " That boy is getting beyond us. He will be fledged earlier than any of us were. We must pray God to guide him with His good spirit."

The retired life of his childhood only increased instead of repressing his ambition to acquire knowledge and obtain influence.

But the limited means which closed the paths of learning to him just at the period when the mind begins to feel its powers, and the necessity that was laid upon him to watch for the leadings of Providence step by step in his career, gave rise to the fact that whatever office he held, it never seemed to satisfy the longings of his soul, that his wishes and aspirations always led him into a sphere beyond that in which his calling lay.

At fifteen he was schoolmaster in various places. But his own thirst for learning often interfered with his teaching ; the originality of his ideas was almost too great for what was expected in a schoolmaster at that day, and often led him to introduce novel plans which gave offence, and his extraordinary passion for reading, and many other tastes and habits annoyed the people.

Admired and censured he went from place to place. When he could not get on at school-keeping he took to working at his trade again, but he soon wearied

of that and longed for a freer and more intellectual
life.   He did not eventually follow either school-
keeping or trade ; at one time he was foreman to a
merchant, in 1770 a medical student at Strasburg,
then a surgeon at Elberfeld, in 1778 professor of
political economy at Kaiserslautern, in 1784 at
Heidelberg, and at Marburg in 1787.   There he appeared to have attained to the summit of earthly
happiness, for he had an income of 1200 dollars, and
a post of honour.   But his religious writings and
pietistic tendencies estranged his hearers until at
last he had but three, just sufficient to form a class.
In 1803 he was for the first time satisfied with his
position, for the Margrave Charles Frederic of Baden
made him aulic counsellor, with a salary, but no
duties, in order that he might devote himself to his
calling of winning souls for the kingdom of God.

During all the vicissitudes of his fortune, he retained the conviction as the star of his life, and to
illustrate which he wrote his history, that God immediately controls the ways of men, in fact, that the
life of a prayerful man is but a tissue of mysterious
leadings and gracious answers to prayer.   He may
often have deceived himself and mistaken his own
inclinations for divine guidance, but in every bitter
disappointment he took refuge in earnest prayer, under the influence of which he returned to walk in
God's ways, so that he was truly justified in considering his life as guided by a divine hand.   He was
not always consistent in his creed.   Although early
rich in religious experience, it was much later before
he became a partaker of the pardoning grace accorded to a condemned sinner ; and though, after
experiencing a sudden awakening in his twenty-

second year, when walking in the street at Solingen, and making on the spot an irrevocable covenant with God to give himself up entirely to His guidance, and though he had been for years in close communion with the " Quiet in the Land," he afterwards adopted the fatalist opinion that all the ways of man are pre-determined by an irrevocable decree. He held these opinions for twenty years, until he was induced to relinquish them by Kant's philosophy. And after he had returned to a God who is heart to heart, he required to be afresh initiated into the doctrine of reconciliation through the blood of Christ.

It was at the time of the French Revolution of 1789, when Christianity was openly rejected, that Stilling renounced fatalism, and returned to a belief in a God who hears prayer and lovingly watches over the destinies of men. He gave up also his belief in the rationalistic explanations of the atonement, and returned to his faith in the blood of the Lamb to cleanse from all sin. He himself relates, " Through the influence of the philosophy of Wolf and Leibnitz, Stilling became entangled in the meshes of fatalism. For more than twenty years he had fought against this giant with prayers and supplications, without being able to vanquish him. He had, indeed, always maintained in his writings the doctrine of the freedom of man's will and actions, and believed it in spite of the suggestions of reason ; he had also always continued to pray, though the giant used to whisper in his ear, 'your prayers are of no use, for that which God has ordained in His counsels will come to pass, whether you pray or not.'"

Nevertheless, Stilling prayed on, but without light

or comfort, even when his prayers were answered, for then the giant whispered, " It is only chance."

It is singular that Stilling was set free from this bondage of fatalism by the same means as Fichte, namely, by the philosophy of Kant. Stilling eagerly studied Kant's ' Critique of Pure Reason.' The arguments adduced therein to prove that beyond the sphere of the senses human reason knows nothing at all, that it encounters contradictions whenever it tries to form conclusions concerning supernatural things, based upon its own premises, appeared to him to be an illustration of the words of the Apostle, " But the natural man receiveth not the things of the spirit of God; for they are foolishness unto him; neither can he know them because they are spiritually discerned."*

With this result of Kant's philosophy, Stilling contented himself. It was a negative result,—merely the conviction that reason of itself knows nothing of things divine. But instead of filling up the void with morality, like Kant, he kept close to the revelation contained in the Scriptures, and felt confirmed in so doing by Kant's words, " You are also right in seeking your only consolation in the Gospel, for it is the inexhaustible source of all truths, which, when reason has exhausted its resources, are to be found nowhere else."

After Stilling had returned to the belief in a God as revealed to us in the Bible, who rules in loving freedom over His free creatures, his views also became clear again on the subject of the atonement, on which he had wavered in consequence of intercourse with a man who held rationalistic opinions upon it.

* 1 Cor. ii. 14.

In the autumn of 1789 he went to Rüsselsheim on the Maine, in Hesse Darmstadt, where he performed an operation on the wife of the pastor Sartorius, and spent nine happy days in his Christian family.

Stilling relates, "Pastor Sartorius belonged to the school of Francke at Halle, and talked in its tone to Stilling of the truths of religion, especially of the doctrines of the atonement and of imputed righteousness.

"Without intending it, he got into an argument on these subjects with the good pastor, and discovered how far he had swerved from the truth. This then was the beginning of his return."

Immediately after this, he resided for a time among the Moravians at Neuwied, which essentially contributed to the confirmation of his faith.

About this period, those opinions which originated in France, of which the tendency was to undermine both Church and State, began to obtain considerable influence in Germany. And as Stilling was then induced to appear as an author of religious works, it was natural that he should endeavour to oppose the new doctrines and uphold the old. His treatise ' On the Revolutionary Spirit of Our Time, for the Instruction of the Burgher Class,' originated in this desire. He points out that pride, luxury, and especially the lamentable immorality and godlessness that prevailed, are the real causes of the Revolution. He says, "Now, my honest German fellow citizens, lay your hands upon your hearts, give glory to God, and say truly, is not the class of people that I have been describing very numerous, and therefore formidable, especially among the learned and people of rank? Unmeasured pride, unbridled sensuality, a secret aversion to Christ and His religion, and a fearful indifference to God, are at once the sources and characteristics of the revolutionary spirit. Titan-like, it presumes to assail the throne of God, and therefore it is not likely that it should submit to the authority of man. Let us first take the beam out of our own eye before we venture to take the mote out of the eyes of our rulers." And again, "My beloved German fellow countrymen, high and low, great and small, there is but one way in which all abuses can be rectified, as far as that is possible in this imperfect world, and this consists in an earnest and general endeavour to attain to moral perfection, to ennoble oneself, and to avoid luxurious living; in a word, in the practical cultivation of real and true religion. This would teach us to submit to those who have the rule over us, and not only to the good and gentle, but also to the froward. It would convince us of our state of moral degradation, and thereby make us humble."

But Stilling's religious writings were much more influential than this political treatise. It is not within our province to treat of the works which have most contributed to his fame, the 'Scenes from the Spirit World,' 'Home-Sickness,' and his romance, called 'Theobald, or the Enthusiast.' The works which had the greatest influence upon public events, were a religious periodical called 'Der Graue Mann,' the greyheaded man, and 'The Triumphant History of the Christian Religion; a Popular Explanation of the Revelation of St. John.'

It appeared in 1799, in the same year as Schleiermacher's 'Discourses on Religion.' Both were the result of newly awakened religious life, but they dif-

fered very widely. It was at first Schleiermacher's
desire, to descend into the depths of his own mind,
in order there to seek for the sources of the religious
life. Stilling, on the contrary, explored the realms
of history, explained passing events, and attempted
to define the nature of the kingdom of God. He
had been accustomed from his youth to occupy himself with the Book of Revelation. In 1798 he made
acquaintance with the interpretation of it by Bengel,
the theologian of Würtemberg, and finding that
some of his explanations were confirmed by the
events of the French Revolution, Stilling adopted
his system, and formed a sudden resolution to make
a new translation of the Revelation from the Greek,
with an exposition upon Bengel's plan. Whilst he
deprecated a hasty application of particular symbols
to passing events, he was firmly of the opinion that
the great conflict was near at hand. According to
his view, the first angel with the everlasting gospel
in the fourteenth chapter is Luther; the second,
Jacob Böhme; the third, Francke. But in the supplement he gives it as his opinion, that Bengel was
the second, who was called to proclaim the fall of
Babylon, and that the third had not yet appeared.
Possibly, in the depths of his soul, he thought that
he was himself the third, for he was convinced that
he had a great and special vocation in the kingdom
of God, and the great acceptance which his writings
found among the " Quiet in the Land," and among
the scattered few who honoured the name of Christ,
could but strengthen his conviction. The key-note
of his prophetic theology was the approach of judgment; and he adopted Bengel's reckoning, according
to which the most distant period at which Christ

should have vanquished his foes was the year 1836. Afterwards, under the excitement of passing events, he thought it was still nearer. If it be asked, what place he assigned to the Emperor Napoleon in his apocalyptic system, he did not consider him to be Antichrist, nor does he speak against him with the indignation that might have been expected from a devout German. Perhaps this is partly explained by his residence in Baden, one of the States of the Confederation of the Rhine. In Würtemberg, where the people were rather inclined to religious speculation, their desire to form a precise estimate of the mission of the French despot, combined with their admiration of some improvements introduced by his government, had led to the delusion that "Napoleon was Jesus Christ, the Son of God, come down to earth the second time to establish His kingdom." Those who fell into this error formed a sect, "who therefore despised all authority, insulted and refused obedience to their rulers, gave out that all preachers, even the most devout, were deceivers and priests of Baal, withdrew from the church and sacraments, wore the white hat and cockade, and adopted all sorts of peculiarities."

Stilling was accused by some journalists in 1807 of being the founder of this sect; this he indignantly repelled, and took the opportunity of explaining his views about Napoleon:—"I consider the Emperor Napoleon to be a great instrument in the hands of Providence, whereby it is God's will to carry out great and important ends, tending to the salvation of the whole world. His history and that of our time renders this so clear that no reasonable man can possibly doubt it. But that he is the Son of God, Jesus Christ, he would himself declare, if he heard it, to be nonsense and blasphemy. None can hold such an opinion but fanatical fools." Stilling could not agree with those who held that Napoleon was Antichrist after his first fall in 1814. Notwithstanding the Peace of Paris, he did not think the tranquillity would be permanent. He thought it possible that the final struggle might yet be near at hand. But, in this case, he held that the man of sin must certainly appear ; and the question therefore arose whether he had not already appeared in the person of Napoleon, but he did not answer it in the affirmative. He said, " The man of sin, or the beast out of the abyss, will reign until the coming of the Lord, when the Lord will slay him with the sword of his mouth, and cast him and the false prophet and all his angels into the lake of fire and brimstone.

" Certainly, Napoleon has been beaten, and that the Lord has done it there can be no doubt ; but we know nothing yet of a false prophet distinguishing himself as such, and the island of St. Helena is not a lake of fire and brimstone."

We have already given our own opinion on the sin of Napoleon, and, while we agree with Stilling that he was not *the* Antichrist, we hold that he was an Antichrist, and that, from a German point of view, Stilling's judgment on him was far too lenient. Long before the alliances of 1812, there were indications in Stilling's writings which prepared the way for the announcement of the Emperor Alexander as the elect of God for the restoration of His kingdom.

In endeavouring to understand the popular reli-

gious movements of that day, we must not overlook
the singular attraction to the East which was felt by
many minds. Because the aspect of the Western
world was dark,—because the ever-increasing unbelief, the resistance unto blood to the powers ordained of God, and all the horrors of revolution,
had come to Germany from the West,—pious people
began to turn their eyes longingly to the East.
There was in Stilling's writings a mysterious pre-
sentiment of this tendency. As early as 1793 he
had foreshadowed an idea that, in His own good
time, God would raise up some great man, who was
destined to lead his people into a place of refuge,
into a land of peace, a Solyma, just as Moses led the
people out of Egppt, and Zerubbabel out of Babylon. He warned people against a carnal millena-
rianism, and premature interpretations; still he
went on prophesying and calling attention to Asiatic
Russia. He looked upon the Moravians as a type
of the church of God, as a beginning of the gather-
ing together of His people; and there was a little
community of them at Astrachan and Sarepta. Stilling thought to himself that God might easily put
it into the heart of the Emperor Alexander to allot
a territory in Astrachan or Georgia where the people
of God, scattered abroad or exiled on religious or
political grounds, might congregate and abide in
safety till the storms were overpast. He wrote,
" All those who honour the Lord from among all
parties, and from every place, would naturally be
attracted to them; and by degrees, or in one great
company, they would all journey to this Solyma or
land of peace, under a prince or leader who would
rule this congregation of the Lord according to their

own laws and the essential principles of the kingdom of God, and thus prepare the way for the establishment of the glorious kingdom."

What at first might have been a half-poetical fancy was afterwards taken for prophecy; at any rate, some of the people were not gifted to distinguish between the poetic form and the prophetic meaning, but endeavoured to put into present practice the foreshadowing of a possible future.

The faithful in South Germany longed for their place of refuge, and began to journey thither. In 1803 George Rapp, of Iplingen, emigrated to America with a large number of his followers. A little later, Mary Gottlieb Kummer, with whom we shall meet again in the life of Mme. de Krüdener, had induced twenty-one persons, with blue ribbons and pilgrims' staves, to set out for the promised land; and now, in 1809, a new movement began, for the Pietists and Millenarians of Würtemberg had taken offence at the introduction of a new hymn-book and liturgy.

A flight from approaching destruction was determined upon, and in 1810 an emigration was begun to Bessarabia, Odessa, and Kaross.

In 1816 and 1817, after Alexander had revealed himself as the coming hero from the East, and had promised protection to the wanderers, 7000 souls took boat to go down the Danube. With a loss of 3000 persons, they arrived in Georgia in 1818. They founded churches, but their emigration proved to be rather a severance from the nursing mother church than a refuge from destruction. The churches fell into confusion, and the remnants of them were succoured by the Basle Missionary Society.

It can scarcely be said that Stilling favoured these undertakings. There was in his character a singular mixture of visionary enthusiasm and common sense. Under the influence of the former he regarded his sanguine expectations as if they were real, and produced the impression upon others that he did so regard them. But no sooner had his poetical prophetic visions escaped him, no sooner had they produced an effect on simple souls, than his common sense induced him to grasp the reins, and to say that he had been misunderstood; that at least the time was not yet come; that the Lord's commands must not be anticipated, etc. In 1805 he wrote :—"Now I earnestly pray you not to seek this place of refuge until the Lord points it out, and not to move until you can stay no longer." And in 1806, just before the great emigration, he gave forth this warning :—"This going to Russia is premature. The true followers of the Lord should remain quietly at their posts, even if the man of sin is revealed and reigns supreme. It is only when they have nobly stood the trial that they are worthy to be received into the place of safety, that they may be protected from the Almighty's vials of wrath, which are designed only for the Antichristian rabble; for the flight of the woman clothed with the sun into the wilderness, does not take place until she has borne the pangs of labour, and brought forth a man child. Not till then is she delivered from her enemy."

It may be imagined with what interest Alexander, the Emperor of the East, was regarded when the course of events suddenly brought him into prominence as the hero called of God to conquer Napoleon. We shall see what great hopes Stilling placed upon him, and what a large place he occupied in the prophecies of Mme. de Krüdener.

Our readers will be glad to get out of this apocalyptic atmosphere into the domain of history. During its stormy course Stilling endeavoured to admonish the people, and to awaken in them a Christian spirit. In the periodical called the 'Grey-headed Man' we have a record of what he had to say from year to year to a large circle of readers.

As to Napoleon, Stilling shared the opinion of some others, especially of Arndt and Rückert, that he perished through hardness of heart, for he was not humbled by the most severe chastisement; was never satisfied with the most advantageous proposals; but scornfully made demands with which it was impossible to comply. Stilling wrote: "This judgment of hardening the heart explains what is meant in the Bible when it says that 'the Lord hardened Pharaoh's heart, so that he would not let Israel go.' The Lord hath also hardened Napoleon's heart, so that he would not accept peace. If he had done so, in a few years he would have regained his power, and then he would have revenged himself terribly on Germany. And who knows what Providence may yet spare him for if he lives?" Stilling had long before predicted divine judgments on the north of Germany, on account of the frivolous spirit that he had observed there, and now he rejoiced that they had produced so good an effect, and fostered a religious spirit in high and low: "It is not the teachers of religion who have effected this," he wrote, "but the acts of the Lord have spoken with a voice of thunder, and the people have hearkened, and heard it. If this text were

now expounded from every pulpit, how many souls
would be won! But it is but rarely done. Some
day severe judgment will be passed on these faithless hirelings.''

In Stilling's writings on passing events we do not
trace the patriotic glow which is so evident in
those of Arndt, Fichte, Schleiermacher, and Schenkendorf. He estimated nations solely by their relation to Christianity, and this sometimes led him
into injustice towards his country. He passed the
most favourable judgments on those parts of the
country where there were the greatest numbers of
the " Quiet in the Land." But around these spots
of light he beheld a great expanse of darkness ;
and, of course, after mixing for seventy-five years
in every grade of society, he was pretty well acquainted with the sins of his countrymen, and he
was not the man to throw over them the mantle of
patriotism. But in other lands, which he had never
visited, he was acquainted only with the Christian
element, for which he wâs always on the look-out,
and the prevailing sins were not so patent to him.
Thus he praises England in most glowing terms, in
consequence of the religious awakening which had
taken place there, and her great zeal for missions
and the circulation of the Bible; but the dark shadows of English life were unknown to him.

He could not deny the ignorance, superstition,
and torpor that prevailed in Russia, but he had
great hopes for the Greek Church, on account of
" its profound reverence for Jesus Christ, and its
just conception of His sublime person."

Several things contributed to inspire him with
special sympathy for religious people in Russia. In

the year 1815 he could relate that he had held important conversations with the Emperor Alexander, and said that the Emperor was firmly resolved to live and die a true Christian, and he accepted the support he gave to the Bible Society as a proof of it. Of the Empress, whom he called the most gracious lady in the world, he reported that she loved religion, and that her ladies of honour, with whom he had had much intercourse, were the most sincere, penitent, and exemplary Christians." In fact, he had seen the Emperor and his court under the most favourable aspect. It was in the beginning of the year 1814, on Alexander's first journey to Paris, that he was often asked by his mother-in-law, the Margravine of Baden, if he would not give an audience to the "privy councillor Jung." The Emperor, however, did not feel any special attraction to the "privy councillor Jung," but at length an idea suddenly flashed upon him, and he asked, "Does not Stilling live here?" And when informed that he was Jung, he said, "I have a great deal to say to him, but I must wait till I come back."

Accordingly, after the Emperor's return from Paris and London, Stilling was summoned to Bruchsal. He greeted the Emperor as the deliverer of Germany, which honour he declined, with the remark:—"The good that has been done came from God, and all the errors belong to us."

Stilling asked for a private interview, as he had important things to say to the Emperor concerning the kingdom of God. An appointment was made for the following day, and Stilling prepared himself for it by prayer. The Emperor received him as an old friend, seated himself close to him as he was rather deaf, and took both his hands in his.

Stilling informed him that the peace would not last long, that the divine judgments would continue to be poured out, until every one was awakened who was capable of being so. He concurred with the Emperor's remark, that great multitudes had already been awakened, but maintained that the mass of the people had only become worse. The Emperor told him of the Bible, Tract, and Missionary Societies with which he had recently become acquainted in England, and promised to do all in his power to advance true and practical religion in his own country. After a humble acknowledgment of his own shortcomings, he asked Stilling what he held to be the real, practical, and essential duties of a Christian. Stilling answered :—" The essential duties of a Christian consist in three things : firstly, in the entire surrender of his own will; secondly, in constant contemplation, and in dwelling in the presence of the Lord ; thirdly, in continual inward prayer." With glistening eyes, the Emperor pressed Stilling's hand, and said, " That is also my firm conviction." To the Emperor's question to which of the Christian Creeds Stilling gave the preference, he answered that the Lord had His people amongst them all, and would not give a decided opinion. He spoke highly of the Moravians on the Emperor's expressing a favourable opinion of them, but without assigning to them the highest place among the visible communities of Christendom. When Stilling congratulated the Emperor on having such pious people about his court, and told him that he had made a compact with Roxandra von Sturza to remain true to the Lord to all eternity, the Emperor rose up, once more pressed his hand,

and said, "Well, we two will also make an agreement to be faithful unto death."

The Emperor afterwards showed himself very friendly to Stilling, lightened the burden of old age by giving him considerable presents, and took one of his sons into the Russian service. Stilling also maintained his intimacy with the Russian court. Amongst the 'Letters from Experienced Christians,' which were published after his death, there were some in French, which appear to have been written by Roxandra von Sturza during the Congress of Vienna. From St. Petersburg, in 1816, the same hand informed Stilling, then near his departure, that "Our Emperor continues to walk in the ways of the Lord. He lives a retired and very exemplary life, and bears with great patience the thorns with which his crown is set. I trust that God will bless him, and enlighten his path, which is beset with more difficulties than you can imagine."

It may be supposed that Stilling, who had been devoted for years to seeking out true Christians in many lands, and to exhorting people to a religious life, took no great pleasure in the hyper-patriotism which prevailed in Germany after the wars of independence, as the natural consequence of the previous cosmopolitanism.

In the last number of the 'Grey-headed Man,' in which, in 1816, he took leave of the "Stilling congregation," he seeks to bring down this Germanizing tendency to a Christian standard. "There is a great deal said now about the regeneration and renovation of the German character. It is said, 'Thank God, we are Germans once more,' etc. But is this true? Have we a just idea of what the German character is? It consists in firm fidelity to God and man, in being that which we seem, and in an insatiable thirst for all kinds of knowledge." He says that this thirst for knowledge will be likely to lead into the dangerous paths of religious doubt, unless the Germans keep close to their Saviour with unswerving fidelity, and this fidelity he finds by no means universal.

Once more he calls to mind how the Lord annihilated Napoleon's army, and continues :—" The thought flashed through the mind of every man, even if not a profound thinker, ' This is a divine intervention.' The Russian crossed himself, put his mouth in the dust and exclaimed, ' Jesus Christ has done this !' A small but most noble portion of the Germans agreed with him. A much larger number said, ' This is a dispensation of Providence ;' a third part said, ' This is a decree from heaven ;' and the fourth, and unfortunately by far the larger part, either thought nothing at all about it, or said, ' The scale of fortune has turned at last on the right side.' Why cannot the Germans exclaim with the Russians, ' Jesus Christ has done this, He has risen up, He has come forth and shown to all the world that He who is truth will keep His word.' He Himself said, ' All power is given unto me in heaven and in earth ;' and St. Paul says, ' He must reign till He hath put all things under His feet.' To ascribe this obviously divine intervention to God or Providence, does not prove a man to be a Christian ; every deist, Turk, or Jew may say that; the true believer will say, ' The Lord Jesus Christ has done it.' "

It was objected to him that the term Lord, by which Jesus Christ was understood, was often thoughtlessly used as a shibboleth by the "awakened." To which Stilling answered, "The Christian should only reverently use the name Lord Jesus Christ when it is necessary to make the distinction between the Father and the Son; but in the case in question it should always be used, especially in the present day, when men have fallen away from Christ, and are attempting to despoil Him of His honours. All the divine government, both in the Church and in the State, is in the hands of our Lord, and it ought to be openly acknowledged on this occasion."

Accustomed as Stilling was to dwell on the Apocalypse, he drew a very definite line between those who were for and against the Saviour; but those were no less justified in their opinion who held that that the acknowledgment of the living God, which at this time became so much more general, was the first step towards the acknowledgment of His Son. Stilling always thought that the great conflict was near at hand, and he naturally supposed that all who did not take a decided stand on the side of Christ would be condemned as His opponents. We now know that the great judgment did not take place; that the course of events was to be still further developed; and that many who then spoke only of God, but who acquired a profound conviction of His overruling presence in the history of nations and men, afterwards turned in repentance and love to Christ.

Stilling's life may well incite us to praise God, who enabled a sinful man to be so useful to his brethren. It is true that traces of human frailty are often to be observed in this instrument of grace, and we sometimes remark with surprise that his duty and inclination, his outward and inward callings, were at variance. But this feeling vanishes when we consider his career of usefulness as a whole.

Without ever making his skill a means of gain, he restored the sight of large numbers by operating upon them for cataract. When the number amounted to 2000 he left off keeping account of them. And to how many was he the restorer of their spiritual eyesight !

His correspondence was entirely devoted to gaining souls for the kingdom and confirming their faith ; he was never weary of sending forth his messengers of peace, although postage often cost him upwards of a thousand florins a year.* By means of his writings he preserved the scattered few who were believers in Christ in unity of spirit.

Many of his doctrines, hopes, and predictions were without any Scriptural foundation, but on the main point he always stood firm.

His childhood had been passed in the midst of a patriarchal life ; and, in his old age, children, grandchildren, and friends assembled around him as the patriarch, and honoured him as their father.

From the year 1806, in accordance with the wish of Charles Frederic, Duke of Baden, who wished to have him near him, and who hoped to employ him for the benefit of humanity, he lived at Carlsruhe ; he had a room in the palace, sat at the Grand Duke's table, and spent most of his time in his company. The Grand Duke preceded his spiritual adviser into eternity.

* About £83.

Stilling had suffered severely for some time from cramp in the stomach and pleurisy, and entered on the year 1817 in much weakness. His illness was developed into water on the chest. He lived for twelve days after giving his wife his parting blessing, continually occupied with the thought of death and of Him who is the victor of death.

His second daughter begged that when in heaven he and her mother would pray for her. The wife then living was not her mother. "Yes," he said; "we must first see what is the custom in the other world, and then we will pray for you." Passion Week had begun. One day, on waking up, he said, "I feel an unspeakable peace in my soul, which my physical misery makes it difficult for you to understand." Soon afterwards, he began to pray for his children and children's children, that God would preserve them as branches in the vine by faith in His Son, so that after the lapse of ages he might find them all united. Then, feeling that his end was drawing near, he earnestly desired to receive the Supper of the Lord with his family; but it was four o'clock in the morning, and there was no pastor of the Reformed Church within reach. After conferring with his eldest son, Stilling decided to take the holy office upon himself.

He asked his family to kneel down, uncovered his head, folded his hands, and, in the power of the Spirit and of faith, he offered a prayer nearly in the following words :—" Thou who didst shed thy blood for us upon the cross, and overcamest death and hell, and forgavest thine enemies, thou divine Mediator, forgive us now if, in our weakness, we are presuming to do that which we ought not to do."

He then distributed the bread and wine, and as he partook last himself of the consecrated cup, he spread out his hands in the attitude of blessing, and said, "The Lord be with you."

The last hour was passed in great anguish from suffocation, but he was continually in prayer, and asking those around him to pray for him. When the sun beamed forth brightly at midday, he drew his last breath, and the aspect of the earthly tenement was dignified and peaceful after the parting spirit had winged its flight. He who had so often experienced a heavenly home-sickness was now blessed for evermore, for he had reached his heavenly home.*

* 'Stilling's Lebensgeschichte und seine sämmtliche Werke.'

CHAPTER III.

BARBARA JULIE DE KRÜDENER.

IT may fairly be questioned what right the portrait of Mme. de Krüdener has to a place among those of the devoted German men and women of the time of the Wars of Independence.

Descended from an ancient German family, she first saw the light in one of the Russian provinces on the Baltic, but her education was neither German nor Russian, but of that European stamp, assuming a French garb, adopted by many of the nobility of the East, who seek to make up for the want of civilization at home by travels in the West, and no longer clinging to their native land, or retaining any of its national customs, they succumb to the charms of a brilliant, seductive, and superficial French life. This is of itself sufficient to prejudice many minds, and it is in truth not easy to turn from the important national events which we have hitherto been describing, to the frivolous life of *salons*, to exchange the smell of the smoke of the battlefield, where men were fighting for freedom, for the delicate perfumes of luxurious entertainments,—to turn away from events

which form part of the world's history, to enter upon
a life where a new romance is an all important topic,
in which there is no more difficult problem to solve
than how to invent new amusements to dispel the
ennui occasioned by their constant succession ; in
which actors, singers, and dancers are the heroes of
the day, and in which the sufferings of humanity are
of no account.

But the life of Mme. de Krüdener, though it gives
us a glimpse of such frivolities, does not always de-
tain us amidst them.

Driven by urgent need, we see her at length at
the feet of the Crucified One, and in conversation
with a poor Moravian artisan. We see how, in communion with simple Christians, she learns to appear
in the character of a prophetess before the great
ones of the earth, in all the simplicity of the Gospel.
We rejoice to see, that grace, whic his no respecter
of persons, has compassion on the distress of a distinguished woman of the world. The conversion of
this lady, which happened during the time of the
French dominion, attracts us to observe her life more
closely from our own point of view, and its importance
is still more evident, when we find that she led thousands of the weary and heavy laden to Christ during
the times of misfortune, and that she obtained great
influence over the Emperor Alexander. The Grand
Duke of Mecklenburg-Strelitz, although from ignorance of the facts he denied that she had any influence upon his sister, Queen Louisa, said of her,
" As for the Emperor Alexander, she had attained
such power over him that the Holy Alliance, which
he projected and carried out, must be regarded as
the work of this woman."   And E. M. Arndt, when

eighty years of age, complained of her power, which, opposed to the more vigorous influence of Stein, appeared to him to be prejudicial to Germany, and only of advantage to France. He wrote, " I went for a few weeks to my friend Schenkendorf, who was living at Carlsruhe and Baden, as a sort of retainer of Stein's. I saw at Carlsruhe, but chiefly at Baden and Heidelberg, the Fieldmarshaless of the Alexandrian ladies. Who was this Fieldmarshaless, who gave the word of command to all the rest ? She was formerly the most beautiful and celebrated nightingale of the diplomatic *salons*, Mme. de Krüdener, who in her youth passed through all the sweets and dangers of *salon* life, and now as a penitent, as which she proclaims herself to everybody, she considers herself called upon to convert herself and all the world. Although her beauty was on the wane, her eye was still powerful, and she has the fine, elegant, and graceful figure of the women of Poland and Curland."

To this woman, and to Jung Stilling, and to the prophecies with which they appeared before Alexander, Arndt ascribes his forbearance towards the French, and injustice to the Germans. At the time when she began to play her part in the world's history, and especially in that of Germany, she was fifty years of age. We must not, however, ignore the history of her previous life, nor how she came to adopt it as her vocation, to endeavour to convert people of all ranks, from the highest to the lowest.

Barbara Julie von Wiekinghoff was born in November, 1764, at Riga, in Curland. Her father, who belonged to an ancient family, had revived the sinking fortunes of his house by the riches acquired in industrial pursuits, and was Russian privy councillor and senator. Her mother, the daughter of Marshal Munich, united to the industry of a housewife the tastes of a woman of the world. Barbara Julie was the second daughter; the eldest was deaf and dumb, and they had three brothers, one of whom died early. She grew up amidst the abundance of her father's house, without any special care being bestowed on her education. Perhaps the best influences of her childhood were derived from those impressions of nature which she received from living in the country, and near the sea. At the age of thirteen, that wandering life began for her which is so critical in its influence upon character. In the summer of 1777 she visited Spa, then the rendezvous of European aristocracy, with her parents. There the chief interest she excited was as an heiress. A residence in Paris during the following winter afforded her all the charms of social life, in which vice concealed itself under attractive disguises, but the only instruction she received was in dancing. In 1778 the family went to England to pay visits at the country seats of their acquaintances. The French governess spoke her language well, had good manners, and was expert in various useless feminine accomplishments, but could confer no greater benefits upon her pupil. But this did not prevent her from exciting universal admiration when she returned to Riga. At sixteen her parents betrothed her to a man whom she did not like. In the anguish of her heart, for the first time she prayed to God. She fell ill, but her recovery was hastened by the news that the gentleman had renounced the engagement. At eighteen she became the bride of Baron Burchard

Alexis Constantine von Krüdener. He was twenty years older than the bride. He had had the good fortune, among other studies at Leipsic, to hear Gellert's lectures on morality. Gellert interested himself in him, and he was so industrious that among his fellow students he obtained the nickname of the " scholar." After leaving the university, he was *attaché* to the Russian embassy at Madrid; at Paris he made the acquaintance of J. J. Rousseau; and after a few months' residence at Warsaw, he was intrusted by the Empress Catherine II. with the office of minister of Curland, which was an important one, as she was endeavouring to incorporate this duchy with Russia. Krüdener had already been twice married and twice divorced. He had a son of nine years of age, who stood in need of a mother, but the girl of eighteen, whom he now married, was not disposed for anything but worldly amusements. She expected from her husband, as she herself expressed it, all that could entertain her mind and gratify her vanity, even if he could not satisfy her heart. He seriously thought of trying to supply the deficiencies of her education, but it gratified her vanity more to dance, and to be seen at the theatre and in society. In 1784 the young wife bore a son, to whom the Grand Duke Paul, afterwards Emperor, stood godfather. In the following year, Krüdener was appointed ambassador at Venice. His wife delighted in the luxurious, idle life in the wonderful city of the sea. One great occupation was furnished by the theatre which the ambassador established in his own house, and in which other distinguished persons took part. Mme. de Krüdener received many attentions, but at first she did not heed them. She was truly attached to her husband, showed him all manner of little attentions, and when he read to her in the evenings, she forgot the book in the reader.

In the spring they went to a charming estate in the country. One sultry day the baron was out, and the lady was impatient of her solitude. A violent thunder-storm came on, and she became intensely anxious about her husband. Night came on, and, as he did not return, she could not rest. At midnight she sent her attendants to bed, became more and more alarmed, fancied she heard cries for help, and rushed out into the darkness to seek her husband. He soon arrived and endeavoured to calm her, but reproached her with her terror, saying, " You should have gone to bed; you will kill yourself with this excitability." The words were kindly meant, but they sent a dagger into her heart. " Ah !" she thought, " in my place he would have gone to bed and to sleep." To so weak and perverse a thing as the natural human heart, untouched by grace, the idea of "not being understood" was an excuse for future unfaithfulness. A young man attached to the embassy, Alexander von Stakieff, conceived a passion for her, but this did not prove a snare to her, for he voluntarily banished himself from her presence. After a residence of a year and a half at Venice, Krüdener was appointed ambassador at Copenhagen, where, after a tour in Italy, he arrived in 1786. In the north as well as in the south the theatre was the favourite diversion at the embassy. Von Stakieff again met with Mme. de Krüdener here, and fled from her again, as he felt that his old passion for her revived with fresh force. He wrote to Krüde-

ner : " I honour her for her affection for you ; from
the moment that you became less dear to her, she
would be only an ordinary woman to me, and I
should love her no more." Krüdener handed the
letter to his wife, who was before in total ignorance
of the attachment of the fugitive, and her unconscious success induced her to enter upon the slip-
pery paths of endeavouring to please. Then she was
" not understood."

Mental agitation occasioned an illness, and, a
confinement occurring soon after, she nearly lost
her life. She was ordered to the south of France,
and left Copenhagen in May 1789, and went first
to Paris. Here she found the need of more
mental culture ; she read the best works that
French literature afforded, and sought the society of
men of taste and science. She lived in the same
house with Bernardin de St. Pierre, the author of
' Paul and Virginia,' and enjoyed the charms of
nature in his company ; and, while she boasted of
her taste for simple pleasures, she contracted a debt
to a celebrated *modiste* of 20,000 francs. In December she left Paris with her children, a governess, and an old professor of medicine, and, after
visiting Avignon, they settled down at Montpellier.
She next became the leader of fashion at Baréges.
She sometimes sat at the gaming-table, and once
electrified the guests by her reading of ' Paul and
Virginia ' in the open air. On returning home they
expressed regret at being no longer able to enjoy
the summer night, and she planned a night excursion, which reminds one of the exuberant spirits of
a party of students. On returning to Montpellier
she formed a fatal acquaintance with the Count de

Frégeville, a young, handsome, and fascinating officer. Arrangements had been made for returning
to Copenhagen, but a thousand hindrances occurred,
and she remained the winter. The count declared
his love; she showed him the door; he threatened
to kill himself, and, just as in a bad French novel, a
sinful relation ensued. And when the governess,
Mdlle. Piozet, who had kept Mme. Krüdener within
bounds, was married to a M. Armand, she was entirely without protection. She resolved to go home,
but informed the count of her intention, and he
persuaded her that she could not travel without an
escort. She had not the will to resist, and he accompanied her on the journey. She had given a
false representation of the relation between them to
her husband, but the nearer she got to him the
more loudly conscience began to accuse her. At
length they met, and the wife confessed that the
sanctity of the marriage tie had been violated. The
husband received the announcement with dignified
grief. Mme. de Krüdener prayed for a separation,
but her husband would not agree to it, and allowed
her to go to Riga to her mother. The count accompanied her to Berlin, and then rushed into the tumult
of war. The sin had made three mortals miserable,
and brought about nothing but separation.

With her mother the daughter found as much
peace as can be found by a soul not yet sensible of
its guilt. She nursed her father on his deathbed,
and wrote frequently to Mme. Armand, and a desire for the peace of God may plainly be traced in
her letters. She wrote: "God has supported me;
religion has tempered my bitter grief; and I am more
disposed for solitude and seclusion from the world."

At Riga she saw Alexander von Stakieff again. He learnt what had occurred, and, as he had before said, all his interest in her vanished. On perceiving this she began to feel the pangs of remorse. But more than ten years went by before she came as a poor sinner to the feet of the Saviour.

We will not enter into many details of this painful time. She met her husband at St. Petersburg. He received her with forgiving kindness, and she was not wanting in humility. At Berlin, whither she had gone on account of her health in 1792, she met Mme. Armand, her best friend, but, not being able to withstand being drawn into society, she retired to Leipsic. In 1794 we find her again at Riga, and in 1796 travelling in Germany and Switzerland. At Lausanne she shone in the society of the French emigrants. The following is a description given of her at this period :—" A charming face, a bright and fascinating mind, her expression varying with the inner thoughts and feelings; of middle height and perfect form; lively blue eyes, which seem to try to look into the past and future; light hair, falling in curls over her shoulders; something quite novel and out of the common in her gestures and movements." Mme. de Staël thus describes a dance with which she often charmed the company :—" Never did grace and beauty produce so great an effect upon a numerous circle. This singular dance has a charm of which nothing that we have seen before can give any idea. It is an Asiatic combination of languor and spirit, of melancholy and vivacity. Often when the music was played more softly Delphine would take a few steps with drooping head and folded arms, as if sad me-

mories or repentance had suddenly intruded themselves into a brilliant feast, but soon returning to
light and lively movements, she would envelope
herself in an Indian shawl, which showed off her
figure to advantage, and, as it drooped from her
shoulders with her long hair, the effect was that of
an enchanting picture." This coquetry went on
till some one else learnt the art, when it lost all its
charms for Mme. de Krüdener. We pass rapidly
over the next few years passed in Switzerland and
Germany, until, in 1800, we find her with her husband at Berlin, where he was ambassador, with the
best intentions of living quietly, but again drawn
into the vortex of society, and striving to outshine
others. But her want of peace within indicated by
such sayings as this :—

" People who would be inconsolable if they had
brought any real misfortune upon us, think it allow-
able to inflict all sorts of little annoyances, which at
last make a mountain more difficult to climb than
any real sorrow."

Vanity, under a garb of religion, is plainly shown
by her ascribing all the honours which are accorded
to her husband to her return to him, and she considered herself his guardian angel. She says, " I
think that God has blessed my husband on account
of our reunion. There is no favour or success which
has not been granted him. Why should I not believe that such favour is accorded to a pious heart
which prays Heaven in simplicity and confidence to
assist him in striving to attain to a higher happiness?"
It would have been very different if this had been
the result of sincere Christian zeal, but very much
was wanting to make it so. In the summer of 1801

Mme. de Krüdener went to Töplitz. Her stay there did her so much good, mentally and physically, that she thought with terror of returning to Berlin, and informed her husband that she wished to travel in Switzerland, but set off without waiting for his answer. At Geneva she received his letter, and found that he highly disapproved of the journey. "I confess," he wrote, "that I had not feared another separation. You cannot conceal from yourself how prejudicial it is to the happiness and interests of our children, and I tell you with the plainness that our friendship demands, that duty has assigned you a place in the bosom of your family. You appear to think your absence a source of economy, as if keeping up two establishments instead of one, could possibly be economical."

At Coppet she met with Mme. de Staël, and at Paris formed an intimate acquaintance with Chateaubriand, who sent her a copy of his ' Génie du Christianisme' two days before it was published, an honour of which she was in the highest degree sensible. These literary acquaintainces stimulated her to carry out some literary projects she had herself formed. But in the midst of these occupations she received the news of the sudden death of her husband, of apoplexy, in June 1802. Here was a fearful chastisement for her neglect of her duties, in order that she might roam about the world at her pleasure. She had been touched by his wishing for her presence, she had wished to return to him, and make his life as happy as she could, but she had postponed the duty so long that death relieved her from it.

She bitterly reproached herself, but was soon again engrossed in frivolity.

The more loudly God called to her, the more entirely she appeared to close her ears, until at length mercy took her by storm. After a two months' mourning, she went to Geneva, and thence to Lyons, where she was delighted with the attentions she received. Her life at this period is mirrored in her correspondence with **Dr. Gay**, her Parisian physician. There were no bounds to the praises she bestowed on this man, but then she hoped for a return. Although luxuriating in vain delights at Lyons, she longed to be at Paris. She wished to give the last touches to her romance ' Valérie,' that it might be published there; but she wished to be summoned, expected, and longed for, and set to work to bring it about. The heroine of a novel she had written, ' La Cabane des Lataniers,' was called Sidonie, under which name she described herself. Dr. Gay was to write an ode to Sidonie, in which he was to say, " Why dwellest thou in the provinces, why does thy seclusion deprive us of thy graces and thy mind? Do not thy conquests summon thee to Paris? There alone art thou admired as thou deservest ?"

This was to appear in the Parisian papers. The complacent doctor fulfilled the task to Mme. de Krüdener's entire satisfaction, and she complied with her own invitation without delay. Her novel appeared in December, 1803. She had taken every possible means to attract attention to it. Devoted friends, journalists, authors, adverse critics, all occupied themselves with it, and still more with the authoress. She drove from *modiste* to *modiste*, asking for bonnets, feathers, scarfs, ribbons, and wreaths *à la Valérie*, and when the serving maidens declared themselves ignorant of the new fashion, she

asked if they had not heard of the novel 'Valérie.'
She had the satisfaction for a short time of being
the talk of the day, and could repose on her laurels,
while she excused her conduct by saying, "Nothing
can be done at Paris without charlatanism." At
length she became weary of this folly, and in the
spring of 1804 she returned to her mother at Riga.
It must be confessed that vanity and self-seeking
could scarcely be carried further, and we fully agree
with her biographer in the following remarks: "We
have hitherto seen Mme. de Krüdener entirely engrossed with self-love and the cultivation of her
charms, seeking nothing but herself, and therefore
ever widening her distance from God. If she turns
to Him for a moment, it it only from weariness and
disgust, not from love to Him or repentance. She
has no idea of self-denial, of bearing her cross, of
following Jesus. Instead of denying herself, she
made self her only object; and instead of bearing
the cross, she wished to be rid of every burden. She
sometimes tries to raise her thoughts to God, but
rather from pride than humility. If she makes the
experiment of exchanging frivolous amusements for
spiritual joys, it is only because, degraded in her
own eyes, she thinks by this course to attain to a
higher happiness and dignity. In a word, literary
success, the tumult of passion, her religious flights
were nothing but varying forms of the same worship
to which she devoted all her powers, and in which
she herself was temple, worshipper, and idol."

"If sin abounded, grace did much more abound."
This was to be the experience of Mme. de Krüdener.
One day she arose as usual weary and melancholy,
and filled with indolent repentance for the past. As

she was watching from her window the autumn
clouds floating slowly over the plain, a nobleman
passed by, one who among the crowds of her admirers had been a special object of her coquetry.
He greeted her, then tottered and fell down in a fit
of apoplexy before her eyes, and was taken up dead.
It was a terrible shock to her. Her thirst for adulation appeared to her as the greatest folly, as the
greatest provocation to God to whom alone worship
belongs. She was seized with such a terror of death
that in the morning she said would God it were
evening, and in the evening would God it were
morning, and she dared not cross the threshold of
the house. To this state succeeded a death-like
apathy. About this time a shoemaker waited upon
her in compliance with her orders. She allowed
him to take the measure without looking at him, but
on his asking some question she took her hand from
before her eyes. His cheerful countenance seemed
like a reproach to her depression; she answered him
shortly, and relapsed into melancholy, but before
long she said to him, 'My friend, are you happy?'
—'I am the happiest of men,' was the answer.
She said nothing, but the tone of his voice and his
beaming look haunted her so that she could not sleep.

"She said to herself, 'He is the happiest of men,
and I am the most miserable of mortals.' She
could not rest till she had sought him out. He was
a Moravian, and with the simplicity which is characteristic of the sect, he preached Christ to her, the
Crucified and Risen one, not in the words that man's
wisdom teacheth, but with the demonstration of the
spirit and of power. She felt that she was loved,
and in place of the avenging God before whom she

trembled, she saw Him who died for sinners. With all the fervour of a forgiven sinner, she loved Him who first loved her. After first tasting of the peace of God among the Moravians, she constantly associated with these simple Christians, and found amongst them what she could not find amidst the most brilliant circles of the world. She wrote to her friend : ' Oh, my dear Armand, pray, pray like a child if you are not yet in this blessed state, pray and entreat for this mercy, which God grants us for the sake of His dear Son's love. It will sustain you and make you feel that man can be happy neither in this world nor in the next without the faith that salvation is only to be had through Him. Religious truth is most simple and sublime, but human pride prefers to rely upon its own pride to humbling itself, and how can man comprehend everything ? ' Ask and it shall be given you,' says the Saviour, ' Seek and ye shall find.' Pray with an honest heart, and everything will become clear to you. Penetrated with these great truths, my heart has gone out towards you, and I have asked that this peace of the soul, this glorious heritage may be yours. My dear Armand, you have not sinned as I have. I have suffered shipwreck on a thousand shoals, but we all have need of the mercy of God."

"En peu d'heures Dieu labeure," is a French proverb. Mme. de Krüdener had experienced a great change, all her powers had received a fresh stimulus. All the warmth and ardour of her nature, for a time extinguished by melancholy, returned to her, sanctified by religion. In her mother's *salons*, instead of seeking to gratify her own vanity, she acknowledged her Lord, avoided worldly society,

and often visited the Moravians. A great part of
her time was devoted to reading the Bible, and
much of the rest to correspondence, in which she
proclaimed her Saviour with the praise and gratitude of a pardoned sinner. And this peace in her
soul was accompanied by Christian conduct. She
introduced method into the arrangement of her
time, her money, and her estate. As her health was
not good, in the summer of 1806 she was ordered to
Wiesbaden. On her return she met Queen Louisa
at Königsberg. Both had been led to the Saviour,
but by very different paths. The Queen, who had
been brought to a sense of a sinful nature without
having fallen into any special sins, and Mme. de
Krüdener, who had gone through so much sad experience of sin, now found each other acknowledging
the same blessed name, and practising the same
charity at the bedsides of the soldiers in the hospitals. The intimacy which was formed at this
time was a lasting one. Mme. de Krüdener went from
Königsberg to Dresden, visited the Moravians at
Kleinwelke, Herrnhut, and Berthelsdorf, and then
went to the south of Germany in order to make the
acquaintance of Jung Stilling.

She arrived with her daughter and step-daughter
at Carlsruhe. There she found Stilling, and enjoyed in his family the peace of a Christian household. While the venerable man was initiating her
into the relations between the spirit world and the
inhabitants of earth, she could not entirely withdraw from the society of the court. She visited
the sick and poor, and at the palaces of the great.
Among these were the Margravine of Baden, mother of the Empress of Russia, her daughters, the

Queens of Bavaria and Sweden, the Grand Duchess
of Hesse, and the Duchess of Brunswick, and she
often saw Queen Hortense, the wife of Louis Bonaparte. When at length for the sake of quiet she
retired into Würtemberg she was placed under the
surveillance of the police on account of her intercourse with the Moravians and other Christian
friends, her letters were intercepted and she returned to Carlsruhe.

The pastor Baumeister at Berthelsdorf had said
to her when he heard of her intention of visiting
Stilling, "Tell Stilling from me that I beg that he
will not invoke you as a saint." If in her intercourse with Stilling she was preserved from imagin-
ing herself to have a special vocation in the kingdom of God, she was soon led to think so by another
acquaintance. There was at that time a pastor at
St. Marien (aux Mines), Frederic Fontaine, who belonged to a Prussian Huguenot family. He was
already well known for his Christian zeal, his devotion to the poor, and the special answers he had
received to prayer, when he formed an acquaintance
with Mary Kummer, an ecstatic peasant, who when
in her ecstasies prophesied and prayed in language
far above her education. She had foretold the visit
of Mme. de Krüdener; and when she arrived, the
pastor greeted her with the words, " Art thou she
that should come, or do we look for another?" and
the prophetess foretold a high vocation for her, in
which she was to be supported by Fontaine. Her
long adhesion to this self-interested prophetess,
and to Fontaine, whose interested motives were
also pretty evident, must be ascribed to the enthusiastic nature of Mme. de Krüdener, but it seems

like a relapse into the old paths, only under a
guise of spirituality. She allowed the prophecies of
Mary Kummer to decide whether she should remain
in a place or go away, and she was once induced by
her to buy an estate in Bonigheim, in Würtemberg, and to found a Christian colony there. In the
beginning of 1809 she went there with Mary Kummer. Crowds of people flocked to them, until King
Frederic, annoyed by the prophesying, had the
house surrounded with gendarmes, and Kummer
sent to prison. Mme. de Krüdener was then compelled to leave Würtemberg, and returned to Baden,
where she was cordially received by the Grand
Duchess Stephanie. Aristocratic society was entertained by her conversation and narrations. They
were interesting and piquant, although they surpassed the standard of piety which was tolerated in
the world; and when, while wandering in the evenings among the ruins of the Schloss, the lady
related stories of visions and spiritual appearances, the hearers were seized with a not unpleasant awe. When Mary Kummer was released from
prison, she also came to Baden, and her prophetic
spirit was not silenced. The life of Mme. de Krüdener was divided between outward difficulties and
spiritual delights, but she found a powerful antidote
to the difficulties of life in the tranquillity which
she found in the writings of St. Theresa, Fénelon,
and Madame Guion. After their example, she cultivated pure self-denying love. "This love," she
wrote, "must burn to ashes all that is impure, personal, and selfish in our hearts. It is opposed
to all self-seeking, and considers it as robbing
God. It wishes to receive everything from God,

in order to give all to Him again. It renders us
capable of the most heroic sacrifices, and effects in
us a devotion to our brethren like that of Jesus
Christ. It advances the glory of the Church, which
is called to reign with Christ for a thousand years
upon the earth. Our Judge is still crucified in His
members. His instruments are despised and persecuted, they are mocked by every one, and not
even acknowledged by many true Christians. They
are a small remnant who seek nothing for themselves, but they are very dear to their divine Shep-
herd. The divine love with which they are filled
causes them to be accused of fanaticism, but it is a
proof of their greatness and noble origin."

Among the sufferings which she had to endure in
consequence of this devotion to her Saviour was
estrangement from her mother. She no longer
wrote to her daughter, who often pictured her
brooding in solitude over her ingratitude. She resolved to go to her, and in August, 1810, arrived at
Riga. It deeply grieved her to find her mother
still engrossed in worldly amusements ; and she and
her friends the Moravians prayed all the more earnestly for her soul. In January she died of apoplexy, after many times exclaiming, " Jesus, dear
Jesus !" In November, 1811, summoned by Mary
Kummer, Mme. de Krüdener returned to Baden.
On her way, she promulgated the doctrine of pure
love at Königsberg, Breslau, and Dresden. She
found Fontaine settled as pastor in the neighbourhood of Carlsruhe, and again gave herself up to his
influence. In consequence of the invitation of numerous friends she went to Switzerland, and thence
in 1812 to Strasburg, to visit her son, who was se-

cretary of the embassy. There she found as prefect the Count de Lezay-Marnezia, with whom and his lady she enjoyed refreshing intercourse. They had been acquainted at Montpellier and Baréges, and the count was not a little astonished at the change which had taken place in Mme. de Krüdener, and she had no more ardent wish than to lead him to Christ.

A visit they paid to Oberlin at Steinthal made a salutary impression upon the count, and a few weeks later Mme. de Krüdener was able to write, "We have had the happiness of seeing the count praying in the midst of us, on his knees before the Saviour of the world. You may imagine what a sensation this has produced. He is pre-eminent in rank, in importance, in character, and in virtues ; and this distinguished man is now thoroughly humbled, and as teachable as a child. He is now truly great ; he is a Christian, a worshipper of the true God and of Jesus Christ the crucified. O adore Him, adore Him !"

When she returned to Carlsruhe, she spent much time among the pupils of a ladies' school, the superintendent of which had been converted through her means. Next she went to Geneva, to visit Mme. Armand, a journey which had great influence upon her future life.

It is well known that the doctrines of rationalism had taken firm hold in the city of Calvin. Even a society of the Moravians, which had long existed there, now only numbered five members. Since 1810, these, with other friends of the Bible, had been in the habit of assembling for prayer. Out of this, at the instigation of M. Bost, arose a meeting for reading the Scriptures, which was attended by some young students of theology, among whom was a young man named Empaytaz. In the year 1810 he had been greatly affected by the death of his father, and through the teaching of one of the Moravian Brethren he had attained to faith and peace. The meetings of the " Friends" were discontinued in consequence of the opposition of the ecclesiastical authorities, but the society of the Brethren increased; and Empaytaz and a friend of his, Guers, who were attached to them, endeavoured to advance the kingdom of God by teaching in a Sunday school. In consequence of this, the " Venerable Company" (the ecclesiastical authorities) informed the father of Guers, that if his son continued to associate with the Brethren he could not be admitted to orders.

Just at this juncture Mme. de Krüdener arrived at Geneva. She stayed with Mme. Armand, who already kept up an intercourse with the Brethren, and took part in their religious *réunions*. Empaytaz, who was assailed on all sides by advice not to ruin his ecclesiastical prospects by connecting himself with the Brethren, was encouraged by Mme. de Krüdener to endeavour to assemble the people of God in Geneva. In September, 1813, they together openly established a meeting. In October, Mme. de Krüdener was obliged to return to Carlsruhe, but she wrote letters to him and to the congregation full of ardent Christian eloquence. " Oh, dear friends," she wrote, "the storm is approaching; the earth trembles under our feet; nation is rising against nation, and the chastisements of a just God are proclaimed in characters of blood.

Woe to us if we do not read them aright! Woe to us if our conversion is not complete! Oh, my best beloved friends, I invite you to come to the cross. The voice to which you have not disdained to listen —the voice of a poor sinner whose hopes are based upon these words of life, ' Thy sins are forgiven thee' —adjures you to unite in prayer with her that Christ will grant us that we may live to Him alone. She adjures you to keep up the meetings faithfully, not to listen to human reasonings; to pray daily to a merciful God that the number of souls saved may be daily increased. She entreats you to remember the wretched, the dying, the widows, and orphans; she adjures you to pray, to pray without ceasing, to implore that sinners may be converted; to pray that God will guide those youths who are preparing themselves for the ecclesiastical office that they may become champions of the truth of the gospel; to pray Him to enlighten those who are in error, to strengthen the weak, to bless the young missionary whom God in His goodness has sent to us. And now I entreat you to pray for me, the most unworthy servant of the Lord, but who prays you in tears and upon her knees to remain faithful to Christ; and to pray that I may practise the virtues which I preach, which indeed I am not worthy to preach, but God my Saviour is my witness that I long to possess them, and to glorify Christ the Crucified. I embrace you, and throw myself with you on the holy bosom of Jesus."

In the meantime the storm was breaking over Empaytaz. He was called upon to decide between giving up either his theological career or the religious meetings. But both appeared impossible to him. In his perplexity he went to consult a professor of theology, who had been friendly to him. Empaytaz asked if he was persecuted on account of his doctrines or the meetings.

"On account of your doctrines as well as the meetings undoubtedly," was the answer.

"What doctrines?"

"You believe that God is too old, and that we should worship Jesus Christ."

"Are you serious?"

"Quite so."

"How can you think anything so preposterous? I believe 'that no one cometh to the Father but by the Son; that he who hath not the Son hath not life, but the wrath of God abideth on him.'"

"Precisely. As I said before, those are the notions you hold; we no longer believe these things."

"No longer believe them?"

"No, I tell you, we do not."

"But they are the words of Scripture."

"I tell you that we no longer believe these things."

"Then, if that is the case, I must tell you that I have nothing in common with you."

Empaytaz went on as before; but one persecution followed another. On the 3rd of June 1814, he was summoned before the "Venerable Company," and informed, that if he continued to attend the meetings, he would be excluded from the ecclesiastical office, and the pulpits were already closed against him. He then left Geneva.

After Mme. de Krüdener left Geneva, she stayed some time at Basle, where she found an attractive sphere of labour. She took part in the efforts of

some zealous Christians to spread the word of God.
It was distributed among the soldiers, who read it
eagerly.   Everywhere there were anxious souls
whom the troubles of war had made susceptible to
the message of mercy.   From Basle she went to
Carlsruhe.   Thence she wrote to Empaytaz to encourage him to remain steadfast, and invited him to
meet her at Steinthal, to visit Oberlin.   He arrived
there before her.   The great events of the time had
given her abundant work to do, both among the
humble and the great.   People crowded to her from
all quarters, and she scattered seeds of comfort
among them from the word of God.

In September she arrived at Steinthal ; and under
the peaceful roof of the venerable Oberlin she and
Empaytaz enjoyed some precious hours employed in
study of the Scriptures, and in labour amongst the
people.   But she was soon called from this placid
yet active life, by the news that Count de Lezay,
while going to meet the Duke de Berri, had been
killed by being thrown from his carriage.

She and her daughter and Empaytaz hastened to
the widow at Strasburg.   The prefect had died a
Christian's death, full of love and prayerful repentance, and in humble faith in the Crucified One.

The visit to Strasburg was taken advantage of to
hold religious meetings, which were conducted by
Empaytaz, and Mme. de Krüdener conversed with
individuals in private.   In November she went to
Carlsruhe, where she daily assembled the Protestant
and Catholic clergy around her, that they might be
edified together.   Fontaine also appears upon the
scene again, and induced her to buy another estate,
Rapenhoff, in Würtemberg ; but she did not come

into possession of it till 1815. The great fatigue
occasioned by the concourse to her of so many
anxious souls, induced her to go to Baden, because
she could have more quiet there. She was accompanied by her daughter, Empaytaz, and Franz von
Berckheim, a young man who, a short time before,
had given up a public appointment in Mayence, in
order to follow a course under the guidance of Mme.
de Krüdener, in which he could work out his own
salvation, and advance the kingdom of God. Every
three hours they desisted from their employments,
in order to unite in prayer. In fine weather they
mounted the hills, reading the Psalms as they
walked ; and when the hour of prayer arrived, they
performed their devotions in the open air. The
time spent at Baden was a refreshing and happy
one. While there, she received a command by revelation, so says her biographer, to go to a mill at
Schlüchtern, in Electoral Hesse, to await a meeting
with the Emperor Alexander. A revival had taken
place in the neighbourhood. The writings of Jung
Stilling and some others had caused such an excitement among the people, that whole communities
were thinking of selling their possessions, and going
to the feet of the Caucasian mountains, to await the
return of the Jews to the promised land. With the
assistance of Berckheim and other good men, Mme.
de Krüdener tried to turn them from such fanatical
projects. She was in full activity here in the spring
of 1815, when she was suddenly called to carry the
message of peace to the Emperor of the East.

Ever since Mme. de Krüdener's intercourse with
Mary Kummer, a desire for the spirit of prophecy
had been awakened in her, and the great events

happening around her, as well as her own spiritual development, conspired to increase it. She had formerly willingly suffered herself to be guided by the peasant prophetess, she now tried to produce an effect upon national events by her own predictions. Of three things she was confident; that after the first Peace of Paris, new storms must burst over Europe; that God had assigned a great part, during the period of them, to the Emperor Alexander; and that she would be called, when the right moment came, to appear before him with a message of mercy for the purification and building up of his own soul. At Carlsruhe she had become acquainted with Roxandra von Sturza, one of the ladies of the court of the Empress Elizabeth of Russia, and had led her nearer to the Saviour. Through a correspondence with her, the voice of this indefatigable woman penetrated into the cabinet of the Emperor at Vienna, perhaps even, indirectly, into the councils of the Congress.

That Alexander, to whom, in 1812, the word of God had struck home, whom the wonderful successes of 1813 had incited to give the praise to God; who, in 1814, had shown himself a magnanimous Christian ruler,—should give himself up to the dissipation and frivolity of Vienna during the Congress,—was to Mme. de Krüdener a bitter grief. She could not get rid of the idea that she had a mission to him. Soon after the opening of the Congress in October, 1814, she wrote to Mdlle. de Sturza, "This is no time for hesitation. Let the giddy multitude amuse themselves, they have nothing but the melancholy pleasures by which they degrade themselves, and which entirely engross them; but Christians must watch and pray. The angel who marks the blood upon the door-posts of the elect passeth by, but the world seeth him not. He counts the number of them; judgment is approaching; it is at hand; we are standing upon a volcano. We shall now see guilty France chastised, which, in accordance with the divine decree on account of the cross given it to bear, has hitherto been spared. Christians must not inflict punishment, and that man alone whom the Eternal has chosen and consecrated,—the man whom we are so happy as to call our sovereign,— can give us peace. But the storm will soon burst. These lilies which the Eternal had protected,—symbols of purity and fragility,—which were crushed by an iron sceptre, because it was the will of the Eternal; these lilies, which should have been a call to purity, and to the love of God, and to repentance, have appeared only to vanish away, and the people —more hardened than ever—dream only of tumult."

She wrote again : " You would like to tell me of the many great and beautiful traits in the character of the Emperor. I think I know a good deal about him already. I have known for a long time that the Lord will give me the pleasure of seeing him. If I live to see it, it will be one of the happiest moments of my life. There can be no more delightful earthly duty than to love and honour those whom God has commanded us to love and honour. I have great things to say to him, for much has been communicated to me concerning him. The Lord alone can prepare him to listen to it. But I do not disturb myself about it. It is my part to be without fear and without reproach; it is his to lie at the feet of Christ, who is truth. May the Eternal guide and bless him who is called to so high a mission !"

Mme. de Sturza hastened to communicate the predictions contained in this letter to the Emperor, who, favourably inclined to the missionary zeal of Christian ladies, from his acquaintance with the Quakers in England, always very susceptible to feminine influence, and specially interested in a lady who felt herself called upon to lead him out of the world to a lofty mission, ardently desired to make her acquaintance.

The prophecies of Mme. de Krüdener were come to pass. The lilies of France had been again dragged into the dust, and the land chastised, but it was not sufficiently humbled, and was to be chastised again.

There was one advantage for Alexander in the return of Napoleon, that it took him away from the enervating atmosphere of the Vienna Congress. The change did not at first suit him. He was depressed. The remembrance of the life that he had led, after experiencing the drawings of God's love; the responsibility which he felt to rest upon him with respect to the destinies of nations, accusing and excusing thoughts produced a melancholy state of mind. He received the honours that were paid him in Bavaria with repugnance, and arrived at his head quarters at Heilbronn. After a day of wearisome festivities he retired early to the solitude for which he was longing. He wrote afterwards to a friend : " At length I breathed freely, and the first thing I did was to take up a book which I always carry about with me, but, in consequence of the dark cloud which rested upon my mind, the reading made no impression upon me. My thoughts were confused, and my heart oppressed. I let the book fall, and thought what a comfort conversation with some pious friend would be to me! This idea brought you to my mind; and I remembered what you had told me of Mme. de Krüdener, and the desire that I had expressed to you to make her acquaintance. I wonder where she is now, and whether I shall ever meet with her. No sooner had this passed through my mind than I heard a knock at the door. It was Prince Wolkonsky, who said, with an air of the greatest impatience, that he was very sorry to disturb me at so unseasonable an hour, but that he could not get rid of a lady who was determined to see me. He said that her name was Mme. de Krüdener. You may imagine my amazement. I thought I must be dreaming, and exclaimed, 'Mme. de Krüdener! Mme. de Krüdener!' This sudden response to my thoughts could not be accidental. I saw her at once; and she addressed such powerful and comforting words to me that it seemed as if she had read my very soul, and they calmed the storm which had been assailing me."

The bearer of divine messages drew aside the veil from the Emperor's mind; she told him of his sins, of the frivolity and pride with which he had entered on his mission. "No, your Majesty, you have not yet approached the God man as a sinner praying for mercy. You have not yet received mercy from Him who alone can forgive sins upon earth. You are yet in your sins, and have not humbled yourself before Jesus; you have not yet cried out, like the publican, 'God be merciful to me a sinner!' and therefore you have no peace. Listen to the voice of a woman who was a great sinner, but who has found pardon at the foot of the cross."

The Emperor shed tears, and hid his face in

his hands. Mme. de Krüdener apologized for her earnestness. "No!" he exclaimed; "go on; your words are music to my soul." Three hours passed in conversation of this nature, and the Emperor implored Mme. de Krüdener not to forsake him. He felt that no one had ever before so touched his conscience, and unveiled the truth to him.

Alexander went on to Heidelberg, and took a small house there, to which he was attracted by a cross in the garden. He invited Mme. de Krüdener to come there, and she hired a little cottage on the banks of the Neckar, where the Emperor spent every other evening. He selected chapters in the Bible for reading, and the conversation was often kept up till two o'clock in the morning. Empaytaz took part in these meetings. It was certainly a singular spectacle to see the Autocrat of All the Russias humbly suffering himself to be guided in the way of peace by the young Genevan; to see how he confessed his weaknesses, and related his spiritual experience. Then Empaytaz would kneel down and pray, and the Emperor would grasp his hand, and say, with tears in his eyes, "Oh, how I feel the power of brotherly love, which unites all the disciples of Christ! Yes, your prayers will be heard, and it will be given me from above to confess my Saviour openly before men."

Alexander's intercourse with Mme. de Krüdener could not remain unobserved, and she was soon subjected to curious visitors. Some were designing and malicious persons, but among them were men of noble character, like Capodistria and Stein.

Arndt maintained that Stein did not approve of the influence of the "Field Marshaless of the *sa-*

lons." It is easy to imagine that he would be pleased that Alexander should visit this lady instead of others, and that he might find his own religion confirmed, and yet that he might feel a patriotic anger, that the Emperor's personal inclinations were unfavourable to Germany. During the important days preceding the battle of Waterloo, Alexander and his friends were reading the Psalms, and conversing on the words of the King of Israel upon the events of his own life.

When news of the victory arrived, they threw themselves upon their knees. After the prayer, the Emperor exclaimed, "Oh, how happy I am! My Saviour is with me. I am a great sinner, but He will employ me to give peace to the nations. Oh, how happy might they be, if they would only understand the ways of Providence, and obey the Gospel!"

The Emperor went to Paris, and invited Mme. de Krüdener to follow him. She employed the last few days of her stay at Heidelberg in carrying the Gospel to some condemned prisoners, and she had the pleasure of giving her daughter her blessing on her marriage with Herr von Berckheim. In July she went to Paris, where the Emperor assigned her a dwelling where he could readily visit her, and the meetings of Heidelberg were continued, though, perhaps, not quite with the same simplicity as in the cottage there. Empaytaz, Berckheim and his lady, and the Countess de Lezay took part in them. Of course people were still more curious than at Heidelberg to penetrate the mystery of this intercourse.

Mme. de Krüdener, who eleven years before had

played a very different part at Paris, had to go through evil report and good report, but she found abundant opportunity for promoting religious revivals after her own manner. There was divine service every evening at seven o'clock in her spacious but plainly furnished *salon*. She took her place among the listeners, always dressed in black or brown. Empaytaz prayed and expounded a portion of Scripture. Mme. de Krüdener helped to preserve Alexander from the seductions of the city, and strengthened him in his peace policy. He instigated France to restore her armies, and when the ministers of the other monarchs remonstrated with him, he answered, " The only policy I adopt is a conscientious and straightforward one."—"You are right," said Mme. de Krüdener. " The more magnanimous you are to others, the more magnanimous will God be to you. I lately wrote to some one, that a holy policy has come down from heaven, and that you are the eagle destined to unravel the tangled policy of the present."—" Oh," he said, " I have only acted in the spirit of the Gospel, which says, ' If any man compel thee to go a mile, go with him twain, and if any man take away thy coat, let him have thy cloak also.' " This sounds very fine, but Alexander forgot that he did not lose his Russian coat by his indulgent policy towards France, while the German cloak was rent afresh by it.

Fontaine and Mary Kummer also came to Paris. She prophesied, and announced a prediction for the following day. While she was waiting for the spirit in Mme. de Krüdener's house, the Emperor came. She addressed him, and the sum and substance of her communication was to ask him to provide funds to establish a religious community at Weinsberg. He had then seen enough of the prophetess, and Mme. de Krüdener also became tired of her. Two days afterwards, she and Fontaine returned to Rappenhof.

During the time of Mme. de Krüdener's residence at Paris, her sympathies were strongly excited for General Labedoyère. His enthusiasm for Napoleon and the empire had attracted the hatred of the royalists. Neither the intercession of Alexander, nor the vows of the accused, the humble entreaties of his wife, nor the unceasing prayer made for him in Mme. de Krüdener's house, availed to incline the hearts of his accusers to withhold the sentence of death. But his death, in reliance on all forgiving mercy, and the consolations which his widow was enabled to derive from the Gospel, were a triumph for the party of Christian brotherly love. Even Chateaubriand was among those who advised the execution of the sentence. And with the same energy with which he advocated the death of the friend of the empire, he sought to gain Alexander's good offices for the restoration.

He wrote to Mme. de Krüdener in delight at the change which was being brought about in France, which was indicated by the new elections, " France will now be preserved for the sake of Christians and of Frenchmen of that ancient sort who enjoyed the esteem of all Europe. Is not that a special favour of Providence? If we profit by this mercy, we may escape destruction. What a triumph it would be for the magnanimous prince, whom I certainly admire as much as you do, if after the success of his arms, and the deposition of our oppressor, he were also to hurl our Revolution from its throne."

Alexander's confidential relations with Mme. de Krüdener attracted a number of people belonging to the best society to her simple *salon*. She was so occupied that she had scarcely time to eat. With every one she conversed of the one thing needful. Heaps of letters covered her table; and though formerly so fond of advocating her Saviour's cause by correspondence, she could find no time to answer them. She visited schools and prisons, and in the evenings Alexander came to her house with his Bible under his arm.

It suited his peculiar character to yield himself entirely to her influence. As he had required the presence of Stein, and allowed himself to be entirely guided by him when it was necessary to exert to the utmost his moral powers in opposing Napoleon, so now he could not be satisfied unless his monitor to repentance, Mme. de Krüdener, was near at hand. He assigned her a place in the Greek chapel,—in order, so to speak, that the breath of her prayers might ascend to heaven with his own.

Before Alexander left Paris, he was very desirous of making a public confession of faith. He wished to acknowledge the Gospel which he had adopted as the guide of his life, as the law also of his political course. It was the wish of his heart to bring his allies to join him in this acknowledgment, and to give permanence in a " Holy Alliance " to the resolutions to which they had been impelled during the last three years by the wonderful dealings of God. History ascribes the first idea of the Holy Alliance both to the Emperor Alexander and to King Frederic William.

Eylert dates its birth from the time of the first unfortunate battles, in the spring of 1813. He says that Alexander related to him that at that period, when retreating towards Silesia, the King and he rode for some time side by side in silence. It was broken by the King with the words, "This cannot go on; we are going towards the East, when we ought to be going towards the West. We shall accomplish it by God's help, but when He does, as I hope He will, bless our united efforts, we will make known our conviction to all the world, that the honour is due to Him alone." Alexander agreed, and gave the King his hand, in ratification of the compact. It has, however, been shown that the carrying out of the idea belongs to the Emperor, after the second entry into Paris; and it is certain that his friendship with Mme. de Krüdener, and the religious zeal which she awakened in his mind, gave the decisive impulse to it. The Grand Duke of Mecklenburg-Strelitz, brother-in-law of Frederic William, considered the Holy Alliance to be the work of that pious lady. "You may be sure," he wrote, "that I should not say so without being assured of the fact."

She herself ascribed it to an inspiration of God. A few days after the review at Vertus, Alexander came to her with a draft of the document, and requested her to examine it. "I wish," he said, "that the Emperor of Austria and the King of Prussia should join me in this act of praise, in order that it may be seen that like the three wise men from the East, we worship the Saviour."

The practical results of the Holy Alliance may have been insignificant; indeed, this attempt to combine religion with politics may often have wrought confusion, but it is a powerful testimony to the religious awakening which took place in the hearts of rulers, and the document is so remarkable that we subjoin a translation of the French text from the life of Mme. de Krüdener.

"PARIS, September 14–26, 1815.

" In the name of the Holy and indivisible Trinity.

"Their Majesties the Emperor of Austria, the King of Prussia, and the Emperor of Russia, in consequence of the great events which have marked the course of the last three years, and in view of the favours which it has pleased divine Providence to grant to those States which have placed their whole trust and hope in God, having acquired a profound conviction that the steps which shall be taken by the Powers in their mutual relations, ought to be regulated by the sublime truths which we are taught by the eternal religion of God our Saviour; declare solemnly that the sole object of the present act is to manifest in the sight of the universe their unalterable determination to adopt no other rule of conduct, either in the administration of their respective states, or their political relations with every other government, than the precepts of this holy religion, precepts of justice, charity, and peace, which, far from being applicable only to private life, should, on the contrary, have a direct influence on the resolutions of princes, and be the guide of all their actions, as being the only means of giving permanence to human institutions, and remedying their imperfections. Their Majesties have therefore agreed to the following Articles :—

"Article 1. In accordance with the words of holy Scripture, which command all men to regard each other as brothers, the three contracting monarchs will be united by the bonds of a true and indissoluble brotherhood; and considering each other as fellow countrymen, on every occasion and in every place they will aid and succour each other; and regarding themselves in relation to their subjects and armies as fathers of a family, they will govern them in the same spirit of fraternity by which they are animated, in order to protect religion, peace, and justice.

"Article 2. The only actuating principle, therefore, whether between the aforesaid governments, or between them and their subjects, will be that of reciprocal service, that they may bear testimony, by an unfailing benevolence, to the mutual affection by which they are animated, and that they consider themselves but as members of one great Christian nation; and the three allied monarchs regard themselves as delegated by Providence to govern three branches of the same family, viz., Austria, Prussia, and Russia; thereby acknowledging that the Christian nation of which they and their people are members, has really no other sovereign than Him to whom all power belongs, because in Him are found all the treasures of love and knowledge and infinite wisdom; that is God, our divine Saviour Jesus Christ, the Word of the Most High, that is to say, the Word of life.

"Their Majesties therefore recommend to their people, with the most tender solicitude, as the only means of partaking of that peace which springs from a good conscience, and which only is lasting, daily to fortify themselves more and more in the principles and in the practice of the duties which the divine Saviour has enjoined upon men.

" Article 3. All the Powers which solemnly acknowledge the sacred principles which have dictated the present act, and who recognize how important it is for the happiness of nations, too long in agitation, that these truths should exercise upon the destinies of man the influence which is their due, will be admitted with equal eagerness and affection into the Holy Alliance.

" Done threefold, and signed in Paris in the year of grace 1815, September 14–26.

" (Signed)   FRANCIS,
" FREDERIC WILLIAM.
" ALEXANDER."

After he had accomplished the project of the Holy Alliance, and given Mme. de Krüdener a warm invitation to St. Petersburg, Alexander left Paris. She had no hope of being soon able to follow him thither, but she did not remain much longer at Paris. During the last few days of her stay there, she had one of those joys which are shared by the angels in heaven. She received indisputable evidence that an old friend of her gay days and literary vanity, and whose admiration she had courted, had begun a life in God. On receiving some touching verses which he sent her, with the motto of St. Bernard, ' O beata solitudo, O sola beatitudo,' she burst into tears, and fell upon her knees, exclaiming, " O my God, his heart still lives, and lives for thee ! "

After Mme. de Krüdener left Paris in October,

1815, a life began for her which must possess great
interest for every friend of the kingdom of God;
but as it is not so immediately connected with our
subject, we shall pass rapidly over it. She went to
Switzerland. Wherever she went crowds of people
who felt their need of salvation crowded round her;
everywhere she testified of her Saviour to the sinner
with the wonderful power derived from a personal
experience of divine mercy. Wherever she went
she excited awakening and stir among the people;
but the singularity and fanaticism of her proceedings, her presumption in denouncing woes upon the
countries where her divine mission was not immediately acknowledged, induced the secular powers
to put police regulations in force against her. Like
a princess in the realms of piety, addressed as
" gracious lady " by thousands of people who came
to her for help, surrounded by a sort of spiritual
court, attended by Empaytaz and her son-in-law,
and sometimes by Professor Lachenal of Basle, but
more often by Kellner, formerly a postmaster, a
man who was entirely devoted to her, and inclined
to every sort of fanaticism, she travelled from place
to place, now persecuted, now hailed with acclamation.

In conjunction with Kellner, Spittler, and Empaytaz, she founded a tract society at Basle. She then
went to Berne, whither she had been invited by her
son, who was Russian ambassador to the Swiss Confederation. But the effect produced by her preaching was so great that the police were frightened,
and even respect for the embassy could not secure
her a peaceful residence there; she was, therefore,
requested in the politest terms to leave the city.

She had more success at Basle. There was daily
service at the hotel where she was staying; there
was singing and prayer, Empaytaz preached, and
the concourse was so great that the largest room
in the hotel would not hold the people. Large
crowds were constantly assembled in the streets,
which excited the alarm of the police. There were
frequent conversions, and not only among girls and
women, strong men also succumbed to the power of
divine grace. Lachenal, professor of philosophy,
went to one of the meetings out of mere curiosity,
to hear what it was that these people were preaching,
and his philosophy melted away like a morning
cloud before the simple preaching of the Gospel by
Empaytaz. He gave his life, his time, his property,
at once to God. A Roman Catholic priest, who had
followed Mme. de Krüdener from Berne, returned
with the remark, "I came here with a Pope, but I
am going away without one." At length she was
driven away from Basle. A pious farmer, on the
border of the territory of Baden, offered her his
country-house at Hörnlein. Mme. de Krüdener and
her party took up their abode there, living in the
simplest possible manner, till April 1816. The
concourse of people was tremendous. Some few
men of education were among them, but it was
principally the country people who flocked to hear
the preaching of Christ. When almost worn out
with fatigue, Mme. de Krüdener gladly accepted an
invitation from two English ladies to go to Aarau,
and on the journey she made the acquaintance of
Pestalozzi. It is well known that this man was inspired by the sincerest love for the people, although
he had not clear Scriptural views of the great
source of love in the mercy of God.

The singing, praying, and preaching, during the journey on which Pestalozzi accompanied the party, appeared to him so delightful that he found it difficult to separate from his new friends. At Aarau the concourse of people began again. The well-known Roman Catholic missionary, Joseph Wolf, was among her hearers, and was confirmed in his Protestant tendencies. By degrees the whole canton, so to speak, flocked to hear her. Just as the authorities were thinking of putting a stop to the meetings, she accepted an invitation to Schloss Liebegg, and her stay there was like a festival for the people in the neighbourhood. On her return to her son and daughter at Hörnlein, she proclaimed free mercy to the pilgrims to Einsiedeln. A woman of 94, who was making the pilgrimage for the fiftieth time, to whom Mme. de Krüdener announced the message of mercy, threw away her rosary, exclaiming, " It is done! it is done! My sins are forgiven. Jesus has saved me !"

About this time famine began to be felt. Mme. de Krüdener sold all her possessions. Her jewels alone fetched 30,000 francs, which, together with the income she received from Russia, she devoted to feeding the poor. Her friends, also, denied themselves for the same purpose. At Unterholz, a gendarme was stationed at her door to see that she only gave away food, and did not preach ; but she quietly continued her work.

The authorities at Baden also endeavoured to silence her by means of gendarmes, but finding it useless, they sent to her a corporal distinguished for his severity.

In the midst of his maltreatment of the poor,

Mme. de Krüdener pierced him with the arrow of
the grace of Christ. He fell upon his knees, and
prayed with her, and the lion became a lamb. The
attacks of the police of Baden and Switzerland continued, and sometimes provoked the people to acts
of violence.

A number of poor people who were living in
Professor Lachenal's house at Unterholz, were
turned out as if they had been criminals, with Empaytaz at their head; and when Mme. de Krüdener
was seeking a little peace at Hörnlein, there arose
a vehement controversy about her in the newspapers.
Wherever she went the people flocked to her; those
hungering after righteousness, as well as those suffering from physical hunger, cold, and nakedness,
and all were relieved, notwithstanding the persecution of the authorities. After she had drunk the
cup of insult and scorn to the dregs without a
murmur, only imbibing fresh strength from it to
persevere in her life of love, she was banished from
Hörnlein and Unterholz.

In the beginning of May 1817, she went to
Warmbach, and was driven thence to Rheinfelden,
where she was mobbed by the people not seeking
help, but incensed that she had helped others; and
she would have been murdered if the police had not
come to her aid. After staying a few days at
Möhlin, she went to Mungtz, everywhere followed
by crowds of people, among whom she distributed
the provisions which Lachenal sent after her. In a
few weeks he spent 100,000 francs on the poor.
From Mungtz she wished to go to canton Argau,
but was forbidden by the Government; then she
went through Laufenburg to Aarau, but the follow-

ing day she was conducted to the frontier by gendarmes.

At length she met with a friendly reception at Lucerne. The same scenes were repeated, but, besides the common people, the priests and pupils at the seminary flocked to hear her. In an address to them which has been preserved, with wonderful eloquence and knowledge of the subject she sketched a picture of a faithful pastor, points out how a man may become one, and relates some particulars of the life of John Tauler.

But an encomium on Mme. de Krüdener, in comparison with the clergy, appeared in the public prints, which incited the authorities to take steps to put a stop to the assemblies which for several successive days had been attended by 3000 people; and, warned to leave the place, she went to Zurich. Her arrival there had been announced some weeks before by a somnambulist, and the crowds that flocked to her were so great that, in spite of the remonstrances of Antistes Hess, she was only allowed to remain twenty-four hours, and was conducted by gendarmes to Lofstätten.

Here she was visited by Maurer from Schaffhausen, who has left a very interesting description of his meeting with her. George Müller also visited her, and candidly expressed his doubts to her about her mission, but was convinced that, though not free from error, her sole desire was to advance the kingdom of God. It is painful to see how she was driven from place to place during the next few weeks. The famine was fearful; all feelings of humanity were quenched by it; thousands were wandering about in the fields and woods, seeking for weeds to appease their hunger. As long as Mme. de Krüdener had anything to give she gave it, but at the same time she offered the people the bread of life; and, under the influence of the fearful times, she admonished them to be converted, and proclaimed the approach of judgment with prophetic zeal; and this it was which caused her to be conducted by gendarmes from one country to another. After being driven out of Switzerland she hastened through Würtemberg to Baden, where she found rest for a few days at Freiburg, in the Breisgau. While there, she was ordered to return to Russia, with permission to take with her Kellner and her daughter, whose husband had preceded them in order to make arrangements for the colonists for the Caucasus from South Germany and Switzerland. Empaytaz and his mother and Mme. Armand went to Geneva; Lachenal and his wife had already been ordered to return home by the police at Basle. Weary with her labours, Mme. de Krüdener travelled through Würtemberg and Bavaria to Saxony, always under the surveillance of the police, as if she had been a prisoner of State. At Weimar she met her friend Mdlle. de Sturza, and she enjoyed rest for a few days among the Moravian Brethren at Neudietendorf. She then went to Leipsic, where, after a few days, the authorities forbade any one to visit her. She would have been glad to spend the winter at Dessau, in order to recruit her health; but she was conducted to Eilenburg, and thence to Lübben. Here, in the presence of a commissary of the police, she was permitted to hold a meeting, and took the opportunity of refuting some of the erroneous opinions which had been circulated about her.

At Mitau the police tormented her by preventing Kellner from accompanying her any further, and sending away other persons in her suite. She spent some time with her brother at Jungfernhof, and at length arrived at her estate of Kosse, where she assumed the office of spiritual mother to the people. While there, during her solitary walks on the shores of the lake, she composed numerous hymns of a somewhat mystical character. She was joined by her daughter and her husband; and Herr von Berckheim has given a lively description of the labours of his mother-in-law among the Esthonians. During her residence there, news of the revolution in Greece, in 1820, reached her, and she hailed it with inspiriting songs. Not long afterwards she received tidings that her son-in-law, who had gone with his wife to visit the Princess Anna Galitzin near St. Petersburg, was seriously ill, and she ardently wished to go to him. She received the Emperor's permission in January, and was soon with her children. Amidst many fervent prayers, her son-in-law recovered.

All those within the borders of the rigid Greek Church in whose minds a certain mysticism had been the means of cherishing religious life, were attracted to visit the celebrated lady. And since the conversion of Alexander, through the circulation of the Bible and other means, true piety and zeal for the kingdom of God had greatly increased. But the weakness of Alexander's character caused him to vacillate between his desire to spread the knowledge of religion among his people, and the fear that their mental emancipation would weaken the imperial authority; and he fell a prey to the priestly party, who hated the mystical and pietistic movements in the church. The excellent minister of worship, Prince Galitzin, was dismissed, and the Bible Society suppressed. All this had occurred shortly before Mme. de Krüdener arrived. It was, perhaps, natural that Alexander should not entertain the same confidence in her at St. Petersburg as he had done in Paris; and her enthusiasm for Greece was not likely to increase it, for he had just been informed by Metternich that the revolution in Greece was not to be supported. Alexander caused her to be informed, in a delicate way, that her residence in his capital could only be permitted so long as she refrained from any expression of opinion on the affairs of Greece, and the relations of Russia with regard to her. She returned to her rural retreat, and added voluntary mortifications to the imposed restriction. She wrote scarcely any letters, but employed her time in praying, reading, singing, and caring for the poor. In the winter of 1822–23 she sat without fire or double windows. She suffered, indeed, in body, but the serenity of her mind increased. The news of the death of Kellner was, however, a great shock to her. She reviewed her past life, and the prospect of death presented itself to her under an aspect of terror, and as an expiation for her sins. But this temptation did not last long, and her readiness to depart returned. Her malady, also, became less painful, and she willingly entered into a plan for going down the Volga towards the Crimea with the Princess Galitzin and her peasant colony. But on the journey her illness increased, and the peculiarities of her character became less conspicuous. When they arrived at Karasou-Bazar she prepared herself for death, under the loving care of her daughter and her husband. She was fond of hearing Tersteegen's hymns, especially the one beginning—

> " Jesu, der du bist alleine
>   Haupt und Hirte der Gemeine,
>   Segne mich dein armes Glied."

> " Jesus, of thy sheep the head,
>   By whose hand Thy flock is fed,
>   Feed me, Thy humble lamb."

The image of the Crucified One was always before her view.

A few days before her death she wrote to her son, " The good that I have done will remain ; the harm that I have done—and how often have I not mistaken the workings of my own imagination and pride for the voice of God !—God in His mercy will wipe away. I have nothing to offer to God or man but my many imperfections, but the blood of Jesus Christ cleanses us from all sin." On the 15th of December, amidst fervent prayers, she took leave of her beloved ones. On the 24th she was unable to speak, and requested by signs, that the sign of the cross should be made over her. At midnight she was told that it was Christmas Day, and with beaming looks and audible voice, she gave glory to God. On that day she died. Her earthly tabernacle was deposited in the Armenian church at Karasou-Bazar, and was afterwards removed to the Greek church, which the Princess Galitzin had built at Koreiss.

Such is the history of Mme. de Krüdener, derived from the only authentic records. We have repre-

sented it as we found it, endeavouring lovingly to
enter into the spirit of her remarkable life. It only
remains to add a few critical remarks. We have
read periodicals, reports, and journals containing
notices of her proceedings. Contemporary opinion
was as various as possible. We do not of course
concur in the judgment of the world, which, not
sharing the angel's joy over a sinner that repent-
eth, is more ready to forgive the sin without repentance than a penitent sinner for preaching it.
But we should consider it to be in good order, that
the more notorious the sin, the more deeply the
sinner should ponder the pardon she has received in
her heart, and not appear before the world with her
newly learnt message of a Saviour from sin, until
she has long and silently communed with it herself.
St. Paul himself only appears to have preached the
Gospel for years after his conversion in small and
private circles. Perhaps a quiet residence in her
home, and confining her labours to her immediate
neighbourhood, would have been better for Mme. de
Krüdener than wandering about the world, although
we grant that if she did so, she could but speak out
of the abundance of her heart. Perhaps she would
then have acquired more taste for domestic life, and
not have fallen into the homeless condition in which
she lived for many years, and which we are inclined
to regard as an evidence of the old leaven in her
character. We do not think that her usefulness
would thereby have been lessened. The spiritual
preaching of mercy when accompanied by a holy life
in God, and devotion to our fellow creatures, is so
shining a light, that let it be placed where it may,
even were it in Russia, it is sure to be seen from
afar, and to attract souls to itself.

And as we regard the perpetual wandering about of the widow as the effect of her early life, we think we recognize in many of her actions during her religious career, the fantastic and eccentric romance writer. She was wanting in Christian sobriety. This was shown by the exaggerated importance she attached to the prophecies of Mary Kummer, and her implicit confidence in Fontaine, who was disposed to turn both the oracle of his prophetess and the credulous enthusiasm of Mme. de Krüdener to his own advantage for earthly and selfish ends. Mme. de Krüdener paid dearly for this, for Alexander became prejudiced against her in consequence of the disastrous result of Fontaine's enterprises, which ended with debt and arrest on the estate of Rappenhof.

Her proceedings in Switzerland were altogether wanting in Christian sobriety. It was shown in her impatient looking for divine judgments, her anxious watching for every report of earthquake, storm, hail, fire, and pestilence, in order that she might proclaim approaching judgment with greater confidence; in her delight in the marvellous, in the way in which she wrested many passages of Scripture to make them suit her own fancy, in the importance she attached to forms, such as the expression, " Praise be to Jesus Christ," to the sign of the cross, and the bending of the knee. The restless haste of her evangelization, very different from the zeal of the apostle; her habit of carrying on several employments at once, reading letters, dictating others, and considering a passage of Scripture, doubtless much to the detriment of each occupation, gave evidence of a great want of soberness. In the persecution which arose against her, there was doubtless much political and ecclesiastical Pharisaism, but there was also a wholesome opposition to a course tending to fanaticism and disorder. What right had she to denounce the social and political state of Switzerland, with which her acquaintance was by no means intimate, as one likely to call down divine judgments? And although in the time of famine she showed her love by her abundant charity, was it wise to entice the people away from their homes and occupations to Russia and the Caucasus?

She was no doubt filled with holy zeal, but her religious character retained a flavour of that of the adventurous woman of the world, the romance writer, the homeless wanderer, whose life had never had the stay afforded by having real work to do.

There was also something incoherent in her creed, for she denied that she belonged to any particular church. The grace of Christ and love to the brethren was the kernel of her Christianity. Her occasional invocation of the Virgin may be ascribed rather to a fantastic enthusiasm than to doctrine, and she was in the main Protestant, or Catholic, according to the original meaning of the word. When in Switzerland she wrote to a Roman Catholic priest, "Love has called me, not only out of the world, but out of a lifeless Christianity, so that I belong neither to the Catholic nor to the Greek Church and thank God have never become Protestant. My great Master has taught me to be a Christian. When the sun of my life began to dawn upon me, I did not think about being a sinner. I loved, and wept in ecstasy over this delightful love. I was unacquainted both with Christian communities and the forms which

people are so ready to adopt. I had heard but little
and learnt but little, but I thought, ' Oh, if He who
is worthy of all adoration did but love me!' Consumed by the divine flame, I did not concern myself
about my own unworthiness; I knew nothing of my
ruined state. I neither knew nor hated my sinfulness, I only kept at His feet like Mary Magdalene."
The love of Christ was the ruling passion of her life.
" Not to love," she said " is to me the epitome of all
horrors. Not love Him who has graven in my heart
the wish that hell itself might learn to love Christ
the conqueror of hell! I have learnt to know the
almighty power of faith and love, not as a heroine
of faith, but as a child. The honour and glory of
my Redeemer are my life. It is my ardent desire to
see all around me saved, that they all might unite
in praising divine love."

This was her universal theme in correspondence, in
private conversation, and among the multitude.

At a time when God was causing His chastisements
to be felt, this remarkable woman, by her preaching
and her self-denying love, accomplished her mission
with wonderful spiritual energy. Her interference
with politics was a mistake, her spiritual labours
were encompassed with many infirmities. But she
advanced the kingdom of God; her own conversion
was a striking instance of the power of grace, and
her unfailing love for the people, in spite of political
and religious persecution, and the testimony she
bore in words and works, all tended to call back the
world to the cross.*

* ' Vie de Mme. de Krüdener, par Charles Eynard.' Paris, 1849.

CHAPTER IV.

FREDERIC PERTHES.

GERMANY has no nobler representative of her citizens' life than Frederic Perthes. Although in his youth his education was limited to that generally afforded to youths destined for trade, yet by his untiring exertions he placed himself on a mental equality with men of learning. Although originally without property, through his energy, ability, and inviolable uprightness, his business became one of the most important of its kind. Without the outward calling of any official position, and solely from his pure and ardent patriotism, he takes his place among the deliverers of his country from the French yoke, and justly shares their fame. From the healthy union in his character of patriotism and religion, he may be regarded as a modern representative of the ancient citizens of the free German cities, in which the preaching of the Reformation, and the spirit of Protestantism took such deep root.

In whatever aspect we regard his life, as the head of a household, as a man of business, patriot, member of the Church, or as a philanthropist,—in every character he displayed zeal, love, and energy; and the conviction is forced upon us that he was a complete man.

Frederic Christopher Perthes was born in April, 1772, at Rudolstadt, where his father was collector of taxes, and his grandfather had been court surgeon. He had to bear the yoke in his youth. His father died early, and his mother, having only a yearly pension of 21 gulden, about £1. 15s. sterling, found a home with some of her friends, and his maternal grandmother took charge of the boy. She died when he was only seven years old, when he was adopted by his maternal uncle, Frederic Heubel, and his sister Caroline. The brother was a man of great animation, taking a keen interest in what was going on in the world, strictly honourable, and devoted to his prince, body and soul; the sister was a woman of great energy and strong will, ready to help every one, but never to accept help herself. In the holidays the boy was fond of staying with his uncle, J. D. Heubel, who was lieutenant colonel and bailiff to the prince, and lived at the castle of Schwarzburg, and roaming about the hills and woods of that beautiful neighbourhood with him, was beneficial both to body and mind. He made but little progress at the gymnasium at Rudolstadt; he had had too little regular instruction before, had no head for figures, and very little for learning languages. But he read with avidity, and a great deal of knowledge was stored up, though unassorted in his mind, when at the age of fifteen he was sent as an apprentice to the bookseller Böhme, at Leipsic. The contract is an interesting relic of a time when religious and moral training was still considered to be the necessary groundwork for success in business.　Böhme promised not only to instruct him in the bookselling trade, but to admonish him to live virtuously and in the fear of God ; and his uncle engaged, besides supplying him with clothes during his apprenticeship, to admonish him to be zealous in advancing his master's interests, to be pious, industrious, and cheerful, to go regularly to church on Sunday, never to go out of the house without leave, day or night, to avoid all bad company, and to fulfil all the duties of a faithful apprentice.　Perthes went to his master at the Michaelmas fair.　He was happy in the family circle, particularly among the young ladies, who were very kind to him.

His chief occupation consisted in going to the other booksellers of the town for the books ordered from Böhme.　If he did not at once understand the titles, his master thundered out, " Don't you understand German ?" but his anger soon evaporated, and he sometimes celebrated a reconciliation by giving him fruit, or sharing his afternoon coffee with him.　The shop was never warmed ; when the master was cold, he stamped his feet and rubbed his hands, but Perthes' feet became frostbitten during the first winter, and his master took no pity upon him till he was no longer able to walk.　The doctor was then sent for, who said that had it been neglected twenty-four hours longer, the foot must have been taken off.　For nine weeks he was laid up in his attic, but his master's daughter Frederica, a charming child of twelve, took pity upon him. Knitting in hand, she chatted and read to him, and a warm friendship sprang up between them.　As may be imagined, the young apprentice in the strange flat town, often suffered from home sickness, when he thought of the hills of Schwarzburg, and when he heard the cowherd of Gohlis blowing his horn, it made him "feel quite curious." It was a great treat to him when his uncle Justus Perthes came from Gotha, and gave him a few groschen to go and see the menagerie, or took him with him to Raschwitz, where the booksellers of the Holy Roman Empire were assembled, and he was introduced to them. "What an honour I have had!" he said to himself, "such as no other of the apprentices can think of."

His mind gradually developed with his years, and his love for Frederica preserved him from the temptations of youth. The intimacy of childhood was replaced by the reserve of riper years. He tried hard to persuade himself that this affection would not lead to anything lasting, and sought to fill the void which this conviction left in his heart by means of friendship. Of his fellow apprentice, Rabenhorst, a well conducted, clever, and business-like youth, he said, "If it had not been for him, the world would have been a hell to me." About this time he became acquainted with some superior young men from Swabia, with whom he read the German poets, and whose friendship was very beneficial to him. He wrote to his uncle, "Yes, I feel a fire in my soul, and if this fire, which now warms me for other subjects, shall some day incite me to religion, perfection, and virtue, all self interest will be done away, and I shall love all men as brothers."

In these expressions we may trace his moral and religious aspirations. Finding that he had got sleepy over French and English grammar during the late hours which were alone at his disposal for self-culture, he took to books which nourished his inner life. He became a philosopher; sought into the grounds and motives of our actions, and formed a conception of the virtues which man should practise.

Perthes conducted himself during his apprenticeship so entirely to the satisfaction of his employer that, at Easter, 1793, half a year before his time expired, he allowed him to take a situation with the bookseller Hoffmann, of Hamburg. With gratitude to God, Perthes reviewed the years at Leipsic. "It was there," he wrote, "that my mind began to be formed, and to have a conception of the dignity of man. I have passed through many evil days, but they have all turned out for my good. When I came here I was a light-minded boy, with many, many faults. I have many still, but many have been corrected or lessened. I thank God for His goodness in putting so many incitements to good in my way, so that my frivolity could not get the upper hand."

When he came to Hamburg he was just twenty-one. There also he had to work hard, but found time to read the works of our great poets; and when at holiday times he gave himself up with cheerful companions to the enjoyment of youth, he tried to make these social pleasures subservient to the perfecting of the inner man. He gained access to the intellectual aristocracy of Hamburg, which assembled in the house of the Sievekings. But intercourse with three friends had a still more important influence upon him,—Speckter, Runge, and Hülfenbeck. They were deeply immersed in the streams of intellectual life which were then rushing through Germany, and they were interested in seeing how eagerly the young bookseller's assistant refreshed himself in their waves. There was something almost effeminate in his slender form, fresh complexion, and the delicate form of the eye, and yet they declared that the little Perthes had the most manly spirit of them all. He congratulated himself on his happiness, and said that he was "like a fish restored to its native element."

But while his pure and youthful mind was in this ferment, he had sufficient decision and circumspection to begin an independent course in business matters. With a young tradesman of Hamburg, and Nessig, a friend of his apprentice years, he founded a business which bore his name alone.

The bookselling trade was then in a very dull state, and Perthes, who thought more of extending intellectual life among the people than of his own gains, selected the bookselling instead of the publishing business. He undertook to obtain any book wherever published, and to deliver it in any place; and, in order to make a visit to his shop attractive, and to forward the interests of literature, he provided copies of every German periodical, and every work of general interest. The booksellers of the Holy Roman Empire, as the young apprentice had once called them, at first regarded with astonishment the young tradesman who, with cheerful confidence, introduced himself to their notice at the Easter fair of 1796. But the ready money with which his Hamburg friends had intrusted him soon helped him over all difficulties.

But it was a less easy task to stem a storm of passionate love which arose just as the little barque of his business was loosed from her moorings, and spreading her sails to the fair breeze. His partner, Nessig, was a rival in his affection for Frederica Böhme, and, with touching disinterestedness, Perthes had allowed him the first claim to her hand, thinking that there was no longer any passion in his love. But when he saw the maiden again at Leipsic, her charms reasserted their power over him. She was now to decide for herself. Her answer was, "I like Perthes and I like Nessig, but I cannot give my hand to either." Perthes felt petrified, and in this state of mind attention to business was a heavy burden. But he controlled himself, did all that was necessary, returned to Hamburg, hired a house in a busy part of the city, took his mother and sister to live with him, and opened his business in July 1796. With his lofty and intellectual conception of his calling, the young bookseller was soon brought into contact with many superior people in the neighbourhood, and in the country in general, and to some of these connections he owed the happiness which soon after bloomed for him. Not long after the opening of the shop it was entered by a distinguished looking man, of about fifty years of age, whose appearance at once inspired confidence. It was F. H. Jacobi, the philosopher, and at one time the centre of a most hospitable literary coterie at Pempelfort, near Düsseldorf. The French Revolution had now sent him northward, and he was living at the castle at Wandsbeck. The first meeting led to a lifelong friendship. He introduced Perthes to the house of Claudius, the author of the 'Wandsbecker Bote.' His eldest daughter, Caroline, though not strikingly beautiful, was pleasing in appearance, and an inner world of imagination, feeling, energy, and repose shone through her light blue eyes. She had been but little in contact with the outer world; had been devoted to domestic duties; had acquired a fair knowledge of languages from her father's tuition; and her beautiful voice contributed to the musical pleasures of the household. A correspondence with her friend, the Princess Galitzin, had directed her attention to the earnest questions of life, and the death of a little sister in the previous year had given her ardent longings for communion with Him who can save us from death. She saw Perthes for the first time in November 1796, and they were at once attracted to each other. At Christmas they met at Jacobi's house, and from that day his heart was decided, though it was not until April that she gave him a favourable answer. In July the betrothal took place, as an ecclesiastical ceremony according to the ancient custom of Holstein, and the Princess Galitzin and Count F. L. Stolberg were among the guests. When the pastor reminded the bride that once betrothed they could only be separated by the Consistory, she replied, " I have long been entirely decided, and for a long time past neither you nor the Consistory would have been able to separate us."

The day before the marriage Caroline wrote to Perthes, " I have been with the pastor to-day. The formulary that is to unite us is neither cold nor hot, neither ancient nor modern, but a disagreeable mixture of the two. But it will not hurt us, dear Perthes. We will ask God for his blessing after the old fashion, and He will bless us in the same manner. Join me in asking for it, dear Perthes, and open your arms wide and hold me fast till you close my eyes. I am yours, body and soul, and trust in God that I shall be happy."

And they did hold each other fast, differing, as they did at first, both in character and from habits of life; but without renouncing their individuality, their communion of spirit continually increased. Through Caroline's influence, Perthes was led to a greater desire for the peace of God, and she learnt from him to put the talent of her hidden life to interest, in the midst of practical activity.

This marriage led Perthes to seek for the pearl of great price, for the charm that attracted him in Caroline's character was derived from the grace of God.

The moral law was a schoolmaster to Perthes to bring him to Christ; and his ideal of spiritual life was a divine influence from the Father to lead him to the Son. He had always aspired to live not after the flesh but after the spirit, and it was needful that he should strive to attain this end with all his might, in order to discover that his own strength was not sufficient for it.

"My dear good uncle," he wrote at eighteen, "heavenly joys are attained by those who labour to improve themselves, and I have often enjoyed times in which, from the contemplation of the works and perfections of God, and from a feeling of my own dignity as a man, I have had a foretaste of the end for which we are destined." But at another time he said, "How often have I bewailed my perversity with tears in my eyes, when, after having resolved to be steadfast in the practice of good, I had fallen away because I could not conquer some passion. At these times everybody appears better than myself, even if they have committed actual crimes, while I have only sinned in thought, for I fancy that if others had the same impulses for good that I have, they would certainly be better than I am." His impulsive, excitable nature could find no satisfaction in the doctrine of virtue, in which merely the understanding is concerned, but when the good to which he aspired appeared to him in the garb of beauty, it gave him fresh zeal to strive to attain it. For this reason he was very fond of Schiller, who endeavours to show that the paths of virtue and beauty are the same. From Schiller, and from intercourse with his friends, his ideas of virtue increased in depth. It no longer appeared to him as the sum total of isolated actions, but as a condition of mind in which the avoidance of evil and the practice of good is a matter of course. But the higher the aim, the clearer became the impossibility of attaining it. "Perthes," said Speckter to him, "all your love is mere delusion, it only assumes the character of a nobler passion, because your feelings are refined and sensitive." Perthes felt compelled to acknowledge that he was right. It was only through Christian knowledge and faith that he could attain peace. What could neither be accomplished by reason, by the feelings, nor by beauty, was to be attained by the divine power of love, which condescends to man in order to lift him up. He witnessed the reflection of the divine light in the house of his father-in-law, in the circles of the pious Lutherans in Holstein, and the devout Roman Catholics of Münster, Reventlow, and Stolberg, Fürstenberg,

and the Princess Galitzin. He wrote to Jacobi,
" He only who is love can solve the problem of our
being, and of our deliverance." But he did not at
first see that it is in Christ alone that reconciling
and rescuing love is revealed to us.

He wrote to his wife, " That there is something
in me that lives, and will live for ever, I feel with a
certainty that words are inadequate to express ; but
I also feel that the immortal *ego* can only find satisfaction in love to God. To every one who is earnestly striving to attain this love, who falls down on
his knees in trembling prayer and thanksgiving, the
Lord will be merciful, even if he worships a piece of
wood, instead of the Crucified One. For since the
invisible is concealed from our view by the visible
world, everything that helps me to draw near to
God is a means of reconciliation, and not idolatry.
The evil principle rages within me, and is very
powerful. My prayers are only signals of distress,
and do not help me, for I am not like you, penetrated by the holiness of the Highest and with His
dazzling brightness ; but I am penetrated with you,
my saint, and through you I shall attain to that
higher love to which I cannot attain without medita-
tion."

But it was not long before Perthes learned that
redeeming love is revealed to us in no other way
than by Jesus Christ. He then wrote to his wife :
" My mental distress requires some one who will
give satisfaction instead of me, and an idea arises
in my mind of a desire for a God who, as man, has
felt the torments of humanity. I have leaned on
many a broken reed, and seen many a star fall from
heaven." The last step of knowledge was now

gained ; he had apprehended the great mystery, " God manifest in the flesh ;" he felt the truth of the saying, " Had Christ been born in Bethlehem a thousand times, but not also in thyself, thou wouldst have been lost eternally." He read the Scriptures with an ardent desire to grow according to his knowledge. He rejoiced in mercy, but was indefatigable in striving to work out the life that had been given him. There is something very edifying in observing how excellent men in that day gained their knowledge step by step, by earnest endeavour, aspiration leading them to knowledge, and further knowledge to more earnest aspiration ; while nowadays some renounce all effort to work out their inner life, content with the everyday experience of their outward existence ; while others, who do accept the proffered truth, accept it so lightly and superficially, that it is impossible to help doubting whether the confession with the lips arises from any real belief in the heart.

While Perthes had thus attained to clearness in his inner life, his business and family had prospered. The first partnership had been dissolved at the end of two years, but he entered into another with J. H. Besser, a man of excellent qualities of the heart, and of greater attainments than he himself possessed, especially in languages. The firm soon became one of the most highly esteemed in Germany. And the house was becoming daily more lively. By the year 1807 seven children had been born to him, of whom one only was lost. His happiness would have been complete, had it not been for the condition of his country.

Perthes' patriotism had never contented itself

with attachment to the little State in which he was born, he was devoted to the Emperor and the empire, and only saw happiness and freedom for the minor States in a great and united Germany. He therefore keenly felt the humiliation of his country, but he was among those who always believed in her renovation. A righteous indignation took possession of him, that some who bore great names in Germany, Goethe, for example, did not feel her ignominy more keenly. In 1804 he wrote to Jacobi, "Our hearts ought to be overwhelmed with shame at the disruption of our country. Instead of arming themselves, and acquiring strength and courage by nourishing this shame, they stifle their feelings, and produce works of art. If the best among us turn a deaf ear like this, our people will no more escape the fate of being vagabonds without home or country, than a sinner can hope for salvation who amuses himself with card-playing in order to escape the pangs of repentance."

But this view of the situation of Germany was only based upon external appearances; his faith perceived strength for a new birth in the midst of desolation. "Should not the fact that we live in this most evil time, stir up our hearts to great deeds?" he once exclaimed. When Austria was so signally defeated in 1805, Perthes urged Johannes von Müller, the historian, whom he would gladly have seen as the leader of all good Germans, to stir up Prussia to come to the rescue of Austria and of Germany. But it was too soon. In the autumn of 1806, Prussia first roused herself up. Not long after the battle of Jena, the French Marshal Mortier entered Hamburg. All intercourse with England was forbidden under pain of death, and the trade and prosperity of Hamburg annihilated for years, and the unbidden guests occasioned enormous expenses to the town by their shameless demands. Between November, 1806, and June, 1808, not less than 7,372,776 marks* were extorted.

About a year after the battle of Jena, Perthes wrote to Jacobi, "My mind becomes daily more free and firm, and so, happen what may, I am cheerful and full of courage. I am a frail mortal, I know, but not an unhappy one,—rather a very happy one, whose lot it is to live in stormy times. Much interest in life and death, much love, much sorrow, many children, many friends, much work and much business, much pleasure and much annoyance, little peace and but little money. Added to all this, a dozen Spaniards in the house, and for three days three gendarmes, who nearly drive me to despair." He often questioned with himself what would be the end of all this frightful overturning of everything. It was his opinion that " it was a necessity that some great power should arise in the midst of the universal weakness and degenerate selfishness of the times, and that it proved victorious, because there was nothing vigorous to oppose it.

" Napoleon is an historical necessity. This mighty spirit of the age is firmer and more secure than any one else, because he cares for nothing but himself; he is of the devil more than any one else, because he has in a greater degree than any one, made self his God." Perthes considered that the world was given over to this demoniacal being, in order that a new birth should arise amidst the terrors of judg-

* About £130,000.

ment. "God is guiding us into a new order of things," he said, "by the paths of trouble and distress. The game cannot be played backwards, and therefore it must go forwards. Let that fall which has not strength to stand. The actors in the great play are playing their parts, but behind the scenes is the great invisible Director, which is a comfort and support for us poor spectators, whose lot is bad enough."

He wrote to Jacobi, "Every support gives way, in order that we may learn to trust in God."

He was desirous of doing everything that was possible to prepare for the future rising in Germany. Before the battle of Jena, he laboured to form a secret alliance in Germany from the Alps to the sea. It was necessary at first to explain his object :—

"If it were once understood," he wrote, "and the way prepared, we shall perhaps, with the aid of the Highest, form an alliance for noble deeds. I have no fear of the spread of it, such a thing rolls rapidly along. But it must be kept together by a few simple, inviolable principles, and cemented by the united judgment of men of talent. The principles must not be printed, but communicated by word of mouth, and by means of correspondence."

When the rising of Austria in 1809 failed to lead to the overthrow of the French yoke, and Germany was not only trodden under foot, but torn in pieces, he set himself to consider how to cherish the sentiment of nationality as the last bond of union, and the first essential for the restoration of unity. By the establishment of a periodical, he hoped to afford the most eminent German patriots an opportunity for discussing learned questions. In the spring

of 1810, the 'Vaterländische Museum' appeared,
and was not only hailed with joy by the most eminent men of the time, but enriched by contributions distinguished by learning, patriotism, and in
a great measure by a Christian tone. Among the
contributors were Heeren, F. W. Schlegel, Arndt,
Reinhold and Jean Paul Richter, Claudius, Mar-
heinecke, Stolberg, and Fouqué. But the periodical
had but a very brief existence. The new Emperor
of the Franks, who regarded himself as the successor of Charlemagne, who is said to have founded
Hamburg, would have considered that he was doing
an injustice to the ancient city if it had not been in-
corporated with the new empire. Hamburg became a French department. The governor, Marshal Davoust, Prince von Eckmühl, made his entry. The 'Museum' no longer appeared, but the
alliance of Germans, which it had helped to cement,
continued.

Perthes managed to carry on his business under
the most difficult circumstances. The book trade
throughout the French Empire was embarrassed
by such a web of police restrictions and supervision as only a French or Napoleonic head was capable of inventing. Thus, if Perthes required a book
from Kiel or Göttingen, for example, or to send
one to any other place in the German States under
French rule, he had first to get a permit from Paris ;
and before the book could reach its destination it
had to run the gauntlet of a whole army of police
regulations. How was it possible for a business to
stand which maintained communication with the
old and new world, and particularly with Holland, the north-west of Germany, England, and the

north of Europe? Two courses were open, either to give in and to wait till the storm was over, or to hold up his head and do as much as was possible, with the dove-like harmlessness of an honourable man, and the serpent-like wisdom of a shrewd man of business. Perthes chose the bolder course.

He wrote to Jacobi, " My situation is very much altered, but in such a way, that notwithstanding the overthrow of my plans, my chief objects as a man of business will be forwarded. As for my inner man, the fulness of life and love has not diminished with years, and as I learn more self-control from day to day, I am able to devote my strength more to outward things, in order to attain the objects which my position places before me. Fear of God and courage among men are one and the same thing according to my philosophy and Christianity." And he infused his own courage into others. Fouqué wrote to him :—

" Your letter has baptized me with fire and water, with tears of the deepest melancholy, but at the same time with the fire of the firmest and most glowing faith and courage." And Niebuhr and Nicolovius, who had the pleasure of seeing their friend at Berlin in 1812, assured him that his visit had had a most strengthening effect upon all who had come in contact with him.

In the meantime the distress in Hamburg had reached the highest pitch, but with it came the hope of relief. Trade and commerce were almost at an end. Of 428 sugar refineries, only a few remained. Cotton printing was given up altogether.

New taxes were being continually invented and exacted with the utmost severity. The charitable institutions were robbed of their incomes, their existence was threatened, and landed property lost its value.

When Napoleon went to Russia, and report after report of victory was spread by the French bulletins, a cloud of melancholy hung over the city. Then all at once on the 24th of December, like a Christmas message of redemption, came the news, which Napoleon's twenty-ninth bulletin could no longer conceal, that the French army was buried beneath the Russian snows. Perthes was greatly excited by this news. Although a Te Deum had been ordered in the churches for the burning of Moscow, it appeared to him like the flames of judgment for the French, and a token of freedom for Germany. He consulted men in whom he could confide, and the question was agitated, whether the weak French garrison might not be driven away. The Swede Von Hess, a friend of Perthes, suggested the idea of arming the citizens. Perthes promoted it. Among the citizens was a plumber named Mettlerkamp, a courageous and decided character, and possessing much influence; he spread the idea of arming amongst his own class, and in a short time a thousand men were ready, and only waiting for the right time. This appeared to be near at hand, but in February the greatest part of the garrison was called to Magdeburg.

It was Perthes' wish that the revolt of Hamburg should be the signal for a general rising against Napoleon in north-west Germany; but to this end countenance in high quarters and a military leader were necessary.

Perthes wrote a request to the Duke of Oldenburg, whose name stood among the highest in Germany, that he would head the movement. While Perthes was on the road to convey the request to the duke, great changes were going on at Hamburg. The Russians were approaching. Caroline Perthes wrote to her father at Wandsbeck,—

"Yesterday morning the Cossacks were at Perleberg, seventeen miles from here. Oh, that I had a thousand tongues to sing, 'Benedictus, qui venit.' The city is all alive, and doubtless great events are before us. I cannot attain to peace or quiet in my room. May God help us further, and fill our hearts with praise and thanksgiving towards Him and towards men, and teach us to act according to His will."

On the 24th of February, the day before Perthes' return, the illwill of the people had already broken out in acts of violence; it was first expended on the custom-houses, then the sons of citizens who had been pressed into French service were set free, and the French eagle, the carrion bird as it was called, was everywhere torn down and trodden under foot. Hess and Besser called the citizens together, and urged them to assemble in the streets to protect the city from plunder. The French authorities, who began to feel uncomfortable, declared that they had no objection. The drums of the militia of the old free city resounded through the streets, and the people of all classes assembled under their former leaders. The following night Perthes returned, and convened a council of the most eminent men at his house. The French authorities agreed that 500 citizens should be armed, but jealousy among the leaders occasioned Perthes to propose that the companies should be disbanded, but the next day he assembled the most decided and trustworthy men in his house for drill. For a short time the French increased their vigilance. The most annoying house visitation was instituted. The prefect had a list of names made out of persons who were to be arrested, and Perthes was among them, but he took care to provide himself with a way of escape, should the hour of danger arrive. But the prefect had not the courage to carry out his orders. When he received instructions to be more severe, he hung himself, and though cut down before he was dead, he remained insane. He had announced that the Emperor would come himself, but instead of that the French took their departure on the 12th of March.

On the 16th, General Morand entered the little town of Bergedorf, only a few miles from Hamburg, and fears were entertained that it might fall into the hands of the enemy again, but Perthes and his friends were determined to oppose any attack by fostering the indignation of the people, which had reached its highest pitch; but the danger passed over.

Morand left Bergedorf, and on the same day 1500 Cossacks entered it, and thirteen of them appeared before the Steinthor at Hamburg. The commander of the Steinthor guard handed over the key of the gate to the leader of the Cossacks, exclaiming, ' Long live Germany and Russia.' The joy soon spread through the city. On the night of the 17th of March news came that the Russians under Tettenborn would enter the city on the following day, but as enemies if they found it under French authority, and the inhabitants joyfully declared themselves free from their rule. Tettenborn was hailed with acclamation.

Caroline Perthes wrote to her father, " My dear papa, how shall I describe the universal joy of old and young, rich and poor, bad and good! It is really a gift of God to have seen, heard, and felt it. Cries of joy burst from the lips of all, and my heart was thankful to God in Heaven and the Russians upon earth. Never, my dear papa, have I witnessed such a unity of feeling proceeding from thousands of hearts. If we could only be so united for the best objects, what a glorious church we should form! People who were before entirely disheartened took heart yesterday, and if the souls of men were more often stirred to their depths like this, I think it would have a good effect. I feel this deliverance more than I shall feel freedom itself, for freedom will not come in the same manner."

That night no guards were posted, no patrols paraded the streets, and the inhabitants went to rest, weary with joy and free from care, under the protection of God. But it was a short-lived repose. Immediately on the departure of the French, the senate seized the reins of government, but it was not easy to restore the old order. A volunteer corps, under the name of the Hanseatic legion, tes‑ tified to the desire of Hamburg to take a share in the deliverance of Germany, but the city which these her brave sons left behind was by no means in safety. A city militia was organized, and by the end of April 6000 men met for exercise, but arms, practice, and skilful leadership were wanting. Tetten‑ born, although a clever cavalry officer, was not fitted to unravel the complicated state of affairs which ex‑ isted in the old Hanse town. And on the other side of the Elbe, only separated from Hamburg by the river and a few islands, Vandamme and Davoust had already besieged Harburg, and were projecting re-taking Hamburg. In this time of danger Perthes' energy was untiring. In the first place, he had to collect funds to arm poor citizens, and provide for their families. Then he directed his attention to the Hanseatic legion. The confidence which he enjoyed occasioned his being entrusted with the supervision of the city militia, and he was made staff major. He had no military knowledge, but he was indefatigably energetic, prudent, courageous, and self-sacrificing. He laboured to foster unanimity, and to overcome petty and selfish considerations in the great cause of the fatherland.

The enemy had established himself on the islands of Wilhelmsburg and Feddel, and the bombardment of Hamburg began. Perthes had sometimes to calm down the impetuous Hess,—now to allay the terrors of the people, and to hurry from post to post to encourage the guards. For twenty-one nights he did not go to bed, and was only now and then in his house for half an hour. His brave wife had to perform her difficult duties without any help from him. She had sent the three youngest children to her mother at Wandsbeck, the four elder ones remained with her. People were always coming in and out and wanting food, and sacks of straw were placed in the large room for the weary to rest upon. Her anxiety led her out day and night upon the balcony to see if her husband or any of her friends were among the wounded, who were continually being carried by.

The danger was constantly increasing. Tettenborn could not hold the city long, Hess was not equal to the occasion, and the hopes which were placed upon the Swedes, Danes, and Prussians by turns all proved fallacious. On the 28th of May Perthes sent his wife and children to Wandsbeck, and they were hardly gone when the bombardment began afresh. The French took the island of Ochsenwärder. On the morning of the 29th of May they were before Hamburg without any great obstacle in the way. Perthes commanded the guard at the Steinthor. At midnight he received news that Tettenborn had withdrawn. Not to flee then would have been a useless sacrifice of the best men in the city to the French. At two o'clock in the morning he was with his family at Wandsbeck, and considered where to send them for safety. His friend Count Moltke had pressingly offered a refuge in the time of danger, and they were sent to Nütschau, an estate belonging to him, but, as the French were so near, it was necessary for Perthes to hasten on. He took a hasty leave, and proceeded during the night. Soon afterwards his wife, with seven children and another expected, accompanied by her sister and a servant, set out, weary to death, in a basket wagon.

She wrote afterwards: "It was a terrible parting. My mother was beside herself, my father deeply moved, the children wept aloud, I was petrified, and could only say continually, 'Now in God's name!'"

In the evening they arrived at Nütschau, near Lübeck, and, as there were only two beds for ten persons, cloaks and bundles of clothes were distributed in order that the children might, at least, have a pillow under their heads. They hoped to have seen Perthes the same evening, but he did not come.

He arrived on the 1st of June, but, as the neighbourhood of Lübeck was dangerous, he had to leave again immediately. The family followed, and on the 7th they met from different directions at Eckernförde, in Schleswig. Not far from this town, on the solitary shore of the Baltic, Count Caius Reventlow had a summer cottage. Here the family found a refuge, and rejoiced in the union of parents and children amidst the loss of all other possessions. On the 30th of May the French re-entered Hamburg. The city was outlawed, and Davoust was allowed to do what he pleased. Forty-eight million francs were demanded, and indescribable burdens were laid upon the city : even the bank was plundered. Perthes lost everything. His business was placed under seal, his other property confiscated ; and, after everything moveable had been taken from his house, a French general took possession of it.

Not long after his name appeared among the list of absentees who were declared to be outlawed. He had no ready money, either for himself or his creditors. He had saved his account books, and tried to reduce his affairs to order. He then joined in the conflict again, for only when his country was saved would he be able to build up his own house afresh. The parting was heartrending. His wife said, " With him, I think, I could bear anything, but without him I do not know what will become of me." But there was no help for it. On the 8th of July Perthes tore himself away from them under the dark shade of the fir trees in the garden. He wrote in his diary : " I am going out into the world again,—a new and unknown world, full of great shadows and much danger,—but my mind is earnest, cheerful, and full of courage. Submission to God, firm convictions and rich experience, a heart full of love, youth and health, truth, uprightness, and constancy of character,—these are ths results and value of my forty years of life. O God, my Lord, I thank thee! Forgive a poor sinner, and lead me not into temptation." At Kiel he met his friend Besser, and they drove together to Heiligenhafen on the Baltic, whence he intended going by water to Rostock. When Besser left him, it seemed to him like the closing of the last door, the screwing down of a coffin; still hope never forsook him. Contrary winds detained him nearly a week in the house of a fisherman. He read much in the Bible, and wrote to his wife: "The Gospel of St. John leads me back to myself. I examine myself strictly, and the conclusion I come to is, that I have been and am in God's hands, however I may have failed in keeping His temple pure."

At last the wind changed, and he crossed over to Warnemünde, and the sight of the waves gave him spirits. He was now in Mecklenburg. He collected a few debts, but needy as he was, that was but a secondary object, and his great desire was to find a point whence he could labour for his country.

His first care was for his fugitive countrymen, and he went hither and thither in order to get an idea of their situation. He soon found that money was indispensable to feed the hungry and provide arms for those who could bear them. Help came from England through Hess, and a society was founded for the proper application of the funds. Perthes' thoughts then turned to the condition of Hamburg, when it should be freed from the French. It was a time of ferment and reorganization. The importance of every State depended upon the value it put upon itself. But at that time Hamburg was annihilated as a State; it had no government to represent it among the powers of the earth, and was ready to fall a prey to any conqueror. The attention of Perthes was therefore directed to organizing a government for the Hanse towns. Not long before the return of the French, Syndicus Gries and Syndicus Curtius, of Lübeck, had been sent as ambassadors to the Crown Prince of Sweden, and were still looked upon by him as the representatives of those cities. Perthes proposed to them to unite with Mettlerkamp, the colonel of the city militia, Dr. Benecke, Dr. Sieveking, and himself, to form a Hanseatic Directory, as a representative of the cities among the leading powers engaged in the war. The plan succeeded, and although the recognition of the government was tardy, this did not hinder it from attending to the interests of the cities. Perthes was very anxious that the Hanse towns should prove themselves worthy allies of the other Germans in arms against Napoleon. But the Hanseatic legion, a noble troop as far as numbers went, but without pay, some of them barefoot and in rags, after wandering about in damp, cold, and mud, and without military discipline, were in danger of getting into confusion. Four-fifths of the legion were composed of noble and courageous young men, but the rabble that was mixed up with them gave the whole legion a bad name. " This must be remedied !" was Perthes' exclamations, "and, as God lives, I will not leave it alone, nor rest till the chaff is separated from the wheat, and I shall succeed."

On his representations, England took the legion into her pay, and, under the command of General Witzleben, it joined the hosts who were fighting for the freedom of Germany. After this matter was settled, the Hamburg civic guard, which was assembled in Güstrow, under Colonel Mettlerkamp, engaged his attention. Proclamations were put forth to induce others to join it; funds were provided, and Perthes headed them as major. It was owing to him that the citizens were permitted to try their strength in the struggle. He thought, " When the name Civic Guard is proclaimed before the gates of Hamburg, they will be opened, and all within will rise."

But after the expiration of the armistice, and the resumption of hostilities, General Vegesack sent the civic guard into garrison at Rostock, and refused, without the most urgent necessity, to expose a corps consisting almost entirely of fathers of families to the dangers of war. Then jealousy arose between the guard and the Hanseatic legion, and it was the part of Perthes to reconcile them. He proposed that they should be amalgamated, which was acceded to, and all difficulties were surmounted.

While Perthes was struggling for his country, his family were struggling to obtain the necessaries of life in the summer cottage on the shores of the Baltic. They had one living room and two bedrooms. Except Count Reventlow's bailiff, there was no human being within two or three miles. They could obtain nothing but milk and butter from him, everything else had to be fetched from long distances by the aunt and the children ; they had no white bread or meat in the house for eighteen weeks. The kitchen, so called, was forty paces from the house, and the cooking utensils consisted of four saucepans, a tin spoon, and a few plates.

The eldest child, Agnes, was just fifteen, the youngest, a boy in arms. Matthias, the eldest son, walked every morning to Altenhof, in order to receive instruction with the sons of the count, but the other children could not receive any teaching. An old servant remained faithful to them. A doctor would have been very welcome, owing to the frequent illness occasioned by the damp situation, but there was none nearer than Kiel, several miles off. The wife's greatest anxiety was about her husband ; her children, her greatest comfort. She wrote, " When I clasped my sweet Bernard in my arms, and looked into his bright young eyes, and saw that he feared nothing, and was not troubled about anything, but only loved me, and was happy, I found my support again, and prayed God to make me like my darling child."

But the father could not share this consolation. He wrote to his wife, " You are only separated from me, but I am parted from so many beings, to lose one of whom would break my heart. The sight of little children always brings tears into my eyes."

Yet he was fully convinced that he must stake life and property for the cause of truth and justice.

Meanwhile Tettenborn had entered Bremen, and Perthes was sent there to see that the cavalry general did not interfere too much with the civic power. All parties had confidence in him. " Do thou, O God, give me wisdom and understanding, and the courage of truth, and let me never forget thee," was his prayer. He strengthened the legion, by inducing the inhabitants of Bremen 'to join it. Then a new task was committed to him. It was necessary to protect the liberties of the Hanse towns from some of the reigning princes, who would have liked to incorporate them with their dominions, especially from the Crown Prince of Sweden and from Hanover.

The allied powers were at Frankfort, whither Stein, who was at the head of the reconquered German provinces, had followed them. To him the deputies of the Hanse towns, among whom was Perthes, were referred, and received not only from Stein, but also from the monarchs, the assurance that the Hanse towns should remain independent, and Perthes and Sieveking took back the welcome news to Bremen, and hastened to communicate it to Lübeck. There he received news of the birth of another son, Andreas. During the Christmas week he travelled towards Kiel, and in the dusk of the evening, after a separation of nearly six months, he unexpectedly rejoined his family. They spent a happy Christmas together, but on the 1st of January he had to leave them again, in order to bring succour to the thousands who were in the greatest distress.

The savage Davoust had nearly filled up the measure of his iniquities. As after the battle of Leipzig, he was more closely confined to Hamburg, he took pleasure in inflicting barbarities, to which his previous extortions were but trifling evils. It is impossible to describe the conflagrations, the devastation, the destruction of houses and gardens, the hunger, the cold, the wretchedness, with which

Hamburg was filled. The Crown Prince of Sweden sent means of help, and intrusted Perthes with the distribution of it. He took up his quarters at Flottbeck, a little beyond Hamburg, and exerted himself to the utmost. "The present is past help," he exclaimed; "May God help us in future!"

At this time he was in much sorrow about his family. He had left his little Bernard ill, the desire of his mother's eyes and joy of her heart, and his own delight when with them at Christmas. He was a child of uncommon beauty and promise. After several weeks' absence, Perthes cheerfully entered the room with "Are all well?" and the mother led him to the body of their darling child, and he gave way to the most bitter grief.

He remained but five days with them, weary in body and mind, and then hastened back to Flottbeck, to assist the miserable, until he succumbed to his excessive exertions. He had been thrown from a carriage, but had not been able to take care of his leg, which was injured. This accident, his great exertions during severe winter weather, the sight of the misery around him, and the loss of his child, all combined to break down his strength. He returned to his family with the germs of typhus fever in his constitution, and when his leg was examined, it was found to be broken. From February to April he was laid low.

When he recovered, the most lovely spring had burst forth, the German troops were marching victoriously through France, and Paris was in the hands of the allies.

Perthes and his family turned their steps homewards. At first they took up their quarters at

Blankenese, in order to await the course of events.
In the middle of May the French took their departure, and the Senate reassumed its duties. The
white banner streamed from Harburg and from the
tower of St. Michael's Church at Hamburg, and the
exiles streamed from all quarters into the city.
Perthes and his family now took possession of the
home which they had not seen for a year, but for
which he had so bravely exerted himself. It was in
an appalling state. The pleasant rooms on the
ground floor had been used for months as a guard-
room for French soldiers. In the middle of the
largest room was a huge fireplace. Trunks of trees
had been thrust in at the window, one end being in
the fire, the other out at the window, and the smoke
made its way out where it could. A French general
had occupied the upper story, but there also the
destruction was dire; all the woodwork had been
torn off for fuel, the dirt was a foot deep on the
floors, and all the furniture which had not been taken
care of by friends had fallen a prey to the French.
Much money would be necessary to make it fit for
habitation. Davoust had placed his seal upon the
books, and had given out that the creditors were to
pay to the French instead of to Perthes. But
Besser, with the help of a faithful servant, had con-
trived to save a good deal. They had now to make
a fresh start. Their well known uprightness pro-
cured them credit everywhere. A wealthy Jew
wrote to Perthes, " If I can in any way relieve you
from the petty cares with which you ought not to
be burdened, in order that you may be at liberty to
labour for good and noble objects, I shall be very
glad to do so. I do not require any special security;

a note from you is quite enough, and I beg you to repay me only at your convenience."

Perthes and Besser went cheerfully to work; in a short time all creditors were paid, and the business became a flourishing and important one.

Perthes had never regarded the book trade as merely a means of making money, but as an important instrument in promoting the intellectual life of the people. He now endeavoured to infuse into it the noble and patriotic spirit which had been fostered by the distress and deliverance of his country. He hoped that literature might prove a common bond, and lessen the antagonism between Austria and Prussia, North and South, Protestantism and Catholicism. But if this was to be the case, it was necessary that some evils in the trade should be reformed, and the greatest of these was the want of a law of copyright. What was required was a general law for the whole of Germany; for of what use, for instance, was Prussian protection when any work could be reprinted in Würtemberg with impunity? The subject had been already mooted at the Congress of Vienna by eighty-one important firms, and it had been resolved by the German Diet that attention should be given to the adoption of measures for the prevention of literary piracy as soon as possible.

Perthes drew up a memorial called "The German Book Trade as the condition of the existence of German Literature."

In the summer of 1816 he made a journey into South Germany, in the interests of this subject, and conferred with the most eminent statesmen, learned men, and booksellers. His object was to prepare watercourses by means of which the whole country might be irrigated by the fertilizing streams of German intellect.

Accompanied by his son Matthias he visited Bremen, Münster, Cologne, and Coblence, whence he visited Stein at Nassau, with whom the affairs of Germany, and especially those connected with the book trade were freely discussed. He then proceeded to Frankfort, Heidelberg, Stuttgard, Augsburg, Munich, Salzburg, and Vienna. In October they turned their faces homeward, visiting Perthes' native place, Rudolstadt, by the way. Here they had a narrow escape from drowning by the breaking down of a bridge over the Schwarza, and a few days afterwards reported their merciful preservation at Hamburg.

It is easy to recognize in Perthes' life how the troublous years of war had fostered Christian faith and charity, and after peace was restored they brought forth rich fruit. We have already spoken of the misery occasioned by the French occupation of Hamburg, and especially by the cruelty of Davoust. Many had perished through it, but the greater number returned after the departure of the enemy. But although restored to their native place, food, clothing, and shelter were wanting; and to remedy this state of things the city contributed large sums, the wealthy families did the same, and help was also received from distant places. But much depended on the proper distribution of the funds, and in consequence of Perthes' reputation for integrity and judgment, he was intrusted with the care of the poor. The memoranda of the distribution which were found among his papers indicate the variety of cases of distress, and the care that was exercised in the minutest details. Among the entries are, " Rent for a blind person, clothing for a girl to enable her to go into service, tools for a carpenter, medical treatment of a girl who had become insane when driven out of Hamburg, education of children whose friends had all perished, support of a widow whose husband had been shot by the French, rebuilding houses which Davoust had ordered to be burnt down, means to enable two industrious women to begin again a trade in fish," etc.

But man does not live by bread alone. Perthes had discovered through his intercourse with the people that they were suffering from more deeply seated evils than physical want. The Bible was very dear, and the people were very ignorant of it. In 1804 the British and Foreign Bible Society had been founded in England, and repeated efforts had been made for the establishment of a similar society in Germany. About this time Messrs. Steinkopf and Patterson came over from England to Hamburg and addressed themselves first to J. J. Rambach the well known writer of hymns, to Gilbert van der Smissen, a man well known to the religious world of that day, and to Perthes.

He interested himself in the subject with his usual aptitude and zeal. He did not care for the imputation of mysticism and pietism which was sure to attach to those who were zealous for a life and faith in accordance with the Bible, but openly introduced the subject to those who held the most important secular and ecclesiastical offices in Hamburg. He represented in a letter to the Mayor that Hamburg had received money from England at the time of her distress, and should not now reject the spiritual gifts which she was proffering, and offered his house for the first conference. He had the satisfaction of seeing the Hamburg and Altona Bible Society founded on the 19th of October, the anniversary of the battle of Leipsic.

The Bible Society brought Perthes into contact with many good men, and they did not forget that the mere circulation of the Bible was not enough, but that it was necessary to impress its contents on the hearts of the people.

The Duke of Holstein-Beck wrote to Perthes, "What can the Bible Societies effect alone if the work is not carried on in other ways? The Prussian church reforms are good, and do not reject the good with the bad like the edicts of Frederic William II. For a spirit of devout piety appears to prevail at present in Prussia, from which much good may be expected if it is nourished by a good liturgy, and good modes of worship; but God grant that we may not be subjected to a new sacrificial service, or a theatrical style of worship. But of what avail will new liturgies, church reforms, and the Bible Societies be altogether, if more care is not bestowed upon the schools, and more pains taken in them to inspire the scholars with love for the religion of Christ, a desire for His word and respect for His servants? It is pitiful in the country to see the children the whole summer tending the cattle in the fields, where they forget all the little they have learnt at school. Besides this, in most of the country schools they learn scarcely anything, and what they do learn is only words not things. When they leave school they learn nothing more of the word of God, for the country people, as well as most of the townspeople, consider it useless, and even ridiculous to go to church. This state of things must be mended." Such words found a ready response in the mind of Perthes. His desire was not only to free the people from a foreign yoke but to deliver them from mental bondage by means of Christian civilization. It was his wish to put good religious instruction in their way, and he considered popular writings an excellent means of doing this.

It was at that time the opinion of the most superior men that the Christian and patriotic spirit should be cherished together among the youth and the people in general.

When Napoleon was dethroned the second time a friend wrote to him : " Are not the bells to-day imploring prosperity for the cause of Germany ?   Is not this the right moment to make a special collection for the poor ?"   Perthes accepted the challenge to take the first step.   He wrote to Fouqué : " We collected 30,000 marks* at once for the instruction of poor children, and hope to get more.   We twelve have now gone through the city, and what numbers of fine children we have found ! God's blessing still rests upon our people. We have already taken charge of 700.   In this age, when everything is regarded in a general kind of way, and human beings are reckoned up like the figures in a sum, such a business is very salutary."

The subject of schools for the poor, which afterwards excited great interest at Hamburg, may be said to have received its first impetus from the collections made for them at this time. Another form

* £1750.

of Christian charity which is still pursued with great
zeal at Hamburg may be traced to this period,—the
labours of the associations of ladies. Perthes wrote
of them as follows : " The associations arose in the
time of great distress, from the just feeling that
when the men and youths were facing death it was
the part of women to succour the helpless. Twice
within a short period these associations have nobly
fulfilled their objects, and we may now trust to
woman's innate feeling and unfailing sense of truth,
that she will also fulfil her vocation in time of
peace, which may God preserve to us ! We Germans, as well as other nations, have gone through a
long and painful apprenticeship : first, a half century of neglect, of shallowness, and mistaken effort ;
then twenty-five years of revolution, war, and confusion. During this period, through the abolition
of monasteries, and the destruction of property belonging to hospitals, poor houses, and orphan
houses, the last remains of the pious institutions of
our ancestors have been annihilated, and their place
has not been supplied either by gift or will. Here
is an endless field of usefulness for women accustomed to works of charity. The associations will
at first work each in its own sphere and place, but
they will soon unite and diffuse a wide blessing as
an alliance of German women. Abundant gifts will
be intrusted to them, for pious souls will, as in
former times, endow them with the means of carrying out their own wishes, and the new institutions
will fare better in the hands of women than under
the protection of men."

These labours of love on behalf of those afflicted
in mind and body have never ceased at Hamburg.

The same city in which Perthes strove to assist the distressed has since given to Germany Amelia Sieveking, the "Hamburg Tabitha," and Dr. Wichern, the father of the Rauhe Haus.

From public life, and these endeavours to relieve the sufferings of humanity, Perthes always turned with delight to his home.

Caroline did not hinder his public activity, her own heart beat too warmly for her country; but her patriotism and faith, and all the gifts with which God had endowed her, shone most brightly in the domestic circle. She had an acute mind and a warm heart; and though her mental powers were highly cultivated, her character was thoroughly simple, and in her fresh and child-like, yet deep and lofty way of looking at life, she was a feminine likeness of her father. Towards God her heart was all thankfulness, and towards man it overflowed with love.

She wrote with Christmas presents to her married daughter and her husband: "Now let us rejoice, and thank God from our hearts, and confide ourselves, and all dear to us, with full trust to His hands. We shall gladly accept your help here to make us thankful. Read that hymn in the name of us all—

"Oh, if I had a thousand tongues!"

"Singing is a great help when we do not know how to give vent to our feelings. This is often my case when I review our twenty-five years." At another time she wrote: "Love always prospers when it is the prevailing feeling, whether in doing or suffering. It is the miracle of miracles, and the only thing which I think of as eternal, for everything else awakes terror when I think of its being perpetuated to eternity."

The love between Perthes and Caroline was always like that of a bride and bridegroom, and those were golden hours when, in the spring, after the cares of the day, they could escape from the city, and take a walk together.

Since the painful experiences of 1813 Caroline's health had not been good. Before she reached the age of fifty she was taken from the blooming circle of her beloved ones, but not before she had seen two daughters happily married, embraced a grandchild, and had accompanied her eldest son on his entrance on his academical career with her prayers and her invaluable advice. She celebrated the last anniversary of her betrothal day with fresh and joyful affection.

"To-morrow is my beloved 1st of May," she wrote, "and I should like to go far among the woods and hills with my dear bridegroom, where I should neither see nor hear any other human being, and thank God that, after twenty-four years, I can celebrate this day with such thorough pleasure. A few sighs would, no doubt, escape me by reason of my shortness of breath; but they would not last long, and I should rejoice afresh continually. Yes, in the green woods I should like to be, but my view here of the blue water, and the sky covered with little clouds, through the young leaves is so pleasant, that when I think of it, it is a shame to wish for anything different. I think we have never had such a luxuriance of beauty in spring,—trees and grass and flowers are indescribably beautiful. And this great change from death to life has come to pass in a few days, I might almost say hours. When one beholds this delightful spring, and gazes on the light green of the trees against the clear heaven, it is almost impossible to believe that there can be so much distress and sorrow amongst and around us. Yes, spring is a joyous time, and, when I have no child ill, it carries my thoughts forward to that land where we cannot imagine any more pain or sorrow." And she was soon permitted to enter it. On her wedding day, 2nd August 1821, she took a walk, although with difficulty, with her dear bridegroom, in the meadow at Wandsbeck. Afterwards she spent an invalid life for a few weeks at Hamburg, and on the 28th of August she died so suddenly that no parting word or look was granted to those around her.

Perthes committed her to God's keeping, but preserved her memory in his heart. He wrote to his daughter, " Grief does not make me spiritless; I wish to make up for the loss of her love, and to help those around me as far as possible;" and through the strength of his affection he seemed still to hold communion with the departed. " She knows now how and in what I have erred, which she could not know on earth, but she also knows the depth of my love. That she knows me now entirely, and helps me to trust in God at all times, and to walk as in His presence, I fully believe because I cannot help it, although I know that this faith has never been revealed to us in any definite form."

It had been always Caroline's most ardent wish to be able to live somewhere with her husband in peace and quietness. But it was not till after her death that he was able to leave the business at

Hamburg in the hands of Besser. In 1822 he removed to Gotha. Two daughters were married
there, and four children were still around him. His
object was to establish a publishing business, but
the leisure which he now enjoyed was not devoted
to business alone ; in order to qualify himself to carry
it on with a view to the highest interests, at fifty
years of age he devoted himself to a wide range of
study, and it was quite in accordance with the
mighty influence of the war of independence that
he published chiefly religious and historical works.
The great conflict of nations, the struggle for national existence, had re-awakened interest in history,
and the sense of religion had been revived by the
experience of human powerlessness and the marvellous help of God. The Bible was by no means
neglected in Perthes' studies; and if in reading it,
many difficulties presented themselves, he had the
right key to the comprehension of it as a whole in
his own need of salvation. "It is only at those
times," he said, " that the meaning of the holy
Scriptures is revealed to us, when we seek to find
in them the means of reconciliation with God, and
help in the conflict with the flesh and the pride of
our hearts." He discovered that it is not chiefly in
the flesh that the devil has his seat, but in the
spirit, by fostering selfishness, pride, and hatred ;
and therefore it was his opinion that the essence of
Christianity did not consist in the abnegation of the
powers given us by God, or in cowardly flight from
the world, but he wished to see human nature renewed in body, soul, and spirit, and in mixing with
the world it was his desire to salt it with the savour
of the divine life. But with deep humility he ac-

knowledged the little progress that he made, and
the need of maintaining the conflict to the end.

To his son, who was pursuing his studies, he
gave advice which he found it constantly necessary
to follow himself, "We must act and suffer, but we
must act and suffer in a spirit of love. When this
spirit has forsaken us, and we have been guilty of
harshness towards others, or of sensuality ourselves,
or of want of humility towards God, we ought to
feel our need of the atonement of Jesus Christ. We
shall have to struggle to the end. If we have escaped the coarser and rougher forms of sin, we shall
still be hourly assailed by it in its more subtle and
refined aspects. This world is not the place for repose after the victory; we must struggle and love,
and trust to the mercy of God."

The same religious and moral earnestness was
also displayed in his calling, and he at once took an
honourable place among his colleagues. He kept a
select assortment of books, especially religious and
historical works. As far as was in his power, he
laboured to forward the revival and deepening of
German theology which had been the result of recent events, and he published the works of modern
theologians, such as Schleiermacher, Lücke, Ull-
mann, Umbreit, and Tholuck. This, and the weight
of his character, brought him constantly into contact with men of mark, and he took the most lively
interest in the general development of his country.

He felt most painfully the solitude in which he
lived, when his third daughter Matilda, who had
kept his house, was married.

About this time Rebecca Claudius, the mother of
his departed Caroline, visited him, and she advised

him to seek a partner for the remainder of his life.
God led Charlotte Becker to him, a widow whom
he had previously befriended in heavy trials, and
the sister of his son-in-law. In May, 1825, the
marriage took place. Seven children were left to
him of the first marriage, and four were given him in
the second. New joys and sorrows awaited him. The
loss of the only son of the new family threw him
into the deepest grief, for he had never before been
able to live with a child and to watch its development,
as he had done with this one. It made him feel that
the evening of his own days was drawing near. He
became more indifferent to the toil and endeavour
of life, and often when pacing up and down his
room, he would exclaim, " My Rodolph, my Rodolph,
where and what art thou now ? " He had chosen a
pleasant retreat for his latter days at Friedrichsroda,
a few miles from Gotha. He delighted in spending
the summer months there with his family, and in
roaming among the Thuringian hills and woods.

Many honours had been awarded him ; he was
adorned with the ribbon of an order, the University
of Kiel had made him a Doctor of Philosophy, and
Leipsic had presented him with the freedom of the
city, but he prized more than any other earthly
honour the freedom of the little town of Friedrichsroda, presented to him by the mayor and corporation. A monument placed there by the family,
still marks the spot near the town where Frederic
Perthes, in the screne evening of his days, loved
to wander, and to listen to the voice of God among
the hills.

On the 1st of January, 1843, Perthes wrote in his
diary, " From the state of my health, it does not

seem likely that I shall write 1844." He suffered from liver complaint and jaundice. By the end of March his strength seemed to have failed entirely, and he arranged everything for his last journey. In those times, when he had had to maintain a perpetual strife with his impetuous spirit, the Epistle to the Romans had been his favourite portion of Scripture; now it was the Gospel of St. John. The parting addresses in the 14th, 15th, and 16th chapters, and the prayer of the Great High Priest in the 17th, afforded him the strongest consolation.

On his birthday, the 21st of April, he was so peaceful and cheerful among the spring flowers in his chamber, that those around him could not but share his serenity.

"When I am dead," he said, after speaking of the mercy of God, "do not mourn for me; I am quite ready to die, and shall die in peace."

> " I've given myself to God, how dear
>   My Father and my Friend!
> There is no life for ever here,
>   All things of earth must end.
> Death has no power to harm,
>   'Tis welcome to my heart;
> If God upholds me with His arm,
>   I shall with joy depart."

During the last few weeks of his life this beautiful deathbed hymn was often on his lips, and he frequently exclaimed :—

> " What heavenly joy and blessing,
>   E'en now await me there!
> For Jesus' love possessing,
>   His blessedness we share.

> Then what can hurt me or alarm,
> 　Christ's peace is in my heart;
> If God uphold me with His arm,
> 　I shall with joy depart."

But the exclamation that most often escaped him was, "God be merciful to me, a sinner, for His dear Son's sake."

Many painful days were before him. Erysipelas set in, and occasioned fearful suffering, and the opiates that were given him to still it, obscured his mental powers. "O Lord, if I could only weep!" he exclaimed; and "Lord, Lord, lead me not into temptation!"

But faith would triumph again, and once when those around him thought that he was in an unconscious slumber, he began in a low and touching voice :—

> "The hour of death draws nearer,
> 　Oh, world, why should I live?
> The joys of Heaven are dearer,
> 　Than aught that thou canst give.
> I have no earthly care, but calm
> 　And ready for the start,
> God will uphold me with His arm,
> 　I shall with joy depart."

At another time he said, "Herder, on his death-bed, asked for one more idea; 'Light, light!' was Goethe's exclamation; it would have been better for them if they had asked for humility and love."

From this time, though his body became weaker, his mind was not again entirely obscured; his affection for those around him burned brighter and brighter, and he rejoiced with ever increasing confidence in his Saviour. "God be praised," he exclaimed, in a low voice, "my faith is firm, and stands fast in death as well as in life. God is merciful to me, a poor sinner, for the sake of His dear Son." On the 18th of May, the doctor told him that he would soon be released. His whole soul was given to prayer, even when he could not pray aloud, and in the afternoon he repeated in a firm voice :—

> "Ye loved ones, bless the Lord for me,
>   And wipe away your tears ;
> You must not weep, for I am free,
>   From sorrow, pain, and fears.
> Steer for the port where storms shall cease,
>   Watching with stedfast heart,
> Then God will fill you with His peace,
>   You shall with joy depart."

In the evening his breathing became slower and more difficult, but he was quiet and without suffering. He prayed aloud for an hour, but with an indistinct utterance, so that only the words "Redeemer," "Lord, pardon," were intelligible.

When a light was brought in, it was evident that a great change had passed over his features, and the last words which caught his dying ear were—

> "What heavenly joy and blessing,
>   E'en now await me there,
> For Jesus' love possessing,
>   His blessedness we share."

One long last breath, one last look of pain, and he had overcome.

He was buried on the 22nd of May, and the favourite hymn quoted above was sung over his grave.

In his life and death he had shown the German people that faith is a living and mighty power, that, to
use the words of Luther, it can make of poor de-
jected sinners, " brave and blessed men who care
neither for the devil, nor for the world, nor for any
misfortunes that can happen to them."*

* ' Perthes, Leben von Clemens Perthes,' 3 Bände.   Gotha : bei
Andreas Perthes.

CHAPTER V.

FREDERIC LEOPOLD STOLBERG.

THE repugnance which Stolberg's conversion to the Roman Catholic faith excites in the minds of Protestants, must not prevent us from recognizing in him one of the foremost representatives of the German mind and its conflicts, at the end of the last and the beginning of the present century, and especially one who advanced the cause of Christianity during a time of general religious declension.

Forty years after he had made a tour with him in Switzerland, Goethe, in conversation with Sulpiz Boisserée, spoke of him as the hero among the proselytes of his day, and expressed his admiration of "his natural character, his magnanimous spirit, the wealth of his human interests."

We must accord him a place among our heroes,—the promoters of religious life,—because he looked at the great events passing around him from a German and Christian point of view, and his religious writings met the wants of those, especially of his own rank, whose minds were opened to receive the message of salvation.

We should be guilty of unfairness if, in portraying the newly awakened religious life at the time of the wars of independence, we were to ignore the tendency which then existed in the Roman Catholic Church in Germany, to turn to the essential and intrinsic doctrines of religion. This tendency cannot be better illustrated than in the character of Stolberg, who took into it a valuable inheritance from the Protestant Church of heartfelt faith, derived from the Bible and founded upon Christ.

Count Frederic Leopold Stolberg-Stolberg was born on the 7th of November, 1750, of an ancient noble family, at Bramstedt, in Holstein. His father, Count Christian Gunther, then warden of the district under the Danish Government, was a branch of the numerous race of Saxon Counts of Stolberg, many of whom were distinguished for their piety. His mother belonged to the Franconian family of Counts of Castell, which boasts of having once given a wife to Charlemagne.

During the whole of his life, Stolberg was distinguished by a strong consciousness of noble birth, but he regarded it as conferring responsibility as well as privileges. His love for his fellow-creatures never forsook him ; and he was not more influenced by the prejudices of his class than his early friend and subsequent opponent, Voss, who assailed him so mercilessly on his change of religion, in his pamphlet, ‘ How was it that Fritz Stolberg became a slave ?” was influenced by the prejudices of the burgher class.

When Frederic Stolberg was six years of age, his father removed to Copenhagen, having been appointed Danish privy councillor and Lord High

Steward to the widowed Queen Sophia Magdelena. To him belongs the merit of being the first nobleman who emancipated his serfs, on his estate of Bramstedt, and, at his suggestion, those on the queen's estate of Kirschholm were also set at liberty. The elder Bernstorf, then Danish minister, following the example of his friend Stolberg, alleviated the condition of the serfs upon his estate of Bernstorf, near Copenhagen, and thus paved the way for the entire abolition of serfdom in Denmark, which was carried out under Bernstorf the younger.

It was in such an atmosphere of humanity and freedom that Frederic Leopold and his elder brother, Christian, grew up ; they lived mostly at a distance from the capital, upon an estate near the sea, the shores of which are clothed with splendid beech woods. Klopstock was an intimate friend of the house, and not only called forth enthusiasm in the minds of the youths for the fatherland and the 'Messiah,' but incited them to fearless riding, and especially to skating.

Count Christian Gunther died suddenly of apoplexy, at Aix-la-Chapelle, in 1765 ; and the friendship of Klopstock was afterwards especially valuable to the widow. He once found the brothers reading a French translation of Cicero's letters, and reproved them for it so sharply that they made strenuous efforts to attain the power of reading the Latin authors in the original. Besides Klopstock, the court preacher and hymn writer, Cramer, assisted the mother in the Christian education of her sons ; as did also the tutor of Cramer's family, Funk, himself an author of hymns, and afterwards councillor of consistory at Magdeburg. Stolberg says himself, " In-

structed in the Scriptures from childhood by God-
fearing parents, I early became fond of them, and
never neglected to read them." Their tutor, Clauswitz, laid a good foundation of useful knowledge in
the minds of the brothers, of whom Leopold was
distinguished for ardour and imagination.

With all the ardour of youth he read German
poetry, the spirit of which was then reviving.
Klopstock read his 'Hermann's Schlacht' to them
before it was printed; and at a striking passage,
Frederic Leopold began to weep, and, full of deep
emotion, pressed the poet's hand. Klopstock was
also moved, and said, as he returned the pressure,
" My boy, this approbation gives me more pleasure
than the praise of all Germany."

In the spring of 1770, these hopeful and aspiring
youths went to the University of Halle, accompanied
by their tutor. Neither philosophy nor jurisprudence,
as then taught, had much attraction for them. The
Muse gave them compensation, and furnished a pretext for their contempt for the wisdom emanating
from the chairs of the professors. In the recesses,
besides visiting their friends at home, they made an
excursion to the Hartz mountains, and to the ancient seat of their forefathers at Wernigerode. One
of the best of Frederic Leopold's poems, the ode to .
the Hartz mountains, dates from this period. A
spirit of Klopstock may be traced in it, but there is
a precision in the form to which Klopstock does not
always attain.

With these poetical tastes, both counts went in
the autumn of 1772 to Göttingen. The sons of the
German nobility flocked to this university, but by
no means with the object of cultivating the liberal

arts. It was the school of conservatism, the seat of historical lore and jurisprudence. The ancient German empire flourished under the fundamental knowledge of its history and laws, as taught by such men as Pütter and Schlötzer at Göttingen. He whose birth entailed upon him the prospect of being one day ruler or minister of one of the hundreds of German States within the compass of the empire, could obtain at Göttingen an insight into the involved relations and manifold diversity of the German constitution and laws. But the Counts Stolberg felt no such necessity laid upon them. No sooner had they arrived at Göttingen than they were strongly attracted to a little set of youths of the burgher class who did homage to the Muses, and to Professor Heyne who was profoundly versed in Homer. These youthful poets, among whom were Hölty and Voss, had already united themselves into a society called the " Hainbund."

On the 12th of September, 1772, during a walk to a neighbouring village, they discovered what they called the national oak of Braga.* They wreathed their hats with oak-leaves, and then, forming a circle round the tree, called moon and stars to be witnesses of their league. Their aim was to be brave sons of their country, to serve it by the practice of religion and virtue, by the love of freedom, truth, beauty, and noble song.

The brothers Stolberg, having grown up in intimacy with Klopstock, and being fired with enthusiasm, were doubtless very welcome additions to this circle, and must have found themselves much at home in it. Voss wrote soon after making their acquaintance :—

* Braga, the god of poetry among the ancient Germans.

"What nice people the Counts Stolberg are! It is
not very common to find among the landowners
and the great, with their Frenchifying tendencies,
people of even moderate taste; but to find, among
this class, people of the most refined sensibilities,
with the noblest hearts that beat for God and their
country, with great poetic talent, and without a particle of pride,—people, in short, who are loved and
valued by Klopstock,—is really a great discovery."
And of Frederic Leopold he says, "I am not proud
of being loved by a count. No; but that my friendship is valued by a German, a gentleman, a poet,
and a friend of Klopstock."

The attention of the brothers at this time was
chiefly occupied with poetry; they troubled themselves very little with jurisprudence, but zealously
studied Greek. One and another of the league occupied himself with the old German Minnesingers,
but Klopstock was regarded as the patriarch of it.
On the 2nd of July, 1773, his birthday was celebrated with great solemnity. Klopstock's chair,
adorned with roses and carnations, stood at the
head of the long table, also decorated with flowers;
on it were placed the works of the poets, while under the chair lay Wieland's 'Idris' torn up. "Cramer," relates Voss, "read some of Klopstock's
odes having relation to Germany; then we took
coffee, and made lighters for our pipes out of Wieland's writings. Even Boie, who did not smoke,
was compelled to light one and to stamp upon the
torn 'Idris.' Afterwards we drank, in Rhine wine,
to the health of Klopstock, the League, Ebert,
Goethe, and Herder, and to the memory of Luther
and Hermann. Klopstock's 'Ode to Rhine Wine,'

and some others, were read. Conversation then flowed freely. With hats on, we talked about liberty and Germany and virtue; you can just imagine how. Then we supped, and finally burnt Wieland's 'Idris' and likeness. Whether Klopstock has heard of our doings, or only guessed at them, I do not know; but he has written to ask for a description of the day."

This happy intercourse did not last more than a year; on the 12th of September, 1773, the anniversary of the formation of the league, they celebrated a parting festival. Overflowing spirits were exchanged for floods of tears. It was midnight when the Stolbergs arrived, and the friends remained together for three hours in a state of mind bordering on frenzy. Frederic Leopold's countenance was torn with conflicting feelings; he tried to look cheerful, but every gesture betrayed melancholy. A parting song was struck up, but their voices were choked with tears. They vowed eternal friendship, and sent greetings to Klopstock. The clock struck three. Voss says, " We then gave full vent to our grief, and tried to enhance it by singing the song again, but were scarcely able to get through it, and broke out into loud weeping. After a dreadful pause, Clauswitz rose up and said, ' Now, my children, it is time to go.' I flew at him, and do not know what I did, but when I had let him go the counts had disappeared. Some of us rushed down the stairs after them, but they had torn themselves away."

The brothers returned to Copenhagen, and lived in the house of their brother-in-law, the younger Bernstorf. In December, 1773, they lost their mother.

They occupied themselves much with Greek, and
Frederic Leopold continued to strike his German
lyre. Some of the best known of his lyrics date
from 1774. Still imbued with the spirit of the
Hainbund, in 1775 they made a tour in Switzerland.
They spent a fortnight at Hamburg, in true Hainbund fashion, with Klopstock, Voss, Miller, and
Claudius. They had announced their intention of
coming to Frankfort to Goethe, whose acquaintance
they had only previously made in the Göttingen
'Almanack of the Muses;' but he was already carrying on the correspondence with their sister Augusta, though they had never met. At Frankfort
they met their friend Haugwitz, afterwards Prussian minister of unenviable notoriety, on account of
his cowardly policy. But now they did not anx-
iously weigh the moral standing of individuals. It
was, as Goethe said, "the joyous season of youth;
they opened their hearts to one another, and, although their mental powers were immature, much
talent was displayed." The brothers and Haugwitz
lived at a hotel, but spent most of their time at the
house of the imperial councillor. At his hospitable
table the young nobles soon disclosed their poetical
hatred of tyrants, and declared that they thirsted
for their blood. Goethe's father laughingly shook
his head, and Mme. Goethe went into the well-
stored cellar, and, bringing up some of her best
wine, exclaimed, "This is the true tyrant's blood;
take your fill of it, but do not let us have any talk
of assassination here."

Goethe determined to accompany them on their
journey. Frederic Leopold hoped that it would heal
the wounds made by an unfortunate love affair, and

Goethe wished to make the experiment whether he could cure himself of his first deep passion, and do without Lili. Merck did not at all approve of Goethe's going with them, and said, "Your going with these youths is a foolish affair. Your aim, and the whole tendency of your mind, is to clothe reality in a poetical garb ; their aim is to realize the poetical, which is sheer nonsense."

Goethe, nevertheless, went with them.

Their stay at Zurich has a special interest, for Lavater, whose enthusiasm for physiognomy was then at his height, took a warm interest in the counts, and took their shadow portraits. The judgment he passed upon Frederic Leopold is certainly not one of the least correct. "Behold the blooming youth of five-and-twenty ! A hovering, floating, elastic being, too lively for repose, not solid enough to stand firm, not strong enough to fly. In the whole outline there is not a single straight line, no firmly arched one, no angular indenture, no rocky prominence in the forehead, no hardness, stiffness, or roughness,—no dominant power, no iron courage,—though there may be courage under excitement,—no searching depth, no patient investigation, no prudent circumspection. He will never stand with the sword in one hand and the scales in the other, yet there is the most perfect rectitude and inviolable love of truth. He is not the man whose penetration will discover, or whose ready recognition will develope new truths. He will ever be floating in space ; a seer, an idealist, one who longs to beautify everything ; to clothe all his ideas in form. A half intoxicated poet, who sees that which he wishes to see." Lavater also said of him to Goethe, "I do not know what you are all thinking about; he is a noble minded, excellent, talented young man, but you represented him to me as a hero or a Hercules, whereas I never saw a more gentle, flexible person, or one more easily influenced."

The travellers pursued their journey amidst the charms of Swiss scenery, after the fashion of men of genius, in that sense of the term which for a long time brought genius into discredit with rational people. Goethe left the Stolbergs in Switzerland, but they rejoined him at Weimar, and the duke offered Frederic Leopold the post of chamberlain at his poetical court. The decision was an important one. Such a character would have been lost in the atmosphere of Weimar; but it was not God's purpose that he should pass from the romantic ardour of youth into a region of cold and intellectual unbelief, but into one of living Christian faith. Klopstock was his good genius. He wrote to Goethe, "Stolberg shall not come if he listens to me, or rather if he listens to himself."

We have purposely described Stolberg's student years somewhat circumstantially. Our sketches would have been incomplete without recalling the spirit of the Hainbund. In the blooming gardens of patriotism during the times of the wars of independence, there was many a flower, the seeds of which were sown by Klopstock and his disciples. Stolberg's youthful enthusiasm for freedom and the fatherland was like a prophecy, which was fulfilied in the days of Germany's struggle for her glory and greatness, against French tyranny. By the year 1813 the fermenting juice was changed into clear and sparkling wine.

In 1776 Frederic Leopold Stolberg received, through the interest of the Duke of Oldenburg and the Archbishop of Lubeck, the office of ambassador and lord high cup-bearer at the court of Denmark, with a salary of 3000 dollars,* and after a journey to Eutin, where he spent some weeks with Klopstock, he took up his residence at Copenhagen. An incident at this period indicates the religious sentiments with which he contemplated important steps in life. Not long after his appointment his birthday occurred. Twenty-four years afterwards he related, " The day induced me to think of my sins, and I seized the Bible and prayed God Himself to direct me to a suitable passage. And behold when I opened it my finger lighted on the words, ' Then spake the chief butler unto Pharaoh saying, I do remember my faults this day.' All must acknowledge that in the whole Bible no passage could have been found more adapted on that day and year to my circumstances external and internal, and as I believe in God's help, I consider that it happened to me through Jesus Christ our Lord."

The ambassador was not much occupied with political affairs, and had abundant leisure to begin a congenial task, in which, however, he was soon rivalled by his friend Voss, the translation of the Iliad into German hexameters, and his own lyre was not neglected. The translation was completed in two years, and was given to Voss for publication, that the profits might assist him in establishing his home.

Stolberg was now thirty years of age. He had hitherto found much pleasure in his love for his fellow men, and in the society of congenial friends,

* £337.

but domestic happiness was still wanting. In the summer of 1781, he met at Eutin with a young maid of honour at the court there, Agnes von Witzleben, a charming maiden, in whose character tender sensibility was combined with a fine understanding. They were soon betrothed, and life opened before them with a bright prospect of love and friendship. Stolberg now fulfilled his duties as lord high cupbearer at the court of Eutin instead of at Copenhagen, and in June the marrige was celebrated.

During the following winter, through Stolberg's influence, Voss received the appointment of rector at Eutin, and the days of the Hainbund were renewed in the daily intercourse, and poetical labours of the friends. They together prepared for publication the poems of their early lost friend, Hölty, and the ladies sat by and gave their advice. Stolberg was engaged in a translation of Æschylus, and often used to rush to Voss in the twilight with a sheet of translation scarcely dry, to ask his friend's opinion of it. During the same winter he began his ' Iambics ;' they were of the nature of satires in which he described his own views, and severely lashed the follies and errors of men. His scorn for faithless priests and wicked princes knew no bounds, and his zeal for religion broke forth in a description of the theologian among the Illuminati,—the elegant mannikin, whose discourses are as ornamental as his curling locks, and who thinks he has penetrated into all the mysteries of religion.

Life at court was not congenial to the poet, and in the summer he went with his Agnes to the house of his brother Christian at Tremsbüttel. There his wife bore her first-born son, and they spent a very quiet winter together, Voss joining them at Christmas.

In accordance with his own wish to enjoy his domestic happiness away from the court and in the seclusion of the country, Stolberg received the appointment of governor of Neuenburg in the duchy of Oldenburg ; and as the official residence required repair, they spent the summer in a journey to Carlsbad. On their return they went through Holstein to Copenhagen, where in a very short time Stolberg finished a drama called 'Timoleon,' wrote another, 'Theseus,' and a third, fourth, and fifth soon followed. Voss felt compelled to remonstrate with his friend against such rapid poetical production. But the poet enjoyed his labours, and wrote to Voss, " It is as impossible to me to make plans as it would be to write a book on the freedom of the will ;" and later, " It may be that in the drama more than in my other poems I have sinned against, or neglected theoretical laws, but none of my other works have ever come so from my inmost soul, or been written so *con amore*, and I consider them the best of my performances. The muse bears witness to my spirit, and that is more to me than anything."   Stolberg's contemporaries received his dramatic writings with a considerable measure of approval, but posterity has forgotten them.

They were scarcely settled at Neuenburg when Stolberg was commissioned to carry the news of the death of the Duke of Oldenburg to St. Petersburg. He met with a flattering reception ; the Empress Catherine appreciated the poetical envoy, and read his Homer with great interest.   Adorned with the cross of St. Anne he returned to his family in 1786.

In a poem called 'The Island,' we have a picture of Stolberg's happy idyl which lasted for three years at Neuenburg. Four children were born to him; nature was an unfailing source of delight, and intercourse was kept up by means of correspondence with numerous friends of note. The sunshine of his friendship with Voss was in some measure clouded when the latter entered the lists with the count by publishing a translation of the Iliad, and it was already threatened by a deeper shadow occasioned by the diversity in their religious opinions.

When Lavater was staying at Bremen in 1786, and the multitude were jeering at a man who was so consumed by his zeal for the kingdom of God, Stolberg expressed a favourable opinion of him, which is of the more value as it contains a criticism on his fanatical tendencies: "I have never seen a man," he said, "who, in a great and good cause, verged so closely on extravagance, and yet so seldom overstepped the boundary." And in an ode to Lavater he reminds him that here below, where we have to be content with faith, we must guard ourselves from being too anxious for sight, and from a taste for the marvellous, and an impatience to see the kingdom of God established in visible form.

At another time he bore a powerful testimony in favour of morality with respect to a romance. He wrote to Halem :—

"Herewith I return 'Ardinghello.' It is written with much spirit and fire, but it is a bad spirit and a fire that consumes, but neither gives light nor heat. If the rights of hospitality permit it I would say, 'Oh, ye men of Oldenburg, if you care

for the virtue of your wives, sisters, and children,
burn this wicked book !'

"Even in libertine Athens no author would have
been allowed with impunity to make such an attack
on virtue as to say that the laws of morality were
only made for the vulgar. But we Germans have
too often taken libertinism for liberty; we flatter
the great, and despise what is really great and
noble. If the book were written with all the genius
to which it lays claim, I should read it with the
same disgust as I should read a clever lampoon on
my father. And should religion and virtue be less
dear to us than a father ?"

Amidst the defections from the Christian faith
of contemporary men of talent, Stolberg remained
stedfast.

He once wrote to Jacobi: "The modern semi-
Christianity which only sees in the Son of God,
God's best and greatest messenger, cannot stand,
for it is contradicted in the Bible in every page."
When Schiller, in his celebrated poem, expressed a
poetical longing for the "gods of Greece," Stolberg's Christianity proved stronger than his love of
classical antiquity. Among other criticisms upon it
he said, "The representations which our religion
gives us of the God who calls Himself our Father,
who offers us a love surpassing a mother's love; of
the Son of God who is our brother, and as such
visibly walked with men; of the Divinity, who, having partially revealed Himself some thousands of
years before, then unveiled Himself completely, and
gave us a moral law in comparison with which all
other moral laws are nought, for it alone is holy,
and based upon love to God and man, who brought

life and immortality to light, and confirmed it by
His resurrection, thus unsealing to us the object of
His life and death;—these representations, I say,
which stand in the closest connection with our im-
provement and happiness, must surely appear to
Schiller, even if he had the misfortune not to believe in them, far more noble and beneficent than
the play of the phantasy of the Greeks, whose my-
thology combined the grossest idolatry with the
most lamentable superstition."

Stolberg's faith in the resurrection was soon put
to a severe test. In November 1788, his Agnes,
the joy of his heart and the sunshine of his house,
was taken from him after a short illness. He
wrote: "I hung with love and joy over her sweet
face, and thought she was asleep—she was dead!
It is not difficult for me to renounce all the joys of
this life, for my Agnes, the essence, sum, and substance of my earthly happiness, has left me. I shall
see her again." His brother Christian hastened to
him, and the mourner returned with him to Tremsbüttel, taking with him the two eldest children.

He did not return to Neuenburg. He received
the welcome appointment of Danish ambassador at
Berlin, and, after spending the winter in Holstein,
he removed thither in the spring. At first he
found his residence there very dreary, for his sister
and his children were not with him. Intercourse
with his friends, his classical studies, and business
sometimes relieved his melancholy for a time, but
again grief for the departed returned in full force.
But in the very midst of this grief, and while he
was cherishing the memory of the wife of his youth,
another lady crossed his path, who ensnared his

heart, so that he projected another marriage. There is something melancholy in this spectacle, but it is one constantly repeated, and it must be ascribed to the needs, the weakness, the weariness, and longing of the human heart, that he whose affections have been most keenly wounded by a separation is sometimes the most ready to enter on another union; that new joys often follow so quickly on the bitterest grief for lost happiness.

In the winter of 1789 Stolberg made the acquaintance of the Countess Sophia von Redern. In a letter to a friend, after extolling her virtues, he says, "I could not remain a widower. I confess to you, my dear friend, that it had been my hope to find my greatest earthly happiness in a lonely life devoted to the memory of my beloved Agnes, but your friend is a weak mortal."

In February, 1790, the marriage took place on an estate belonging to the Redern family.

The young wife sympathized with the religious views of her husband, which, about this time, became more decidedly confirmed. The poet Von Halem, in conjunction with two ecclesiastics, was commissioned to carry out a scheme which found much favour in those days, the revision of the Oldenburg Hymn Book.

Although not a believer in the doctrines of the Church, Von Halem not only put his own hand to the work, but sought for helpers among his friends, and applied to men of such widely differing opinions as Voss and Stolberg. The latter returned the following excellent answer:—" With a noble candour worthy of our friendship and of your character, you have often told me that you had doubts about the

Gospel history. My dearest friend, how is it possible that you can make a selection of hymns for congregations whose hopes for this world and the next are all founded upon it! Is it your wish to expunge from our hymns all that appears to you like a delusion, like a pious, or shall I say impious fraud, and as far as you can do it, to deprive the people of all that is to them most holy? Do you mean to reject hymns which have sustained thousands in suffering and death, because they appear to you to be based on what is legendary, or do you propose to adopt what appears to you to be of that character? I know that it would be quite possible to make a collection of hymns to suit all classes of worshippers, just as Basedow has written such; but that would not satisfy any Christian congregation whose faith and hope are founded on the Gospel? But," he continues "if you do persevere in the attempt, I wish from the bottom of my heart that the hymns which you undertake to criticize may induce you not so much to think, as first to believe and feel. May it happen to you, as it did to the king of Israel who came to disturb the prophets, and began instead to prophesy himself; or as it did to the learned West, who took the pen to write against the resurrection of Christ, and became its most zealous advocate?"

Stolberg's mind was so filled with religious fervour about this time that the condition of unbelievers greatly excited his compassion. He wrote to Jacobi, "It is a melancholy spectacle, and depresses me exceedingly to see people trying to live without God;" and when the faith of his friend Halem was beginning to dawn, he took advantage of his correspondence with him to endeavour to confirm it, that it might shine more and more unto the perfect day. He especially commended to him the practical test whether the doctrine of Jesus was of God, of endeavouring to do His will, saying that this had had great effect upon his own mind, in conjunction with the testimony to the truth of the Gospel which he had witnessed in the life, the love, and the death of his Agnes.

We may certainly expect from Stolberg the resolve, " As for me and my house, we will serve the Lord ;" and from the spirit in which he sought a tutor for his children, it is evident how earnest was his desire to give a Christian tone to his household. He wrote to Jacobi, " I require in a tutor purity of morals, or rather purity of heart, and biblical Christianity, kindliness and cheerfulness, and sufficient ability to prevent his pupils from too soon getting the start of him. I should like him to read the classics fluently, and with that appreciation that makes the works of a superior man ennobling to the mind. But if you write to your brother or Schlosser to make inquiries for me, tell them that I would not have a neologist, even were he as learned as Aristotle and as wise as Xenophon ; when the question is of a tutor for my children, I am intolerant. Whether he is intended for the Church or the law I do not care, nor whether he professes the Lutheran or the Reformed faith, but he must believe the Gospel." And at another time he wrote, " If the young man accepts the Scriptures with simplicity of heart, and places his hopes on Him to whom every knee shall bow, we shall not come into collision about systems. But if he does not, I would

not venture to intrust my children to him, even had
he been rendered invulnerable in the Styx of philosophy, or baptized with Homeric fire."

It had been Stolberg's wish to secure the services
of Nicolovius as tutor, a young man in whom were
combined child-like faith and profound learning,
and whose experience of life was far beyond his
years. Some private reasons had at first prevented
his accepting the charge, but he afterwards consented, and went to Holstein in 1791.* Stolberg
had returned thither in the previous year, having
concluded his mission to Berlin, and negotiated for
his appointment as ambassador at Naples. Tremsbüttel and Emkendorf were his favourite residences
in Holstein. In the latter place the Count and
Countess Reventlow lived, and Stolberg was attracted to it, not only by the bonds of friendship
and relationship, but it was the home of sentiments
which opposed to revolutionary illusions the lessons
taught by history, and to the blinding glitter of the
doctrines of enlightenment, faith in the Bible and
the creed of the Lutheran Church.

While Stolberg was awaiting his commission to
Naples, and looking forward with pleasure to going
to Italy, the death of the President of the Government at Eutin altered his plans, for the Prince-
Bishop offered him the post. He was installed into
his office in June, 1791, having relinquished his
connection with the government of Copenhagen.

* Nicolovius was afterwards in the service of the Prussian Government at Königsberg, and later, in 1808, a member of the Ministry of the Interior at Berlin, in the department of public worship and
instruction. He was a friend of William von Humboldt and Niebuhr.—Tr.

But he obtained leave of absence to make a tour in
Italy, on which he was accompanied by his wife, his
son Ernest, and Nicolovius. He went through Osnabruck to Münster. Perhaps no step had a more
decided influence on Stolberg's after life than his
entrance within the gates of Münster, for there the
Roman Catholic Church was presented in its most
favourable aspect to the eyes of the Protestant who
was accustomed to see much discord in his own. It
was the home of a Catholicism in which the Christian
element far outweighed the Roman, and which was
making noble efforts to advance the education and
prosperity of the people. The excellent minister,
Baron von Fürstenberg, and the pious Overberg,
had made the district a model in matters of education. The Princess Galitzin had found there her
spiritual home. She was the daughter of Field-
Marshal Count von Schmettau, and was born at
Berlin in 1748. She was educated in all external
worldly accomplishments, but was very early possessed with an ardent thirst for knowledge. She
was married at twenty to Prince Demetrius von Galitzin, Russian ambassador at the Hague, a man
possessing the culture of the French encyclopædists.
When in Holland she had, with great determination,
withdrawn from the world, and devoted herself to
study and the education of her children; and, at
the invitation of Prince Fürstenberg, she had gone
to Münster, hoping to benefit by his advice in the
education of her son Demetrius. She found there
far more than she sought; for, after having been for
years steeped in philosophy without any belief in
revelation, and having maintained a close intellectual
friendship with the Dutch philosopher Hemsterhuys,

after a recovery from a severe illness, her feet
rested on the firm foundation of faith in Christ.
This lady, then forty-three years of age, who in the
very prime of life had renounced the pomps and vanities of the world in order to foster her own inner
life and that of her children, made a profound impression upon Stolberg. His admiration was very
great of a life based upon religion, and, in allusion
to Socrates, he henceforth called her his Diotima.

After visiting friends and making the acquaintance of eminent men in various places, Stolberg
and his party went southwards. We must not linger
to describe the delight which a man of Stolberg's
tastes found in the scenery, the people, the treasures
of art, and the historical associations of Italy. That,
as a Lutheran, he took so little exception to the aspect of the Roman Catholic Church, that it is but
seldom that any satirical word escapes him respect-
ing it, though we frequently meet with some ap-
proving remark, must be attributed to his suscep-
tibility to the impressions of the moment and to his
visit to Münster. After he joined the Roman Catholic Church in 1800, he stated that he had given
the subject seven years' consideration before deciding
to do so. According to this, he must have begun to
entertain the idea on his return from Italy to Eutin in
the beginning of 1793. After that date, besides the
old association with members of the Protestant
Church, an animated intercourse was kept up with
his Münster friends, particularly with the Princess
Galitzin. In the summer of 1793 she and Overberg
came to Eutin, and at first their enthusiasm for
popular education made them welcome guests even
to Voss; and in 1794 the Stolbergs visited Münster.

About this time Stolberg translated a series of the Dialogues of Plato, for his love for the Greeks was never extinguished by his religious interests.

These pleasant studies and social intercourse were interrupted in 1797 by a second embassy to St. Petersburg, to take to the Emperor Paul the congratulations of the Duke of Oldenburg and the Prince Bishop of Lübeck, on his accession to the throne. Soon after his return, the Princess Galitzin and Overberg again visited Eutin, but this time they were viewed with suspicion by Voss.

There is no doubt that during this visit, the different creeds of the friends were the subject of discussion. In 1798 Stolberg and the countess, and his two eldest sons, made a journey to Carlsbad, and visited the Moravians in the Lausitz; perhaps with the hope of finding within the narrow bounds of this community, which in a time of religious declension was full of faith in a crucified and risen Redeemer, that rest for his soul which he could not find in the Lutheran Church. But it had no such result. On the contrary, he applied to J. R. Asseline, the fugitive bishop of Cologne, to solve some of his doubts; but he had as yet given no public evidence of dissatisfaction with his mother Church.

In December, as President of the Government, he inducted Götschel into his office as head preacher at Eutin, and gave an address on the occasion full of glowing faith and appreciation of the ministerial office. What a surprise then it was for his friends and the public to whom he was well known as a poet, when in the spring, the news went forth that ' Stolberg had become a Catholic.'

He gave the following account of the circumstance:—" In April, 1800, I and my wife, my two eldest sons, and my daughter Julia, who was nine years of age, went through Oldenburg to Münster, which we reached on the first or second of May. I could not announce the change in my religion either to the Prince Bishop or his minister, my old friend Count von Holmer, for the simple reason that it had not taken place. Neither my wife nor I thought we should be able to subscribe to certain doctrines of the Catholic Church. During the time that we spent at Münster, in intercourse with many estimable people, we entered at leisure on the serious consideration of them, and became convinced, and in the beginning of June we made our profession of faith. My sons knew nothing of it, for they were in the country with a friend. We afterwards proceeded on our journey through Wernigerode, where my eldest daughter had gone with my sister in May."·

The step was taken at Whitsuntide, in the private chapel of the Princess Galitzin, and Overberg received the confession of faith.

Stolberg's conversion to the Roman Catholic Church is remarkable, and requires elucidation. Until the moment of his taking the step, he had not been known either in his letters or his works to express a sentiment which was incompatible with the creed of the Protestant Church, nor a need that could not have been satisfied within its bounds.

The ground of it lay neither in the want of anything in the one Church, nor in the superiority of the other; it lay in Stolberg's own nature; in his want of clear judgment; in his dependence on the impressions made on his susceptible heart and lively imagination; in a short-sighted impatience, which caused his views to be confined to a restricted sphere, and the passing moment of the history of the Church, instead of taking in her historical development in all its length and breadth.

We will hear what he says for himself in a letter to Count Schmettau, brother of the Princess Galitzin. "Ever since my childhood, I have believed in revelation. My faith was shaken for a time, and this led me to make researches which served to confirm my convictions the more they were assailed. I was a Protestant by birth, and saw with grief that Protestantism was going to ruin. It was going to ruin in consequence of its inherent weakness. It bore within itself the seeds of decay.

"Even the name, though an expressive one, having a negative meaning, indicates a restless and turbulent spirit more disposed to pull down than to build up. It soon turned its own weapons against itself; it renounced venerable doctrines which it had until then held in honour; it exchanged them for doubts, and at length advanced far on the road towards Atheism, whose efficient servant I hold Kant to be, far rather than the founder of a new sect. The Catholic religion, stedfast and unchangeable in its very nature, neither was nor could be assailed by the principles of philosophy. The Catholic ceases to be one, when he gives up even the most insignificant dogma; for the system of true religion founded upon truth, can but be one, it cannot give up its character of unity. It is like a sphere; if you take away the smallest particle, it ceases to be a sphere. As soon as this idea struck me, I was convinced, and I saw that the Catholic comes much nearer to tho morality which the Gospel demands than the Protestant. I admired the spirit of unity which had preserved the same idea through 1800 years, and which gives courage and power to model the life in accordance with it.

"I was struck with and affected by the great spectacle which has been presented to our view. We have seen this Church, which the unbeliever considers unfruitful by reason of age, bring forth faithful confessors and noble martyrs. The sublime yet simple code of morality of the Gospel is adopted by all Christian communities, but it was only among the Catholics that I saw men who faithfully acted up to it. In every age I beheld simple, admirable, heroic, yet humble minded men; in short, saints. While the virtue of the Catholic is nourished on the memory of these great exemplars, and the springs of their actions, the Protestant who has not yet abjured Christianity finds himself destitute of any guide, and is compelled to allow himself to be illumined by the light dispersed through the works of the Catholics."

It must be confessed, that if these were Stolberg's reasons, they were very weak ones, and the change must be attributed to his own peculiar nature. He did not look at the essential character of the two Churches, but compared an exceptionally favourable aspect of the one with an exceptionally unfavourable aspect of the other.

He speaks as if there were none but bad rationalistic preachers in the Protestant Church, and in the Roman Catholic none but the most saintly characters like the Princess Galitzin, Overberg, and Fürstenberg.

A weaker reason than the superior morality of

the Roman Catholic Church could hardly have been adduced. When it is considered how strongly he had been opposed to Catholic France; that he had traversed Italy from north to south, which, at the end of the last century, was not distinguished for morality or ability; that he must have been pretty well acquainted with the ecclesiastical court of Mayence and other centres of Catholic power; that he well knew of the existence of a cloud of Protestant witnesses, who had lived to the glory of God, and cheerfully suffered martyrdom for their faith, one is tempted to think that he scarcely could have been serious in adducing as a ground of his defection the superior holiness of life of the Roman Catholics. That the unity and unchangeable doctrines of that Church should attract him is more intelligible. He wanted a tangible security in a sphere where faith only can afford it. He wanted to be delivered from all doubt, not as the result of wrestling with his difficulties, but by means of an institution which should come to the aid of his weakness. He wanted, as he wrote to Lavater, to find "a Church led by the Spirit of God, and therefore infallible." He had not the acuteness or the energetic will which, had he recognized the remedies which exist in the very constitution of the Protestant Church as well as her defects, would have made him a rallying point for the most profound spirits within her borders. Lavater said that he had never seen a more gentle flexible person, or one more easily influenced. He could not bear any contradiction. Jacobi said that if any one assailed his favourite opinions, it would cause his colour to change and his lip to quiver; it made him feel insecure in what he had considered an undisturbed possession. It suits such characters to be simply subject to some external authority. They are not content with divine support; they want some individual or community who will undertake to pacify their spirits, and to silence their mental conflicts, before they could themselves have concluded peace. Stolberg expected to find all this in the Roman Catholic Church. He wrote to the Princess Hohenlohe: "I had been investigating the subject for seven years, and still had doubts which I could not conquer. My wife, on the contrary, was quite convinced. One day, when I felt less than usually inclined to join the Roman Catholic Church, God suddenly removed my scruples. On that day the children had prayed for my wife and myself at their first communion. It was the last resource that the Princess Galitzin and Overberg had in reserve, and the result was in accordance with the mercy of God."

Fifty years later Stolberg would have found what he lacked in the Lutheran Protestant Church. Not only the presence of Christ, more especially in the Sacrament of the Lord's Supper, but also a more stringent authority, as indicated in a creed rendered in some respects more defined. But he was too impatient to wait. What he had once blamed in Lavater was the basis of his own error,—the desire to see realized a visible kingdom of God at a time when faith must suffice us. It was an error which had been long before condemned by Luther. In 1530 he wrote from the fortress of Coburg: "I have at length seen two miracles; the first, that when I looked out of the window I saw the stars of

heaven and the glorious vault of God, and yet I
could no where see the pillars on which the Master
had supported it; still the heavens did not fall, and
the vault stood secure. But they quiver and tremble,
just as though they would really fall, only because
they can neither grasp nor see the pillars. If they
could grasp them, they would stand firm without
quivering and trembling."

We refrain from recalling the impression which
Stolberg's conversion made upon his friends and
the eminent men of his time, attractive as such a
review might be of every shade of opinion, from
Voss's vehement disapproval to Lavater's easy ac-
quiescence. We will abide by the opinion of such
men as Claudius, Perthes, and Nicolovius, his best
friends, who attributed the step to a false estimate
of his needs, but still recognized in him after it had
been taken the sincere Christian, full of faith and
good works. Having brought his life to this point,
when his religious opinions became fixed in the
form which, in essentials, they retained to the end,
we must hasten to give some idea of his influence
upon the religious life of his time.

After making profession of the Roman Catholic
faith at Münster, Stolberg went with his wife to
Wernigerode, where his eldest daughter, Mary
Agnes, was staying with the parents of her betrothed, Count Ferdinand. Her parents informed
her of what had taken place, but could not induce
her to follow their example. In August he returned
to Eutin, and, after giving up his official position
there, left the place where he had enjoyed so much
affectionate intercourse with Voss and afterwards
with Jacobi, and removed to Münster. Here, and

during the summer months at Lütjenbeck, not far
distant, he lived for the next twelve years, in association with the Princess Galitzin, Overberg, the
brothers Droste, and their tutor, afterwards Professor Katerkamp.

A young priest, Kellermann, soon became an in-
mate in his own family, and was for many years
highly valued and beloved as tutor and domestic
chaplain.

The father gave lessons in Greek to both tutor
and pupils, but his attention was chiefly devoted
to religious questions, and mainly to Church history. At the suggestion of his friends, C. A. Droste-
Vishering and the Princess Galatzin, he undertook
to write a 'History of the Religion of Jesus Christ,'
which was the principal occupation of his latter
days. This work, which appeared in several successive volumes, and which, beginning with Adam,
embraced the preparation of the world for Christianity and the planting of the Christian church, gave
him renewed opportunities of addressing the public.
And as he was not unwilling to sacrifice vigour and
terseness of style to discursive addresses of an edifying character, he frequently took occasion to introduce remarks on passing events in the midst of
the history. By this means he acquired considerable religious influence, particularly among those
of his own rank and religious profession.

It may readily be imagined that Stolberg, with
whose youthful ardour for liberty we have made acquaintance, did not greet the first appearance of
the French Revolution with less delight than his
intellectual father, Klopstock. But he did not long
remain in the same mind. His religious feelings

were harrowed by the horrors by which the course
of the Revolution was stained, and his patriotic sentiments outraged by the cosmopolitanism which continued to regard with complacence the building of
castles of liberty in the air, when the builders were
already threatening his country's freedom. He maintained that liberty must be founded upon law, law
upon morality, morality upon religion, and that it
was "the most hazardous enterprise to attempt to
balance the constitution of a ruined nation upon the
point of a needle, or upon the ideal mathematical
point of a politico-metaphysical axiom."

It astonished him to see the indifference with
which sensible and good men viewed what was
taking place in France, and saw horror and dis-
aster striding towards them. He thought it was his
duty to endeavour to gather together the seven
thousand men who had not bowed the knee to Baal,
and wrote several stirring and patriotic odes, which
were watch-words against the enemies of religion
and of Germany.

Meanwhile, Germany proceeded in her downward
course. Her ignominy closely affected Stolberg;
for when, after the peace of Luneville, the German
princes were indemnified for their losses on the left
bank of the Rhine by the bishoprics, monasteries,
and ecclesiastical foundations on the right, Münster
fell to the share of Prussia. As Stein was intrusted
with the task of taking possession of the new territory, he and Stolberg were brought into contact.
They often met, and though Stein's religious views
were decidedly opposed to those of Stolberg, he
willingly recognized his sincere love of truth, and
the resignation with which he sacrificed so much.

Münster did not belong to Prussia for many years; after the defeat at Jena, it fell to the French kingdom of Westphalia under Jerome, and in 1808 to the Grand Duchy of Berg, under Murat.

It may be readily imagined with what grief Stolberg witnessed all these changes, but he regarded them as God's chastisements for the correction of Germany. He wrote in answer to a spirited letter from Perthes, " Yes, the dead leaves must fall, that the slumbering promise for the future spring may be preserved. If we could only see the first sign of its budding."

And in the third volume of his ' History of Religion,' published about the same time, he says, " Have we any right to be amazed at what we are passing through? Public misfortune, subjection to enemies that we are accustomed to conquer, is often the last means employed by a merciful Providence. And it is only reasonable that nations which, having forgotten their God, rely upon riches or upon an arm of flesh, should be brought to themselves by misfortune and distress; by great misfortunes, if they will not give heed to lesser ones. They swallow ignominy like water, and yet it does not bring them to reason."

When, in 1809, Perthes tried to unite the best of his countrymen in a peaceful mental alliance by means of a periodical, Stolberg readily took part in it. His contribution to the ' Patriotic Museum,' " On our Language," shows that the patriotism of the sexagenarian was as fresh as we have seen it in his youth. The following is an extract from it :—" The wealth of our language embarrasses the worldling, for it obliges him to make choice of words, and ill-

chosen words betray a want of judgment. Perhaps
our language, more than any other living tongue,
affords a test of the mind and heart of him who uses
it. What an indiscretion ! Such a language cannot possibly be agreeable to the worldling ; it is
distasteful to him because it shames him ; but for
those who love it, it is truly a living language. Or
it may be compared to a full suit of armour, with
weapons offensive and defensive, under the weight
of which the weakling succumbs, but which fits the
strong man like a skin, and like the armour of
Achilles, forged for him by a god, of which we are
told by Homer, that far from oppressing him, it
suited the hero well, and bore him as on wings
aloft. Let our rich, noble, and vigorous tongue be
a bond of union to us when all other bonds are torn
asunder. Many noble-minded men have clothed
in it great thoughts and warm feelings. They form
a common property to us. Let us follow their example, and thus lay up treasure for our children and
children's children.''

The circumstances which rendered the continuation of the ' Patriotic Museum ' impossible, the in-
corporation of the Hanse towns and North-Western
Germany into the French empire, also affected Stolberg. Münster as well as Hamburg became a
French town, and like Perthes, Stolberg had to
submit to the tyrant. It became difficult for him
to remain at Münster. His sentiments were so well
known that his words and actions were closely
watched by the police. And since his friend Caspar
Maximilian Droste, the suffragan Bishop of Münster,
had ventured to urge on the Council of Paris the
freedom of the Church and the liberation of the

Pope, Stolberg was more than ever an object of suspicion.

Governed by a French prefect, Münster lost many of its attractions ; and when the countess was informed by a friend that her husband was to be still more closely watched, he resolved to seek for some residence in the country, where he should be further from the sharp eyes and ears of the police.

He therefore removed in 1812 to Tatenhausen, a nobleman's seat not far from Halle.

Meanwhile God's judgments were preparing for Napoleon in Prussia, and the year 1813 arrived. At the time when Germany rose against her oppressor, Fouqué entered into correspondence with Stolberg, and in the days of their country's victories, the bond between the German bards became more and more closely cemented. So was also that between Stolberg and his brother Christian. There is something inspiriting in the sight of these two brothers, both already upwards of sixty, whose affection nothing had ever disturbed since their childhood, emulating each other in tuning their harps in the service of their country. Frederic Leopold had the satisfaction of having four sons, "worthy of Germany," engaged in the conflict. Two had been in the army before, and two entered it during the campaigns of 1813 and 1814.

Soon after the battle of Leipsic, his son Christian left his father's house, which was within the boundaries of the French territory, by night, accompanied by his father's blessing and a letter to Nicolovius at Berlin. His father wrote, "In his eighteenth year I allow this dear son to depart, to enter upon a high and holy calling ; with a heavy heart indeed, but

full of hope.   It was not his fault that he did not go
long before.   I trust that God will be with him,
whether in life or in death.   In our retired but
closely watched corner, we have shared your cares,
your hopes, your dangers, and the glorious deliverance.   God will crown your efforts with unity, wisdom, and moderation, and that holy fear which alone
gives power to tread all other fear under foot."

Nicolovius joyfully received the son of his old
friend into his house, though it was crowded with
soldiers quartered in it, and sent him with a letter
of introduction to Blücher.

In January, 1814, exactly a thousand years after
the death of Charlemagne, Stolberg could proclaim
victory over the tyrant who was fond of considering
himself Charlemagne's successor, and the patriotic
lyre of the grey-headed bard resounded with tones
of youthful vigour.

The course of events proceeded; and when Paris
was taken, Stolberg wrote to Fouqué, " The light of
God's countenance has so visibly shone forth for us
out of the darkness—with His mighty hand and outstretched arm He has so led and strengthened our
armies—He has given unity to the great triumvirate
of Europe, and sustained it thus far—and, best of
all, He has given us not only courage, but humility
and fear, that, as it seems to me, we may and must
hope ; yes, that we may indulge in glorious expectations, soon to be fulfilled."

Besides his great work on ecclesiastical history,
and the poetic effusions called forth by passing
events, Stolberg found time for a work, which was
at once patriotic and Christian, ' The Life of the
Anglo-Saxon, Alfred the Great,' who in his own
kingdom sought to advance the kingdom of God.

When Napoleon again appeared upon the scene, Stolberg sent his son Christian, who had begun to study at Berlin under the auspices of Niebuhr, and his younger son Caius into the field. He wrote cheerfully to Fouqué, "Four of my sons and a son-in-law are gone to the war. I am of good courage; I look confidently forward to victory. God give us wisdom, humility, unity, and Christian feeling afterwards. May He give us that regeneration that we so much need!"

Victory cost Stolberg dear, for his son Christian fell at Ligny.

"The Lord hath done all things well," he wrote, when he received at the same time the news of the victory of Waterloo and of the death of his son. "He has rewarded my Christian for his faithful service, after having permitted him to attain an earnestness and childlike humility far surpassing anything that we could have expected. Desolate as it looks to see his place empty, and much as my heart is torn, still I can praise God, and consider myself a happy father, for he is with his Redeemer, the fountain of love, in whose mercy and merits alone he trusted."

In the negotiations which followed peace, Stolberg was one of those who boldly demanded that all Germany's possessions should be restored to her; but he did not consider that her security rested upon one fortress more or less.

"Such soul-less defences," he wrote about this time in his 'Church History,' "and every garrison is soul-less which relies upon walls and ramparts, are of little advantage. It is manly sentiments that are a check to an enemy. Such sentiments have at length broken the first fetters that Germany ever bore, and what contemptible fetters they were! Let us then preserve the same state of mind. Let us put our trust in God. Else, neither Luxembourg, nor Mayence, nor Wesel, can defend us from the West Huns."

Stolberg was not called by Providence, like his younger friends Niebuhr and Perthes, to play an active part in the history of his time. God had granted him a more peaceful lot, whence he watched the stream of historical events as it rushed past. He heard the voice of God in it, it deeply moved him, and he earnestly besought his countrymen to give heed to it, that it might not be drowned in the noisy tumult of the nations. During the most exciting years of the wars of independence, he was very diligent as an author, and seized every opportunity offered him by his 'History of Religion' of arousing the consciences of the people.

This work had a large circulation; it appeared at a time when, even in the Protestant Church, there was no work distinguished by a keen appreciation of the great exemplars of ecclesiastical history; and as it was published by Perthes, who, while keeping the one thing needful clearly in view, was not a zealous Protestant partisan, it was favourably received in pious Protestant circles, especially among the nobility.

Stolberg received the thanks of many such, who dated the confirmation of their faith from the perusal of his book. The history only reached to A.D. 430, for it began with Adam, and embraced the whole period of the Old and New Testaments.

This delight in biblical study was an inheritance

from Stolberg's mother church, but he was a faithful son of his adopted church; he declared in the preface that he was ready to recall any expression that was not in accordance with her doctrines; he deeply regretted that all those whom he loved were not of the same faith, but nothing that the Church had to offer him as a means of grace was so precious as the Bible.

He felt pleasure in the desire which was awakened after the war to spread the Scriptures among the people, and could not understand how one of his fellow professors could see "fresh incendiarism" in it. He wrote to Perthes, "I am sorry that so many Catholics view the Bible Societies with distrust. The members of them will certainly have to proceed with circumspection in Catholic countries, but according to my opinion the universal spread of the Scriptures can only be productive of great good."

When the time arrived when even he to whom long life is granted must look forward to his end, Stolberg found the task of continuing his history too severe, and turned his attention exclusively to the Bible. In his sixty-ninth year, "like the aged farmer who no longer cultivates his fields, but confines himself to his garden," he gave his attention to the 'Paradise of the Holy Scriptures,' and published 'Meditations and Reflections' upon them. This work, like many of the former ones, is dedicated to his children. He said in the dedication, "I wish, my dearly beloved children, who are my hope and joy, now in the evening of my days, before I pass through the dark valley, guided, I hope, by Jesus Christ through the mercy of God, to talk to you of this mercy which He has shown us in His Son, and revealed to us by His Spirit."

This dedication to his children reminds us that we must say a word on Stolberg's family life, by means of which, as it was an exemplary one, he contributed not a little to the renewal of religious life. The Christian father who has no calling to active service for his country, can yet render it most valuable service by guiding well his own house. As Luther said—

> "If every one his task doth know,
> Order and peace the house will show."*

And Rückert,—

> "When the rose herself adorns,
> She adorns the garden."

The wealth of human interests which Goethe admired in Stolberg is well illustrated in his family life. His first wife bore him four, his second fourteen children. Of the whole number thirteen survived him, of whom several were married, and had presented him with a goodly number of grandchildren. At the time when most of the children were still under their father's roof, when foster-children and visitors were often added to the family, with the requisite number of servants, it constituted a little community of itself. All daily assembled round the private chaplain; for the family always sought strength for their work and renewal of their love in daily worship.

Yet there was no narrow exclusiveness. Stolberg,

---

* "Ein jeder lern sein Lection,
So wird es wohl im Hause stohn."

as we have seen, was heartily attached to his church
and his country; he corresponded so diligently both
with his friends and others who sought his aid, that
he spent 1000 dollars a year in postage. He and
his wife were most liberal dispensers of alms; he
disbursed not less than 20,000 dollars for the Sisters
of Mercy at Münster. But he considered his family
his most important sphere of labour. He met them
in the morning at family worship, again at dinner
after the morning's work and ride, then old and
young took recreation together in riding, bathing,
or roaming about the woods. In the evening an
hour was often devoted to reading Greek poetry,
when tutor and children all sat at Stolberg's feet,
and at a later hour they met again for worship.

How anxious he was to aid his children in uniting
themselves to God their Saviour is shown by a letter
which he gave to his eldest son on his leaving home
at twenty-one years of age, to enter the Austrian
service. We give a few extracts:—

"Begin the day with the morning, and close it
with the evening prayer; but if you use them as
prayers in earnest, you will not be satisfied with
these alone. Devote a quarter of an hour daily to
the contemplation of God and divine things. Try
to realize His greatness and love, and your own
insignificance, and then His love and mercy in
giving us His only begotten Son, and the thought of
Jesus Christ in Gethsemane and at Golgotha will
produce their right effect. Then will the love of
the Holy Ghost fill your soul if you will permit
Him to cleanse it from all impurity.

"Before the evening prayer, review your thoughts,
words, and actions during the day. Commend your-

self daily to the Mother of God and your guardian angel, and ask them to pray for you. May you always go to confession with a contrite heart, and return with a lighter one. Let the word of God be a guide to your feet, and a lamp to your path. Christ desires that we should be closely united to Him and take counsel of Him above every other. He desires that we should 'strive to enter in at the strait gate that leadeth unto life.'

" Nothing is so dangerous to youth as false shame. Be always chaste in word. If you allow yourself to take part in impure conversation, you will be in danger of falling into impurity yourself.

" Never drink wine to excess, or allow it to lead you into folly. Go to bed early, and rise early. Take daily exercise, and do not neglect swimming and leaping. Ask permission to break in the young horses of the squadron. Continue to study the science of war in all its branches. Be sure to devote some time every day to reading, and keep up your knowledge of the ancient languages, since you have made so much progress in them, and mind and preserve fluency in Latin. Increase your acquaintance with the Greek Testament, and let Homer be your constant companion.

" If opportunity offer for the chase, it is well to avail yourself of it, but do not let it become a passion. Always have a good horse, a good sword, and a good watch. You should regard your horses with affection, and when they have shared with you the labours of the day, see that they are well cared for, before thinking of yourself."

Then recurring to admonitions relating to his soul's health, he says, " Faithful is he that calleth you who also will do it.   Pray for me, for your mamma, your brothers and sisters, for our friends, your superiors, for heretics, for all men.   Pray for the souls in purgatory, for any of us who die before you, for those of us who are already dead.   May God the Father in heaven bless you ; may Jesus Christ our brother, our Lord, and our God, bless you, and be your eternal high-priest.   May the Holy Ghost bless you, and fill you with His love. Amen."

Although the Roman Catholic element in these admonitions may be repulsive to us, we can scarcely fail to admire the Christian and patriotic tone of them, nor their noble and chivalrous spirit, since it is combined with religion.

Not long before his death, Stolberg wrote, " God has always given me great—yes, very great—pleasure in my children.   I may surely hope that they will stand firm in the conflict that has been long preparing, and which will summon the children of God into the field.   It will be a conflict in which the follower of the Cross will be victorious if he remain true to his colours, even if it please God that he should not appear so in the eyes of the world."

In 1816, Stolberg exchanged his residence at Tatenhausen for one at Sondermühlen, near Osnabruck, in Hanover, where he passed the evening of his days.   His dying song was ' The little Book of Love,' an illustration of the Scriptural doctrine of love, as it could only be given by one whose soul had been fed, not only on the writings of St. Augustine and the Christian mystics, but who was profoundly versed in the Scriptures; although, in our view, it contains some things not in accordance with their teaching. It was written in October 1819. On the 7th of November he kept his seventieth birthday with his family at home. A week later he received the derisive pamphlet of his former friend Voss, entitled, ' How was it that Fritz Stolberg became a slave ?' Before Stolberg left Eutin it was painfully evident that a deep gulf was opening between the friends. Neither the memory of their enthusiastic friendship in the days of the Hainbund, nor their love of the Greek classics, neither Stolberg's noble sentiments, nor Voss's honourable character, could keep those united who were separated in spirit.

The man who, in his home in Mecklenburg, had heard the evils of serfdom cry aloud against the oppression of the nobles, was confronted with one who wore his nobility with a good conscience, because he knew himself to be free from the selfish prejudices of his class ; cold intellect came in contact with warmth of feeling, sober judgment with imagination, superficial enlightenment with an absorbing contemplation of the mysteries of saving grace. The " arch-inquisitor of rationalism," as Perthes called Voss, lifted up his voice against his friend, whom rationalism had driven into the Roman Catholic Church.

Voss's long pent up ill-will broke forth on the publication of an article by Stolberg on the ' Spirit of the Age,' in Adam Müller's periodical. The views expressed in it were open to criticism by those who did not share them ; but Voss's violent attack on Stolberg can only be explained as the result of fanatical irritability. However disinclined he might be to the task, Stolberg felt himself obliged to reply in order to correct misrepresentations and errors in matters of fact. But from this contest, which was none of his own seeking, he was soon withdrawn by the hand of God, for he was laid upon his dying bed. His illness lasted from the 29th of November to the 7th of December, and he was fully conscious to the last. He was surrounded by his wife, many of his children and grandchildren, and Kellerman, who for fifteen years had been the friend and chaplain of the household, happened to have just arrived on a visit. The patient lay like a patriarch admonishing and blessing his children; and, with childlike humility, he allowed himself to be prepared for his last journey by the Scriptures and the sacraments of the Church. His end, as recorded for us by some of his children in their diaries, was so edifying and striking that one of the doctors said, "I cannot imagine the wretch who would not have been converted by the sight."

To a Protestant there is naturally something repulsive in the dread of purgatory, the invocation of Mary, and his frequent requests to his family to pray for him often after his death; but all this is overcome by the testimony that was borne to the Scriptures, and to Jesus Christ of whom they testify.

At first the patient liked to have the writings of his beloved Wandsbeck Messenger, and Klopstock's devotional hymns, read to him, but the Bible soon took the place of everything else.

The last few days were like converse between God and the dying man, only interrupted by occa-

sional conversation with his family, and to the words
of comfort from the Scriptures read to him by
Kellerman, he responded with keen comprehension
and deep experience.   And when he addressed
himself to God in prayer, it was not only the
prayers of the Roman Catholic Church that were
used, he derived refreshment from many of the
hymns of the Protestant Church ; and once, when
Kellerman had not the breviary at hand, his daughter
Julia knelt down and prayed in the words of Paul
Gerhardt's parting sigh,—

> " Oh, when Thou call'st me to depart,
>   Turn not away Thy face."

On the 7th of December he commended his spirit
to his Saviour's love.   His last words were a
thanksgiving for His mercy to sinners, and with
the exclamation, " Praise be to Jesus Christ," he
departed.*

* ' Der Graf Friedrich Leopold Stolberg und seine Zeitgenossen,
von Dr. Theodor Menge.'   2 Bände.   Gotha : 1862.

CHAPTER VI.

JOHN FALK.

SOME of the most valuable fruits which ripened in German soil after it had been fertilized by the blood shed during the wars of independence, were the loving labours expended in rescuing poor children whose minds and bodies were alike neglected. What Pestalozzi had previously attempted in Switzerland, John Falk accomplished with great success in Germany. Saxony had for the third time the honour of giving a mighty impulse to practical religion in Germany. It was from Wittenberg that Luther's call to faith had first gone forth; it was at Halle that Francke had furnished an example to his countrymen of the faith that worketh by love; and now, at Weimar, Falk showed that the intellectual progress of the age, which had its chief seat in the town on the banks of the Ilm, was not sufficient to raise the people,—that it is only by the love which the Saviour inspires that they can be effectually helped.

John Falk's life has a claim on the warmest sympathies of our readers. As in the account which

Stilling gives of his youth, a striking effect is produced by the affinity between his poetical nature and the rural scenes which he describes, so the particulars which Falk gives of his youthful experiences, with all the simplicity of nature, have quite a poetical charm.

The idiosyncrasy of Stilling's character caused him to find favour in Goethe's eyes, and he also honoured with his intimacy the open, impressible, and aspiring Falk. Falk drank much more deeply than Stilling of the poetic spring, and it excites our warmest interest when, in the days when the universal distress knocked so loudly at the doors of all true friends of the people, we see the friend of Wieland and Goethe, the author of songs and satires, suddenly changed into the loving father of a number of ragged and starving children who were ripening for every species of crime.

John Daniel Falk was born in October, 1768, at Dantzic, where his father was a wig-maker. His mother, whose maiden name was Chalion, was a member of a family from Geneva which had settled in Dantzic, professing the reformed faith, but she was attached to the Moravians. His father appears to have belonged to the Reformed Church, as it was in this that Falk was baptized. A spirit of sober piety, in accordance with the father's faith, reigned in the house ; the discipline was severe, and the children were carefully guarded from the evil influences of the world. Little John's ardent and aspiring mind was oppressed by the strictness of his training. His whole nature soared far above his father's workshop, but at eleven years of age he was taken from school and set to work. It was expected that all his time should be occupied by his trade, and if ever he did take a book in hand it was to be a religious one. The boy suffered severely under this mental oppression. It induced him to save up his pence, and take them to the circulating library; and he read the books by the light of the street lamps, even in severe weather, when his hands were so cold that he could hardly turn over the leaves. Wieland's translation of Lucian had been given him, and he devoured it ravenously. He wrote to his cousin, "Like me, he was the child of poor, insignificant people, and like me, he worked at a trade, and yet he afterwards became a learned and famous man. When I read this, my heart leaped for joy, but I cannot have the pleasure of letting my parents share my happiness." His taste for reading and study was so great that he looked wistfully back to some happy days when, having broken his leg, he was obliged to lie still, and could read to his heart's content.

God preserved the youth from many dangers, both moral and physical. In consequence of his taste for music and his skill in playing on the violin, when twelve years old, he joined the choir of the Roman Catholic Church. One day, Father Lambert, who had taken a fancy to him, took him into his cell. "Listen to me, John," he said; "would you like to be confirmed, and to become a Catholic?" John was alarmed, and said, "No, reverend father; I was baptized in the name of Christ and Calvin, and I intend to die in the same faith." And the tears rolled down the little confessor's cheeks. The Father then continued, in gentler tone, "Well, well, my son; you need not be frightened. A question leaves you quite free, and the Church compels no one." And, as he spoke, they heard the tuning of the violins in the choir. "Come with me," said the Father; and the danger of Falk's becoming a Roman Catholic was over for ever. Other perils, however, assailed him. His father had an apprentice, whom John calls the Mannheimer. Wishing to give his master's strictly-kept son a treat, he asked leave to take him with him to the Christmas fair. With a warning against frivolity his father consented. They had seen folly enough at the fair, but the Mannheimer was not content, and proposed to spend the evening at a place of public resort of evil repute. The way in which our young friend was restrained in these scenes of danger indicates the depth of his poetical nature. In the midst of a dissolute crowd he found himself standing before a young, pretty, and well-dressed girl, who appeared to be in no little embarrassment at her position. John stood still; they looked at each other, but neither spoke a word; and with clenched fist he prevented any one from touching her. This seemed to please her, for, when the crowd was over, she stood for a moment longer, and turned to him with a pleasant blushing look as she went away. A ray of the light which beamed on Dante when he beheld the youthful Beatrice had darted into his soul. The idea of holy love had dawned upon him, and how could he walk in the paths of sin? As he was passing by the Nonnenkirche on his way home, the door was open, a bright lamp hung in the midst, and a voice was singing in the choir. His parents then came into his mind, and the words, " When sinners entice thee consent

Q 2

thou not." He went in; his heart became lighter; he wept much, and whichever way he looked he seemed to see the maiden pleasantly smiling at him. The music went on; the lamp shone like the moon; and it seemed to John as if he saw heaven opened, and the angels ascending and descending, and rejoicing to see him there.

But this was not the last time that he tried to escape from the restraints of his father's house. His imagination was excited by the sea and the shipping, and the desire to see distant lands possessed him like a home-sickness. Once he begged a seaman to take him with him, but without answering a word, he loosed the vessel from her moorings before his eyes. John gazed after it as long as it was in sight, and then poured forth his longings in the following lines :—

> " Little bird ! little bird !
> Oft I see thee come and go,
> O'er the Baltic to and fro ;
> Hast thou ne'er my prayer heard?
> Take, O take me, let me see
> Other fairer lands with thee,
> Little bird ! little bird !

On the day of the festival of Corpus Christi, his father gave him permission to go and see the procession, if he would be very industrious during the day. He fulfilled the condition, but when the time came, his mother made objections, probably from Protestant scruples, although she had before given her consent. John was irritated, so far forgot himself as to use angry words, and ran away, vowing never to enter his father's house again. He hastened to the Roman Catholic church. On the way he fell in with an old sailor's wife, who told him to come to her again, and she would put him in the way of escaping to the East Indies. When he went into the church the procession had already begun. He took his place and looked on, but the women would not let him rest till he knelt down; and as he did so, he saw in the distance a crimson canopy, under which the Queen of Heaven was to appear, and as it approached him, he recognized in a white robe, and with a crown of myrtle on her head, the same maiden who had already appeared to him in the crowd at the Christmas fair; and she looked at him again with her mild blue eyes as if she would ask where he had been so long. And as she went slowly by, he tried to rise from his knees, and could not; and the lights in the church flickered in the clouds of incense, and the organ sounded to him like a trumpet, and the singing almost took away his breath. Thus God touched his heart, and he prayed earnestly, and vowed never to run away secretly from his father's house again, but to bear his lot with patience.

If Falk recognized in this circumstance the protection of a guardian angel, he had soon afterwards to acknowledge God's hand in delivering him from the jaws of death. In December, 1785, he went skating with his younger brother; the ice broke, and he fell into the water. He thought that it was all over with him, and after commending his soul to God, he felt a great curiosity to know what would become of it when separated from the body. His first thought was, " So I am to lose my life in this pitiful way;" the second, " O my poor parents, my dear mother and dearly beloved father, to think

that I should cause you this sorrow in your old age !"
the third, "I hope brother Charles will not meet
with the same misfortune ;" the fourth, "Lord Jesus
to thee I live, to thee I die; I am thine now and for
all eternity ! "   He was just about to say, "Amen,"
when he suddenly felt the grasp of a hand; it was
that of his little brother. The sailors had warned
him of the danger, but he had followed the impulse
of his heart, had seized his brother by the hand,
and would not let him go, though the weight pulled
him down upon the ice. He was up to the middle
in the water, the ice cut him in the face and arm till
the blood flowed, he screamed and called, but would
not let go his brother's hand. The sailors called
out to him, "You see you cannot save him, for
God's sake let him go," but he only screamed the
louder, and prayed more earnestly, till some fishermen came with hooks and poles and pulled them
both out. And when John came to himself and
asked his brother what had made him bleed so, he
did not tell him, but fell on his neck and hugged
and kissed him, and rejoiced to see him revived.
And he got up many times in the night and went
to his brother's bed, and listened to his breathing,
and then went and told his parents, "Yes, he is
alive." And they all thanked God for the wonderful deliverance, and his aunt, Anna Marten, who,
like his mother, was attached to the Moravians,
said to him, "John, God has been with you again ;
He will not leave you nor forsake you, if you do
not forsake Him, for I feel quite persuaded in my
mind that the Lord has chosen you for His service."

Falk had been rescued from his mental bondage

before this deliverance occurred. His mother, and
an English teacher of languages of the name of
Drommert, had told his father that he ought to
allow his son to study. His father at length consented, on condition that he should work at his
trade every day for a few hours. The son was delighted, and went twice in the week to Drommert.
Some of the sons of the wealthy patricians, with
swords at their sides and feathers in their hats,
turned up their noses at him, and would not allow
him to look over their books, so he looked over the
master's book, and soon put the boys to shame by
getting before them; and when the teacher said
that he had made a better translation of a passage
from Ossian than any of the others, and had even
put it into verse, he was ready to cry for joy.
Drommert took the exercise forthwith to the head
pastor of St. Peter's church, and obtained permission for him to enter the High School, at Easter,
1785, that he might study theology. Now that this
path was open to him, he would not allow himself
to be deterred from it. One day the churchwarden
of St. Peter's met him in the street, and asked him
if it was true that his father was allowing him to
study theology. "Yes, your Excellency, with your
permission," answered Falk, with a deep obeisance
and uncovered head. "But how—without money?"
And then, after a pause, as if he could not recover
from his astonishment, "and what then?"—"With
your Excellency's leave I think of going to the
Gymnasium here."—"And what then?"—"I mean
to go to the university."—"And then?"—"I shall
be a candidate."—"What a simpleton you are!"
"Yes, if it please your Excellency; but that is just

the reason why I wish to study, that I may not always be one."

The purse-proud contempt that was poured upon
him cost him bitter tears; but he persevered in his
course. When he was at the Gymnasium, he promised himself much pleasure in hearing a lecture on
style, announced by the professor of poetry. He
had a certain horror of philosophy, because, according to the opinion of a physician, the philosophy of
Kant had affected the nerves of a professor, and
hastened his death; but the poetic art, at which he
had already tried his hand, had great charms for
him. He could scarcely sleep the night before the
lecture, and entered the room with the expectation
of wonderful revelations. But there sat a tall, thin
man, constantly sucking the knob of his walking-
stick, with hollow eyes, and a still more hollow
voice, and he was reading from his papers a lecture
devoid of all spirit or interest. Nevertheless, after
the lecture, Falk ventured to call on him, and opened
his heart to him, which was warm with anticipa-
tion of the delights of poetry. But the professor
told him, that through God's merciful preservation,
he had never composed a stanza, and always warned
his hearers against it, because people who gave
themselves up to verse-making, generally became
good for nothing. After this, if any one asked
Falk if he had ever written any verses, he used to
feel inclined to say, " God forbid! I have not come
to that," but he never did say it; and during close
study, he still cultivated the art of pouring out his
youthful feelings in song. At length the time came
for going to the university. The town council of
Dantzic provided the funds; and just before his

departure he received a solemn summons to appear at the town hall, before the burgomaster and councillors. They were seated in the great hall, in their stately robes of office, and John Falk stood in their presence with dignified modesty, and tears of gratitude in his eyes. They shook hands with him, and gave him their blessing; and one of the old men, as he held the boy's hand in his, uttered the striking words, "John, you are now going hence, God be with you! You will always be our debtor, for we have adopted you, and affectionately cared for you as a poor child. You must not fail to repay this debt. Wherever God may hereafter lead you, and whatever may be your future destination, never forget that you were once a poor boy. And when some day, sooner or later, some poor child knocks at your door, you must consider that it is we, the dead, the grey old burgomaster and councillors of Dantzic, who are standing there, and you must not turn us away from your door."

Falk's youth contains the germs of the life of love which unfolded in his mature years. The simple and needy burgher life in which his youth had been passed, rendered it easier to him to adapt himself to the people. He had experienced the special temptations of childhood. The remembrance of the help which had been extended to him and the words of the old councillor were indelibly engraven on his mind. And the wonderful help of God seemed to him like a revelation of eternal love, which was continually extended to him afresh, and which he extolled in words and works. But the poetic vein which ran through his youth was never exhausted, and his manner of carrying on his benevolent labours was strongly influenced by it. But it was a long time before the course of his life was directed into its original channel ; between his youth and his later labours of love, there is a period which was entirely engrossed by poetic interests. It is not easy to follow the thread of his life from the time of his leaving Dantzic, till the beginning of his philanthropic career, a period of about twenty years.

It is certain that he went to the University of Halle in 1787, in order to study theology, but that he did not persevere in it. Like many others, he was probably deterred from the theological career by the superficial tone and want of spirituality that prevailed in matters of divinity.

The study of languages, which promised to unlock for him the springs of poetry, had received a fresh impulse from the labours of such men as Friedrich August Wolf, and under his guidance Falk zealously studied the ancient classics. He probably supported himself while at Halle by authorship and giving lessons, and perhaps was among the men of rising talent who received assistance from Gleim of Halberstadt. At any rate, his first poem of any length, on 'Man,' is dedicated to Gleim, and the dedication concludes with the words, " Gleim was my father and my friend." We find him at Halberstadt in 1798, and at Weimar in 1801. In 1797 he was married to Caroline Elizabeth Rosenfeld, at Halle. At Weimar he made the acquaintance of Herder and Schiller in their later years. With Wieland, and especially with Goethe, he maintained the confidential intercourse of an enthusiastic disciple, but he nevertheless knew how to retain his independence.

We shall best supply the want of information about his outward life by endeavouring to trace his mental development by means of his poetic effusions. As a boy of fifteen, he produced songs which indicated a popular talent. The later offspring of his muse comprises a large number of sea-pieces, poems, tales, and letters, which partly belong to his Dantzic life, but mostly to that at Halle and Weimar. Love is the topic of almost all his poems, partly drawn from the imagination, but certainly in part from experience. The form of his pieces sometimes reminds us of Goethe, and the contents of the excessive *naïveté* of Wieland. The lyrical pieces always indicate talent, whether they speak the language of passion or are narrative or satirical.

No definite religious element is to be found in them, but no mockery, and there is unmistakable trace of the poet's deeper feelings, and of an aspiration to a higher life. The unconscious piety of childhood has vanished, and the conscious religion of a riper age is yet undeveloped. If we seek for the influences that have formed the peculiar character of his mind, the views of Rousseau may be traced in Falk's writings of this period. It certainly reminds us of Rousseau when Falk, in his satire on 'Man,' describes him as the most ridiculous of creatures, and pretends to prove by a long series of examples that man is surpassed by animals in all his best qualities ; and he paints in the liveliest colours the perversity of the human race. Another satire, 'The Heroes,' although dedicated to Herder, and bearing marks of the influence of this great thinker, concludes with the words :—

"Mid rocks and caves, away from man, away!"

Disgust with the world induced a feeling of scornful self-reliance and retreat into himself. He boasted that he owed nothing to the great ones of the earth; but he seems to have forgotten the wonderful preservations of his youth, for which he had then been so thankful to God. But the "portentous times" were the means in God's hands of putting an end to this state of mind. Like the man who, weary of life, intended to drown himself, but was recalled from his intention by the sight of a drowning man,—or the alpine traveller in momentary danger of succumbing to the cold, whose own circulation was restored by rubbing the limbs of a frozen man whom he discovered in the snow,—so John Falk's zest for life returned when his feelings were aroused by seeing his countrymen in danger of sinking into misery and bondage.

For he had never been without affection for humanity; his powers were only waiting till the sphere for their exercise should be indicated to him. No sudden change is to be observed. As in the days of his self-reliance, though disgusted with his fellows, he never turned against God, so, after his return to religious faith, he never abjured the treasures of mental culture. The interesting book which was published after his death, ' Goethe, from intimate personal Acquaintance,' shows that the hero of the home mission was still in close association with Wieland, and especially with Goethe.

On the day of Wieland's funeral, Falk found Goethe in a particularly open, grave, and tender mood. Falk asked him, " What do you suppose Wieland's soul to be occupied with at this moment ?" " With nothing mean or unworthy," was the answer; " nothing incompatible with the moral greatness which he maintained throughout his life. But, that I may not be misunderstood, as I seldom speak of these things, I must expatiate further on the subject." And Goethe gave his friend a full account of his views on the subject of man's life after death. They were essentially based upon natural grounds, but did not ignore the confirmation of them by faith.

The tender mood which had disposed the poet to this open expression of his opinions, remained after he had finished speaking. Contrary to his custom, on Falk's taking leave he kissed him on the forehead, would not suffer him to go down-stairs in the dark, but held him by the arm till a light was brought, and when just going out he warned him to beware of the cold night air. Falk went home and wrote down his thoughts on the conversation,—or, as he expressed it, he worked it up into some results which were not without effect upon his after life. He wrote, " It is really true, then, and a man of so superior a mind as Goethe is constrained to make the humiliating confession, that on this planet, which is our dwelling-place, all our knowledge is but fragmentary. All our keenest and most careful observation of any department of nature can no more give us an adequate idea of God and the universe, than the fish at the bottom of the sea, even if he were in the possession of reason, could form to himself a correct notion of the human race, or free his ideas from the influence of scales and fins so long as he lives in those watery realms. But what do we mean by nature? Does it only include the coral insect in the South Seas, or the vegetation of a toadstool? Is that sublime mental height, higher than the highest Alps, which we climb in order to obtain a view of nature, somewhere outside of nature? Is not man, perhaps, to use that beautiful expression of Goethe's, 'the first converse that nature holds with God'? And must not, therefore, the place where it is held be more sacred to us than any other? And if this is the case, can it be well for this higher and seraphic nature in man to ask counsel of the coral insect and the toadstool in matters that concern his own inward being, the will, the omnipotence, and omnipresence of God? If God speaks to us in the recesses of our minds,—and who will dare to deny it? it may be asked,—does God learn from man, or man from God? (Job xxxviii., xxxix., xl.) How little it is that man can teach God, we have abundantly seen from the foregoing, so let us investigate what God teaches man.

" If the heavenly voice that speaks within us is right, all-pervading love, and not blind force, is the law of the universe. All its laws are dictated by love. Love calls and entices her lost children to return to her arms. Forbearance and compassion towards all created beings are indelibly impressed upon our hearts. If we do violence to the dictates of conscience, it revenges itself by sending evil spirits to us, who allow us no peace, and pursue us day and night.

" As the criminal is alarmed at every rustling leaf, so all those who obey the divine commands enjoy an unruffled peace. There must, therefore, be higher natures somewhere, who approve and are filled with joy when their heavenly mandates are obeyed, and are displeased when they are neglected. How different must be the view of the universe obtained from this high moral elevation, to that which can be reached by the closest observer on earth, who looks upwards from the lower spheres of nature! What a benign influence must pervade a whole community, when each individual fulfils his duties faithfully, and is daily and hourly obedient and responsible to a higher power!

"Faith, hope, and charity—these voices so unmistakably divine—must be followed as sure guides by all who bear the name of man. Let us never indulge in sophistry when we owe implicit obedience to a divine command, communicated immediately to our minds. Having discovered the limits which are imposed upon humanity, I shall be able to comprehend the expression of that blessed and loving spirit, that messenger from God, who, in two poor words, 'Our Father,' announced to us that God's love extended to all the universe, and taught me how, by a sincere use of them, to please my Father in heaven."

In these extracts from Falk's diary we see the nature of his views of God and the world, their essentially moral character, their benignity and mercy; but there is no mention of the Name in which are hid all the treasures of wisdom and knowledge, but we afterwards see him turn to the cross of Christ, as the most striking illustration of the love which was the medium through which he looked at life.

The gradual change which took place in Falk's inner life, was a thoroughly practical one. It was not the result of a process of thought, but it was brought about by means of the great events by which God proclaimed Himself to that generation, as the eternal though oft-forgotten Disposer of events. Falk was a zealous patriot before he was a vital Christian, and the patriot's grief aided the development of his Christian character.

The lash of satire which he had previously aimed at his fellow-creatures was laid down at the advance of Napoleon's power, and he began to call on his countrymen to repent. In 1801 he drew a comparison between that year and 1701. " Then piety, now scepticism ; then propriety of conduct, now wantonness ; then patriotism, now coquetry with France ; then well furnished coffers and moderate expenditure, now luxury and empty purses." He does battle with the tendency of the Germans to construct systems, and says, that though they think profoundly on all subjects, it does not result in action ; and he inveighs against a mode of education which communicates mere learning, but infuses no vital power. He had a clear insight into the causes of the approaching calamity, which he ascribed principally to the want of spirit and national character in the army. He says of merit and nobility, " They should never be opposed to each other. Nobility is previous merit ; merit, future nobility. The time is come when the pedantry of the parade-ground cannot save the State from destruction. Fear of corporal punishment is not favourable to winning laurels, and the government of the stirrup must cease, or the rider, through sheer subordination, will sink to the level of his horse. It is no idle dream. Motives very different from these must lead the German armies into the field, and help them to win glorious victories. Mere hired soldiers can do us little service at the present crisis. These are novel ideas, but Buonaparte has taken care that they shall become better known, and at the battle of Austerlitz he wrote them so plainly in the heavens in characters of fire, that they will still be legible to the cherubim at the day of judgment."

After the battle of Jena, Falk gave up writing for action. His warm heart occasioned him to turn his attention to helping his enslaved and impoverished countrymen. The French had taken possession of Weimar and the surrounding country, and, according to their custom, were exacting large sums of money. The French officials required an interpreter, to enable them to collect the imposts demanded in money and provisions. Wieland advised that Falk should be secretary to the French commission; and he accepted the office, in the hope of being of service to his countrymen. He exercised his functions with equal courage and prudence, and especially endeavoured, with his loving sympathy for the oppressed, to shield them from severity and outrage. His labours amongst the country people acquired for him the name of the "kind councillor," and in consideration of them, the Grand Duke of Weimar afterwards gave him the title of Councillor of Legation, the order of the Falcon, and a salary. He lived through the years of bondage, after the misfortunes of 1806, without mental subjection to Napoleon; indeed, we have evidence that he confidently hoped for the overthrow of the tyrant by the hand of God. The year of deliverance came. Just before the battle of Leipsic, the army, under the Duke of Ragusa, lately arrived from Spain, came

into the Duchy of Weimar. They disposed of the
produce of the fields, the houses, and even of the
inhabitants, in the most despotic manner. The
people were panic-struck, and wandered about in
terror amidst the smoke of burning villages.

Falk's heart was touched by the misery around
him, and, in order to try to lessen it, he left his
family, and rushed into the tumult; and, though
single-handed, his trust in God and love for his
fellows made him a host in himself. Whenever any
special tyranny was being practised he was quickly
on the spot. He courageously snatched the booty
from the soldiers, and restored it to the owners.
His capacious pockets were stored with purses,
watches, and wedding-rings, intrusted to him by the
people. Wherever he went his eyes were met by
dire distress. Whole wheat-sheaves were thrown
to the horses instead of straw, and the roads were
strewn with ears of corn. Horses were stolen and
sold again for a few florins; flocks of sheep were
shorn, and then roasted; oxen were taken from the
plough to the fire. When wood was scarce, the
soldiers sometimes tore down the stairs to feed the
surrounding fires. Falk felt that this state of things
must be altered. If compassion did not lead to it,
it must be brought about by the fear that the people,
driven to despair, might rise in rebellion, when a
general slaughter would ensue. He wrote to the
French general, De Cœhorn, who had discretion
enough to place a company of soldiers at Falk's
disposal. He went with them through the Duchy
of Weimar and the surrounding country, and, as far
as possible, defended the people from cruelty and
oppression, and restored law and order.

The battle of Leipsic changed the scene. Advancing and insolent troops were replaced by wretched fugitives. The French army was scattered throughout Thuringia. Pestilence was now the scourge which, like a pale angel of death, hovered over the land. The fugitive soldiers felt that he was pursuing them; he shook the deadly poison from his wings over towns and villages, where the inhabitants were already half dead with fright and hunger. In one village there were sixty orphans mourning for their parents. The pale messenger also knocked at Falk's door, and called away four of his six blooming children; he was himself seized with illness, and was so sick at heart that he was ready to wish for death. "But that is just like us poor mortals," he said. "We are all ready to make tabernacles, that we may abide on Mount Tabor with Moses and Elias, but we do not like the nights on Golgotha, nor to watch through the trying hours with our Lord at Gethsemane, nor to bear the cross nor the crown of thorns after Him, nor to sweat blood. No, this brings terror and dismay into the heart of the natural man. Oh! it is very hard in hours of such bitter trial to say 'Thy will be done' with a truly honest and resigned heart." Falk recovered his health entirely, and was also cured of his errors, of his contempt for society, and his indifference towards God. National and family sorrows had opened his heart for the glad reception of the streams of love which flow from the cross. From the year when Germany regained her independence his whole life was devoted to helping the distressed. He had gained the confidence of the people through his previous exertions; and now artisans wanting help before they could go to work again; peasants in need of seed corn; and, above all, hundreds of orphaned and desolate children, who could only keep themselves from starving by begging and stealing, came to him for aid. He established the "Society of Friends in Need." He put forth appeals at Weimar, Jena, Eisenach, etc., and sums of money were subscribed monthly to form a fund for placing out poor boys to learn a trade.

Various good works, which were afterwards divided into separate departments, were combined in embryo in Falk's labours. His original idea was not to place children in an asylum, but to find homes for them in families, and he succeeded in placing out hundreds in this manner. But he could not altogether dispense with the plan of an institution. He had always about twelve children in his own house. He kept the new ones there for a time that he might become acquainted with them; he did not like to give up those who were especially destitute, and youths who were to receive a better education, to fit them to become pastors, belonged to his family. They were expected to assist him with the children, and may be regarded as the origin of the societies of lay brothers.

In course of time more children were gathered around him in a house built for the purpose, and he kept up regular intercourse with those who were otherwise provided for. Every evening he held a Bible class with those who were destined to enter the Church, and music and singing were also practised. For the girls there was a sewing, knitting, and spinning school. All children under the care of the society were expected to attend a Sunday school at the institution.

Thus a beautiful work of Christian charity grew out of the prevailing distress. It was a fresh manifestation of the love with which August Hermann Francke had devoted himself to children a hundred years before. It sprang from the same source, the love of God revealed to us in Christ, and the object was the same, to train souls for the kingdom, but the manner of carrying it out was very different.

Falk's religion was far removed from ecclesiastical orthodoxy. His horror of the hideousness of sin, which met his eyes in a thousand forms, was combined with admiration for the natural goodness of the human heart, and he seemed sometimes to assume a mysterious good or evil destiny for particular persons, as if his views retained a trace of his early education in the predestinarianism of the Reformed Church. The rationalistic doctrine, that all men might be made good by education, excited his indignation, and he would not allow his pupils to attend the preaching of a rationalistic minister at Weimar. But, on the other hand, he did not accept the Scriptural doctrine of the atonement. He did not realize the wrath of God at the sight of sin, the necessity of a sacrifice, or the immensity of the fact that the Son of God should die for sinners.

Love was everything to him; it was his God. In his Saviour he beheld the incarnation of everlasting love; and when he gazed upon the cross, as he often did, he had less of the feeling that it was "for me" than that it was "an example to me," and it gave him fresh strength to follow his Saviour.

But it was not so much that he was opposed to the doctrines of the Church as that he had not attained to them. Many of the noble philanthropists of his day were more disposed to assist him in his labours, because they were not repulsed by an odour of orthodoxy; yet at Weimar he was regarded as a mystic, and the orthodox party were certainly justified in giving him their support. "God has diverse sorts of flowers in His garden of Paradise," said Blockmann, a pious man at Dresden, and he rejoiced in Falk's labours of love. And surely not without reason. If he was wanting in the definite Christian doctrines which were peculiar to pietism, there was more of cheerfulness in his system, and an absence of constraint. There was something depressing and gloomy in the pietistic mode of education. It laid too much stress on sorrow for sin, and the need of renouncing the world; it did not attain to being in the world, but not of it, to receiving with gratitude all the creatures of God, and to rejoicing in adoption as His sons.

There was not sufficient allowance made for children; they were expected to have an experience of sin and grace which can only be looked for in mature years, and as the result of the purifying fires of sorrow.

It was considered wrong to play and to give way to naturally joyous spirits, and the pleasures of music were denied them, unless it breathed the tone of the most decided Christian faith.

It was very different under Falk's rule. He brought to his work a warm heart, full of love for the people, but he preserved all the freshness and versatility of his poetical nature, and in his efforts to train up the children, to gain their affections, to make goodness attractive to them, and to deliver them from sin and the snares of the devil, he knew how to avail himself of every resource, and could turn to account old things and new, youthful troubles, and the trials of mature age, gravity and laughter, national dialect and popular songs.

He lived with the children; he devoted to them the very best that he had to bestow. He was engaged early and late in guiding the household both in moral and in temporal matters; letters were continually being despatched as messengers of Christian love, or as admonitions to others to exercise it; daily and hourly there was some one to be taught, comforted or punished, or there were disputes to be adjusted. And when a new child came he had a wonderful tact in feeling its pulse and discerning its disposition by the most natural conversation.

Thus the son of a farmer, a little boy from Poppendorf, once came to him, who already had an idea of being a minister, and considered it beneath his dignity to help to drive in his father's cows. Falk asked him whether Poppendorf was a town or a village. "A village."—"Then I wonder you should have come to Weimar to find out what a cow is. Or do you know how much we have to thank these good creatures for? It does not seem to me that you do. But now to change the subject. When a good maid rises early, and goes out with her basket and sickle into the green meadow, and cuts the dewy grass, it makes a rustling noise, does it not?" "Yes."—"And when a wealthy sluggard dozes all the beautiful morning inside his silken curtains, they rustle too, do they not?"—"Yes."—"And which sort of rustling do you suppose is most pleasing to the

Lord God, the rustling of the dewy grass under the sickle, or the rustling of the sluggard's silk curtains?"—"The rustling of the grass."—"Good; but why so?" Here the little man seemed to have come to the end of his ideas. "I will tell you, my son. Suppose the silk curtains rustle for ten or twelve years, what will become of it?"—"Nothing." "But if the sickle sparkling in the morning light rustles for six or seven years, and the basket filled with clover is faithfully taken to the cowhouse, what will become of the little calves and yearlings who look for the flowery food from the hands of the good maid, and lick them in their gratitude?"— "Fine large cows."—"And they fill the pantry with milk and butter and cheese, and the children have rosy cheeks, and are thriving and merry, and the flocks and herds disport themselves in the green fields, and praise the Lord who created us all, and they can in no wise do without the good maid as an instrument of their support. How, my boy? and so you do not like in fine bright weather to help to drive in such noble creatures, to whom we owe so much? My town boys know better than that. They know that the calling of a farmer is a high one. Now, boys, strike up our fine old song in praise of a country life, that this little boy from Poppendorf may hear it, and be ashamed of his pride." And the boys sang a song of Falk's. "Did you understand it? Who was Moses?"—"A man of God."— "And David?"—"Another man of God, who made psalms which we learn at school."—"You do not look to me as if you were ever likely to be a David, or to make psalms and hymns, and yet you disdain to do things that these men of God undoubtedly did, for Moses kept the flock of Jethro, his father-in-law, forty years, and David kept his father's sheep when his brothers were encamped with Saul against the Philistines. Off with you; you are such a simpleton, that you do not even know what a good maid is entrusted with in the care of an earthly flock, and how should the Lord intrust you with His sheep, or take you for His servant?"

However cutting such a reception might be, its effect was generally like the wound of a barbed hook which holds the victim fast. The liberty which the children enjoyed proved their strongest bond. Falk said, "All our chains are forged from within; we disdain the use of those that are put on outside, for it is written, 'When Christ shall make you free, ye shall be free indeed;' but then the converse must also be true, 'When Christ puts you in fetters you must be content to forego wandering over hill and dale. We cannot too greatly enlarge the kingdom of Christian freedom. Do fathers and mothers ever lock the door to prevent their children from running away from them? Then if this is not necessary at home, why in other places? Or is human nature twofold, and at variance with itself in the matter of love? No, it cannot be so, but Christ and the Scriptures are right in saying that love overcomes everything—doors, locks, drawbridges, gates, and wicked men."

In this confidence in the power of love, he once said to a pupil who had run away several times, after pointing out his folly, "God is all-powerful, and yet He does not compel any one to be saved! Now, listen to me. In order that you may not lose your way when you run away, if that is still your intention, I will tell you that there are two gateways here; if you wish to go to Frankfort, the nearest way is through Luther's Alley; but if you are going to Leipsic you should go through the other gate. They are opened at six in the morning, and shut at ten at night; so now you can act accordingly." The boy actually ran away once more, but came back in tears, and ever after humbled himself before God.

It was undoubtedly the love, of which the children could not fail to be conscious in Falk's presence, that kept them from running away. His mode of teaching was never dry and abstract; he brought everything vividly before the view of their minds; and when he talked to them of the love of God, it was illustrated by familiar examples.

The boys sang hymns at their work, many of them composed for them by Falk. He wrote a history of Luther for them in rhyme, in the style of Hans Sachs, and interspersed it with spirited songs. He often took his children out to roam with him over the Thuringian hills, that they might be familiar with the sacred lessons taught by the stars of heaven and the flowers of the field, and with the voice of God in the wailing of the wind and the rustling of the forest.

Falk devoted himself entirely to this work of rescuing poor children. Everything that happened in his own family seemed to give him a fresh impulse to take up their cause. In March, 1819, God took from him his own Edward, a hopeful youth of nineteen. Overwhelmed with grief, the parents and brothers and sisters were sitting by the lifeless body. An hour after his death, some one knocked at the door. "Oh," exclaimed the poor mother, "if I could but see you coming in at the door, my poor Edward, but once more!" A boy of fourteen came in, saying, "You have taken pity on so many poor children from our neighbourhood, do take pity on me. I have had neither father nor mother since I was seven years old." And the address, which began in tears, ended in sobs. The poor mother, who was still prostrate at the feet of her son, started up, and raising her weeping eyes to heaven, exclaimed, "Oh, my God! thou still sendest us the children of strangers, whom we so willingly take in, and takest away our own!"

The boy was received; but the parents, and particularly the mother, were so affected by this grief, that they were advised to try for a time the quiet of a country life. They went to the foot of the Wartburg, near Eisenach, and were refreshed by the pleasant country and the inspiriting memories connected with the castle. After visiting Frankfort, they returned to their children in the autumn.

For two years God granted them rest from sorrow, but then their daughter Angelica, a girl of sixteen, died after a short illness. They were well practised in saying, "Thy will be done," and did not weary in the work which God had given them to do.

And, just at this juncture, fresh courage was needed in carrying it on. The landlord of the house in which Falk had conducted his refuge suddenly gave them notice to quit.

He sought diligently for another, but could find no suitable place. A report was spread that Falk was going into Luther's Alley. There was in this place a large, old, ruined, and desolate house, which had formerly belonged to a Count von Orlamünde. Falk's first remark when he heard the report was, that he "would not wish to be there if he were dead." But not having been able to find any other house, the thought darted into his mind, "Suppose I do go into Luther's Alley, and, with the children's help, turn the old house into a new own." It was no sooner said than done. The house was bought; 5000 dollars were to be paid within a given time, and there was not a farthing in hand; and then there was the building to be set about. "Trust in God, trust in God, my friends," said Falk; "if we consider our plans well in God's name, and put our hands cheerfully to a work which is pleasing to Him, we get all that we want, and often even more."

And he did put his hand bravely to the work. He sent messengers through Germany and Holland, furnished with printed accounts of what he was doing, and they sent home the funds that were intrusted to them. Falk contributed more than 3000 dollars himself from his own property or the profits of authorship. And while he and his assistants were thus providing the funds, the pupils were hard at work on the new building.

From that time every boy lived for half a year in Falk's house before being apprenticed to a master, and journeymen who could not get work found employment with him. The old house was pulled down, and the foundation-stone of the new one laid in 1823.

The following benediction, sealed with Falk's seal, was laid with the stone :—

> "May no fire destroy thee!
>   No floods overflow thee!
> May'st thou prosper, House Weimar!
> May the Fatherland honour thee!"*

It was built in accordance with the following resolution :—

"A house shall be built in Luther's Alley, in which every tile on the roof, every lock on the doors, every chair and table in the rooms, shall be the work of Falk's sons."

His benediction, when it was finished, was in these words :—"As long as this house is open to poor children, the blessing of God will rest upon it it and its inhabitants ; but from the moment when its doors are unmercifully closed against them, His blessing will depart from it."   And a black marble tablet was placed upon it, with this inscription :— "After the battles of Jena, Lützen, and Leipsic, the 'Friends in Need' caused this house to be built by two hundred rescued boys, as an everlasting thank-offering to the Lord."

And when the house itself was built, Falk devoted himself with more zeal and spirit than ever to building up the characters and caring for the souls of the youthful fraternity.   It enabled him to keep a larger number of them around him.   He had much satisfaction in his pupils.   Many an honest master workman, efficient schoolmaster, and devoted pastor, were indebted to him for rescuing them from poverty and neglect, and training them up to be useful members of society.

> * "Kein Feuer zerstöre dich !
>   Kein Wasser verheere dich !
>   Haus Weimar mehre dich !
>   Und das Vaterland ehre dich !"

One of Falk's pupils, John Denner, has given us an account of his life. He was a poor boy, who was induced by his great desire for knowledge to leave his home near the forests of Thuringia, and in the year 1822 he was adopted by Falk, and was before long employed to assist him in writing, and honoured with his affection. He was afterwards sent out as a travelling collector for Falk's institution. After Falk's death he experienced many remarkable leadings of Providence, and at length attained to the long-wished-for office of a pastor in Würtemberg. From Denner's life we have a picture of Falk in his later years. Nothing could be more amiable and confiding than the intercourse which the friend of Goethe, with all his learning and knowledge of the world, maintained with this young man. He wrote charming letters to him, varying in tone from genial humour to deep seriousness. "When you get to the Baltic, and hear the murmur of its waves, give my love to it, and tell it that the poor John who came from its shores has hushed the tears and sighs of many, but he has shed many a tear and heaved many a sigh himself. You wished for a long and large letter, and yet you are so little yourself; but I cannot refuse it to you. God bless you, my dear fellow, in all your ways. May an invisible escort of angels encompass you, and bear you up in their hands, lest you dash your foot against a stone."

"P.S.—By mistake, you will get a letter on gilt-edged paper. Do not be puffed up by it, and, when your pockets are empty, you can cut off the edge; and then you can at least say that you are never without gold. If I had any gold dust, I would powder the whole letter with it."

When Denner wrote to him of his stay in the island of Rügen, he answered, " My dear faithful Elisha! (2 Kings ii.) While I have been sitting here on Mount Carmel, and looking up to the Lord, you have been at Rügen, and have been listening to His voice in the murmurs of the Baltic waves! May God lead you on in health and happiness, and open hearts to you which, like ours, beat warmly for humanity, and which belong not to the day or to the hour, but to all eternity. When God calls me hence, whether it be in the thunder or in the gentle breeze, if I can leave you a little bit of my mantle I shall rejoice to do so. Then you shall smite the waters with it, and pass dryshod through all the sea of troubles which men have to go through here on earth! You have not only been taught by, but have learnt from your master to believe firmly in God, and to trust in Him at all times, good or bad. I am so glad, my dear, good Denner, that even in youth you had a pure heart, for the pure in heart shall see God. The pious Spener says, ' Prayer is the breath of the soul. Without it the soul perishes, just as the body perishes without the breath.' It is the heart that prays with groanings that cannot be uttered. Watch and pray then, my son, for from the pleasure you take in prayer you will be able to judge how you stand with God. The more freely your soul can breathe, the nearer it is to God. You say that you often have to talk to learned men by the hour about our institution. Take comfort and courage, my dear Denner. Your heart is faithful to God, and full of nature, truth, and simplicity. They will judge from you what we are doing for popular education here in Luther's Alley ; that we are not turning out crafty, cunning rogues, or puffed-up fools, but honest and true men, whose calling it is to speak truth with simplicity, and, still better, to do good with simplicity of heart. We must humbly submit to everything that the Lord requires from us in His service.

"Now, my dear good Denner, may the Lord bless your going out and your coming in, as He has done hitherto. He who was so gracious to shepherds and fishermen can extend the kingdom of His love by means of poor boys out of Luther's Alley if it be His will. Ungodly men may hiss at us and gape upon us with their mouths, but the Lord will not suffer us to be put to shame."

When Denner was making his second journey in Holland and the Rhenish provinces in 1825 and 1826, Falk could not conceal from him in his letters that he was very ill. On October 25th he wrote, " Pray for your sick father, who, as he lies awake many an hour on his couch, commends you to the protection of the Almighty." And a week later, " I can neither walk, stand, nor sit, nor scarcely move at all. I cannot sleep a wink the whole night. All my appetite is gone, and the least movement makes me feel as if pierced with a thousand knives. They call this dreadful disease, which is worse than death, sciatica, and it grinds a poor man to nothing. May God, who has laid this new and heavy cross upon me, help me to honour Him by bearing it with patience and composure." And then he says, in touching words, how it comforts him in his sufferings to know that, through the exertions of the young men who are collecting for it, the institution will be provided for.

Four weeks later he wrote, " God has heard my prayers, my dear son; the burning pain in my bones, like the fires of hell, has ceased. And to the letter, which was dictated to his daughter, he added with his own hands a few lines in rhyme, expressive of his affection for Denner, and his conviction that he should be spared to see him again.

But the disciple did not see his master again on earth. His illness returned. He wrote, "If you want to know my condition read the 102nd Psalm."

But his strong faith kept his mind clear. " Look around you, my son," he wrote again. " We live in a lazaretto, where there is no end to the sighing and dying, the parting and heart-breaking. But the children of this world give little heed to it. They are like frivolous French commissioners who could arrange a dance in the upper rooms while the groans of the dying were heard in those below. Yes, sound the trumpets lest the cries of the dying should reach your ears, and your delicate nerves should be pained and your pleasure marred while merry dances and intoxicating drinks have sent you into the third heaven. There, my dear Denner, you have a picture of the world and its miserable frivolity. God sent us into the world to oppose this state of things, and through fearful trials He has marked me out as a man of sorrows. Blessed are they who through great tribulation enter into the kingdom of heaven !"

He preached a most powerful sermon by his patience, and triumph over suffering. As he said, he went through the experience of Job ; but he resisted the tempter, and employed every moment of ease in praising God and exerting himself for his children. They came to his bedside for their lessons ; and until the very last day, he ruled the house, and dictated.

He dictated a poem on the 'Invincible Armada' of Philip II., in the destruction of which he clearly traced the hand of God, and three days before his death he wrote the preface to his 'Lutherbüchlein,' in which he had related the story of the reformer in popular rhymes. He then made his will, and let his daughter read it in the presence of an attorney. When she came to the epitaph which he had composed for himself, she burst into tears; he repeated it himself, and then said, " Go on, my daughter; be a heroic girl ! "

On the 14th of February he wished to take the communion. It was administered to him by one of his greatest opponents, who afterwards became one of his warmest admirers. Soon the last conflict began, and only unconnected words were intelligible,—God — popular—faith—short—Christ—full stop.

The victory was won.

Three days afterwards Falk's pulpils laid his body to rest in the family vault. The epitaph on a simple stone still marks the spot where he lies under the shadow of the lime-trees.

The author of this sketch will not soon forget the fine June morning on which he paid a visit to Falk's grave. In going through Weimar he had lingered before the houses in which our great poets, Falk's friends, once lived, and the monuments which a grateful posterity has erected to their memory. He had gazed upon the frescoes in the grand ducal palace in which the painter has represented the subjects of the most remarkable poems of the mighty men who were once assembled at Weimar, and Schwind's wonderful sculpture representing the legend of the seven ravens. Then he wandered into the churchyard, which rises gently from the town. The princely vault was shown to him in which the poet princes repose side by side with the princes of Saxony.

There were fresh garlands on the coffins, but it was cold and gloomy, and the soul was seized with a melancholy conviction that all the glory of man fadeth as the flower of grass. But it was more cheerful outside ; thousands of roses bloomed amongst the graves, the birds were singing, and the blue sky extended over the city of the living and the resting-place of the dead, and the wanderer was consoled when under the shadow of the lime-trees he found on the churchyard wall John Falk's epitaph, which gives the glory to the Saviour.

> " Where the limes their shadows trace,
> Pardoned through his Saviour's grace,
> Hath John Falk his resting-place.
>
> " He who left his friends and home,
> By the distant Baltic's foam,
> With a sacred call to roam.
>
> " Stranger children, here who tread,
> Lightly o'er his resting head,
> Breathe a blessing o'er the dead.
>
> " ' Holy Father, thou wilt bless,
> Him who was in our distress
> Father of the fatherless !
>
> " ' As he did for children care,
> May he in thy mansions fair,
> All thy children's blessings share.' "

CHAPTER VII.

SULPIZ BOISSERÉE.

WE conclude the series of our sketches with one of
the most efficient promoters of German Christian art at the time of German ignominy. An essential element would be wanting in our delineation of
renewed religious life, if we were to omit notice of
the fresh impulse which was given to Christian art.
There is an intimate connection between Christianity and art. From the earliest times, the reception of the Gospel by a nation has given a new
meaning and a higher tone to art, and art has ever
been at the service of religion. And it is not only
in the Roman Catholic Church, in which the outward and visible predominates over the inward and
spiritual, that art can render service to religion; we
have in the Protestant community the words of the
great Reformer as a watchword to incite us to strive
after perfection in art. "Neither am I of opinion
that all the arts should be neglected and perish for
the sake of the Gospel, as some over-zealous ecclesiastics hold; on the contrary, I should like to see
all the arts, especially music, in the service of Him
who gave and created them."

Herein lies the connection of art with religion, that the arts are a gift and creation of God. The more clearly an artist perceives that art is a gift of God, the more he will aspire and, as it were, stretch out his arms to Christ, the unsullied likeness of God, the express image of His person; the better qualified he will be to represent scenes from the blessed life of the Son of God and man, and from the lives of his followers, and to create foretastes, in an artistic sense, of the perfecting of our life in the heavenly kingdom.

As long as man realizes in his heart that the Word was made flesh and dwelt among us, so long will human hands strive to make the Word flesh by artistic representations, to clothe eternal love in visible form, to permeate matter with spirit, to elevate the natural into the sphere of the spiritual life.

But when religion has lost its power to bring down the divine into our life, to consecrate the things of sense by raising them to the regions of the divine,—when Christianity has become an empty name, and the Church a mere form, art becomes powerless also.

In past centuries German Christian art was very fertile. But when Christianity and nationality were at a low ebb, not only had creative power disappeared, but all appreciation of the monuments of art was lost, of the old German pictures with their holy simplicity, of the ancient churches with their symbolic details, and the powerful impression they produced of aspiration towards heaven.

Uhland's legend of the lost church had become a truth. Service was still heard in the church, but

who accepted the message that was delivered in it?
The churches were still standing, but who knew
that they were wonderfully beautiful?　But as the
poet relates of himself, that as he wandered alone,
looking upwards to God from amidst the ruins, the
lost church revealed itself to his mind, so Sulpiz
Boisserée wandered alone, or but with few companions, amidst the ruins of our nationality and religion, amidst the still standing but unappreciated
monuments of ancient glory, and the lost church
was again revealed to him.

> " The heavens were clear and darkly blue,
> 　The sun was shining full and bright,
> A proud cathedral to my view
> 　Rose glowing in the golden light.
> I thought the clouds that floated by,
> 　Like angels' wings, were gliding o'er,
> And far into the tranquil sky,
> 　The pinnacle appeared to soar.
>
> " Now tolled the bell, with solemn clang,
> 　It swung melodious in the tower ;
> Yet, 'twas no human hand that rang,
> 　It was the storm's supernal power.
> It seemed to strike my heart, which beat
> 　With mingled wonder, joy, and pain ;
> With strange delight and trembling feet,
> 　I stepped into the lofty fane."

Although the massive form of the cathedral of
Cologne must always have made it a conspicuous
object, Sulpiz Boisserée had, as it were, to show it
again to his countrymen ; and he may be said to
have discovered the ancient German pictures, though
they were everywhere to be seen in churches, monasteries, and halls.

It was the great work of his life to direct atten-

tion to the treasures of ancient German painting
and architecture, and we class it among those which
contributed to the renewal of religious life. This
sketch will introduce us to one of the most amiable
of our countrymen; to a devout Christian, whose
mind was open to the manifold interests of humanity; to a Roman Catholic, who appreciated every
incitement to a higher life wherever found; to an
enthusiast in art, whose interest in it was not merely
fugitive and transitory, but who devoted to it a long
life of most effective labour.

The French-sounding name of Boisserée owes its
fame to two excellent Germans, the brothers Sulpiz
and Melchior. The family came from near Liége,
anciently a constituent part of the German empire.
Hadrian Boisserée, the grandfather of the celebrated
picture collector, was a government *employé* of some
note, first at Huys and afterwards at Stockem, near
Maestricht. A wealthy and childless maternal uncle,
Nicholas de Tongre, invited Hadrian's son Nicholas
to Cologne, where he was introduced into his uncle's
business, and became his chief heir. He married
Mary Magdalena Brentano, the daughter of an eminent merchant of Cologne. Eleven children were
born to them, of whom but one died in infancy.
The youngest were the brothers Sulpiz, born in
1783, and Melchior, three years younger. Their
mother was a devout Roman Catholic, who was fond
of associating with priests and nuns, and they were
always welcome at her house. She died before
Sulpiz was seven years old, and the father, who took
a high position, not only as a merchant but as a
member of the town council, followed her three
years afterwards.

The little orphan grew up under the care of his grandmother, and amidst the influences of the Catholic city. His youthful mind was very susceptible to the charms of nature. He shouted for joy, when, on the occasion of a visit to the monastery of Langwaden, he first saw a forest; and every autumn he revelled in the delights of a country life on his parents' estate at Wesseling; and the mountains and rocks on the banks of the Upper Rhine made a deep impression upon him. But it was the influence of the Roman Catholic Church, by which he was so surrounded in his native city, that gave the prevailing colour to his youthful days.

His godfather, John Sulpiz Pols, was the provost of Langwaden. When the boy paid him a visit, he considered it a great honour to wait upon him when he performed mass, and the nuns at the nunnery almost smothered the provost's godchild with caresses. When the provost came to the city, the grandmother always had the best guest chamber, with the crimson silk curtains and coverlet, prepared for him; and Sulpiz was pleased to have the honour of kissing his hand, and of admiring the beautiful sapphire ring which he wore as an ensign of his dignity.

The eldest son of the Boisserée family had chosen the Church as his profession, and often took Sulpiz with him on his visits to churches and monasteries. When the boys went to school they were taught by ecclesiastics. Gorgeous processions, churches, and monasteries were continually before their eyes.

Sulpiz was confirmed in his seventh year, and in his twelfth, "well prepared, but not without anxious scruples," he partook of the communion. On this

occasion his brother, the priest, gave him Stolberg's
'Homer,' an indication that poetry was not excluded
from this ecclesiastical atmosphere. Moreover, at
that time, people adhered to ecclesiastical usages
and institutions rather from habit than from any
profound conviction of their importance. There
was nothing strict or gloomy in the aspect of the
Roman Catholic Church. When Sulpiz visited
Bonn he saw the elector and archbishop, only con-
descending to witness the procession of the festival
of Corpus Christi from a balcony; and he sometimes merely drove up to a church door to hear
mass, and listened to it from outside, whip and
bridle in hand.

Soon after his first communion Sulpiz was expected to begin work in the counting-house, but he
still had some lessons to learn as well, and, although
so young, he read Jean Paul and Shakspeare with
his bosom friend. The family, however, thought it
best to send the boy from home for a time. Hamburg was selected, and it would have been difficult
to find any place where the influences would have
been in greater contrast to those of Cologne, especially when it is considered that Hamburg was then
the seat of a newly awakened philosophical and
poetical life.

Sulpiz obtained introductions to the families of
Sieveking and Reimarus, and arrived in the old
Hanse town, in 1798, when he was just fifteen years
of age. His situation did not give him much to do,
and he took lessons in the laws of commerce, mathematics, physics, and in architectural drawing.
His visits to the houses of Reimarus and Sieveking
introduced him to the intellectual life which was

then stirring in Germany. During the latter part
of his residence at Hamburg he lived in the house
of Elise Reimarus, but his favourite haunt was
Perthes' shop. There the newest publications were
always to be found, and those that were well spoken
of in the reviews stood ready bound for sale. Intercourse with the bookseller himself was improv-
ing, and incited the youth to mental culture. Perthes' own circumstances had been somewhat similar
to those of Sulpiz, and, with his characteristic kindness and readiness to serve others,—the man of ripe
experience condescended to the boy,—aided him in
his course of reading, and gained his lasting affection. With enlarged ideas and loftier aims, as the
result of his two years' residence at Hamburg,
Sulpiz returned to his native city. With anxious
care, his brothers, aided by their grandmother's advice, sought to make home pleasant to him. A
horse was at his disposal, and some pleasant rooms
were prepared for his own private use in an ancient
house which stood in the garden. As far as was
possible he continued his Hamburg life, surrounded
himself with pictures, books, and reminiscences of
it, and corresponded with Perthes about completing
his collection of books. A spark of intellectual
aspiration, which could not be satisfied with an
ordinary business life, had fallen into his mind, and
it soon burst into a flame. It was in the summer of
1801 that he met at his bookbinder's a young man
with curling hair and sparkling eyes, who arrested
his attention by his spirited and intellectual remarks
upon literary subjects. This stranger was under
the influence of the brothers Schlegel, who were
just then setting up new criterions of poetic merit,

and daring boldly to tear off laurels, the possession
of which had been hitherto undisputed, and to distribute them afresh. Sulpiz, who was accustomed
to the more sober judgment of the Hamburg circles,
entered into a friendly dispute with this disciple of
the romantic school, which was continued on their
way home.

This was the beginning of a friendship with his
fellow-citizen, John Baptist Bertram, which lasted
during the whole of their lives, and was much
blessed by God. Bertram was seven years older
than Sulpiz, and their daily intercourse caused the
mind of the latter to emerge from its chrysalis
state. Bertram made him acquainted with the modern romantic school; directed his attention from
the sphere of every day life to the realms of poetry;
from conventionalism to the freedom of nature;
and from a mere interest in humanity in general to
the claims of patriotism. While Sulpiz was from
home at Aix-la-Chapelle he and his friend kept up a
diligent correspondence, and discussed the most important questions of life. On his return to Cologne
Sulpiz had made up his mind that nothing but a
course of study could satisfy his mental longings,
and Bertram assured him that it was not too late
for a zealous youth of nineteen to lay the necessary
foundation. His elder brothers did not approve of
the scheme, but his grandmother and guardian consented, and he began diligently to study the Latin
authors and philosophy, in the hope of going to the
University of Jena in the autumn of 1803.

But God directed Sulpiz Boisserée into another
path, which led to that which he was ultimately to
follow.

His brother Melchior, whose mind was infected
with the enthusiasm of Sulpiz and Bertram for
mental culture, was obliged by matters of business
to reside for nine months at Antwerp. Sulpiz went
to see him there, and visited the glorious monuments of the architecture of the middle ages, in that
city, Louvain, Brussels, and Malines. The few pictures which had not been taken to Paris excited the
desire to see the spoils which had been collected
there. After his return, these ideas were strengthened by the perusal of works on art by various disciples of the romantic school, which to some were like
sealed fountains, to others springs of living water.
The works of Goethe, Tieck, Wackenroder, and Schlegel, increased the desire of Sulpiz to see the art
treasures of Paris. Artists and connoisseurs were
going thither in swarms. The young enthusiasts
of Cologne, whose tastes had been confirmed by
acquaintance with Hofman, the artist of that city,
and Peter Cornelius at Düsseldorf, were eager to
follow their example; and like a party of students
merely making an excursion, they suddenly set out
on their journey on foot, in the autumn of 1803.

We may be sure that the young Germans enjoyed
to the full the treasures of art of which so many
lands had been spoiled. But, again, things did not
turn out according to their expectations.

They made the acquaintance of Frederic Schlegel,
who had betaken himself to Paris to pursue his
studies in Indian literature.

An eruptive complaint from which Sulpiz had
previously suffered, returned, and confined him to
the house, so that the plan of going to Jena was
abandoned. Schlegel proposed to the young men

to spend the winter in Paris, and to live with him, and he promised to give them lectures.

They agreed. Sulpiz found a careful nurse in Schlegel's wife, and all three derived great advantage from the lectures which he delivered to them on Greek philosophy and ancient and modern literature. Under his guidance they visited the works of art, and studied Winkelmann, while Mme. Schlegel cultivated their taste for music.

The household, and the various visitors who came and went, formed a little German colony in the French capital,—altogether German in its sentiments, although only a year later Mme. Schlegel was captivated with the French Emperor at Cologne. In the city which considered it to be its prerogative to give the tone in modes of life and thought to the world, a little handful of Germans maintained their own national tone; among the works of art collected from all countries, the spirit was unconsciously strengthened which afterwards demanded their return; under the eyes of the man who was then intending to assume the imperial crown as a signal that he considered himself a universal monarch, the independent powers of these aspiring youths were ripening which afterwards fitted them to take part in the conflict which hurled the tyrant from his throne.

In their intercourse with Schlegel, perhaps Sulpiz and Melchior Boisserée were merely recipients, but Bertram, who was their senior, and who was distinguished by a clear and forcible manner of communicating his ideas, was capable of imparting new ones to the man of genius. He interested him in Cologne; told him of its numerous monasteries and ecclesiastical foundations, of the churches and religious services, and the peculiar life in the old city on the Rhine. The church of Notre Dame, to which Schlegel's attention had just been drawn by his young friends, excited his desire to see the glorious cathedrals of Belgium, and in the Rhenish provinces. And as Cologne was likely to afford him opportunity of turning to account his unusally rich and varied learning, he was easily persuaded by his friends to go there.

He at once found temporary occupation at the University, and began giving lectures, and the trio of enthusiasts for German art began the labours which were to be the occupation of their lives.

The French dominion on the left shore of the Rhine led, as is well known, to the abolition of the prince-bishoprics, and of numberless monasteries and religious foundations.

While the friends were at Paris the monasteries and churches had been robbed of their pictures; those that had not been taken away by the displaced occupants, or sequestered by the government commissioners, had been, as Sulpiz relates, hastily sold to dealers. Like the German empire, the art treasures of Germany had suffered shipwreck; the broken pieces of the ship were tossed ruthlessly about by the waves; whoever found anything worth saving was at liberty to save it, if perchance some new thing might be modelled after the old pattern.

The three friends were fired with the desire to save as much as possible from the wreck, and they had made a discovery which revealed to them what treasures there were to save.

Sulpiz relates, " Bertram had a recollection of the

large altar-piece in the Chapel of the Rathhaus, which
was highly spoken of in all the old books about
Cologne. For several years it had disappeared. The
office of patriarch, as the chaplain of the Town
Council had been called, and with it divine service,
had been abolished. During that period of commotion Professor and Canon Wallraf, who took great
interest in the antiquities of the city, had had the
picture removed into an out of the way vault,
whereby it was saved from destruction. Upon in-
quiry, we found that the picture had been lately re-
instated in its place in the council-room ; we hastened to see it, and we and Schlegel were greatly
struck with its originality and beauty."

The impression made upon them by this picture
excited their desire to save others, and a beginning
was soon made. The following account is given by
Sulpiz himself of the incident which was an era in
the history of his own life, and that of modern
art :—

" During the first few months after our return, as
we were walking with Schlegel in the Newmarket,
the great square of the city, we met a truck loaded
with all sorts of furniture, among which was an old
painting, in which the glory round the head of a
saint was seen glittering from a distance. It was a
picture of the bearing of the cross, with the weeping
women and Veronica, and seemed to possess some
merit. I was the first to notice it, and asked after
the owner. He lived in the neighbourhood, and, as
he did not know what to do with it, he was glad to
get rid of it for the price he named. Then arose the
question how to get it home ; and, in order to avoid
observation and banter, we resolved to take the

dusty old treasure in at the back door. But just as
we reached it, who should come up but my grandmother? and, after looking at it for a little while,
she said to the new and somewhat embarrassed
owner, ' That is a touching picture you have bought ;
you have done well to buy it.' It was a benediction
at the beginning of an eventful future.''

From that time Sulpiz and Melchior Boisserée
devoted themselves to seeking out and buying old
pictures. When funds ran short, little treasures
were sacrificed. At first their only idea was to get
possession of anything that was offered them, and
they bought without plan, but by degrees their
practical interest in art led them to distinguish the
style of various schools and the development of the
art of painting, and they purchased and arranged
their treasures so as to constitute a history of
art.

Diligent mental culture went hand in hand with
the practical energy that became the sons of a mercantile house. After a visit to Mme. de Staël at
Coppet, and another winter spent at Paris, Schlegel
returned to Cologne in 1805, and gave private lectures to his friends upon the whole range of philosophy, the laws of nature, and politics in the highest
sense of the term. During the following winter
universal history was added to the course, and in
1806 he gave public lectures on logic, and critiques
on the various systems of philosophy. The history
which was then passing before the eyes of the
nations, the unsparing criticism which annihilated
decayed systems, the powerful logic of facts, prevented the young men from falling into a habit of
mere philosophical speculation, and the writings of

Gentz and Johannes Müller, and especially Arndt's 'Spirit of the Age,' kept their patriotism aglow.

About this time Tieck's 'Minnelieder,' and Hagen's 'Nibelungen' were published, and found many admirers; and in 1807 Schlegel drew the attention of his pupils to this department of literature. Thus, just when German nationality was being trodden underfoot, fresh elements of strength for its resuscitation were being developed unobserved. Continued occupation with ancient German art led to the discovery that the old paintings at Cologne by the brothers Van Eyck, like those of the contemporary Italian school, were after the style of the old Byzantine models, although it was developed with great originality, and this led to a project of making " as complete a collection as possible of the ancient German school of Cologne." Thus, a systematic aim was added to the occupation of the brothers with art as mere amateurs.

It was not long before a desire was excited to do something for Cologne cathedral,—that unfinished, ay, even decaying, monument of the enthusiasm and noble projects of our fathers. Sulpiz relates:

" In the spring of 1808 I got quite into a ferment about it. Schlegel's lectures were over. I was engrossed with art, with the collection of old German paintings, and with the study of the history of art, especially the architecture of the Middle Ages. I undertook to take measurements of the cathedral, and began to dream of a scheme for completing this fine monument of German greatness which had been so mournfully interrupted."

A host of difficulties, however, appeared in the way of the career on which he would fain have entered.

Bertram was too rash and impulsive ; Melchior too young, and too much under Bertram's influence to be looked to for assistance. He could depend upon Schlegel's support, but since he had joined the Roman Catholic Church he had removed to Vienna. There was also Reinhard, the ambassador, whom Sulpiz had induced to settle at Cologne ; and about this time he formed a friendship with Dr. Schmitz, an intelligent young physician, which was of great value to him. He introduced Sulpiz into musical circles, and hearing the compositions of Handel and Mozart put him into such a state of rapturous enthusiasm, that for a month he almost daily noted down some outpouring of the heart. If, according to an expression of Görres, architecture is congealed music, we need not wonder that, at the time when Sulpiz was gazing in admiration at the cathedral, in which he beheld, as it were, the aspirations of the soul expressed in stone, he should listen eagerly to the harmonies which respond to them.

We will listen to the account he gives himself of his state of mind at this period :—

"I was overwhelmed with profound melancholy, to which my frail health may have contributed. I felt myself forsaken and alone, like one who has had to renounce all the joys of life, but who is yet thankful for the hope held out to him that (like a poor miner) he may be able to help forward a work which his happier brethren shall complete and enjoy, and then lovingly think of their departed comrade. It was in words like these that I clothed my ideas about Cologne cathedral. In my rapturous effusions I gave expression to the deepest feelings

of the heart, the most subtle ideas of the mind, and
discussed the profound questions of faith.

"The deep expression which, in nature as well as
in art, lies in the eye and mouth, was at one time
the subject of my rapt attention, and Raphael's pictures seemed to hover as illustrations of it before
my sight. At another time I was engrossed with
the power and significance of music. How wonderful did its power appear to me in symphonies and
concertos, when it expresses strength, might, and
glory, sorrow, melancholy, and aspiration, and finally
pleasure, joy, and triumph ! What a life of the soul
is revealed in song ! What a world of wealth in
dramatic, what sublimity in sacred music !

" At that time I began to apprehend, that a more
or less conscious endeavour on the part of man to
produce a new creation to the honour of God is the
true origin of art. Architecture creates the dwelling-place ; painting and sculpture people it with
representations of plants, animals, and men ; music
fills it with tones of harmony, and bears aloft to the
triune Lord of Heaven the voice of prayer and
praise. All my researches in the history of art and
of the world, and the progress of the human mind,
led me to observe the aspiration to a higher life
which has always characterized civilized nations,
and still continues to characterize them,—a perpetual desire to build up the city of God.

"It will be quite intelligible, therefore, that in
this state of mind my enthusiastic effusions of poetic
prose were concluded with an endeavour to give a
lofty symbolic signification to the project of the
completion of the cathedral of Cologne."

God grants success to honest endeavour. Boisserée did not content himself with poetic dreams, and it was granted him to see the result of his projects and energy,—to see the continuation of the cathedral undertaken in earnest.

He had measurements and drawings of it made, and views of it executed as it would be when completed. He succeeded in having the picture in the council-chamber, before mentioned, removed into the cathedral, where, under the name of the Cologne cathedral picture, it is still the delight of all beholders.

"On Epiphany Sunday, 1810," he relates, "I had the pleasure of seeing this ancient treasure shining in all its glory in the cathedral, and all the world hastening to worship and admire. It was one of the greatest pleasures I have ever experienced."

In March, 1810, he set out on his travels with the drawings, and took up his quarters at Heidelberg. The university there was the seat of the romantic school, and new views on the subjects of religion and art had gone forth thence into the world. Boisserée expected to find more sympathy there for the passion of his life than at Cologne. But he did not remain stationary; he made excursions into all parts of the country where noteworthy architectural remains were to be found, and, wherever he went, he took his map and drawings of Cologne cathedral. He exhibited them to Schelling at Stuttgard, who said, to Boisserée's great satisfaction, "It is really a mental gain to have seen these views; they open up quite a new page of life, and a page of noble German life it is. This building is altogether great and glorious, like a work of nature; indeed, one may almost say that it is a work of nature," etc.

Sulpiz next negotiated with the publisher Cotta, and with skilful artists about the publication of the views. Having been thus successful with Schelling, he was very desirous of interesting Goethe in his schemes, the poet to whom almost regal honours were paid. As a young man he had written pages on Strasburg cathedral imbued with a patriotic and artistic spirit; and though his interests had been turned away from Germany to the ancient classics, his sympathies were still warm for art.

In May, 1810, Boisserée had sent him the drawings with an explanatory letter. Goethe gave him a friendly answer, and invited him to Weimar, but the visit did not take place till the spring of 1811.

Sulpiz wrote to his brother Melchior, " I am just come from Goethe, who received me coldly and stiffly; but I was nothing daunted, and was stiff and by no means obsequious in return. He kept me waiting some time, and then came in with powdered hair, and with his ribbons in his button-holes, and addressed me as loftily as possible. I had a number of messages for him. ' Very good,' he replied. Then we spoke of the drawings, copperplate engraving, the difficulties, the publication by Cotta, and all external matters connected with the subject. ' Yes; yes, indeed—hem, hem.' Then we got to the work itself, the fate and history of ancient art. I had determined to be as lofty as he was, and spoke of the beauty and excellence of the work in the cathedral as shortly as possible, observing that he must be already acquainted with it from the views. But he looked all the while as if he was ready to devour me. He did not thaw in the least till we got upon the subject of ancient painting."

At length the old gentleman became more friendly, and invited his visitor to dinner the next day. "Another visitor was announced," Boisserée continues, "and he gave me one or two fingers; but I think I shall soon have the whole hand. As I passed into the ante-room, I saw a little old gentleman in black, and with silk stockings, go in with a profound bow. With him Goethe's loftiness would be in place. It is a wonder that a man who is constantly surrounded with flatterers and admirers, and who is looked upon by great and small as a star of the first magnitude, should be so ceremonious; but it ceases when he is confronted with any one who, while acknowledging his eminent merit, does not forget his own dignity."

A few days afterwards Boisserée wrote, "I am getting on capitally with the old gentleman. If I had but one finger the first day, the next I had the whole arm." Before leaving Weimar, Boisserée had entirely gained Goethe for his cause, and he says, "I experienced the rare pleasure of seeing a mind of the first order delivered from an error in which he had been untrue to himself." As Boisserée warmed with his subject, Goethe's heart warmed also, and this intercourse was the beginning of a friendship of which we have a memorial in the interesting correspondence which was continued till Goethe's death, in which his kindliness, often obscured by advancing age and polite formalities, shines brightly forth, and in which Sulpiz Boisserée wins our admiration at once by his childlike devotion to the great man and his independent bearing in his presence.

The labours of the brothers Boisserée and Bertram, on behalf of old paintings and the cathedral, took place in the latest years of our country's ignominy. It is quite intelligible that these apostles of art, who were very practical men, did not wait for better times; indeed, we consider it to be an honour to them that they endeavoured to turn the unfavourable circumstances in which they were placed to account. With the cathedral especially, which in one part was in danger of falling down, delay would have been disastrous. All difficulties would be surmounted if Napoleon's government could be interested in the restoration. In the autumn of 1811, after Boisserée left Weimar, he went to Cologne, and Napoleon's mother was there also. A French newspaper reports, " Yesterday the most honourable and happiest of mothers came *incognito* to our city. To-day she visited the port, and afterwards the treasures of our ancient cathedral. After the mass, Mr. Sulpiz Boisserée had the honour of exhibiting to her some views intended for a splendid work which he is going to publish in France and Germany, on this glorious monument of Gothic architecture. A number of our inhabitants looked on at a distance with reverence and admiration, and tried to discern in the countenance of the exalted princess the features of the adored ruler, whom we venture to hope we shall one day see again." Sulpiz describes the audience as the most hurried and confusing that he had ever had; it was all over in six minutes, but the lady was as friendly and gracious as this distinguished haste permitted. Sulpiz did not fail in making himself agreeable in the interests of his work. When the princess remarked that it was a pity the cathedral was unfinished, he answered, " Nothing is required to finish it, but the mandate of his Majesty, your son ;" and he relates that such a ray of joy lighted up every feature of the imperial maternal countenance, that it was as if he had performed a miracle."

In the evening the prefect said to him, " Your cause prospers wonderfully. Madame will praise your work, and she is the third person in the empire, so it will be sure to succeed."

The daughter of the last of the German emperors seems to have received the adulation which was offered her as Empress of the French in the ancient German city, with deep emotion. About 15,000 persons were in the cathedral. The Empress was received by the dean, with the choir and a crucifix under a canopy, and at the first sound of the drum, there was a mighty chorus of vivas, trumpets, drums, and military music. The Empress, deeply moved, proceeded with downcast and tearful eyes to her throne, where she threw herself upon her knees, and hid her face in her hands. After the Te Deum, she saw the cathedral treasures, and gave a few minutes' attention to Boisserée, and assured him that she would willingly accept the dedication of his work. Before it was published, however, the French rule was at an end.

The feelings of this genuine German, while pleading for the cathedral before the French powers, because it was under their rule, are shown by some expressions in his letters.

In January, 1812, he wrote the following gloomy words to his young friend Behr :—" Your faithful, friendly, patriotic words have cheered my heart ; it seldom happens to me that the affection I show to my young friends leaves so lasting an impression.

Our ancient national virtue of constancy lives in but few breasts now ; may these few cherish the treasure all the more carefully, though the heavens grow darker above us, and our minds more deeply depressed day by day. It is the only rock which stands secure against the storms of passion, and all the conflicts and troubles of life, for it is but another manifestation of the faith upon which God has built His everlasting Church. Had the Germans, like loving children of the same family, not lost faith in one another, if they had not given way to selfish suspicion and grovelling doubt, they would have remained to this day the greatest nation in the world, one and united ; and we, their unhappy posterity, should not have been suffering the judgments of God. Do not think it strange, dear Behr, that I reply in this grave and solemn strain to the joyous expression of your patriotism. Whenever these sentiments are awakened, it calls forth my deepest grief, that with all her splendid talents and careful culture, torn asunder by discord and strife, like her most precious monument, our cathedral, our poor country lies in fragments, exposed to all the vicissitudes of fate."

One year more passed by, and as the edifice of German nationality was being again upreared, Sulpiz Boisserée began to indulge new hopes for the restoration of the cathedral. The year 1813 was spent in earnest energetic labour for the furtherance of this end. When princes and statesmen were assembled at Frankfort after the battle of Leipsic, Sulpiz was soon among them, and the question arose, what was to become of Cologne, of the cathedral, and of the collections of ancient works of arts ? What a

different task it was to bring the subject before the
German princes, from introducing it, as it had been
needful to do, to the French?

"The life and stir here make one's heart leap,"
Sulpiz wrote from Frankfort to his brother Melchior. "Germans of all nations rejoicing together,
—Bavarians, Würtembergers, Austrians, and Prussians, all one in the cause of deliverance and freedom. Thoughts of the Imperial progress to Bra-
bant, and the arrival of the French at Cologne,
came involuntarily into my mind, and I am continually praising God who has so ordered everything.
In comparing that time with this, the change is so
marked and instructive that it is impossible not to
recognize the hand of God and His justice in the
events of the last twenty years, and to feel one's
heart overflowing with holy reverence for His severe
goodness."

He found among the eminent men, princes, ministers, and generals, a better reception than he anticipated for the cause he was advocating. The Crown
Prince of Prussia, the Grand Duchess Catharine,
afterwards Queen of Würtemberg, and the Emperor
Francis were interested in it, and Boisserée's hopes
rose high.

It would have been most in accordance with his
wishes to have again made his home with his pictures at Cologne. During the progress of the victorious armies on the left shore of the Rhine he
made many efforts on behalf of his native city. He
hoped that it would be a centre of patriotic sentiments, and of German art and learning. He wrote
to Rühle von Lilienstein: "That in this case we
should return with our collection you may readily

suppose, and we should be able to make ourselves very useful in other spheres besides those of art and literature, for our openly expressed patriotism and our collections have brought us into contact with the people and the ecclesiastics, and by rescuing the antiquities from destruction, we gained their esteem and affection, while the merchants and other educated people were laughing at us for spending so much money, time, and pains on these old and despised objects." A letter to privy councillor Willemer at Frankfort, in 1814, gives evidence of his conviction that popular art must have its root in popular religion : "It is that strength of feeling, that enthusiasm which lifts man above the earthly and transitory, which has produced all that is great and good. Faith and patriotism are the unfailing springs of life ; earthly joy and heavenly hope, with their daughter art, will make their home with us again. It was one of the great perversions of a self-deluded age to regard art as a branch of culture independent of religion. The history of all nations, the history of art itself, proves that it has its true foundation in religion. Art that does not at once satisfy the refined taste of the educated, and interest the simple citizen, cannot be genuine art; it has failed of its true purpose ; like all ultra-refinement, it is a sort of aristocratism. All art, on the contrary, having its origin in religion, whether it be the religion of heathendom or Christendom, has always in its day been popular, intelligible, and pleasing."

And it appeared as if these valued patrons of art, religion, and patriotism had again appeared in Germany. Sulpiz complained, indeed, to his brother

Melchior that it was said at Cologne "better French than Prussian," but he was able to report that thoroughly patriotic rejoicings resounded through his native city when news was received of the capture of Paris. For three days and nights there was firing, shouting, ringing of the cathedral bell, and illuminations. The Grand Duchess Catharine came with her future husband, the Crown Prince of Würtemberg, in the summer of 1814, to Cologne. Boisserée showed her his views of the cathedral, and acted as guide to the art treasures. The Grand Duchess said she thought the French should have been laid under contribution for the preservation and continuation of such buildings. Regrets were then expressed that the art treasures had been left for the French to take possession of, and the lady said, "I have scolded my brother finely for leaving them for them."

Soon afterwards Cologne and the cathedral received a visit which was the most promising of all for future results. The Crown Prince of Prussia came with Gneisenau, Knesebeck, Ancillon, and their suites. They made the tour of the cathedral, saw the painted windows in the choir and the nave, the celebrated picture, the tomb of the three kings, and went out upon the roof. The Crown Prince was delighted, and said that nothing that they had seen in France, England, or the Netherlands surpassed this building. He would have liked that the continuation of it should be immediately begun, and orders were at once given that it should be preserved from further decay.

It was the most beautiful spring, summer, and autumn that had been known for ages. Victory had inspired the Germans with a spirit of progress, and everywhere there was stir and commotion. Many came to Heidelberg to see the collection of old German paintings. Among them were the poet Schenkendorf, who commemorated his visit in song, and E. M. Arndt. He encouraged the brothers in their work of collecting memorials of the past. "For, unfortunately," he said, "it is the object of most of the governments of the present day to reduce all places and things to a pitiful uniformity, and, by means of a paper government, to reduce the hearts of men to paper also."

But the greatest conquest that the brothers made with their pictures was that of the "old gentleman," Goethe. He came to Heidelberg in September, 1814, and remained a fortnight. The effect of these devout old German paintings upon the man whose predilection had been so great for the heathenism of antiquity, and who had passed himself off for a heathen, was magical. He had never seen any of the works of John van Eyck, nor, indeed, any of those of the old German masters, except Kranach and a few of Dürer's."

"Ah, children," he would exclaim almost every day, "what fools we are, what fools we are! we fancy our grandmothers were not so handsome as people now-a-days, but the men of those days were finer fellows than we are; now we have found out their worth, we will sing their praises,—they are worthy that princes and empresses and all nations should come and bow down and worship them."

The good brothers looked upon Goethe's delight in the pictures as a real conversion. A friend wrote to them, " You are blessed and happy men that in your labours there for your pictures a success has been accorded you, which thousands of preachers and authors have striven for in vain. Give the glory to God, that the work may be a witness of the Lord's mercy in its progress and results, and eternally praise and proclaim it."

If Boisserée was inspired with hopes for the success of his work by the sympathy of great men, the universal sympathy of the people must have been still more encouraging. He lived and laboured for German architecture and painting for forty years, after the excitement of the wars of independence.

His letters and diaries give us a clear insight into the artistic, poetic, political and religious life of those days through the eyes of many of the most eminent men of the time. But we must not follow these remarkable records in detail. Having indicated, according to our aim, that even under French bondage the indomitable German spirit began to appreciate the value of the Christian works of art that it had previously produced, and that bright hopes dawned for it when Germany rose up against her oppressor, we must content ourselves with giving a few particulars of the further progress of the work which Boisserée had been carrying on.

At first, under the excitement occasioned by the events of 1813–14–15, and the bringing back of the art treasures from Paris, it appeared probable that the pictures and their collectors would have been gained for Prussia, either for the Rhenish provinces or Berlin.

In the summer of 1815, Stein having intercepted Goethe at Nassau, the two old men went down the

Lahn into the Rhine and thence to Cologne in a boat. Goethe had planned to write a treatise on the art and antiquities of the Rhine, in the first place for the Chancellor Hardenberg, and afterwards for the benefit of the public. For this object he obtained the assistance of Sulpiz Boisserée, who furnished him with the particulars of every branch of the subject in writing, and Goethe and his young friend remained together for nearly three months in Wiesbaden, Frankfort, Heidelberg, and Carlsruhe.

In 1816 Schinkel, at Berlin, concluded a treaty with Sulpiz Boisserée; everything seemed in train when the minister became alarmed at the sum of money required for the purchase of the collection, and King Frederic William III., with his timid nature, was not the man to do anything extraordinary for art and antiquities in times of difficulty.

The art-loving trio and their pictures remained at Heidelberg till 1819, when they removed to Stuttgard, in order to be able to exhibit their treasures to better advantage, to be in the neighbourhood of more eminent artists, and always in the hope of establishing a centre of past German art, which should be an instructive incitement to present progress. Had they been willing to sacrifice the idea of their lives to their own advantage, it would have been easy to have realized the sums they had spent in the purchase of pictures by selling them to private collectors. But they wished to keep the collection together for the benefit of the nation at large.

Seven years had been passed by these excellent men at Stuttgard; they had had abundant opportunity of exhibiting the pictures to visitors from all nations; in intercourse with the artists and poets of the Swabian capital, they became more and more confirmed in following out their plan, and Sulpiz made frequent journeys.

In June, 1826, Von Dillis, the director of the picture galleries at Munich, deputed by King Louis, suddenly made his appearance at Stuttgard. He compared the collection with the catalogue, and was enraptured with the pictures. What had not been practicable even in the revived patriotism which took place after the war, because the man was wanting who had both the courage and the means to carry out the wishes of the lovers of art, was achieved from his own resources by an art-loving king.

For 50 of the best pictures selected he offered 180,000 florins;* for the whole collection of 213, 240,000 florins,† and a copyright for ten years for the lithograph copies which the brothers had undertaken to publish. In February, 1827, the contract was signed, "not," as Sulpiz relates, "without great emotion." Observing this, Von Dillis said, "Well, we are not going to part, and we will hope for much enjoyment together in friendship and peace."

The King exclaimed over and over again, "What a collection I shall have, gentlemen, what a collection I shall have, when it is all together!" He wished that the price given should not be mentioned in the papers, "For," he said, "if you lose your money at play, or spend it on horses, people think it is all right, but if you spend it on art, they begin to talk of extravagance."

* £15,000.   † £20,000.

The brothers Boisserée and Bertram now settled
with their treasures at Munich, and one of the three,
who had all previously lived for their calling alone,
without any household cares or ties, now entered
into the married state. Sulpiz was married to Matilda Rapp, of Stuttgard, whose acquaintance he
had made in the artistic circles there.

She was a Protestant, but she was as much disposed to accommodate herself to the Roman Catholic faith, where it did not clash with her own, as he
was to acknowledge all genuine Christianity in the
Protestant community.

Meanwhile the work on the cathedral was pro-
gressing. Endless pains were expended on the
views. After being engaged for years in securing
the services of artists to execute, and of Cotta to publish them, Sulpiz made several journeys to Paris to
excite an interest in the work there.

The religious state of mind of many Frenchmen
during the restoration, the interest which the royal
family had acquired for the monuments of Gothic
architecture during a visit to England, and the penetration of connoisseurs, secured him a favourable
reception. He was elected a member of the Aca-
demy of Arts, in the department of architecture.
He had already received the honour of being made
a Doctor of Philosophy by the university of Heidelberg. The work was completed in 1824. King
Frederic William III. sent Boisserée a gold snuff-
box, with a few words of thanks. Alexander von
Humboldt spoke to him of " this miserably formal
fashion, which was peculiar to the Prussian Court,"
but explained that the object of showing the King's
approval was attained, for, according to Berlin no-

tions, a gold snuff-box was a magnificent present.
But it was not for personal honours that Boisserée
cared ; it was for his cause. It was a reward for
him that he had succeeded in calling attention to
the dilapidations of the cathedral, and that, under
Schinkel's auspices, the most necessary steps were
being taken for its preservation.

But the time arrived when the nation awoke to
fresh hopes ; when Prussia especially was inspired
with a fresh breath of life ; when the national and
religious enthusiasm found a symbol in the idea of
the completion of the cathedral. In 1840 King
Frederic William III. had closed his eyes, and after
his " time in disquiet" had found his rest in God.
King Frederic William IV., the patron of German
Christian art while Crown Prince, had ascended the
throne. Ruler and people joined hands in rebuilding the cathedral, and funds from the royal treasury
were added to those of the society which had been
formed for its completion. In the evening of his
days a rich harvest succeeded to the laborious seed-
time for Sulpiz Boisserée. He had often visited his
beloved Rhine land. For years he and his brother
had owned the Apollinarisberg near Remagen, until
they sold it to Von Fürstenberg. But it was not
until his fortieth year that he found a general appreciation of the object of his life among his countrymen.

" An entire change seems to have come over
our countrymen," he wrote to his brother from Cologne in 1841, after he had been serenaded the evening before. " When I was lying here in the window
during the singing last evening in the well-known
family room, it brought back the thought of many

things which I had gone through here with my grandmother, my parents, and brothers and sisters, with Bertram and other acquaintances, and, abobe all, it brought all the past and the singular course of our destiny, with all its joys and sorrows, so vividly to mind, that I could not but feel the deepest emotion; and it cost me some pains to regain my equanimity."

The great day of rejoicing for him was in the autumn of 1842, when the King and the Archduke John of Austria came to Cologne to lay the first stone of the restoration of the cathedral.

Sulpiz was present in the government house during the first reception of the King; and when it was proposed to introduce the best friend of the cathedral to him, he exclaimed, "Is he come? is he here? Where is he?" Sulpiz thanked him for thinking of and inviting him. "Of whom should I think, if not of you?" answered the friendly monarch. "How many years is it since I first made your acquaintance?"

"Twenty-nine years; it was at Frankfort in 1813."

"Yes; I remember it well. Your views of the cathedral kept me awake for three nights."

A sudden gravity overspread Boisserée's features. On this festive occasion, on which he was called to take part, his feelings entirely overpowered him, and he buried his face in his hands; the King's words had had the effect of an electric shock upon him.

He wrote to his brother, "I can only compare the eventful present with the days of 1813, 1814, and 1815, when all classes were united in one bond,

all minds pervaded with the same sentiments. It
is like the evening glow of that great time, but it is
also the dawn of a brighter day, and, if we do not
deceive ourselves, of a hopeful and blessed future.
On Sunday there was not a dry eye among us. The
old generals who were standing near me, the Archduke John, even Humboldt, and Metternich himself
after his own fashion, were moved. Humboldt told
me that Metternich remarked upon the King's
speech, ' This is a mutual infatuation, which is perhaps more dangerous to him who produces it than
to the rest.' With these and many others I was
brought into contact, as in those old times. Dear
Melchior, why were not you here too? You who
have, as it were, borne me up in all my sorrows and
distresses, have guarded and watched over me, and
ever inspired me with fresh courage."

A few days afterwards Sulpiz received an invitation from the King to go up the Rhine with him,
from Stolzenfels to Rheinstein.

Sulpiz related that, wherever the vessel passed,
there was firing and ringing of bells, singing and
shouting, flags, garlands, and decorations ; the
whole voyage was a triumphal progress. After dinner, which was served on deck, the King addressed
Sulpiz, asked kindly after his brother Melchior, and
regretted that he was not with them. Then, taking
a case out of his pocket, he said, " Boisserée, you
were the first protector of the cathedral ; I must
give you a memorial of it for your button-hole."
And he presented him with the order of the Red
Eagle of the third class.

Sulpiz answered, " I have only tried to treasure
up a few seeds of the flower of ancient German art,

to recall the memory of its grandeur, and they have taken root in your generous heart, and are growing up into a great tree. May God add His blessing."

With his cold Mephistophelian spirit, Mettornich called the enthusiasm of those autumn days "a mutual infatuation." But Germany breathed freely in them, and they inspired her with courage. So great was the desire for a great and united national life that even Protestant Christians regarded the building of the cathedral as a symbol of unity. Before the cathedral *féte*, Frederic Perthes wrote to Boisserée, " The cathedral of Cologne, a corner stone which has been a stumbling-block to many, has become a symbol of that unity, without which all effort after agreement is vain and fruitless, unity in the Church of Christ. According to the external aspect of things, the prospect of this unity is very distant, but when we look at essentials, firm foundation stones may be descried."

After the *féte* he wrote, " The attention paid by both parties to the deepest questions of Christian life and being is so grave and searching, that a return to an indifferent existence side by side is impossible.

" Because God is guiding us, we may hope to reach the goal, but the conflict will and must be a long one. The cross of a *united* Church of Christ on the spire of the cathedral of Cologne, would be a symbol of the victory, as well as an evidence of the completion of the cathedral."

Perhaps the time when Catholics and Protestants shall have attained to unity may be more distant than the planting of the Cross of Christ upon the spire of the finished Cathedral; but that need not prevent our rejoicing in the successful labours of the man who devoted his life to German Christian art, and we see in these labours a precious fruit of the great days when we regained our independence, a fruit which tended to the advancement of a deeper and richer religious life through the mediation of art.

King Frederic William IV., after summoning many valuable men into his kingdom, attracted Sulpiz Boisserée to return to his native land. He gave him an honorary office at Bonn, where he resided from 1845 until his death. In August, 1848, together with the Frankfort legislators, he attended the cathedral *fête*. This occasion was like a few bright days in the midst of long continued stormy weather, for the events of that year were very painful to his devout and patriotic spirit. In 1851 he was deprived of the faithful companionship of his brother. Bertram had died before, and in 1853, Sulpiz visited Cologne and the cathedral for the last time. Fifty years had passed by since he took the first picture of his collection in at the back door. The *Bignonia Catalpa*, which he had planted in the garden, was in full bloom and beauty; in the cathedral, the wall of the south window was closed in, and was, as he said, "mighty to behold." Throughout a long life, God had given him strength for much exertion and many long journeys, in spite of his poor health.

A heart complaint now brought death near to him.

He received the last sacraments of his Church, and then said to his wife, "Let us look into each other's eyes once more, and then look forward to meeting again."

He had prayers read to him till the close. Clement Perthes, the son of his old friend, had just left, when his wife observed that the patient drew a deep breath. She grasped his hand, and as she repeated the Benediction, he breathed out his soul into God's loving keeping on the 2nd of May, 1854.

The builders and workmen employed on the cathedral came over from Cologne, and, followed by many friends, they took him out and buried him beside his brother Melchior.

In the churchyard at Bonn, which contains the mortal remains of so many distinguished Germans, the graves of Sulpiz and Melchior Boisserée are to be seen, and may remind us what energy, uprightness, and devout faith can enable individuals to achieve for their country.*

* 'Sulpiz Boisserée;' Stuttgart, 1862.

CHAPTER VIII.

EFFECTS OF THE WARS OF INDEPENDENCE.

THE time immediately after the wars of independence was one of the happiest periods in the long annals of the German nation.

As there are hours in the mental history of individuals, when their vocation, like a hitherto buried germ, becomes evident to them,—hours in which that which is to be the leading idea of their lives reveals itself in royal pre-eminence, as the result of the healthy exercise of all their powers, and of their earnest endeavours to ascertain it, hours, the remembrance of which is always an incitement to good,—so are there times in the course of a nation's history when it clearly perceives what is the calling for which it is designed by God, and feels its strength renewed to fulfil it. " Ritornar al segno," a return to the first watchword, is, as Machiavelli says, the law of the development of history. It may deviate from its course, but returns to the original starting point, and makes amends for the error by increased progress.

The watchword of the Germans was the union of

nationality and religion, and the wars of independence resulted in a return to it. Every power was
in healthy exercise, and there was a prevailing conviction that the nation could not fulfil its vocation
independently of religion, and that the Church
would be powerless if she did not adapt herself to
the national wants.

In 1786 the youthful Spalding wrote to F. H.
Jacobi that he had heard Biester say, that "we
must not relax our efforts, and then in twenty years'
time the name of Jesus, in a religious sense, would
no more be heard." And exactly twenty years
later came the chastisement at Jena, and with it
many earnest people returned to the Saviour of sinners; and thirty years later, how often the name of
Jesus occurs in the hymns of Arndt and Schenkendorf; how powerfully it was proclaimed by many
from the pulpit; how efficacious it proved among
the people in the lecture rooms of the philosophers,
as well as among the congregations of the faithful!
And that kingdom began to be established, concerning which we have the promise that it shall endure when all the kingdoms of the world shall have
passed away.

From the moment when religion took the place
among the nation from which it had been deposed,
a wonderful impulse was given to all the nation's
powers. Science and art, learning and education,
political and mercantile life, all began to flourish
anew.

After the war, Germany was like a field that has
been well ploughed, sown with good seed, and
richly watered with the tears of sorrow. The seed
was already sprouting; there was every prospect of

a good harvest, though much would depend upon future weather.

It is beyond our purpose to record in detail the religious results of the wars of independence; we shall only indicate a few of them in the various departments of religious life. In the first place, we will give an example of the fact that many earnest Christians, who afterwards rendered effectual aid in building up the Church, received their first incitement to spiritual life in the times of the war.

Ferdinand Charles von Bülow, born at Lüthe, in Hanover, in 1789, had studied law, and was intended by Savigny, of Berlin, who thought highly of him, for an academical career. But when in February, 1813, the King issued his appeal for volunteers, although Bülow's health was poor, he could not remain behind, but hastened with hundreds of his fellow students to Breslau. There he bought a Testament, which accompanied him in all the battles in which he was engaged. There is on the fly-leaf, in his handwriting, a record of the course of the war, and then follow the words, "This book has been my constant companion, and has often given me divine support. 'O praise the Lord, for He is good, and His mercy endureth for ever.' Lord, forgive me my sins."

Thus equipped, he fought as a volunteer jäger at Grossgörschen and Bautzen, as an officer at Grossbeeren and Dennewitz, and in 1815, when war broke out again, as adjutant to General von Dobschütz. After the second peace of Paris he entered the diplomatic service, and died as privy councillor of legation at Berlin in 1853.

He evinced his faith, not only by various hymns

which he composed, but by the keen interest he took in many good works of Christian charity. He was a member of the committee of the Missionary Society, vice-president of the Protestant Book Society, and of the Society for the Care of Discharged Prisoners, and he aided in building the church of St. Matthew in Berlin, now a favourite haunt of earnest Christians, especially among the nobility. Thus, in the person of Bülow, we see the religious awakening which took place in 1813 in immediate connection with the interest in the Church which has been so general since 1848. And this is but one instance out of many.

Not during the war itself, but under the influence of its warning voice, another Prussian officer was led to embrace the faith, whose conversion influenced first his own family, and then a whole neighbourhood, like the ever widening circles produced when still waters are set in motion.

Gustavus von Below, the son of a landed proprietor in Pomerania, born in 1790, being a talented youth, was designed for the service of the State, and had sat at the feet of Fichte, at Berlin.

Utterly devoid of any interest in religion or the Church, in 1813 he entered the army as a volunteer jäger. He served in Prince William's regiment of dragoons, then as adjutant in General Gneisenau's staff, and won the Iron Cross.

Led into serious reflection by the grave experiences of war, after his return from the campaign he felt aspirations towards a higher life which could not be satisfied with Fichte's philosophy. He was brought into contact with a circle of serious young men, among whom were Clemens Brentano, and the three brothers Von Gerlach. But it was a former comrade in the regiment, Götze, who divined the state of his mind, and one day said to him, "My friend, I wish you would read the Bible;" and in the words of Wangemann, "So near had God's love and mercy drawn to men after the great events and distress of the war, so thin was the partition between man's averted will and God's outstretched arm, that the perusal of the Gospel of St. Matthew sufficed to effect an entire change in the life of a young officer of the guards."

He searched the Scriptures further, read other religious works, and was soon entirely converted to Christ. His correspondence at that time is an evidence that Fichte, although he had not himself attained to the knowledge of salvation in Christ, did in reality lead many to Him by reason of the moral earnestness and religious enthusiasm by which his philosophy was pervaded. Von Below relates that after his return from the war to Berlin, he read some of Fichte's works with earnest attention; for when he compared his own faith with that of some of his devout friends, it did not seem to him to be sufficiently firm, and he longed to attain to their standard. "But I doubt," he continues, "whether this would have effected any change in my views, for it seemed only to confirm them the more. In the meantime I renewed my acquaintance with some of my former fellow students and others besides, and discovered that in intercourse with spiritually minded and excellent men, one gains more than from any books. Among others, I will mention G.——, whom you know; he served in the same detachment of jägers, and was severely wounded at Dennewitz. I cannot

undertake to give you a description of this delightful man. I saw a good deal of him, and admired in
silence the serene and cheerful peace, and the sted-
fastness which pervaded his whole being. I very
soon discovered that a firm unshaken faith in the
doctrines and promises of the Holy Scriptures, a
deep sense of religion, unmixed with any philosophical jargon, was the foundation and essence of
his life. By his means I was led to the Bible and
the church; all my philosophy retreated into the
background, and served only as a foil to faith. And,
God willing, that shall henceforth be its place. It
is now my undivided and earnest endeavour to uphold and confirm these views; to imbue my whole
mind and being with faith.

"Happily, my former philosophy does not hinder
me in this work of sanctification, because there is
nothing in it detrimental to the interests of faith.
It goes as far as human insight and reason can go,
it leaves off where the other begins, and my error
consisted in trying to engraft faith on philosophy,
and to permeate the latter with the former. Faith
shall now be the groundwork of all my life and
thoughts, and if God only grant me strength I hope
to find mercy."

In May, 1817, his words sounded like those of
one who *had* found mercy. He wrote to a friend,
"There is no other life for us but in and through
faith in our Lord and Saviour, and the forgive-
ness of sins through his blood. There is no true
love, but that which flows fresh and free from the
wells of life and mercy; there is no other truth,
there is no other way to God and to everlasting life,
but through Him. There is no other virtue but

that which has its foundation in the Lord, and which is practised for His sake. Dear S., if your heart has not yet been enlightened by these truths, I pray you for God's sake, and for the sake of your soul's salvation, acquaint yourself with the divine revelation in the holy Scriptures, and if the perverse understanding rebels against the reception of the proffered mercy, I beg you to meditate on the following sayings of a divinely gifted man :—

" When thou gazest on the sun and findest it too bright,
　'Tis thy eyes that are in fault, and not the brilliant light."

" Man, when thy heart is soft as wax, and like it pure and fair,
　The Holy Spirit will impress the Saviour's image there."

" O man, thou must a child become, else thou wilt never go
　Among the children of thy God, the door is far too low."

In proportion as Gustavus von Below was thankful that he had been delivered from the kingdom of Satan, the more zealous was he to save the souls of his brethren. " Have you a Bible, dear S. ?" he wrote, " or have you read it with simplicity and humility of heart ? If not, do so now, and you will soon discover that it is a divine revelation, and not what many theologians of modern times proclaim it to be, who deserve rather to be called the slaves of Satan than the servants of God. I had read some parts of it before myself, but in much the same spirit in which I should have read Plato or Cicero. The years of war and misfortune have caused a great stir and commotion amongst us ; in the first place only in a political sense, but like the widening eddies in a pool when you throw in a stone, it will soon spread itself into every department of life."

At the time of his conversion Gustavus von Below had a father and two brothers.

From the year 1818, when he was married, he had taken possession of the estates of Reddintin and Symbow, while Charles had the larger estate of Gatz, and Henry those of Serhoff and Pannekow, their father having retired to that of Brünnow. Gustavus sent forth his earnest exhortations to faith in Christ on all sides, at first without visible result. The desolating breath of rationalistic teaching, and the worldly lives of the rationalistic clergy, had produced disastrous effects in Pomerania; but there were still some few souls who, like Gustavus von Below, valued the ancient treasures of consolation. He became more and more confirmed in his biblical Christianity, which may be described as Lutheranism tinged with Pietism. His brother Henry was the first to be won over in 1819. One day, in an idle mood, from mere *ennui* he took up Tersteegen's 'String of Pearls;' and the exposition of the fifteenth chapter of Luke made such an impression upon him, that he said to himself, "I am the prodigal son!" He called his family together, and said to them, "We have all been hitherto going the wrong way; if we do not alter our course, and are not converted, we shall all be lost." He gave up smoking, cards, and wine; banished things not in themselves sinful out of his house; searched the Scriptures diligently, and read the works of Luther, Arndt, and Francke. About the same time, Charles was converted also. One of them wrote, "We three brothers have now agreed to rule our households, as far as God gives us grace to do it, as faithful followers of Christ; that His word shall be prized above everything,

and diligently put in practice; and by God's help
we have already made a successful beginning."
There was soon no member of the large family who
did not share in this new life; and when the incre-
dible report was noised abroad that family worship
was held in these noble houses, it came to the ears
of the "Quiet in the Land," and they praised God
for the grace He had given. The excitement in the
neighbourhood continually increased, and was regarded with great enmity by the clergy. The only
pastor within range of these Lutheran nobles who
understood them was Metger, of the Reformed
Church, the court preacher at Stolpe, the successor
of Schleiermacher. The minister at Pannekow carried his rationalistic doctrines so far, that Henry von
Below one day said to him after service, at the
church door, "Are you fully convinced of what you
have been preaching to-day, that it is not necessary
to salvation to believe in the Lord Christ?"—"Certainly I am fully convinced of what I have been
preaching," was the answer.—"Well, then," said
the patron, "I hereby renounce you, for it is my
duty to avoid false doctrine. Henceforth I shall no
longer attend your ministry." Then, mounting
upon a grave mound, he said to the congregation,
"Do not believe him; he is a false prophet."

From this time the movement took a free course
independently of the ruling powers. The nobles
themselves preached, and multitudes came to hear
them; other laymen, servants and labourers, did
the same, and a great revival took place. The
Government sent gendarmes to arrest the work of
the Spirit; but neither they nor the rationalistic
clergy could set bounds to it. All the concomitant

circumstances usually observed when a sudden awakening occurs in a whole neighbourhood took place here; prophesying and violent bodily contortions. All the arrows which, with an only too natural rancour, those who have felt constrained to separate themselves from a lifeless community are apt to discharge at the national Church and its servants, were sent forth here. And the revivalists in Pomerania had also to pass through all those perils which are generally the lot of those who separate themselves from the Church. First, open rupture with the clergy; then, when more faithful pastors were sent, a desire to be reconciled with the Church, but these again were regarded with suspicion if they did not go through thick and thin with the revivalists. After the great awakening, the promoters of it sank into a state of mystical theosophical contemplation, and the clergy endeavoured to rule their congregations according to order. We cannot follow further the history of this " Spiritual stir and strife on the shores of the Baltic," as it has been called by Wangemann.* Charles von Below died in 1842, and Gustavus in 1843. Their study of the works of Böhme and Gichtel had given them a distaste for these religious commotions. Henry, who was the most energetic character, came in contact with the Lutheran Separatists in Silesia, and at length formed his followers into a sort of congregation. He died in 1855. We cannot fail to regret that the spiritual life which was awakened by the brothers Below in Pomerania, when the national Church was, as it were, too old a skin to contain the

* Wangemann, ' Geistliches Regen und Ringen am Ostseestrande.' Berlin, 1862.

new wine, assumed so disorderly a character; but we must give the promoters of it the credit of faithful discipleship to the end. And if the preaching of the Gospel takes deep root to this day in Pomerania,—if faithful pastors find the ground well prepared for their labours,—and if, in many of the mansions of the chief families, conservative political sentiments are adorned with the doctrines of the cross,—it is fair to seek the source of this state of things in the days of the wars of independence.

The newly-awakened religious life was clearly evinced in those works of charity which were so greatly needed in the universal distress. Here was a sphere for the Christian patriotism of women. Some few men, like Perthes and Falk, whose souls were pained by the distress of whole towns or districts, worked on a large scale, and sent forth far and wide their urgent appeals for help. But there was abundant room for works of mercy in detail for the hands of girls and women. In the periodicals of the day we meet with papers by women who take a just view of the position of the German woman judged by a historical and religious standard. 'What does regenerated Germany require of her Women?' is the title of a little book by a governess, Betty Gleim, published at Bremen in 1814, for the benefit of the fugitives from Hamburg. And where their duties were not thus theoretically discussed, women did not doubt that it was their part to sustain the men by helping to equip them for the war, and by caring for the wounded and for widows and orphans. The angel of mercy followed closely on victory, war, scarcity, and pestilence. In November, 1813, the young

ladies of Leipsic established a society "for the succour of those who are fighting and suffering in the
good cause." Their plan was to work for the
society, and raise funds by the sale of the work.
"Contributions in money," they said, "unless it
were first earned, could not be of the same value as
the industry of German girls for the cause of their
country."

No sooner had their appeal been issued than a
gold chain, a pin, and an anchor were sent by a
young lady in the country. She wrote with them
to her "dear sister" at Leipsic, that she would fain
have followed her brothers to the war in the service
of Prussia, but that, being an only daughter, she
was obliged to stay at home, and, being too busy in
working for her brothers to send work, she had
sent her ornaments instead. "If I could only send
things of greater value," she added; "but if many
would follow my example we should soon have a
good sum. The sacrifice would not be great, for
what is the use of these glittering trifles? A flower
or a ribbon is far more ornamental."

Patriotism and religious feeling led in those days
to simplicity of dress, and especially to the avoidance of French fashions.

We have seen in Falk's life how the misery occasioned by the war called forth works of mercy in
Thuringia. Gerd Eilers, a tutor in the wealthy
merchant families at Frankfort, has given us a description of the labours of women in clothing the
naked, feeding the hungry, and nursing the sick in
the old imperial city, and in the valley of the Maine.
"While the citizens of Frankfort were patiently
bearing the burden of having soldiers quartered

upon them," Eilers relates, "their utmost sympathies were excited by the misery and distress which prevailed in the district around the city. Typhus fever had consorted itself with want, and many families had lost both father and mother.

"A large hospital in the city, in which hundreds of fever patients were lying, took fire. The sick had to be saved, and there was no course open but to remove them into the houses of the citizens. Fear of infection brought natural self-love and love of our fellow creatures into collision, and, to the honour of the inhabitants of Frankfort be it spoken, humanity gained the day. The sick were all provided for, except a few who perished in the flames.

"Perhaps no one had better opportunities than I had in the circles in which I was then living, of admiring the mental power and moral strength in the characters of noble women in the midst of this urgent distress. It filled me with the highest esteem when I saw how, without the least cant, they kept the law of Christian liberty, and walked in deed and in truth in that more excellent way which St. Paul showed to the Corinthians."

The Frankfort Ladies' Association, which celebrated its jubilee on the 2nd of February, 1864, was instituted in those days, and is a living evidence that the influence of the benevolence which was called forth during the war time has extended to our own days. For a moment we cast our eyes from the south to the north, to remind our readers of the activity of the Hamburg ladies narrated in the life of Perthes, and then return to Würtemberg to observe how, under the auspices of Queen Catherine, works of Christian charity were extended over a whole country. This princess was the daughter of the Emperor Paul of Russia, and her mother was the Empress Mary, a princess of Würtemberg. The Emperor Alexander was her brother. Like him, she had been deeply impressed by the grave events of the times in which she lived. She was greatly shocked by the murder of her father, and it led to her living a retired country life with her mother, and her youth was passed in serious study instead of idle vanities.

Her marriage with Prince George of Oldenburg, who settled as governor-general at Twer, on the Volga, gave her increased opportunity of exerting herself for the good of her dependents. When Napoleon advanced towards Russia, and the Prince prepared to defend his territory, the Grand Duchess equipped a corps of her serfs at her own expense. After the burning of Moscow, when the hospitals at Twer were filled with the wounded, the Prince constantly visited them, and was himself seized with typhus fever.

His wife nursed him faithfully until his death, when she fell ill herself from grief and over exertion. Having recovered her health at the baths of Bohemia, in 1813 she took an eager interest in political events, and when the allied armies entered Paris she laid aside her widow's weeds.

In January 1816 she married the Crown Prince of Würtemberg, who succeeded to the throne in October of the same year. Being now queen, there was no outward hindrance to her following the dictates of her loving woman's heart. Her mind was peculiarly fitted to rule, and her keen, masculine insight into the position of affairs enabled her to animate and regulate the works of benevolence throughout the country.

In the year 1817 a network of beneficent institutions was spread over Würtemberg, but she was only permitted for two years to be the mother of the country. Nevertheless, at her death in 1819, the work was so well established, and intrusted to such faithful hands, that it has endured, and is to this day an example to other lands.*

Although blessing flowed and continues to flow from the labours of women, men were not wanting who walked in the same steps. From the year 1816, Count von der Recke Volmerstein followed in Falk's footsteps. He at first endeavoured to rescue neglected children by placing them out in families, but, as that proved impracticable to a sufficient extent, in 1819 he founded an asylum on his estate at Overdyk, with which, since 1822, the larger institution at Düsselthal has been connected.

From 1819 Reinthaler carried on the labours of his friend Falk at the Martin's Stift at Erfurt. And while, in Northern Germany, charity was directing her blessed steps hither and thither, reconnoiterers were standing on the southern boundary of Switzerland, not to see whether Germany was open to attack, but for the reception of streams from the fountain of beneficence then open at Basle. There is at Beuggen, near Basle, but in the territory of Baden, an institution for training teachers for the schools of the poor, with which an asylum for neglected children is connected. It did not, like Falk's labours, originate in the war time, but it was a branch of a society, called the "German Christian Association,"

* Merz, 'Frauenbilder.' Stuttgard, 2 Bände.

which had been founded in Basle in 1780, and from which ramifications had spread into Germany. It was an association of earnest Christians for the promotion of Christian knowledge and godliness of life. But its establishment has some connection with the commotions of the time and with the foundation of the Basle Missionary Society, so that we will say a few words on that institution. The leading members of the Christian Association, especially Steinkopff, and after he was elected minister of the Savoy church in London, Spittler and Blumhardt had long had it in their hearts to establish a missionary training school at Basle. It is sometimes said that it originated as follows :—That at the siege of Hüningen some devout men formed a vow that if Basle were spared the horrors of war, they would establish a seminary for training missionaries to be sent among the Calmucks and Tartars who were among the allied armies. This, however, is not correct, though the events of the war caused the long-cherished plan to be carried out. From 1803, Blumhardt and Spittler had worked together in the service of the Christian Association. When Blumhardt's father died in 1800, he placed his hands on the head of his son, then a student, with the prophetical words, " The Lord will bless thee, and so prepare thee with the gifts of His Spirit, that thou wilt one day become a blessed instrument in carrying His grace to the heathen." A few years later, Steinkopff asked him, on behalf of the London Missionary Society, to go out as a missionary. His weak health precluded him from this, but he began to take a special interest in missions, and sent contributions and pupils to the mission school which

Jänicke had established at Berlin in 1801. He had
not thought of establishing one himself, but it had
been proposed by Spittler, and only some fresh
impulse and a suitable opportunity were wanting to
induce them to lay the proposal before the public.
Albert Ostertag relates that, in the year 1814, a
man looking something like a German student, half
gentleman half vagrant, came into Spittler's room
with a letter of introduction from Gossner. He
made inquiries about the Christian Association, and
asked if he could be in any way employed in it.
This was that singular, zealous, and powerful man,
Kellner, with whom we have made acquaintance
in the sketch of Mme. de Krüdener. During the
French rule he had been postmaster at Brunswick,
but had incurred the wrath of the foreign power,
partly by objecting to the shameless opening of
letters, partly from some patriotic expressions which
had escaped him.   He was imprisoned in the fortress
of Cassel, where he daily expected the fate of many
of his fellow-prisoners who were shot under his
window. In this situation he took up the only
book that had been left him, a Bible. He had
before been a materialist, but, in reading it, he
found that liberty, compared with which the liberty
which he had hitherto been striving to attain was
but a delusive shadow. The events of 1813 released
him, and after various adventures, he came to
Spittler at Basle. Spittler received him gladly, and
found him to be possessed, not only of a richly-
gifted and cultivated mind, but of the fiery zeal
which was just what was wanting to fan into a
flame the embers which were smouldering in Spittler's thoughts. He enthusiastically took up the

idea of a missionary institute, but the fitting occasion for making it public had not yet arrived.

It was so ordered by God that some of the bombs of
Hüningen, maliciously thrown into the town, should
inflame the hearts of the inhabitants with zeal, instead of setting fire to their dwellings ; and the
plan of the missionary institute was matured in
those days of deep anxiety, and under the influence
of the unusual presence of foreign hordes, some of
them from Russian Asia. After the storm had
blown over, Spittler's first letter to his friend Blumhardt, then a pastor in a remote country place, gives
him the joyful news of the establishment of the
institute, and says, " And you must be inspector."
And inspector Blumhardt became.

It was on the 21st of October, 1816. The autumn leaves were falling, and the fading aspect of
everything turned the mind to serious thought.
Two friends, zealous promoters of the kingdom of
God, Spittler and Zeller of Zofingen, director of the
school at Aargau, were walking under the trees behind the cathedral at Basle.

They had just come from the Missionary Institute,
where they had seen the ten pupils destined to go
to the heathen. Just then some late birds of passage were taking their flight towards the south,
and brought the young missionaries afresh to mind.
" Ah," said Zeller, " these young men are soon
going to the heathen, and amid the growing apo-
stasy we want efficient labourers for the harvest in
our churches and schools at home." Then he described the spiritual destitution in Switzerland and
Germany, the need of suitable instructors in the
existing institutions, the number of neglected chil-

dren, and suggested the idea that an institution for training teachers for home work should be combined with the Mission Institute. Winter and spring passed by. At Easter, Spittler wrote to Zeller at Zofingen, to ask him to draw up a paper setting forth his ideas on the subject. The conference of the friends at Basle on the paper resulted in the decision that the Training School must be a separate society from the Mission Institute. On the evening of the 31st of October the friends kept the festival of the German Reformation, and constituted themselves a society for a voluntary association for training schoolmasters for the poor.

A gold snuff-box was soon sent for the object, which, being three times raffled for,—for twice the successful competitor presented it to the Society again,—brought in a sum of 3200 francs, and other gifts flowed in.

They tried to find a site for building near the town, but as land was dear, they turned their thoughts to Beuggen, an old German château a few miles above Basle on the Rhine, in the territory of Baden. For the last three years it had been used as a lazaretto for sick soldiers, and was an abode of misery and desolation.

In 1819 the friends Spittler and Zeller had a personal interview with the Grand Duke Louis of Baden, and obtained permission to occupy the castle for a rental of 60 florins a year. By April 1st, 1820, it was to be ready for the reception of the inmates, and a mother was found for them in Mrs. Mary Salome Fäsch, widow of Professor Fäsch of Basle, a lady of property, but who had previously found her greatest pleasure in instructing poor children.

Zeller, of Zofingen, was requested to undertake the office of Director, and he and his wife took possession of a corner room in the upper story, which had before been the special haunt of typhus fever. Their first act was to throw themselves on their knees, to thank God for His guidance, to dedicate the whole house to Him, to pray Him to dwell in it by His grace and His holy Spirit, and to change it from an abode of misery, pestilence, and death, into a blessed sanctuary for many poor creatures. There were pupils from six years of age to thirty, clever and stupid, attractive and repulsive, those who had been well brought up, and wild neglected beings, well dressed, and ragged ones. There were ten boys and ten girls intended to be trained for teachers. Zeller devoted himself entirely to this work until his death in 1860, at the age of eighty-one.

One of the pleasantest incidents in the annals of the institution was a visit from the aged Pestalozzi in 1826. From his correspondence with Nicolovius we see how this man, so possessed by a spirit of love, but to whom it was not granted to carry out his loving projects, rejoiced to see them carried out by younger, and, as he readily acknowledged, more practical men.

How he must have delighted in the spectacle presented to him at Beuggen! and may we not rejoice to observe how the mantle of an Elijah is ever bequeathed to an Elisha, and how link is added to link in the chain of works of charity, until the coming of the Lord !

"We shall never forget," Zeller reports, "the moment when the venerable man entered the room, and passing between the double row of seventy-

eight children and twenty-two youths, who greeted
him by singing a hymn, he walked feebly up the
stairs, and with tears of emotion in his eyes, took
his seat in the pulpit in the great schoolroom; we
shall not forget how he declined the wreath of oak-
leaves that was offered to him, and placing it on
the head of my little son, pressed him to his heart,
with the words, 'Not for me, not for me; garlands
belong to innocence.'   His voice was choked with
tears when the youthful choir sang, in soft and
touching voices, the following stanza from 'Ger-
trude and Lienhard :'—

> " Thou who cam'st from heaven above,
>   Thou who all our anguish stillest ;
> Thou who with the richest love,
>   Evermore the poorest fillest,
> I am weary, give me rest,
>   Bid my anxious wanderings cease ;
> Send unto my troubled breast,
>   All Thy promised grace and peace."

Then, still almost overcome with emotion, he blessed
the children. And during the four days that he spent
with us, the advice he gave us from the rich harvest
of his experience will never be forgotten, nor his
affectionate interest in the poor and their children
at so advanced an age. May God comfort the venerable father ! "*

Another work of charity was the circulation of
the Bible. It was originally a genuine German one,
the sense of the need of which was first practically
shown by Luther in his translation of the Bible,
and it was afterwards promoted by the Canstein
Bible Society, which was a result of the pietism

* Ostertag, ' Ueber den Ursprung und die Entwicklung der Deut-
schen Christenthums-Gesellschaft in Basel, in den Beiträgen zur
vaterländischen Geschichte.' Basel, 1850.

of the Halle school. Since the beginning of the century, it had been carried on with great success in England, and had found since the war a fruitful soil in Germany. We have looked through the reports of the British and Foreign Bible Society, and the narratives of the English agents Pinkerton and Paterson, and the German agents Steinkopff and Schwabe; the correspondence from all parts of the country, gives so interesting an insight into the religious condition of Germany at that period, that we regret that space will not allow us to reproduce more than a few features of it.

Before the war, the indifference to the word of God which prevailed among the upper classes had penetrated to the lower, but after it, a desire for the Scriptures was everywhere felt.

At Wernigerode, Dr. Schwabe found the count's family just returned from banishment, and mourning that the French rule had at once stifled the growth of religion and lessened the means of promoting it. The aged countess herself undertook to distribute Bibles. " The blessings of young and old," she exclaimed, "will be joined with mine on the Society which gives me the pleasure of offering them this book; it was from this alone that we derived strength and comfort during a time of repeated losses and distress, and it taught us to bear our fate with resignation and even cheerfulness. I will take the book myself to the houses of the poor, and tell them when I give it them, that God has raised up benefactors for us in a distant land."

Leander van Ess, Catholic Professor of Theology at Marburg, author of a translation of the New Testament, which, with the assistance of the British and Foreign Bible Society, he circulated among the Catholic population, wrote, in March 1813 : " Never were the minds of the people so ready to receive the Word of Life ; never was the need of consolation so deeply felt ; never did the door of the kingdom of heaven stand wider open than at present. Oh, my dear friends, do satisfy this hunger with the bread of life !"

A pastor near Eisenach wrote : " One of the saddest effects of the war is the loss of the means of instruction which many of our poor families have sustained, and they cannot replace them. After the retreat of the French many fathers and mothers came to me, and complained that they had lost all their Bibles, hymn-books, and other religious books, and begged me to furnish them with some books of consolation. The condition of the children is still worse. One schoolroom cannot be used at all, and most of the children have to stay away from another because they have no books, and their parents are unable to buy any. The minister at Fortha assured me that he had been robbed of all the books used in divine worship, that he had not a single Bible or Prayer-book left."

The distress was indeed great; but, as soon as peace was restored, as soon, in fact, as any hope of it dawned, there was great readiness to help. The agents of the Bible Society, in their travels through Germany, had only to shake the ripe fruit from the trees.

Wherever they went they found people ready to take up the work. Ministers of State and generals united with the most eminent of the clergy, and princes, under the influence of the spirit which had

found its expression in the Holy Alliance, and with
a settled conviction that nothing but religion could
permanently close the pit of misery, afforded protection to the Bible Society, and often gave it their
sympathy and blessing. A network of societies was
soon spread over Germany, from Wupperthal to Königsberg, and from Hamburg to the remote south.

The work of Bible circulation promoted the
increased inclination for union between various
Churches which existed at that period. Pinkerton
reports, in the year 1814: "In Hanover, as well as
at St. Petersburg, I saw the Lutheran, Calvinistic,
and Catholic clergy all joining hands in the good
cause, and, after the meeting, some of them assured
me that, though they had been for years teachers of
the same religion in the same town, they had never
before had an opportunity of conversing together.
Oh, what a blessed undertaking it is which thus
brings the different sections of the Christian Church
together! When the head of the Catholic clergy
at Hanover came into the room he came straight up
to me, shook me heartily by the hand, and said,
with a beaming countenance, 'I rejoice to have an
opportunity of taking part in so glorious a cause.
I am decidedly of opinion that the Scriptures
should be in the hands of all classes, and that especially the lowest and poorest should have it in their
power to draw water from the fountain head of
divine instruction.'"

The love of the Scriptures was especially strong
in the Catholic circles in Bavaria, who gathered
around Sailer and Wittmann, and later around
Gossner, Boos, and Lindl.

We must not allow ourselves to dwell on the Protestant awakenings which took place in Catholic Bavaria, since it has no special connection with the wars of independence; but, just to give an idea of it, we cannot refrain from making an extract from a description of a visit which Anna Schlatter, of St. Gall, paid to the revivalists of Bavaria in 1816:—

"I shall always rejoice in having undertaken this journey. It seemed to me when I was sitting at the table among the brethren and fathers as if I were amongst a community of the early Christians. I could be entirely simple and unconstrained as I am by nature. Knowing that I should go to the château of a wealthy baron, I took my best clothes with me, but was ashamed to wear them amongst these simple Christians, who had renounced all love of the world. Our minds and conversation were engrossed with one topic,—with Him who gave His life for us. Since I have seen so many very poor believers in these parts, who, in the midst of extreme poverty, feel themselves so rich in Christ, I feel that my own faith has never been put to the test. I wish that some others could have seen them. It went straight to my heart when some poor old labouring man or woman, or a girl who worked in the stables, recognized me at once as a sister, and kissed and embraced me with heavenly words. It was a foretaste of heaven. One thing is needful, a living active faith in Christ, the crucified Son of God. Where He lives in the heart, all is well."

History has taught us that for believers in the Bible in the Romish Church, at any rate, for her priests, no other union with the Protestant Church is possible than that of joining themselves to her community.

There is no doubt that the union within the borders of the Protestant Church which has been effected in many parts of Germany since 1817 was the result of the feeling of Christian communion during the war. We can but regret that in many cases it has been brought about rather by indifference to the distinctive doctrines than from a unity of spirit based upon a deep feeling of the need, and an experience of the blessings of salvation.

We can only allude to the commemoration of the Reformation when there was a strong sentiment of unity between the Lutheran and the Reformed Churches. The whole course of our narratives indicates the influence of the wars of independence upon the re-awakened recognition of the true significance of the Reformation. The religious movements of the last few years had opened men's minds to the comprehension of Luther's work of faith; the struggle with Napoleon had called to mind the struggle with the Pope; the heroes of the war had revived the memory of the old heroes of faith; the popular commotions, the waves of which were scarcely stilled, had recalled the popular movements at the time of the Reformation.

An appeal had been made to the whole nation, to the nobles, the citizens, and the labouring classes to rise against a foreign yoke; an appeal to their conscience, in opposition to romantic unscrupulousness, and to faith in a living God and Saviour in opposition to unchristian practice and unchristian views of life. "The restoration of the synthesis of Protestantism through the newly awakened moral sense;" as Hundeshagen expressed it, was a result of the war. After having long been taught that faith was a mere assent of the understanding, and virtue a course of action independent of the effect of the grace of God, our people once more clearly apprehended that religion and morality are essentially one, that upon the basis of this divine harmony man must advance to the fulness of the divine life. As at the time of the Reformation, a fresh revelation had been vouchsafed to the Church, for God had inspired the people anew with His spirit, and had afresh proclaimed His word by the eloquence of mighty deeds.

In recalling the results of the war, and in reviewing the spiritual blessings which flowed from those years into the succeeding ones, we must not overlook the energetic and aspiring youth who had grown up in the heat of the conflict.

Görres wrote in the 'Rhenish Mercury' in 1814, "It is a pleasure to look at these daring and vigorous youths. There is a conscious dignity and magnanimity in their mien ; they have accomplished and suffered something in the world; their lives have not run on in a course of empty idleness, they have lived through an exciting period of history, and the consciousness of their power and of what they have gone through, gives them that noble and military bearing which has taken the place of the old obsequiousness. One sees that their minds are inspired with an animating idea, that they know that they are working in a noble cause, and that they, therefore, cheerfully bear all the penalties and dangers of their arduous calling.

" The brotherly affection which exists among these young people is also very pleasant to behold. Indeed youths whose dawn of life has fallen in these eventful times, who have shared so much enthusiasm and so many sufferings, who have stood together amid the thunder of so many eventful battles, cannot fail to regard each other with affection. Their whole lives will be nourished on the remembrance of their youth, and their friendship will never grow cold.

"Supercilious vanity has been succeeded by an honourable pride, based on the conscious possession of hardly-won treasures ; and therefore are they the pride of their country."

If any one takes exception to the pride of these young men, it must not be forgotten that among the best of them, it was, if we may so call it, a holy pride, that noble consciousness of dignity as a free Christian man which may be combined with deep humility before God.

For the youths who returned from the war were Christians. If with some love for their earthly, and with others for their heavenly country was predominant, a union of patriotism and religion was the basis of their sentiments. Not that in this period of fermentation there was always perfect harmony between their impulses and their actions ; and who can wonder if here and there some excitable mind lost its equilibrium ?

The German Students' Association (*Burschenschaft*), formed by the young men who were penetrated with the spirit evoked by the war, exercised an important influence.

Our opinion of this Association, so early nipped in the bud, has long ago been expressed by the veteran of those days, Karl von Raumer. He says, "The effect of the war upon the universities was incalculable. The youths, thousands of whom in response to the King's appeal had joined the army, and honourably fought in the great battles, returned to the universities in 1815 and 1816 to resume their studies. In the short space of three years, during which Europe lived through more than three centuries of ordinary time, our youths were entirely changed. They had been spell-bound by commonplace and ignoble academical notions, but now the spell was broken by what they had gone through. They were delivered from the tyranny of a false honour, and viewed its code of laws in their true light, like Titania her lover after the disenchantment. Genuine honour and courage devoted to the fatherland had taken the place of that spurious honour which is always morbidly taking offence, and giving challenges about trifles. In what a light must these pitiful notions, derived partly from the French, have appeared to men who had fought at Dennewitz and Leipsic! Purer thoughts, and morals also, replaced the previous immorality of the students. They had been face to face with the grave questions of life and death, and it had had its effect upon them. The bullying, obscene, mawkish, sentimental student songs had given place to pure, vigorous, and patriotic ones.

" Reverence for religion went hand in hand with patriotism, a feeling, even if it were but a vague and undeveloped one, that without religion Germany would be lost. Were not the words, ' With God for King and Fatherland,' the motto of the war?"

The students at Jena were the first to attempt to embody this new life in an Association in June, 1815; and it was from them that the invitation proceeded to the festival of the Wartburg on the 18th of

October, 1817. Their main idea was to associate the commemoration of the Reformation and of the battle of Leipsic; and it was, therefore, a genuinely religious and patriotic one. As such it proved itself during the course of the *fête*, for it was surely no small thing that 500 students from all parts of Germany comported themselves with seriousness and dignity during the whole time.

Amidst the ringing of bells they wended their way up to the Castle in solemn procession. Afte a few moments of solemn prayer in the great hall they sang,—

> "Ein' feste Burg ist unser Gott."
> "A mighty castle is our God."

A student of theology from Ratzeburg, who had earned the iron cross at Waterloo, made a speech, in which he called to mind the victories of the 18th and 31st of October, and exhorted his comrades to the practice of Christian and patriotic virtues, and closed with an earnest prayer. Then

> "Nun danket alle Gott."
> "Now let us all give thanks."

resounded through the ancient hall. A professor from Jena then gave an address by request, and after a prayer for a blessing on the occasion, the assembly dispersed.

These "Sons of the Fatherland" then partook of a banquet, but they did not linger long over it, for they hastened to attend the commemorative services in the churches, after which they amused themselves with gymnastic exercises in the market-place, and in the evening assembled round a blazing bonfire. It was then that a freak took place, which was by no means a preconcerted thing, but was improvised by a few hot-headed students,—the burning of a basket containing books, a bodice, a pigtail, and a corporal's stick.

On the following day they again assembled on the Wartburg, discussed the subject of the Association, and concluded by forming a "bond of brotherly union," which was sealed by partaking of the Holy Communion.

The burning of the books was immediately taken hold of to stir up the government against the Association; the storm however blew over, and on the 18th of October, 1818, the "Universal German Association of Students" (*Burschenschaft*) was instituted, with the object of "Cultivating, in a Christian and patriotic spirit, every power mental and physical for the service of the Fatherland." All went well; the influence of the Association was evidently beneficial to the moral and intellectual character of the students, when Kotzebue was murdered by Karl Ludwig Sand, and this abominable deed, for which all the German youth were held responsible, nipped the Association in the bud. It is true, indeed, that Sand's deed indicates that there was in the mind of this young man a caricature of holy things, a perversion of Scripture, a religion without repentance, full of self-glorification, and a hallucination on the subjects of bondage and liberty. It is true that Sand's deed was an indication of tendencies which existed in the minds of a small section of German youths, the tendencies of the "Unconditionals," of which Karl Follen may be said to be the representative, whose desire it was to sacrifice everything unconditionally, even the purity of Christianity, to their republican idea of German liberty. It must be allowed that in many of the hymns which emanated from this sect, there is an unhallowed zeal, not kindled by the spirit of God. Scriptural words are used, but in an unrepentant and distorted sense; and as in the hymns of Arndt, Rückert, Körner and Schenkendorf in the war time, there were appeals to break fetters and to shed blood; but what fetters and what blood could be meant? The foreign yoke had been thrown off, and therefore it could only be intended to incite Germans against Germans, and malcontents to rise against their rulers. Expressions which had always been used in the service of religious faith, were given a high-sounding, mystical, and pantheistic meaning, and what they called prayer, was nothing but a mental excitement against their opponents, no true lifting up of the soul to God. This was that caricature of the Students' Association, of which by reason of man's sinfulness and infirmity, there lurks a germ in every human institution, but it would never have been so mischievously developed had more confidence been awarded to the genuine religious and patriotic Association. It came out scathless from all the investigations which were instituted, nevertheless severe measures against it were resolved upon by the Prussian Diet, and published in October, 1819.

We have recorded individual examples of the religious results of the war, in order to give an idea of the deep and manifold effect of that great time upon the spiritual life of our people. But we must not overlook the grand result, the most important of all, that Germany again became conscious of her dignity as a national individualism, conscious that

she still retained within herself the germ of the
greatness assigned to her by God, and all her
powers were strained to cause it to spring up and
bear fruit. A new spirit was infused into every department of life. It was not only at the universities
that the principles of education and instruction received a new impulse.

Gymnastic exercises had been practised before,
but it was now taught by Jahn, the father of the
gymnastic system, to whom the credit belongs of
having aroused German nationality in the midst of
French bondage, that physical strength and agility
should be cultivated for the sake of the Fatherland.

Pestalozzi had endeavoured to raise his pupils
from selfish isolation to considering themselves members of the great community of men, but they now
learned that it was by seeking their country's good
that advantage would be gained for humanity.

Learning, which had hitherto looked down upon
common life, began to have a beneficial effect upon
it, and to see that its true aim is to advance its interests, and in order to do so it turned its attention
to the history of our country.

The nation saw itself reflected in lively colours,
and with distinct features, in the mirror which was
held up to it by the researches of Pertz and others
under the sanction of Stein, and through the labours
of the brothers Grimm, who so diligently devoted
themselves to removing the accumulated rubbish
from the springs of national lore.

Art, too, was revived; the beauty of the ancient
German pictures and cathedrals was discovered, and
appreciation of them inspired the desire to create
new ones. Architecture, painting, and sculpture

received a new impulse. Art must have for its exercise, a country, a national life, and heroes, and these were all regained. Our poetry was inspired with a spirit of patriotism; the effect of the songs of the war-time was not lost. Uhland became the favourite of the nation, because he knew how to unite Schiller's spirit of liberty, the spirit of the romantic school, imbued as it was with the recollection of ancient German glory, and the spirit of the wars of independence. And the German youths began to take an interest in Siegfried and Dietrich, as well as in Achilles and Hector, in Chriemhild and Kudrun, as well as in Penelope and Andromache.

The national ballads from the boys' "Wunderhorn," breathing the spirit of the woods, again resounded through the land, and the old fairy tales were revived which had been banished as too antiquated from the nursery.

In the church, too, there was new life. Rationalism, which had not been without a blessing during the great days, and had become less cold and more devout, was indeed also revived and spread far and wide, but even then its strength had departed. The sense of sin had been too profound, God had revealed Himself too plainly, many had too devotedly attached themselves to the Captain of their salvation, the influence of the old hymns was too powerful, too many fervent prayers had been offered, to allow that frigid system, the opinions of which were as superficial as its faith was weak, to assume the old ascendancy. Not that there was unanimity of opinion among the faithful. The commemoration of the Reformation, at which the union of the Lutheran and Reformed churches was effected revived the subject of the differing creeds. Steffens, once a partisan of Schleiermacher, became again a Lutheran. Harms, who had, as he said, received an impulse to perpetual motion from Schleiermacher's ' Discourses on Religion,' also joined the ranks of the Lutherans, but earnestness, enthusiasm, faith, love, and life were promoted in the church.

There was once more a moment in the life of the people, when inspired by the spirit of God, they turned to God Himself to receive of His fulness, grace for grace.

" Son of man, can these bones live ?" was the question which God had put to the best men in our nation, when its limbs appeared to be torn asunder and scattered abroad like dry bones. And they answered, " O Lord God, thou knowest." And the living God displayed the power of His might, " And the breath came into them, and they lived, and stood up upon their feet, an exceeding great army."

Let us return to the watchword which God has given us, Patriotic Religion, and Religious Patriotism. May the promotion of it be the vocation of this book ! While we have been writing it, it has often seemed to us as if Germany was already retracing her steps. There are many who would like to separate the banner of 1813 and 1814, to preserve the portion on which Fatherland is inscribed, and leave that bearing the name of Christ to whomsoever cares to have it. But the victorious banner must be kept intact. He who rejects Christ is not a true patriot, and he who is not a true patriot cannot stand before the Lord who wept over Jerusalem.

THE END.

A LIST OF BOOKS

PUBLISHED BY

STRAHAN AND CO.

56, LUDGATE HILL, LONDON.

By ALFRED TENNYSON, D.C.L.
POET LAUREATE.

1. POEMS. Small 8vo, 9s.
2. MAUD, and other Poems. Small 8vo, 5s.
3. THE PRINCESS. Small 8vo, 5s.
4. IDYLLS OF THE KING. Small 8vo, 7s.
   ———————————————— Collected, small 8vo, 12s.
5. ENOCH ARDEN, etc. Small 8vo, 6s.
6. SELECTIONS FROM THE ABOVE WORKS. Square 8vo, cloth extra, 5s.
7. THE HOLY GRAIL, and other Poems. Small 8vo, 7s.

IN MEMORIAM. Small 8vo, 6s.

POCKET VOLUME EDITION OF MR. TENNYSON'S WORKS. 10 vols. in neat case, £2 5s.

CONCORDANCE TO MR. TENNYSON'S WORKS. Crown 8vo, 7s. 6d.

By HENRY ALFORD, D.D.
DEAN OF CANTERBURY.

1. THE NEW TESTAMENT. Authorized Version Revised. Long Primer Edition, Crown 8vo, 6s. Brevier Edition, Fcap. 8vo, 3s. 6d. Nonpareil Edition, small 8vo, 1s. 6d.
2. ESSAYS AND ADDRESSES, chiefly on Church Subjects. Demy 8vo, 7s. 6d.
3. THE YEAR OF PRAYER; being Family Prayers for the Christian Year. Crown 8vo, 3s. 6d.; Small 8vo, 1s. 6d.
4. THE YEAR OF PRAISE; being Hymns with Tunes for the Sundays and Holidays of the Year. Large type, with music, 3s. 6d.; without music, 1s. Small type, with music, 1s. 6d.; without music, 6d. Tonic Sol-Fa Edition, 1s. 6d.
5. HOW TO STUDY THE NEW TESTAMENT. Three Vols., small 8vo, 3s. 6d. each.
6. EASTERTIDE SERMONS. Small 8vo, 3s. 6d.
7. MEDITATIONS; Advent, Creation, and Providence. Small 8vo 3s. 6d.
8. LETTERS FROM ABROAD. Crown 8vo, 7s. 6d.
9. THE QUEEN'S ENGLISH; Stray Notes on Speaking and Spelling. Small 8vo, 5s.

By the DUKE OF ARGYLL.

1. THE REIGN OF LAW. New Edition, with Additions. Crown 8vo, 6s.
2. PRIMEVAL MAN. An Examination of some Recent Speculations. Crown 8vo, 4s. 6d.

By ROBERT BUCHANAN.

1. THE BOOK OF ORM THE CELT. Crown 8vo, 6s.
2. LONDON POEMS. Crown 8vo, 6s.
3. IDYLS AND LEGENDS OF INVERBURN. Crown 8vo, 6s.
4. UNDERTONES. Small 8vo, 6s.

By the Rev. SAMUEL COX.

THE RESURRECTION. Crown 8vo, 5s.

By PERCY FITZGERALD.

PROVERBS AND COMEDIETTAS, Written for Private Representation. Crown 8vo, 6s.

By EDWARD GARRETT.

OCCUPATIONS OF A RETIRED LIFE. Popular Edition. Crown 8vo, 6s.

By WILLIAM GILBERT.

1. DE PROFUNDIS. A Tale of the Social Deposits. Crown 8vo, 6s.
2. DR. AUSTIN'S GUESTS. Crown 8vo, 6s.
3. THE WIZARD OF THE MOUNTAIN. 2 vols. post 8vo, 21s.
4. THE MAGIC MIRROR. A Round of Tales for Old and Young. With Illustrations. Crown 8vo, 5s.
5. THE WASHERWOMAN'S FOUNDLING. With Illustrations. Square 32mo, 2s. 6d.

By DORA GREENWELL.

1. ESSAYS. Crown 8vo, 6s.
2. POEMS. Enlarged Edition. Crown 8vo, 6s.
3. THE COVENANT OF LIFE AND PEACE. Small 8vo, 3s. 6d.
4. THE PATIENCE OF HOPE. Small 8vo, 2s. 6d.
5. TWO FRIENDS. Small 8vo, 3s. 6d.

By THOMAS GUTHRIE, D.D.

1. STUDIES OF CHARACTER FROM THE OLD TESTAMENT. Crown 8vo, 3s. 6d.
2. THE PARABLES READ IN THE LIGHT OF THE PRESENT DAY. Crown 8vo, 3s. 6d.
3. MAN AND THE GOSPEL. Crown 8vo, 3s. 6d.
4. OUR FATHER'S BUSINESS. Crown 8vo, 3s. 6d.
5. OUT OF HARNESS. Crown 8vo, 3s. 6d.
6. SPEAKING TO THE HEART. Crown 8vo, 3s. 6d.
7. THE ANGELS' SONG. 18mo, 1s. 6d.
8. EARLY PIETY. 18mo, 1s. 6d.

SAVING KNOWLEDGE. Addressed to Young Men. By THOMAS GUTHRIE, D.D., and W. G. BLAIKIE, D.D. Crown 8vo, 3s. 6d.

By Sir J. F. W. HERSCHEL, Bart.

FAMILIAR LECTURES ON SCIENTIFIC SUBJECTS. Crown 8vo, 6s.

By J. S. HOWSON, D.D.
DEAN OF CHESTER.

THE METAPHORS OF ST. PAUL. Crown 8vo, 3s. 6d.

By the Rev. JOHN HUNT.

RELIGIOUS THOUGHT IN ENGLAND from the Reformation to the End of Last Century. A Contribution to the History of Theology. Vol. I. Demy 8vo, 16s.

By EDWARD IRVING.

1. COLLECTED WRITINGS. 5 vols., demy 8vo, £3.
2. MISCELLANIES FROM THE COLLECTED WRITINGS. Post 8vo, 6s.
3. PROPHETICAL WRITINGS. Vols. I. and II. Demy 8vo, 15s. each.

By JEAN INGELOW.

1. STUDIES FOR STORIES, FROM GIRLS' LIVES. With Illustrations by Millais and others. Crown 8vo, 5s.
2. A SISTER'S BYE HOURS. With Illustrations. Crown 8vo, 5s.
3. STORIES TOLD TO A CHILD. With Illustrations. Square 32mo, 3s. 6d.

By the Rev. HARRY JONES, M.A.

THE REGULAR SWISS ROUND. With Illustrations by WHYMPER. Small 8vo, 3s. 6d.

By J. T. K.

THE LEGENDS OF KING ARTHUR AND HIS KNIGHTS OF THE ROUND TABLE. Compiled and Edited by J. T. K. Small 8vo, 1s. 6d., or in paper wrapper, 1s.

By GEORGE MACDONALD, LL.D.

1. ANNALS OF A QUIET NEIGHBOURHOOD. Crown 8vo, 6s.
2. THE SEABOARD PARISH. Crown 8vo, 6s.
3. THE DISCIPLE, and other Poems. Crown 8vo, 6s.
4. UNSPOKEN SERMONS. Crown 8vo, 3s. 6d.
5. DEALINGS WITH THE FAIRIES. With Illustrations by ARTHUR HUGHES. Square 32mo, 2s. 6d.

By NORMAN MACLEOD, D.D.

1. EASTWARD. Travels in Egypt, Syria, and Palestine. With Illustrations. Crown 8vo, 6s.
2. THE STARLING. A Scotch Story. With Illustrations. Crown 8vo, 6s.
3. REMINISCENCES OF A HIGHLAND PARISH. Crown 8vo, 6s.
4. THE OLD LIEUTENANT AND HIS SON. With Illustrations. Crown 8vo, 3s. 6d.
5. THE EARNEST STUDENT: being Memorials of John Mackintosh. Crown 8vo, 3s. 6d.
6. THE GOLD THREAD. A Story for the Young. With Illustrations. Square 8vo, 2s. 6d.
7. PARISH PAPERS. Crown 8vo, 3s. 6d.
8. SIMPLE TRUTH SPOKEN TO WORKING PEOPLE. Small 8vo, 2s. 6d.

By H. L. MANSEL, D.D.
DEAN OF ST. PAUL'S.

THE PHILOSOPHY OF THE CONDITIONED; Sir William Hamilton and John Stuart Mill. Post 8vo, 6s.

By GERALD MASSEY.

A TALE OF ETERNITY, and other Poems. Crown 8vo, 7s.

By the Rev. CHARLES MERIVALE, D.C.L.
DEAN OF ELY.

HOMER'S ILIAD in English Rhymed Verse. 2 vols., Demy 8vo, 24s.

By J. E. MILLAIS, R.A.

MILLAIS' ILLUSTRATIONS. A Collection of Drawings on Wood. Demy 4to, cloth gilt extra, 16s.

By E. H. PLUMPTRE, M.A.

1. BIBLICAL STUDIES. Post 8vo, 7s. 6d.

2. CHRIST AND CHRISTENDOM. Being the Boyle Lectures for 1866. Demy 8vo, 12s.

3. THE TRAGEDIES OF ÆSCHYLOS. A New Translation, with a Biographical Essay, and an Appendix of Rhymed Choral Odes. 2 vols., crown 8vo, 12s.

4. THE TRAGEDIES OF SOPHOCLES. A New Translation, with a Biographical Essay, and an Appendix of Rhymed Choruses. Crown 8vo, 7s. 6d.

5. LAZARUS, and other Poems. Crown 8vo, 5s.

6. MASTER AND SCHOLAR, and other Poems. Crown 8vo, 5s.

7. THEOLOGY AND LIFE. Sermons on Special Occasions. Small 8vo, 6s.

8. SUNDAY. Sewed, 6d.

By the Rev. ADOLPH SAPHIR.

CONVERSION ILLUSTRATED FROM EXAMPLES RECORDED IN THE BIBLE. New Edition. Small 8vo, 3s. 6d.

By M. B. SMEDLEY.

1. POEMS (including "Lady Grace," a Drama in Five Acts). Crown 8vo, 5s.

2. OTHER FOLK'S LIVES. Crown 8vo, 5s.

By ALEXANDER SMITH.

1. ALFRED HAGART'S HOUSEHOLD. Crown 8vo, 6s.

2. A SUMMER IN SKYE. Crown 8vo, 6s.

3. DREAMTHORP: A Book of Essays written in the Country. Crown 8vo, 3s. 6d.

By A. P. STANLEY, D.D.
DEAN OF WESTMINSTER.

SCRIPTURE PORTRAITS, and other Miscellanies. Crown 8vo, 6s.

By ANTHONY TROLLOPE.

1. RALPH THE HEIR. Now appearing in Sixpenny Monthly Parts.

2. PHINEAS FINN. With Illustrations by MILLAIS. 2 vols., demy 8vo, 25s.

3. HE KNEW HE WAS RIGHT. With Illustrations by MARCUS STONE. 2 vols., demy 8vo, 21s.

By SARAH TYTLER.

1. CITOYENNE JACQUELINE. A Woman's Lot in the Great French Revolution. Crown 8vo, 5s.
2. DAYS OF YORE. Crown 8vo, 5s.
3. GIRLHOOD AND WOMANHOOD. Crown 8vo, 5s.
4. PAPERS FOR THOUGHTFUL GIRLS. With Illustrations by MILLAIS. Crown 8vo, 5s.
5. THE DIAMOND ROSE. A Life of Love and Duty. Crown 8vo, 5s.
6. THE HUGUENOT FAMILY IN THE ENGLISH VILLAGE. With Illustrations. Crown 8vo, 6s.

By C. J. VAUGHAN, D.D.

MASTER OF THE TEMPLE.

1. LAST WORDS IN THE PARISH CHURCH OF DONCASTER. Crown 8vo, 3s. 6d.
2. EARNEST WORDS FOR EARNEST MEN. Small 8vo, 4s. 6d.
3. PLAIN WORDS ON CHRISTIAN LIVING. Small 8vo, 2s. 6d.
4. CHRIST THE LIGHT OF THE WORLD. Small 8vo, 2s. 6d.
5. CHARACTERISTICS OF CHRIST'S TEACHING. Small 8vo, 2s. 6d.
6. VOICES OF THE PROPHETS ON FAITH, PRAYER, AND HUMAN LIFE. Small 8vo, 2s. 6d.

By SAMUEL WILBERFORCE, D.D.

BISHOP OF WINCHESTER.

HEROES OF HEBREW HISTORY. Post 8vo, 9s.

By SARAH WILLIAMS (Sadie).

TWILIGHT HOURS. A Legacy of Verse. With a Memoir by E. H. PLUMPTRE, M.A. Crown 8vo, 5s.

By JOHN YOUNG, LL.D.

1. THE CHRIST OF HISTORY. New and Enlarged Edition. Crown 8vo, 6s.
2. THE LIFE AND LIGHT OF MEN. Post 8vo, 7s. 6d.
3. THE CREATOR AND THE CREATION, HOW RELATED. Crown 8vo, 6s.

STRAHAN AND CO., 56, LUDGATE HILL, LONDON.